Samuel Johnson, George Birkbeck Norman Hill

Wit and Wisdom of Samuel Johnson

Samuel Johnson, George Birkbeck Norman Hill

Wit and Wisdom of Samuel Johnson

ISBN/EAN: 9783337275211

Printed in Europe, USA, Canada, Australia, Japan

Cover: Foto ©Andreas Hilbeck / pixelio.de

More available books at **www.hansebooks.com**

WIT AND W█████

OF

SAMUEL JOHNSON

Selected and Arranged

BY

GEORGE BIRKBECK HILL, D.C.L.

PEMBROKE COLLEGE, OXFORD

Oxford

AT THE CLARENDON PRESS

1888

INTRODUCTION.

NO man has ever held the same place as Johnson. Dryden was gazed at with distant veneration by Pope; Pope's hand was touched with reverence by Reynolds[1]. Each of these poets was in his own time the acknowledged head of the world of letters. But Johnson was more than this. He was the unrivalled talker, the master of the art of life, the oracle whom all men could consult, the dread of the fool and the affected, the founder of a great school of truthfulness and accuracy, the profound teacher of morality. Death laid his hand on him in vain; for though Johnson was gone the land became more and more *Johnsonised*[2]. Great though his fame was in his life-time, it is greater still in his death. It is his singular fortune among authors that his reputation is founded not on his own writings but on those of his disciples and friends. As Edmund Burke justly maintained, 'Boswell's *Life* is a greater monument to Johnson's fame than all his writings put together[3].' His written wisdom was indeed great, but it is in his spoken wisdom that he lives. A few of his writings still hold their ground and are likely to hold them, for it is not easy to believe that the day will ever come when the world will be wholly indifferent to *London* and *The Vanity of Human Wishes*, or will suffer the *Lives of the Poets* to sink into neglect. *Rasselas* has been translated into at least ten languages[4], and can be

---

[1] Boswell's *Life of Johnson*, Clarendon Press ed. i. 377 *n.* 1.
[2] *Ib.* i. 13.   [3] *Ib.* i. 10 *n.* 1.
[4] Italian, Spanish, French, German, Dutch, Modern Greek, Hungarian, Russian, Polish, and Bengalee. *Ib.* ii. 208; vi. lxiv.

read

read not only on the banks of the Volga[1] but also on the banks of the Ganges. Nevertheless it is true that when we talk of Johnson it is not of Johnson's Johnson, but of Boswell's Johnson, that we are thinking. The extraordinary interest which the skill of the biographer has raised in his hero has led us no doubt to study his character in all the lights that are cast upon it. In the pages of Hawkins, Murphy, Mrs. Piozzi, Mme. D'Arblay, and a host of others, we see qualities and peculiarities which Boswell either altogether passed over or traced with far too light a touch. In Johnson's own writings, if we care to study them, we come upon many a passage in which the author, while describing the character of another, is at the same time describing his own. Tradition too, before it was too late, came in with her delightful aid. From the memories of men who had visited at Bolt-court and at Streatham, or had enjoyed ' the manly conversation and the society of the brown table ' of the Literary Club[2], was gathered many an interesting anecdote of the grand old sage. The result of all these varied labours has not been in vain, for we now know Johnson as no other man is known to us. It is with the characters of fiction alone that we have the same kind of friendly and close intimacy. Our acquaintance with him is not as with Dryden or Pope or Gibbon, but as with Falstaff and Don Quixote, with Sir Roger de Coverley and my Uncle Toby.

If it is by the wonderful skill of the biographer that his life

---

[1] ' Johnson. "O! Gentlemen, I must tell you a very great thing. The Empress of Russia has ordered the *Rambler* to be translated into the Russian language; so I shall be read on the banks of the Wolga. Horace boasts that his fame would extend as far as the banks of the Rhone; now the Wolga is farther from me than the Rhone was from Horace."' Boswell's *Life of Johnson,* iv. 276. The report that the *Rambler* was translated into Russian was not well founded.

[2] *Ib.* iii. 128 *n.* 4.

still

still lives and glows, yet that skill would have been of no avail had it not had for its subject a man whose character was noble in itself, and was marked in the deepest and strongest lines. Striking and even wonderful though this character was, yet it seems to be understood only by the English-speaking races. Of Boswell's *Life of Johnson* no translation, so far as I know, has ever yet been made. No foreigners come to worship at the shrine of the rugged idol whom we have set up. His wit, his humour, his strong common sense, his truthfulness, his roughness, his tenderness, are known to us and us alone. Boswell was indeed right when he so often spoke of him as 'a true-born Englishman[1].' Of all Englishmen he was the most English—in his bad qualities as well as in his good, in his prejudices as well as in his wisdom. The interest of the portrait that Boswell draws of him is heightened by the biographer's freedom from all insular narrowness. The young Scotchman was as far removed as possible from being—

'A Scot if ever Scot there were[2].'

With perfect justice he boasted that he was 'a very universal man[3].' He was as easy with Rousseau as he was with Johnson, with Paoli as he was with Jack Wilkes. 'I can drink,' he boasted, 'I can laugh, I can converse in perfect humour with Whigs, with Republicans, with Dissenters, with Independents, with Quakers, with Moravians, with Jews[4].' He would have been the last man to agree with 'Old Meynell' when he exclaimed:—'For anything I see foreigners are fools[5].' In his *Tour to the Hebrides*, while he describes Johnson as 'at bottom much of a *John Bull*, much of a blunt *true-born Englishman*[6],' writing of himself he says:—'I am, I flatter myself, completely a citizen of the world. In my

---

[1] Boswell's *Life of Johnson*, v. 20.　　[2] *Ib.* ii. 306.
[3] *Ib.* iii. 375 *n.* 2.　　[4] *Ib.*　　[5] *Ib.* iv. 15.　　[6] *Ib.* v. 20.

travels

travels through Holland, Germany, Switzerland, Italy, Corsica, France, I never felt myself from home[1].' He often boasted of his descent from Robert Bruce. But this universality, which was one of his greatest merits, may have come to him from his 'great-grandmother, Veronica, Countess of Kincardine, a Dutch lady of the noble house of Sommelsdyck[2];' certainly it is not often found north of the Tweed. In whatever way it came, he had it in a large degree. By means of it he saw the striking contrasts in his hero's character, but he saw them not with anger or contempt, or even with mere toleration. So far from being shocked by them, he had his interest all the more aroused.

As Johnson is marked off from all other men as the typical Englishman, so is he distinguished from all other Englishmen, by the prominence of 'the contradictory qualities[3]' that were found in him. Horace Walpole describes him as 'the representative in epitome of all the contradictions in human nature[4].' With all his contradictions, however, he never exhibited those unhappy variations which trouble us in some of the greatest of men. One of his friends praising the originality of his talk said :—' In general you may tell what the man to whom you are speaking will say next. This you can never do of Johnson[5].' Though you could never tell what Johnson would say, yet in all the greater questions of right or wrong every one could know what Johnson would do. Here there were no wanderings, no strayings to one side or to the other. There was the strait gate, and here was the narrow path leading to it. The gate he kept ever in view, and along the narrow path he doggedly plodded his way. Who has

---

[1] Boswell's *Life of Johnson*, v. 20.   [2] *Ib.* v. 25 *n.* 2.
[3] *Ib.* iv. 426.   [4] Walpole's *Letters*, viii. 538.
[5] Boswell's *Life of Johnson*, iv. 421 *n.* 1.

not

not sorrowed over the miserable failings of some of the noblest of men? But with Johnson's whole life lying open before us as no other great man's life lies, we can say:—

> ' Nothing is here for tears, nothing to wail
> Or knock the breast, no weakness, no contempt,
> Dispraise or blame, nothing but well and fair[1].'

This uniformity in the main of character heightens still more the contrast which exists in the minor parts. It not only heightens it but it renders it far more pleasing.

The most striking quality in Johnson was his wisdom, his knowledge of the whole art of life. Gibbon describes ' the majestic sense of Thurlow[2].' If common sense can be thought of as invested with majesty, it is seen in all its stateliness much more in the dictionary-maker than in the great Lord Chancellor. But mere common sense would never have made Johnson all that he is to us. Benjamin Franklin had more common sense than the frame of any single man seems capable of containing or supporting. But who loves common sense when it stands alone? It must be dashed by the failings of men of like affections with ourselves. It must at times be crossed by the playful extravagances of a wayward humour. It must be joined not with a cold and calculating selfishness, but with a tenderness and a pity for those whose want of it has brought them to misery. No one understood better than Johnson the art by which we arrive at such happiness as life admits of; no one felt more compassion for those who, through the infirmity of will, failed to practise this art. It is perhaps this union of the strongest common sense and a real tenderness of heart that more than anything else endears him to men who are wide as the poles asunder. Macaulay did

---

[1] *Samson Agonistes*, l. 1721.
[2] Gibbon's *Miscellaneous Works*, i. 222.

not

not delight in him more than did Carlyle, and Mr. Ruskin, I believe, would set him scarcely below the high level on which he is placed by the Master of Balliol.

Round about his common sense and his tenderness, and mingled with them in endless variety, his humour and his wit are ever playing. If he ever wearies us it is when he has a pen in his hand. When he speaks we wish that he could have gone on speaking for ever. He is wholly free from all affectation, all cynicism, all moroseness, all peevishness. He is as far removed from the savageness of Swift, as from the querulous irritability of Carlyle. He never snarls and he never whines. He is never 'guilty of sullenness against nature[1].' Life, he holds, is unhappy, it must be unhappy. But what of that? Something can be done to make it happier, and that something we must each one of us steadily do. The worst thing of all is to sit down and whine. It is of small things that life is made up, and it is in these small things, and in them alone, that we can find such happiness as we are allowed here on earth to attain. He would never have cried with Swift *Vive la bagatelle,* nor would he have applauded a life of conscious and intentional trifling. We are to attend to trifles, or those things which are accounted trifles, because it is of them, in all their variety and their multitude, that human existence is composed.

> 'Small sands the mountain, moments make the year,
> And trifles life[2].'

He accepts life as it is; 'he takes existence on the terms on which it is given to him[3].' He never expects from life more than life can afford. He always refuses to hide from himself the real state of things. He puts up no screen between

---

[1] Milton, quoted in Johnson's *Dictionary* under *Sullenness.*

[2] Young, *Love of Fame,* satire vi.

[3] Boswell's *Life of Johnson,* iii. 58.

himself

himself and the truth. He has what Rousseau calls 'that rarest kind of philosophy which consists in observing what we see every day[1];' and he looks at it just as steadily whether it gives him pleasure or pain. He belongs to the most accurate class of the observers of human nature, for he never confounds what is with what ought to be. Happiness is not, he maintains, the unfailing consequence of virtue. 'We do not always suffer by our crimes; we are not always protected by our innocence[2].' He never throws the veil of the poet or the moralist over the evils of life. He will not allow either his hopes or his fears to fool his reason. He 'lays no flattering unction to his soul.' He may 'be suspended over the abyss of eternal perdition only by the thread of life[3];' but great though is his terror he cannot cheat himself. The most that he can do is to turn his mind from constantly dwelling on mortality. 'The whole of life,' he said, 'is but keeping away the thoughts of death[4];' but when he does think his 'obstinate rationality[5]' will not allow him to flatter his soul. That there is no Hell he would have admitted was a matter for argument, though in all likelihood he would have refused to allow it to be argued in his presence. But that there is a hell, and that it need not be the constant object of our terror, he would have 'passionately and loudly[6]' denied. To the evils of this life he refuses to shut his eyes. Poverty he steadily maintains is a great evil. He likes Crabbe's *Village* because the poet never varnishes rustic vice and rustic misery, but

<blockquote>'paints the cot
As truth will paint it, and as bards will not[7].'</blockquote>

He dislikes all affectation, all 'studied behaviour[8].' He is the great lexicographer, the great moralist, the 'Guide,

---

[1] Morley's *Life of Cobden*, i. 308. [2] *Works*, iv. 121.
[3] *The Rambler*, No. 110. [4] Boswell's *Life of Johnson*, ii. 93.
[5] *Ib.* iv. 289. [6] *Ib.* iv. 299. [7] *Ib.* iv. 175. [8] *Ib.* i. 470.

Philosopher,

Philosopher, and Friend [1],' 'the majestic teacher of moral and religious wisdom [2],' 'awful, melancholy, and venerable [3]'; yet 'his throne of felicity is a tavern chair [4].'   He never acts up to a part.   'I never considered,' he says, 'whether I should be a grave man, or a merry man, but just let inclination for the time have its course [5].'   In Fleet-street, in the silence of the night, he bursts into such a fit of laughter that he has to cling to a post for support [6].   At Langton he lays himself on the ground, and has a roll down a steep hill [7].   In a stage-coach he at once begins to talk without reserve [8].   'Great Kings,' he said, 'were always social [9].'   He, 'the monarch of literature,' was as social as the greatest among them.   'Let a man,' he says, 'be *aliis laetus, sapiens sibi*.   You may be wise in your study in the morning, and gay in company at a tavern in the evening.   Every man is to take care of his own wisdom and his own virtue, without minding too much what others think [10].'   He was the most humorous of men, 'incomparable at buffoonery,' full of 'fun and comical humour, and love of nonsense.'   His 'laugh was irresistible [11].'   'He gives you,' says Garrick, 'a forcible hug, and shakes laughter out of you, whether you will or no [12].'   He spends a whole night in festivity at a tavern, to do honour to an authoress's 'first literary child.'   He orders 'a magnificent hot apple-pie and has it stuck with bay-leaves.'   He 'invokes the muses by some ceremonies of his own invention, and encircles her brows with a crown of laurel.'   At five in the morning 'his face still shines with meridian splendour.'   He 'rallies the company to partake of a second refreshment of coffee,' and it is near eight

---

[1] Boswell's *Life of Johnson*, iii. 6.   [2] *Ib.* i. 201.   [3] *Ib.* ii. 262.
[4] *Ib.* ii. 452 *n.* 1.   [5] *Ib.* i. 470.   [6] *Ib.* ii. 262.
[7] *Ib.* i. 477 *n.* 1.   [8] *Ib.* iv. 284.   [9] *Ib.* i. 442.
[10] *Ib.* iii. 405.   [11] *Ib.* ii. 262 *n.* 2.   [12] *Ib.* ii. 231.

o'clock

o'clock before he goes home to bed[1]. He gets up at three on a summer morning 'to have a frisk' with those young dogs, Beauclerk and Langton, and joins in drinking 'a bowl of that liquor called *Bishop* which he had always liked[2].' With this entire absence of all 'studied behaviour' he combines the most 'inflexible dignity of character[3].' Perhaps there never was a man more entirely free from what is known in this age as 'snobbishness.' In the days of his poverty his clothes might be little better than a beggar's, and his chairs might have lost a leg; but 'no external circumstances ever prompted him to make an apology, or to seem even sensible of their existence[4].' He reproaches Mrs. Thrale with her 'despicable dread of living in the Borough[5].'

It is this freedom from affectation which gives such weight and such interest to his criticisms. He has none of 'the cant of those who judge poetry by principles rather than perception[6].' He is never afraid to speak what he holds to be the truth, however great may be the author whom he reviews. When George III asked Miss Burney whether 'there was not sad stuff in Shakespeare,' he added :—'I know it is not to be said, but it's true. Only it's Shakespeare, and nobody dare abuse him[7].' There was no author whom Johnson dared not criticise with honest boldness. 'A quibble,' he writes, 'was to Shakespeare the fatal Cleopatra for which he lost the world, and was content to lose it[8].' No one has bestowed loftier praise on Milton than Johnson, no one has done him more 'illustrious justice[9].' He speaks of him as 'that poet whose works may possibly be read when every other monument

---

[1] Hawkins's *Life of Johnson*, p. 286.
[2] Boswell's *Life of Johnson*, i. 251.   [3] *Ib.* i. 131.
[4] *Ib.* i. 328 *n.* 1.   [5] *Piozzi Letters*, ii. 92.   [6] *Works*, viii. 343.
[7] Boswell's *Life of Johnson*, i. 497 *n.* 1.
[8] *Works*, v. 118.   [9] Boswell's *Life of Johnson*, i. 227.

of British greatness shall be obliterated[1].' Yet of *Paradise Lost* he writes, 'None ever wished it longer than it is. Its perusal is a duty rather than a pleasure. We read Milton for instruction, retire harassed and over-burdened, and look elsewhere for recreation; we desert our master, and seek for companions[2].' This truth, if it be a truth, most men would have hidden from themselves, and all other critics would have hidden from the world. Nowhere does his dislike of affectation show itself more strongly than when he finds it among authors. Whether it takes the form of allegories, or visions, or pastorals, whether it shows itself in the idle attempt to revive a diction which has become obsolete, it equally meets with his scorn. In every shape he attacks it as 'a fashion by which idleness is favoured and imbecility assisted[3].' His criticisms are often wanting in insight, but they are at all events his own. Among the servile herd of imitators[4] he is never found.

He is no lover of singularity. 'There is in human nature,' he says, 'a general inclination to make people stare, and every wise man has himself to cure of it, and does cure himself[5].' He is not ashamed to own his natural feelings. Carlyle says of him that he 'prized Fame as the means of getting him employment and good wages; scarcely as anything more[6].' Johnson would never have said this of himself, for it was not true. On the contrary he describes fame as that 'which no man, however high or mean, however wise or ignorant, was yet able to despise[7].' 'The applause of a single human being is of great consequence' he said, when a letter was read to

---

[1] Boswell's *Life of Johnson*, i. 230.   [2] *Works*, vii. 135.
[3] *The Rambler*, No. 121.
[4] 'O imitatores, servum pecus.' Horace i. *Epistles* xix. 19.
[5] Boswell's *Life of Johnson*, ii. 74.
[6] Carlyle's *Miscellanies*, ed. 1872, iv. 114.
[7] *The Rambler*, No. 151.

him

him that was highly in his praise[1]. Praise from those who were entitled to give it was as pleasant to him as it is to all men. 'He loved it,' says Boswell, 'when it was brought to him; but was too proud to seek for it[2].'

He makes us see 'the shame of imposing words for ideas upon ourselves or others[3].' He clears our mind of cant. We may talk foolishly, but we are not to think foolishly[4]. To use Sir Joshua Reynolds's striking words; 'he brushes the rubbish from our minds[5].' Against no kind of cant is he severer than against 'the cant of sensibility[6].' We do not feel for the distresses of others as we feel for our own. 'It would be misery to no purpose[7].' Who 'eats a slice of plum-pudding the less because a friend is hanged[8]?' We are not 'to be duped' by those who lay claim to this excess of sympathy. 'You will find these very feeling people are not very ready to do you good. They *pay* you by *feeling*[9].' He distinguishes between 'inexcusable lies and consecrated lies.' The news arrives of some great battle lost. 'Every heart,' we read, 'beats, and every eye is in tears. Now we know that no man eats his dinner the worse, but there *should* have been all this concern; and to say there *was* may be reckoned a consecrated lie[10].' Perhaps he nowhere better exhibits his rough common sense than in these frequent appeals to appetite as a measure of feeling. Author though he is, he has no respect for 'the cant of authors[11]' in their affected contempt of critics. He attacks the 'despicable cant of literary modesty[12].' He scorns Pope for feigning a 'contempt of his own poetry[13],' and Swift for his 'affectation of

---

[1] Boswell's *Life of Johnson*, iv. 32.   [2] *Ib.* iv. 427.   [3] *Works*, vi. 64.
[4] Boswell's *Life of Johnson*, iv. 221.
[5] *Life of Reynolds* by Leslie and Taylor, ii. 461.   [6] *Works*, viii. 248.
[7] Boswell's *Life of Johnson*, ii. 94.   [8] *Ib.*   [9] *Ib.* ii. 95.
[10] *Ib.* i. 355.   [11] *Works*, viii. 238.   [12] *Ib.* vii. 433.   [13] *Ib.* viii. 315.

familiarity

familiarity with the great[1].' He laughs at both for their letters from which 'it might be inferred that they, with Arbuthnot and Gay, had engrossed all the understanding and virtue of mankind; that their merits filled the world; or that there was no hope of more[2].' He lays bare the real aim of self-depreciation. 'All censure of a man's self is oblique praise. It is in order to show how much he can spare. It has all the invidiousness of self-praise and all the reproach of falsehood[3].' We may be at first sight astonished when we find him maintaining 'that there is very little hypocrisy in the world.' Our surprise lessens, if it does not pass altogether away, when he goes on to say that 'we do not so often endeavour or wish to impose on others as on ourselves[4].' Other writers have laid bare other conspiracies. He is the first to tell us of 'the universal conspiracy of mankind against themselves[5].'

In the art of 'the management of the mind[6]' he is one of the greatest masters. He upholds everything that is innocent, however trifling it may be, that 'drives on the system of life[7].' He envies the advantage which women have 'that they may take up with little things without disgracing themselves; a man cannot except with fiddling[8].' He will allow no one 'to think with a dejected indifference of the works of art, and the pleasures of life, because life is uncertain and short[9].' 'If the world be worth winning,' he writes to Mrs. Thrale, 'let us enjoy it; if it is to be despised, let us despise it by conviction. But the world is not to be despised but as it is compared with something better[10].' Are we troubled with unhappy thoughts, we are not 'to attempt to think them down,

[1] *Works*, viii. 225.   [2] *Ib.*
[3] Boswell's *Life of Johnson*, iii. 323.   [4] *The Idler*, No. 27.
[5] *Works*, iv. 47.   [6] Boswell's *Life of Johnson*, ii. 440.   [7] *Ib.* iv. 112.
[8] *Ib.* iii. 242.   [9] *Ib.* iii. 164.   [10] *Piozzi Letters*, i. 242.

for

for it is 'madness'[1]. Do disappointments come upon us, let us drive them out of our mind. 'Even to think in the most reasonable manner is for the present not so useful as not to think[2].' We are not to resist gaiety, for 'those who resist gaiety are likely to fall a sacrifice to appetite[3].' 'Gaiety is a duty when health requires it[4].' He is 'a great friend to public amusements, for they keep people from vice[5].' We are not to nurse sorrow. However great the bereavement may have been, we are not 'to continue gloomy. Grief has its time[6].' 'Grief is a species of idleness[7];' while 'the business of life is to go forwards[8].' Of all diseases the most to be dreaded is the 'sickness of leisure. Rather to do nothing than to do good is the lowest state of a degraded mind[9].' Has a man greatly sinned, it is not to a life of solitude and sadness that he must flee for repentance. 'Gloomy penitence is only madness turned upside down[10].' 'The life of a solitary man will be certainly miserable, but not certainly devout[11].' In every way we are to make the most and best of our lot. 'We are to be well when we are not ill, and pleased when we are not troubled[12].' We are not to torment ourselves with either suspicions or the expectation of coming ills. 'Suspicion is very often a useless pain[13],' and 'all useless misery is certainly folly[14].' If we do suffer we are not to trouble the world with our complaints, but to remember 'that those who do not feel pain seldom think that it is felt[15].' He is 'no croaker, no declaimer against the times[16].' He never complains of the world. 'It is not,'

---

[1] Boswell's *Life of Johnson*, ii. 440.
[2] *Piozzi Letters*, i. 202. [3] Piozzi's *Anecdotes*, p. 106.
[4] Boswell's *Life of Johnson*, iii. 136 *n.* 2. [5] *Ib.* ii. 169.
[6] *Ib.* iv. 121. [7] *Ib.* iii. 136 *n.* 2. [8] *The Idler*, No. 72.
[9] Boswell's *Life of Johnson*, iv. 352. [10] *Ib.* iii. 27.
[11] *Rasselas*, ch. xxi. [12] Boswell's *Life of Johnson*, iv. 379 *n.* 3.
[13] *Ib.* iii. 135. [14] *The Idler*, No. 72.
[15] *The Rambler*, No. 48. [16] Boswell's *Life of Johnson*, iv. 383 *n.*

he maintains, 'so unjust or unkind as it is peevishly represented[1].' In the time of his greatest necessities 'it is not
without some satisfaction that he can produce the suffrage
of Savage in favour of human nature'—of Savage, whose 'knowledge of life was his chief attainment[2].' He is willing to accept
the well-considered judgment of the world, 'for about things on
which the public thinks long, it commonly attains to think
right[3].' 'The world,' he says, 'has always a right to be
regarded[4].' 'The man who threatens it is always ridiculous[5].'

While he is thus ready to listen to the general judgment he
is always protesting against the general inaccuracy. Few
things anger him more than the love of 'catching greedily at
wonders[6].' He brought people, as Reynolds said, 'to think
rightly[7].' He is rigidly truthful himself, truthful both in small
matters and in great. 'He inculcates upon all his friends the
importance of perpetual vigilance against the slightest degrees
of falsehood[8].' He at once brings everything to the test
of truth. He loves arithmetic because it overcomes a
thousand stories[9]. He is reproached with credulity, but it
never goes beyond a willingness, at times even an eagerness,
to believe what is in itself incredible. He has, to use Boswell's
words, 'an elevated wish for more and more evidence for
spirit[10].' But when the evidence is brought before him he puts
all his wishes on one side, and sifts it strictly. He never
'helps his unbelief.' One single instance of the appearance
of a ghost would settle a host of doubts, but he has to admit
that 'it is still undecided whether or not there has ever been
an instance of the spirit of any person appearing after death.

---

[1] *Piozzi Letters*, ii. 199.   [2] *Works*, viii. 188.
[3] Boswell's *Life of Johnson*, i. 200 *n*. 2.   [4] *Ib.* ii. 74 *n*. 3.
[5] *Works*, viii. 281.   [6] *Works*, vi. 455.
[7] *Life of Reynolds* by Leslie and Taylor, ii. 461.
[8] Boswell's *Life of Johnson*, iii. 229.   [9] *Ib.* iv. 171 *n*. 3.   [10] *Ib.* ii. 150.

All

'All argument is against it, but all belief is for it[1].' Few things anger him more than the idle praise of some golden age either in the past or in the wilds of the world. He scoffs at Lord Monboddo's belief in the superiority of our ancestors and at Rousseau's praises of savage life. 'Honesty is not greater where elegance is less[2],' he maintains after travelling in the Hebrides. 'We are as strong as our ancestors, and a great deal wiser[3]' he tells Monboddo. Rousseau no doubt 'talks his nonsense well,' but Boswell is not to imitate him 'in talking such paradox. It cannot entertain, far less can it instruct[4].' He will never for one moment tamely put up with that indistinct state of the mind in which people praise a state of life which they could not endure for a single day. A shop, he says, in London 'affords no image worthy of attention; but in an island it turns the balance of existence between good and evil[5].' He loves civilisation—civility he would have called it—and he will never allow it to be attacked by those who enjoyed its gifts as much as he did himself.

He is full of the most ardent curiosity. He has 'a mind like Dryden's, always curious, always active[6].' Like him too 'he gleans his knowledge from accidental intelligence and various conversation, by a quick apprehension, a judicious selection, and a happy memory, a keen appetite of knowledge, and a powerful digestion[7].' Unlike most other gleaners, whatever he gathers he scatters with a lavish hand. He is equally ready to explain the processes of brewing, tanning and granulating gunpowder and to discuss questions of poetry, of law, of theology and of philosophy. 'His attention never deserts him[8],' and he never wearies the attention of his hearers. His talk 'is a

---

[1] Boswell's *Life of Johnson*, iii. 230.   [2] *Works*, ix. 38.
[3] Boswell's *Life of Johnson*, v. 77.   [4] *Ib.* ii. 74.   [5] *Ib.* v. 27 *n.* 4.
[6] *Works*, vii. 306.   [7] *Ib.*   [8] *Ib.* viii. 187.

 perpetual

perpetual fountain of good sense[1].' He does not always convince ; he does not indeed always wish to convince, for he often talks for victory. But he always instructs, even when he is in the wrong, for he makes his hearers examine the foundations on which their opinions rest. There are indeed few parts of practical wisdom in which he is not our teacher. We listen to him all the more readily, because he does not sit solitary and apart on some lofty peak of wisdom, but is a man of like passions with ourselves. He has, he owns, 'a great reluctance to go to church[2],' and to this reluctance he very readily yields. He is enticed by the gay, dissipated Beauclerk, to saunter about the whole of one fine Sunday morning, till at length 'in the time of divine service he lays himself down at his ease upon a tomb-stone in the churchyard.' We smile as we thus see 'the great lexicographer playing the part of " Hogarth's Idle Apprentice[3]." ' We are amused with 'his ingenious defence of his dining twice abroad in Passion Week,'—at the houses of bishops, too[4]. We are, perhaps, a little more perplexed when we find that he frowns even at the mention of the virtuous Priestley[5], but is ready to dine a second time with the shameless Jack Wilkes, whom a few years earlier he had openly charged 'as a retailer of sedition and obscenity[6].' We forgive him, when we remember that 'Jack has great variety of talk, Jack is a scholar, and Jack has the manners of a gentleman[7],' and that at their first meeting he had so delightfully turned Johnson's 'surly virtue' into complacency by means of the roast veal, the stuffing, the gravy, the butter, and the squeeze of the lemon[8]. We see once more the truth of the words of Imlac, the philosopher in *Rasselas*—

---

[1] Dryden, in the preface to his *Fables*, thus describes Chaucer. Bell's *Dryden*, ii. 244.   [2] Boswell's *Life of Johnson*, i. 67.

[3] *Ib.* i. 250.   [4] *Ib.* iv. 88.   [5] *Ib.* iv. 238.

[6] *Ib.* iii. 64. *n.* 2.   [7] *Ib.* iii. 183.   [8] *Ib.* iii. 69.

the

'the teachers of morality discourse like angels, but they live like men[1].'

In all his greatness it is along the common ways of men that he moves. In every circle he is the first, yet the companions of his home life, whose society for many a long year he seeks with pleasure, are a poor blind lady and 'an obscure practiser in physic.' He delighted as much as he excelled in the rough game of talk, yet he maintained that 'that is the happiest conversation where there is no competition, no vanity, but a calm quiet interchange of sentiments[2].' He is as much struck by a brilliant spectacle as Miss Burney's heroine, the youthful Evelina. 'When I first entered Ranelagh,' he said, 'it gave an expansion and gay sensation to my mind such as I never experienced anywhere else[3].' 'The *coup d'œil*,' he told Boswell, 'was the finest thing he had ever seen[4].' He is as eager to inspect a new manufactory as an old black-letter volume. He visits some iron-works in North Wales. 'I have enlarged my notions,' he records in his Diary[5]. He would have felt none of Carlyle's scorn had he seen such a sight as the Great Exhibition of 1851, 'the world's fair' in Hyde Park. 'For such a thing as this,' Mr. Froude tells us, 'Carlyle could have no feeling but contempt.' Carlyle himself in his journal mocks at '"all nations" crowding to us with their so-called industry or ostentatious frothery[6].' Johnson's nature was wider than this. He could find 'good in everything.' His curiosity would have been excited, and at the same time gratified, by the almost countless fabrics and the various processes of manufactory. He would have taken pleasure in watching 'the full tide of human existence[7],' as it

[1] *Rasselas*, ch. xviii.　　　　[2] Boswell's *Life of Johnson*, ii. 359.
[3] *Ib.* iii. 199.　　　　[4] *Ib.* ii. 168.　　　　[5] *Ib.* v. 442.
[6] Thomas Carlyle. *A History of his Life in London*, 2nd. ed. ii. 79.
[7] Boswell's *Life of Johnson*, ii. 337.

ebbed and flowed. He would have pointed perhaps some sad moral, but in some way or other he would have maintained that every one had their shilling's worth of pleasure[1]. The hopes that were commonly formed that by such an Exhibition, universal peace and brotherhood could be established, would have seemed to him wild but not despicable. He scoffed at no aspiration after good. When a fund was raised to buy the necessaries of life for the starving French prisoners of war he wrote :—'The relief of enemies has a tendency to unite mankind in fraternal affection[2].' The same tendency he might have discovered in this Exhibition. In his writings he speaks of 'the great republic of humanity[3],' and 'the universal league of social beings[4].' War he hated as much as he did heroes and conquerors. 'I would wish Cæsar and Catiline, Xerxes and Alexander, Charles and Peter huddled together in obscurity or detestation[5].' He would have delighted in the hopefulness which for a few brief months in 1851 swept over England like sunshine between showers, for 'hope itself is happiness, and its frustrations, however frequent, are less dreadful than its extinction[6].' He never discourages either himself or anyone else. At all Carlyle's complaints, could he have seen his journal, he would have scoffed as mere 'foppish lamentations[7].'

He neither lives in a mist nor does he ever try for a single

---

[1] ' "I said there was not half a guinea's worth of pleasure in seeing this place." JOHNSON. " But, Sir, there is half a guinea's worth of inferiority to other people in not having seen it." BOSWELL. " I doubt, Sir, whether there are many happy people here." JOHNSON. " Yes Sir, there are many happy people here. There are many people here who are watching hundreds, and who think hundreds are watching them." ' Boswell's *Life of Johnson*, ii. 169.

[2] *Works*, vi. 148.   [3] *The Rambler*, No. 77.   [4] *Ib.* No. 81.

[5] *The Adventurer*, No. 99.   [6] Boswell's *Life of Johnson*, i. 368 *n.* 3.

[7] Piozzi's *Anecdotes of Johnson*, p. 105.

moment to throw one round him. He thinks clearly, and he states with perfect clearness what he thinks. He always knows what he means to say, and his readers and hearers always understand what he does say. He never 'delights,' like Dryden, 'to tread upon the brink of meaning[1].' It is true that he often 'talks paradox,' but whether he is right or wrong he is as clear as the day. With all this clearness there is no shallowness. The awe which overwhelms him as he gazes into infinitude, the thoughts which rise in him as he meditates on life and death, and

> 'The undiscover'd country from whose bourn
> No traveller returns,'

belong to a nature that is as deep as it is wide. That his mind has great defects, that it is wanting in fancy and imagination, that it is insensible to the arts of the musician and the painter, and is little open to the beauties of nature, cannot be denied. To him who, nursed in the modern school of thought, reproaches Johnson for the qualities which he does not possess, I would answer in his own words :—'Sir, there is no end of negative criticism[2].' We must take him as he was, 'the true-born Englishman,' whose greatness is not understood by the other nations of the earth, but who perhaps for that very reason is all the dearer to those to whom the English language is their mother tongue.

---

[1] *Works*, vii. 341.
[2] Boswell's *Life of Johnson*, v. 222.

SAMUEL JOHNSON.

[1709–1784.]

Accounting for Everything Systematically:

OF Dr. Hurd, Bishop of Worcester, Johnson said to a friend, 'Hurd, Sir, is one of a set of men who account for every thing systematically; for instance, it has been a fashion to wear scarlet breeches; these men would tell you, that according to causes and effects, no other wear could at that time have been chosen.' Boswell's *Life of Johnson*, iv. 189.

Acquaintances:

NOTHING is more common than mutual dislike where mutual approbation is particularly expected. There is often on both sides a vigilance not over benevolent; and as attention is strongly excited, so that nothing drops unheeded, any difference in taste or opinion, and some difference where there is no restraint will commonly appear, immediately generates dislike. *Piozzi Letters*, ii. 110.

.·.

'I REMEMBER a man [1],' writes Mrs. Piozzi, 'much delighted in by the upper ranks of society, who upon a trifling embarrassment in his affairs hanged himself behind the stable door, to the astonishment of all who knew him as the liveliest companion and most agreeable converser breathing. "What upon earth," said one

---

[1] Mr. William Fitzherbert.

 at

at our house, "could have made ———— hang himself?"
"Why, just his having a multitude of acquaintance,"
replied Dr. Johnson, "and ne'er a friend." '

Piozzi's Synonymy, i. 217.

'Action' in Public Speaking:

ACTION can have no effect upon reasonable minds.
It may augment noise, but it never can enforce argument. If you speak to a dog, you use action; you hold
up your hand thus, because he is a brute; and in proportion as men are removed from brutes, action will have
the less influence upon them.   Boswell's Life of Johnson, ii. 211.

Addison's Use of Wit:

IT is justly observed by Tickell, that Addison employed
wit on the side of virtue and religion. He not only made
the proper use of wit himself, but taught it to others; and
from his time it has been generally subservient to the cause
of reason and of truth. He has dissipated the prejudice
that had long connected gaiety with vice, and easiness of
manners with laxity of principles. He has restored virtue
to its dignity, and taught innocence not to be ashamed.
This is an elevation of literary character, 'above all Greek,
above all Roman fame[1].' No greater felicity can genius
attain, than that of having purified intellectual pleasure,
separated mirth from indecency, and wit from licentiousness; of having taught a succession of writers to bring
elegance and gaiety to the aid of goodness; and, if I
may use expressions yet more awful, of having 'turned
many to righteousness[2].'   Works, vii. 451.

---

[1] Pope, *Imitations of Horace*, ii. 1. 26.   [2] *Daniel*, xii. 3.

Advice:

Advice :

ADVICE, as it always gives a temporary appearance of superiority, can never be very grateful, even when it is most necessary or most judicious. But for the same reason every one is eager to instruct his neighbours. To be wise or to be virtuous, is to buy dignity and importance at a high price; but when nothing is necessary to elevation but detection of the follies or the faults of others, no man is so insensible to the voice of fame as to linger on the ground.

> — *Tentanda via est, qua me quoque possim*
> *Tollere humo, victorque virum volitare per ora.*—VIRG.[1]

New ways I must attempt, my grovelling name
To raise aloft, and wing my flight to fame.—DRYDEN.

Vanity is so frequently the apparent motive of advice, that we, for the most part, summon our powers to oppose it without any very accurate inquiry whether it is right. It is sufficient that another is growing great in his own eyes at our expence, and assumes authority over us without our permission; for many would contentedly suffer the consequences of their own mistakes, rather than the insolence of him who triumphs as their deliverer. *Rambler*, No. 87.

. · .

THE advice that is wanted is commonly unwelcome, and that which is not wanted is evidently impertinent.

Piozzi Letters, ii. 139.

. · .

THE mischief of flattery is, not that it persuades any man that he is what he is not, but that it suppresses the influence of honest ambition, by raising an opinion that honour may

---

[1] *Georg.* iii. 8.

be gained without the toil of merit; and the benefit of
advice arises commonly not from any new light imparted
to the mind, but from the discovery which it affords of the
public suffrages. He that could withstand conscience is
frighted at infamy, and shame prevails when reason is
defeated.   *Rambler*, No. 155.

Advocates:

'I ASKED him whether, as a moralist, he did not think
that the practice of the law, in some degree, hurt the nice
feeling of honesty. JOHNSON. "Why no, Sir, if you act
properly. You are not to deceive your clients with false
representations of your opinion : you are not to tell lies to
a judge." BOSWELL. "But what do you think of supporting a cause which you know to be bad?" JOHNSON. "Sir,
you do not know it to be good or bad till the Judge deter-
mines it. I have said that you are to state facts fairly; so
that your thinking, or what you call knowing, a cause to be
bad, must be from reasoning, must be from your supposing
your arguments to be weak and inconclusive. But, Sir,
that is not enough. An argument which does not convince
yourself, may convince the Judge to whom you urge it : and
if it does convince him, why, then, Sir, you are wrong, and
he is right. It is his business to judge; and you are not to
be confident in your own opinion that a cause is bad, but to
say all you can for your client, and then hear the Judge's
opinion." BOSWELL. "But, Sir, does not affecting a warmth
when you have no warmth, and appearing to be clearly of
one opinion when you are in reality of another opinion,
does not such dissimulation impair one's honesty? Is there
not some danger that a lawyer may put on the same

mask

mask in common life, in the intercourse with his friends?"
JOHNSON. "Why no, Sir. Everybody knows you are paid
for affecting warmth for your client; and it is, therefore,
properly no dissimulation: the moment you come from the
bar you resume your usual behaviour. Sir, a man will no
more carry the artifice of the bar into the common intercourse of society, than a man who is paid for tumbling upon
his hands will continue to tumble upon his hands when he
should walk on his feet."'   Boswell's *Life of Johnson*, ii. 47.

Affectation :

IT is not folly but pride, not error but deceit, which the
world means to persecute, when it raises the full cry of
nature to hunt down affectation. . . . Affectation is to be
always distinguished from hypocrisy, as being the art of
counterfeiting those qualities which we might, with innocence and safety, be known to want. . . . Hypocrisy is the
necessary burthen of villany, affectation part of the chosen
trappings of folly; the one completes a villain, the other
only finishes a fop. Contempt is the proper punishment
of affectation, and detestation the just consequence of
hypocrisy.   *Rambler*, No. 20.

.·.

SCARCE any man becomes eminently disagreeable, but
by a departure from his real character, and an attempt at
something for which nature or education have left him
unqualified.   *Rambler*, No. 179.

Allegories :

ALLEGORIES drawn to great length will always break.

Works, vii. 323.

Allegorical

Allegorical Paintings:

I HAD rather see the portrait of a dog that I know than all the allegorical paintings they can show me in the world.

Works (ed. 1787) xi. 208.

Ambition: generally proportioned to capacity:

IT is, I believe, a very just observation, that men's ambition is generally proportioned to their capacity. Providence seldom sends any into the world with an inclination to attempt great things, who have not abilities likewise to perform them.   *Works*, vi. 275.

Ambulatory Students:

TOM RESTLESS has long had a mind to be a man of knowledge, but he does not care to spend much time among authors; for he is of opinion that few books deserve the labour of perusal, that they give the mind an unfashionable cast, and destroy that freedom of thought and easiness of manners indispensably requisite to acceptance in the world. *Tom* has therefore found another way to wisdom. When he rises he goes into a coffee-house, where he creeps so near to men whom he takes to be reasoners as to hear their discourse, and endeavours to remember something which, when it has been strained through *Tom's* head, is so near to nothing, that what it once was cannot be discovered. This he carries round from friend to friend through a circle of visits, till, hearing what each says upon the question, he becomes able at dinner to say a little himself; and, as every great genius relaxes himself among his inferiors, meets with some who wonder how so young a man can talk so wisely.

At

At night he has a new feast prepared for his intellects; he always runs to a disputing society, or a speaking club, where he half hears what, if he had heard the whole, he would but half understand; goes home pleased with the consciousness of a day well spent, lies down full of ideas, and rises in the morning empty as before. *Idler*, No. 48.

Amendments:

AMENDMENTS are seldom made without some token of a rent. Boswell's *Life of Johnson*, iv. 38.

Amusements:

I AM a great friend to publick amusements; for they keep people frcm vice. *Ib.* ii. 169.

Ancestors:

REASON, indeed, will soon inform us, that our estimation of birth is arbitrary and capricious, and that dead ancestors can have no influence but upon imagination: let it then be examined, whether one dream may not operate in the place of another; whether he that owes nothing to forefathers, may not receive equal pleasure from the consciousness of owing all to himself; whether he may not, with a little meditation, find it more honourable to found than to continue a family, and to gain dignity than transmit it; whether if he receives no dignity from the virtues of his family, he does not likewise escape the danger of being disgraced by their crimes; and whether he that brings a new name into the world, has not the convenience of

playing

playing the game of life without a stake, and opportunity of winning much though he has nothing to lose.

Adventurer, No. 111.

Anecdotes:

' DR. JOHNSON had last night looked into Lord Hailes's *Remarks on the History of Scotland.* Dr. Robertson and I said, it was a pity Lord Hailes did not write greater things. His lordship had not then published his *Annals of Scotland.* JOHNSON. " I remember I was once on a visit at the house of a lady for whom I had a high respect. There was a good deal of company in the room. When they were gone, I said to this lady, ' What foolish talking have we had !' ' Yes, (said she,) but while they talked, you said nothing.' I was struck with the reproof. How much better is the man who does anything that is innocent, than he who does nothing. Besides, I love anecdotes. I fancy mankind may come, in time, to write all aphoristically, except in narrative; grow weary of preparation, and connection, and illustration, and all those arts by which a big book is made. If a man is to wait till he weaves anecdotes into a system, we may be long in getting them, and get but few, in comparison of what we might get." '   Boswell's *Life of Johnson*, v. 38.

Antipathies:

THERE is one species of terror which those who are unwilling to suffer the reproach of cowardice have wisely dignified with the name of *antipathy*. A man who talks with intrepidity of the monsters of the wilderness while they are out of sight will readily confess his *antipathy* to a mole, a weasel, or a frog. He has indeed no dread of harm from an insect or a worm, but his *antipathy* turns

him

him pale whenever they approach him. He believes that a boat will transport him with as much safety as his neighbours, but he cannot conquer his *antipathy* to the water. Thus he goes on without any reproach from his own reflections, and every day multiplies *antipathies*, till he becomes contemptible to others, and burdensome to himself. It is indeed certain, that impressions of dread may sometimes be unluckily made by objects not in themselves justly formidable; but when fear is discovered to be groundless, it is to be eradicated like other false opinions, and antipathies are generally superable by a single effort He that has been taught to shudder at a mouse, if he can persuade himself to risk one encounter, will find his own superiority, and exchange his terrors for the pride of conquest.

Rambler, No. 126.

Antiquaries :

A MERE antiquarian is a rugged being.

Boswell's *Life of Johnson*, iii. 278.

Anxious Cleanliness :

THERE is a kind of anxious cleanliness which I have always noted as the characteristic of a slattern; it is the superfluous scrupulosity of guilt, dreading discovery, and shunning suspicion: it is the violence of an effort against habit, which, being impelled by external motives, cannot stop at the middle point.   *Rambler*, No. 115.

Appetite :

A MAN who rides out for an appetite consults but little the dignity of human nature.   *Works* (ed. 1787) xi. 204.

Arguments

Arguments and Understanding:

JOHNSON having argued for some time with a pertinacious gentleman; his opponent, who had talked in a very puzzling manner, happened to say, ' I don't understand you, Sir:' upon which Johnson observed, ' Sir, I have found you an argument; but I am not obliged to find you an understanding.'

Boswell's Life of Johnson, iv. 313.

Army:

I DOUBT not but I shall hear on this occasion of the service of our troops in the suppression of riots; we shall be told by the next pompous orator who shall rise up in defence of the army that they have often dispersed the smugglers; that the colliers have been driven down by the terror of their appearance to their subterraneous fortifications; that the weavers in the midst of that rage which hunger and oppression excited fled at their approach; that they have at our markets bravely regulated the price of butter, and sometimes in the utmost exertion of heroic fury broken those eggs which they were not suffered to purchase on their own terms.

Debates, x. 52.

.·.

IT is not without compassion, compassion very far extended, that I consider the unhappy striplings doomed to a camp from whom the sun has hitherto been screened and the wind excluded, who have been taught by many tender lectures the unwholesomeness of the evening mists and the morning dews, who have been wrapt in furs in winter and cooled with fans in summer, who have lived without any

fatigue

fatigue but that of dress, or any care but that of their complexion. Who can forbear some degree of sympathy when he sees animals like these taking their last farewell of the maid that has fed them with sweetmeats and defended them from insects; when he sees them dressed up in the habiliments of soldiers, loaded with a sword and invested with a command, not to mount the guard at the palace, nor to display their lace at a review; not to protect ladies at the door of an assembly-room nor to show their intrepidity at a country fair, but to enter into a kind of fellowship with the rugged sailor, to hear the tumult of a storm, to sustain the change of climate, and to be set on shore in an enemy's dominions?

Debates, x. 63.

Assertors of Uncontroverted Truth:

Tom Steady was a vehement assertor of uncontroverted truth; and by keeping himself out of the reach of contradiction, had acquired all the confidence which the consciousness of irresistible abilities could have given. I was once mentioning a man of eminence, and, after having recounted his virtues, endeavoured to represent him fully, by mentioning his faults. *Sir*, said Mr. *Steady, that he has faults I can easily believe, for who is without them? No man, Sir, is now alive, among the innumerable multitudes that swarm upon the earth, however wise, or however good, who has not, in some degree, his failings and his faults. If there be any man faultless, bring him forth into public view, shew him openly, and let him be known; but I will venture to affirm, and, till the contrary be plainly shewn, shall always maintain, that no such man is to be found. Tell not me, Sir, of impeccability and perfection; such talk is for those that are strangers in the world:*

world: I have seen several nations, and conversed with all ranks of people: I have known the great and the mean, the learned and the ignorant, the old and the young, the clerical and the lay; but I have never found a man without a fault; and I suppose shall die in the opinion, that to be human is to be frail. To all this nothing could be opposed. I listened with a hanging head; Mr. *Steady* looked round on the hearers with triumph, and saw every eye congratulating his victory; he departed, and spent the next morning in following those who retired from the company, and telling them, with injunctions of secrecy, how poor *Spritely* began to take liberties with men wiser than himself; but that he suppressed him by a decisive argument, which put him totally to silence.

Idler, No. 78.

Attention:

You are now retired, and have nothing to impede self-examination or self-improvement. Endeavour to reform that instability of attention which your last letter has happened to betray. Perhaps it is natural for those that have much within to think little on things without; but whoever lives heedlessly lives but in a mist, perpetually deceived by false appearances of the past, without any certain reliance on recollection.

Piozzi Letters, ii. 319.

Attorneys:

Much enquiry having been made concerning a gentleman, who had quitted a company where Johnson was, and no information being obtained; at last Johnson observed, that he did not care to speak ill of any man behind his back, but he believed the gentleman was an *attorney.*

Boswell's Life of Johnson, ii. 126.

Audacity

Audacity the last Refuge of Guilt:

To revenge reasonable incredulity by refusing evidence [1] is a degree of insolence with which the world is not yet acquainted; and stubborn audacity is the last refuge of guilt.

Works, ix. 115.

Authority:

It must always be the condition of a great part of mankind to reject and embrace tenets upon the authority of those whom they think wiser than themselves ; and, therefore, the addition of every name to infidelity in some degree invalidates that argument upon which the religion of multitudes is necessarily founded.

Ib. vi. 501.

.˙.

The general story of mankind will evince that lawful and settled authority is very seldom resisted when it is well employed. Gross corruption or evident imbecility is necessary to the suppression of that reverence with which the majority of mankind look upon their governors, and on those whom they see surrounded by splendor and fortified by power. For though men are drawn by their passions into forgetfulness of invisible rewards and punishments, yet they are easily kept obedient to those who have temporal dominion in their hands till their veneration is dissipated by such wickedness and folly as can neither be defended nor concealed.

Rambler, No. 50.

---

[1] Johnson had challenged Macpherson to produce the original Erse manuscripts of the poems of Ossian.

Authors :

Authors :

THERE seems to be a strange affectation in authors of appearing to have done everything by chance.

Works, viii. 24.

.˙.

MY character as a man, a subject, or a trader, is under the protection of the law; but my reputation as an author is at the mercy of the reader who lies under no other obligations to do me justice than those of religion and morality. If a man calls me rebel or bankrupt I may prosecute and punish him; but if a man calls me idiot or plagiary I have no remedy; since by selling him the book I admit his privilege of judging and declaring his judgment, and can appeal only to other readers if I think myself injured.

In different characters we are more or less protected; to hiss a pleader at the bar would perhaps be deemed illegal and punishable, but to hiss a dramatic writer is justifiable by custom.

Ib. v. 463.

.˙.

THE writer who thinks his works formed for duration mistakes his interest when he mentions his enemies. He degrades his own dignity by shewing that he was affected by their censures, and gives lasting importance to names, which, left to themselves, would vanish from remembrance.

Ib. vii. 294.

.˙.

THERE is nothing more dreadful to an author than neglect, compared with which, reproach, hatred, and opposition, are names of happiness.

Rambler, No. 2.

'DR. JOHNSON

'DR. JOHNSON said he expected to be attacked on account of his *Lives of the Poets.* "However (said he) I would rather be attacked than unnoticed. For the worst thing you can do to an author is to be silent as to his works. An assault upon a town is a bad thing; but starving it is still worse; an assault may be unsuccessful; you may have more men killed than you kill; but if you starve the town, you are sure of victory."'   Boswell's *Life of Johnson*, iii. 375.

.˙.

IT is advantageous to an author, that his book should be attacked as well as praised. Fame is a shuttlecock. If it be struck only at one end of the room, it will soon fall to the ground. To keep it up, it must be struck at both ends.   *Ib.* v. 400.

.˙.

'MRS. COTTERELL having one day asked Dr. Johnson to introduce her to a celebrated writer, "Dearest Madam," said he, "you had better let it alone; the best part of every author is in general to be found in his book, I assure you."'   *Ib.* i. 450 *n.* 1.

.˙.

A TRANSITION from an author's book to his conversation, is too often like an entrance into a large city, after a distant prospect. Remotely, we see nothing but spires of temples and turrets of palaces, and imagine it the residence of splendour, grandeur, and magnificence; but, when we have passed the gates, we find it perplexed with narrow passages, disgraced with despicable cottages, embarrassed with obstructions, and clouded with smoke.   *Rambler*, No. 14.

No vanity can more justly incur contempt and indignation than that which boasts of negligence and hurry. . . . Among the writers of antiquity I remember none except Statius who ventures to mention the speedy production of his writings, either as an extenuation of his faults, or a proof of his facility. Nor did Statius, when he considered himself as a candidate for lasting reputation, think a closer attention unnecessary, but amidst all his pride and indigence, the two great hasteners of modern poems, employed twelve years upon the Thebaid, and thinks his claim to renown proportionate to his labour.

> *Thebais, multa cruciata lima,*
> *Tentat, audaci fide, Mantuanæ*
>   *Gaudia famæ.*

> Polish'd with endless toil, my lays
> At length aspire to Mantuan praise.
>
> *Rambler*, No. 169.

.·.

Nothing is more common than to find men whose works are now totally neglected mentioned with praises by their contemporaries, as the oracles of their age, and the legislators of science. Curiosity is naturally excited, their volumes after long inquiry are found, but seldom reward the labour of the search. Every period of time has produced these bubbles of artificial fame, which are kept up a while by the breath of fashion, and then break at once, and are annihilated. The learned often bewail the loss of ancient writers whose characters have survived their works; but, perhaps, if we could now retrieve them, we should find them only the

Granvilles,

Granvilles [1], Montagues [2], Stepneys [3], and Sheffields [4] of their time, and wonder by what infatuation or caprice they could be raised to notice. *Rambler*, No. 106.

. ˙ .

THE chief glory of every people arises from its authors: whether I shall add anything by my own writings to the reputation of English literature must be left to time : much of my life has been lost under the pressures of disease; much has been trifled away; and much has always been spent in provision for the day that was passing over me; but I shall not think my employment useless or ignoble, if by my assistance foreign nations and distant ages gain access to the propagators of knowledge, and understand the teachers of truth ; if my labours afford light to the repositories of science, and add celebrity to Bacon, to Hooker, to Milton, and to Boyle.

When I am animated by this wish, I look with pleasure on my book [5], however defective, and deliver it to the world with the spirit of a man that has endeavoured well.

Works, v. 49.

. ˙ .

I HAVE been often inclined to doubt whether authors, however querulous, are in reality more miserable than their fellow mortals. The present life is to all a state of infelicity; every man, like an author, believes himself to

---

[1] George Granville, Lord Lansdowne.
[2] Charles Montague, Earl of Halifax.   [3] George Stepney.
[4] John Sheffield, Duke of Buckinghamshire. They were all four 'raised to notice' by being included in Johnson's *Lives of the Poets*.
[5] *The Dictionary of the English Language.*

merit more than he obtains, and solaces the present with the prospect of the future; others, indeed, suffer those disappointments in silence of which the writer complains to show how well he has learnt the art of lamentation.

Adventurer, No. 138.

NEVER let criticisms operate upon your face or your mind; it is very rarely that an author is hurt by his critics. The blaze of reputation cannot be blown out, but it often dies in the socket; a very few names may be considered as perpetual lamps that shine unconsumed.

Piozzi Letters, ii. 110.

IT is one of the common distresses of a writer to be within a word of a happy period, to want only a single epithet to give amplification its full force, to require only a correspondent term in order to finish a paragraph with elegance and make one of its members answer to the other: but these deficiencies cannot always be supplied; and after a long study and vexation, the passage is turned anew, and the web unwoven that was so nearly finished.

Adventurer, No. 138.

IT is commonly supposed that the uniformity of a studious life affords no matter for a narration: but the truth is, that of the most studious life a great part passes without study. An author partakes of the common condition of humanity; he is born and married like another man; he has hopes and fears, expectations and disappointments, griefs and joys, and friends and enemies, like a courtier or a statesman;

nor

nor can I conceive why his affairs should not excite curiosity as much as the whisper of a drawing-room, or the factions of a camp.

Idler, No. 102.

MEN of the pen have seldom any great skill in conquering kingdoms, but they have strong inclination to give advice.

Works, vi. 260.

WE are blinded in examining our own labours by innumerable prejudices. Our juvenile compositions please us because they bring to our minds the remembrance of youth; our later performances we are ready to esteem because we are unwilling to think that we have made no improvement; what flows easily from the pen charms us because we read with pleasure that which flatters our opinion of our own powers; what was composed with great struggles of the mind we do not easily reject because we cannot bear that so much labour should be fruitless.

Rambler, No. 21.

MANY causes may vitiate a writer's judgment of his own works. On that which has cost him much labour he sets a high value because he is unwilling to think that he has been diligent in vain; what has been produced without toilsome efforts is considered with delight, as a proof of vigorous faculties and fertile invention; and the last work, whatever it be, has necessarily most of the grace of novelty.

Works, vii. 110.

TEDIOUSNESS is the most fatal of all faults; negligences or errors are single and local, but tediousness pervades the

whole;

whole; other faults are censured and forgotten, but the power of tediousness propagates itself. He that is weary the first hour is more weary the second; as bodies forced into motion, contrary to their tendency, pass more and more slowly through every successive interval of space. Unhappily this pernicious failure is that which an author is least able to discover. We are seldom tiresome to ourselves; and the act of composition fills and delights the mind with change of language and succession of images; every couplet when produced is new, and novelty is the great source of pleasure. Perhaps no man ever thought a line superfluous when he first wrote it, or contracted his work till his ebullitions of invention had subsided. And even if he should control his desire of immediate renown, and keep his work *nine years* unpublished, he will be still the author, and still in danger of deceiving himself: and if he consults his friends, he will probably find men who have more kindness than judgment, or more fear to offend than desire to instruct.

Works, viii. 18.

.•.

THERE is indeed some tenderness due to living writers, when they attack none of those truths which are of importance to the happiness of mankind, and have committed no other offence than that of betraying their own ignorance or dulness. I should think it cruelty to crush an insect who had provoked me only by buzzing in my ear; and would not willingly interrupt the dream of harmless stupidity, or destroy the jest which makes its author laugh. Yet I am far from thinking this tenderness universally necessary; for he that writes may be considered as a kind of general challenger whom every one has a right to attack,

since

since he quits the common rank of life, steps forward beyond the list, and offers his merit to the public judgment. To commence author is to claim praise, and no man can justly aspire to honour, but at the hazard of disgrace.

Rambler, No. 93.

Wit and Wisdom of Samuel Johnson.

.·.

To deliver examples to posterity, and to regulate the opinion of future times, is no slight or trivial undertaking; nor is it easy to commit more atrocious treason against the great republic of humanity than by falsifying its records and misguiding its decrees.

Ib. No. 136.

.·.

'A SHILLING was now wanted for some purpose or other; and none of them happened to have one. I begged that I might lend one. "Ay, do," said Dr. Johnson, "I will borrow of you; authors are like privateers, always fair game for one another."'

Boswell's *Life of Johnson*, iv. 191 *n.* 1.

.·.

A WRITER who obtains his full purpose loses himself in his own lustre. Of an opinion which is no longer doubted the evidence ceases to be examined. Of an art universally practised the first teacher is forgotten. Learning once made popular is no longer learning; it has the appearance of something which we have bestowed upon ourselves, as the dew appears to rise from the field which it refreshes.

Works, vii. 301.

.·.

HE by whose writings the heart is rectified, the appetites counteracted, and the passions repressed, may be considered as not unprofitable to the great republic of humanity,

even

even though his behaviour should not always exemplify his rules. His instructions may diffuse their influence to regions in which it will not be inquired whether the author be *albus an ater*, good or bad; to times when all his faults and all his follies shall be lost in forgetfulness among things of no concern or importance to the world; and he may kindle in thousands and ten thousands that flame which burnt but dimly in himself, through the fumes of passion or the damps of cowardice.   *Rambler*, No. 77.

.˙.

'LADY MACLEOD objected that the author[1] does not practise what he teaches. JOHNSON. "I cannot help that, Madam. That does not make his book the worse. People are influenced more by what a man says, if his practice is suitable to it,—because they are blockheads. The more intellectual people are, the readier will they attend to what a man tells them. If it is just, they will follow it, be his practice what it will. No man practises so well as he writes. I have all my life long been lying till noon; yet I tell all young men, and tell them with great sincerity, that nobody who does not rise early will ever do any good. Only consider! You read a book; you are convinced by it; you do not know the author. Suppose you afterwards know him, and find that he does not practise what he teaches; are you to give up your former conviction? At this rate you would be kept in a state of equilibrium, when reading every book, till you knew how the author practised." "But," said Lady MacLeod, "you would think

---

[1] Dr. Cadogan, the author of a *Dissertation on the Gout*.

better

better of Dr. Cadogan, if he acted according to his principles." JOHNSON. " Why, Madam, to be sure, a man who acts in the face of light is worse than a man who does not know so much; yet I think no man should be the worse thought of for publishing good principles. There is something noble in publishing truth, though it condemns one's self." [1] Boswell's *Life of Johnson*, v. 210.

THE reciprocal civility of authors is one of the most risible scenes in the farce of life.

Works, vi. 478.

WRITERS commonly derive their reputation from their works; but there are works which owe their reputation to the character of the writer. The public sometimes has its favourites, whom it rewards for one species of excellence with the honours due to another. From him whom we reverence for his beneficence we do not willingly withhold the praise of genius; a man of exalted merit becomes at once an accomplished writer, as a beauty finds no great difficulty in passing for a wit.

Ib. viii. 77.

THIS censure [1] time has not left us the power of confirming or refuting; but observation daily shows that much stress is not to be laid on hyperbolical accusations and pointed sentences, which even he that utters them desires to be applauded rather than credited. Addison can hardly be supposed to have meant all that he said. Few characters

---

[1] Censure passed by Addison on Rowe.

can bear the microscopic scrutiny of wit quickened by anger ;
and perhaps the best advice to authors would be that they
should keep out of the way of one another.   *Works*, vii. 415.

.·.

His[1] works afford too many examples of dissolute licentiousness and abject adulation ; but they were probably, like
his merriment, artificial and constrained ; the effects of study
and meditation, and his trade rather than his pleasure.

Of the mind that can trade in corruption, and can de-
liberately pollute itself with ideal wickedness for the sake of
spreading the contagion in society, I wish not to conceal
or excuse the depravity. Such degradation of the dignity
of genius, such abuse of superlative abilities, cannot be
contemplated but with grief and indignation. What consolation can be had Dryden has afforded by living to repent,
and to testify his repentance.   *Ib.* vii. 293.

.·.

The wickedness of a loose or profane author is more
atrocious than that of the giddy libertine or drunken
ravisher, not only because it extends its effects wider, as a
pestilence that taints the air is more destructive than poison
infused in a draught, but because it is committed with cool
deliberation. By the instantaneous violence of desire, a
good man may sometimes be surprised before reflection can
come to his rescue ; when the appetites have strengthened
their influence by habit, they are not easily resisted or suppressed ; but for the frigid villany of studious lewdness, for
the calm malignity of laboured impiety, what apology can

---

[1] Johnson is speaking of Dryden.

be

be invented? What punishment can be adequate to the crime of him who retires to solitudes for the refinement of debauchery; who tortures his fancy and ransacks his memory only that he may leave the world less virtuous than he found it; that he may intercept the hopes of the rising generation, and spread snares for the soul with more dexterity?

Rambler, No. 77.

He that is himself weary will soon weary the public. Let him therefore lay down his employment, whatever it be, who can no longer exert his former activity or attention; let him not endeavour to struggle with censure, or obstinately infest the stage till a general hiss commands him to depart.

Ib. No. 207.

The promises of authors are like the vows of lovers.

Works, vii. 450.

An author and his reader are not always of a mind.

Ib. viii. 371.

No man but a blockhead ever wrote except for money.

Boswell's *Life of Johnson,* iii. 19.

Avarice:

Avarice is generally the last passion of those lives of which the first part has been squandered in pleasure, and the second devoted to ambition. He that sinks under the fatigue of getting wealth lulls his age with the milder business of saving it.

Rambler, No. 151.

HE

HE [1] was censured as covetous, and has been defended by an instance of inattention to his affairs; as if a man might not at once be corrupted by avarice and idleness.

Works, vii. 483.

．•．

AVARICE is an uniform and tractable vice: other intellectual distempers are different in different constitutions of mind; that which soothes the pride of one will offend the pride of another; but to the favour of the covetous there is a ready way; bring money and nothing is denied.

Rasselas, ch. 39.

Balance of power:

WE have suffered our trade to be destroyed and our country impoverished for the sake of holding the balance of power; that variable balance in which folly and ambition are perpetually changing the weights, and which neither policy nor strength could yet preserve steady for a single year.

Debates. Works, xi. 294.

．•．

I HOPE our ministers will in time think it no advantage to their fellow-subjects to be doomed to fight the battles of other nations, and to be called out into every field, where they shall happen to hear that blood is to be shed. I hope they will be taught that the only business of Britain is commerce, and that while our ships pass unmolested we may sit at ease whatever be the designs or actions of the potentates on the continent; that none but naval power can endanger our safety, and that it is not necessary for us to inquire how foreign territories are distributed, what family

---

[1] John Sheffield, Duke of Buckinghamshire.

approaches

approaches to its extinction, or where a successor will be found to any other crown than that of Britain. . . . Had these principles been received by our forefathers we might now have given laws to the world; and perhaps our posterity will with equal reason say, How happy, how great and formidable they should have been, had not we attempted to fix and hold the balance of power and neglected the interest of our country for the preservation of the House of Austria.

Debates.—Works, xi. 300.

Beauty:

'I MENTIONED a friend of mine having resolved never to marry a pretty woman. JOHNSON. "Sir, it is a very foolish resolution to resolve not to marry a pretty woman. Beauty is of itself very estimable. No, Sir, I would prefer a pretty woman, unless there are objections to her. A pretty woman may be foolish; a pretty woman may be wicked; a pretty woman may not like me. But there is no such danger in marrying a pretty woman as is apprehended: she will not be persecuted if she does not invite persecution. A pretty woman, if she has a mind to be wicked, can find a readier way than another; and that is all."'

Boswell's Life of Johnson, iv. 131.

Benevolence:

To act from pure benevolence is not possible for finite beings. Human benevolence is mingled with vanity, interest, or some other motive. *Ib.* iii. 48.

Bet Flint:

'"I WONDER," said Mrs. Thrale, "you bear with my nonsense. "No, Madam, you never talk nonsense; you have as much sense and more wit than any woman I know."

"Oh,"

"Oh," cried Mrs. Thrale, blushing, "it is my turn to go under the table this morning, Miss Burney." "And yet," continued the doctor, with the most comical look, "I have known all the wits from Mrs. Montagu down to Bet Flint." "Bet Flint!" cried Mrs. Thrale. "Pray, who is she?" "Oh, a fine character, Madam. She was habitually a slut and a drunkard, and occasionally a thief and a harlot." "And, for Heaven's sake, how came you to know her?" "Why, Madam, she figured in the literary world too. Bet Flint wrote her own life and called herself Cassandra, and it was in verse;—it began:

> 'When nature first ordained my birth
> A diminutive I was born on earth:
> And then I came from a dark abode
> Into a gay and gaudy world.'

Mrs. Williams," he added, "did not love Bet Flint, but Bet Flint made herself very easy about that."'

Mme. D'Arblay's Diary, i. 87, 90.

Biography:

THE mischievous consequences of vice and folly, of irregular desires and predominant passions, are best discovered by those relations which are levelled with the general surface of life, which tell not how any man became great, but how he was made happy; not how he lost the favour of his prince, but how he became discontented with himself. Those relations are therefore commonly of most value in which the writer tells his own story. He that recounts the life of another commonly dwells most upon conspicuous events, lessens the familiarity of his tale to increase its dignity, shows his favourite at a distance, decorated and magnified like the ancient actors in their

tragic

tragic dress, and endeavours to hide the man that he may produce a hero. *Idler*, No. 84.

.˙.

IF the biographer writes from personal knowledge and makes haste to gratify the public curiosity, there is danger lest his interest, his fear, his gratitude, or his tenderness, overpower his fidelity, and tempt him to conceal, if not to invent. There are many who think it an act of piety to hide the faults or failings of their friends, even when they can no longer suffer by their detection; we therefore see whole ranks of characters adorned with uniform panegyric, and not to be known from one another but by extrinsic and casual circumstances. 'Let me remember,' says Hale, 'when I find myself inclined to pity a criminal, that there is likewise a pity due to the country.' If we owe regard to the memory of the dead, there is yet more respect to be paid to knowledge, to virtue, and to truth. *Rambler*, No. 60.

.˙.

THE necessity of complying with times, and of sparing persons, is the great impediment of biography. History may be formed from permanent monuments and records; but lives can only be written from personal knowledge, which is growing every day less, and in a short time is lost for ever. What is known can seldom be immediately told; and when it might be told, it is no longer known. The delicate features of the mind, the nice discriminations of character, and the minute peculiarities of conduct, are soon obliterated: and it is surely better that caprice, obstinacy, frolic, and folly, however they might delight in the description, should be silently forgotten, than that by wanton merriment and unseasonable detection, a pang should be

given

given to a widow, a daughter, a brother, or a friend.   As
the process of these narratives[1] is now bringing me among
my contemporaries, I begin to feel myself 'walking upon
ashes under which the fire is not extinguished,' and coming
to the time of which it will be proper rather to say 'nothing
that is false than all that is true.'   *Works*, vii. 444.

.·.

I HAVE often thought that there has rarely passed a life
of which a judicious and faithful narrative would not be
useful.   For not only every man has, in the mighty mass
of the world, great numbers in the same condition with
himself to whom his mistakes and miscarriages, escapes and
expedients, would be of immediate and apparent use; but
there is such an uniformity in the state of man, considered
apart from adventitious and separable decorations and disguises, that there is scarce any possibility of good or ill but
is common to human kind.   *Rambler*, No. 60.

.·.

'MR. FOWKE once observed to Dr. Johnson that, in his
opinion, the Doctor's literary strength lay in writing biography, in which he infinitely exceeded all his contemporaries.   "Sir," said Johnson, "I believe that is true.   The
dogs don't know how to write trifles with dignity."'
                    Boswell's *Life of Johnson*, iv. 34 *n.* 5.

Bolingbroke and Mallet:

'ON the 6th of March[2] came out Lord Bolingbroke's
works, published by Mr. David Mallet.   The wild and
pernicious ravings under the name of " Philosophy," which

---

[1] *The Lives of the Poets.*   [2] 1754.

                    were

were thus ushered into the world, gave great offence to all well-principled men. Johnson, hearing of their tendency, which nobody disputed, was roused with a just indignation, and pronounced this memorable sentence upon the noble author and his editor :—" Sir, he was a scoundrel, and a coward: a scoundrel for charging a blunderbuss against religion and morality ; a coward, because he had not resolution to fire it off himself, but left half-a-crown to a beggarly Scotchman to draw the trigger after his death !" '

Boswell's *Life of Johnson*, i. 268.

Bonds:

IF we consider the present state of the world, it will be found that all confidence is lost among mankind, that no man ventures to act where money can be endangered upon the faith of another. It is impossible to see the long scrolls in which every contract is included, with all their appendages of seals and attestation, without wondering at the depravity of those beings who must be restrained from violation of promise by such formal and public evidences, and precluded from equivocation and subterfuge by such punctilious minuteness. Among all the satires to which folly and wickedness have given occasion, none is equally severe with a bond or a settlement.   *Rambler*, No. 131.

Books:

IT was the maxim, I think, of Alphonsus of Aragon that *dead counsellors are safest.* The grave puts an end to flattery and artifice, and the information that we receive from books is pure from interest, fear, or ambition. Dead counsellors are likewise most instructive, because they are heard with patience and with reverence. We are not unwilling to

believe

believe that man wiser than ourselves from whose abilities we may receive advantage without any danger of rivalry or opposition, and who affords us the light of his experience without hurting our eyes by flashes of insolence.

Rambler, No. 87.

.˙.

'JOHNSON said that Baretti had told him of some Italian author, who said that a good work must be that with which the vulgar were pleased, and of which the learned could tell why it pleased; that it must be able to employ the learned, and detain the idle. Chevy Chase pleased the vulgar, but did not satisfy the learned; it did not fill a mind capable of thinking strongly. The merit of Shakspeare was such as the ignorant could take in, and the learned add nothing to it.'   Windham's *Diary*, p. 18.

.˙.

WHOEVER has remarked the fate of books must have found it governed by other causes than general consent arising from general conviction. If a new performance happens not to fall into the hands of some who have courage to tell and authority to propagate their opinion, it often remains long in obscurity, and perishes unknown and unexamined. A few, a very few, commonly constitute the taste of the time; the judgment which they have once pronounced, some are too lazy to discuss, and some too timorous to contradict: it may however be, I think, observed, that their power is greater to depress than exalt, as mankind are more credulous of censure than of praise.

Adventurer, No. 138.

.˙.

IT is not by comparing line with line that the merit of

great

great works is to be estimated, but by their general effects and ultimate result. It is easy to note a weak line, and write one more vigorous in its place, to find a happiness of expression in the original, and transplant it by force into the version : but what is given to the parts may be subducted from the whole, and the reader may be weary, though the critic may commend. Works of imagination excel by their allurement and delight; by their power of attracting and detaining the attention. That book is good in vain which the reader throws away. He only is the master who keeps the mind in pleasing captivity; whose pages are perused with eagerness, and in hope of new pleasure are perused again ; and whose conclusion is perceived with an eye of sorrow, such as the traveller casts upon departing day.   *Works,* vii. 337.

IT is observed that *a corrupt society has many laws*; I know not whether it is not equally true, that *an ignorant age has many books.* When the treasures of ancient knowledge lie unexamined, and original authors are neglected and forgotten, compilers and plagiaries are encouraged who give us again what we had before, and grow great by setting before us what our own sloth had hidden from our view.

Idler, No. 85.

WHAT is good only because it pleases cannot be pronounced good till it has been found to please.

Works, vii. 252.

To works of which the excellence is not absolute and definite, but gradual and comparative ; to works not raised

D   upon

upon principles demonstrative and scientific, but appealing wholly to observation and experience, no other test can be applied than length of duration and continuance of esteem. What mankind have long possessed, they have often examined and compared; and if they persist to value the possession, it is because frequent comparisons have confirmed opinion in its favour. *Works*, v. 104.

Brandy:

'JOHNSON harangued upon the qualities of different liquors; and spoke with great contempt of claret as so weak, that "a man would be drowned by it before it made him drunk." He was persuaded to drink one glass of it, that he might judge, not from recollection which might be dim, but from immediate sensation. He shook his head, and said, "Poor stuff! No, Sir, claret is the liquor for boys; port for men; but he who aspires to be a hero (smiling) must drink brandy."' Boswell's *Life of Johnson*, iii. 381.

Brentford:

I ONCE reminded Johnson that when Dr. Adam Smith was expatiating on the beauty of Glasgow, he had cut him short by saying, 'Pray, Sir, have you ever seen Brentford?' and I took the liberty to add, 'My dear Sir, surely that was *shocking*.' 'Why, then, Sir, (he replied,) YOU have never seen Brentford.' *Ib.* iv. 186.

Building:

THE happiness of building lasted but a little while, for though I love to spend, I hate to be cheated; and I soon found that to build is to be robbed. *Idler*, No. 62.

Burlesque:

Burlesque:

BURLESQUE consists in a disproportion between the style and the sentiments, or between the adventitious sentiments and the fundamental subject. It therefore, like all bodies compounded of heterogeneous parts, contains in it a principle of corruption. All disproportion is unnatural; and from what is unnatural we can derive only the pleasure which novelty produces. We admire it a while as a strange thing; but when it is no longer strange, we perceive its deformity. It is a kind of artifice which by frequent repetition detects itself; and the reader, learning in time what he is to expect, lays down his book, as the spectator turns away from a second exhibition of those tricks of which the only use is to show that they can be played. *Works*, vii. 155.

Bustle of Idleness:

WHEN Tom Restless rises he goes into a coffee-house, where he creeps so near to men whom he takes to be reasoners as to hear their discourse, and endeavours to remember something which, when it has been strained through Tom's head, is so near to nothing, that what it once was cannot be discovered. This he carries round from friend to friend through a circle of visits, till, hearing what each says upon the question, he becomes able at dinner to say a little himself; and as every great genius relaxes himself among his inferiors, meets with some who wonder how so young a man can talk so wisely. At night he has a new feast prepared for his intellects; he always runs to a disputing society, or a speaking club, where he half hears what, if he had heard the whole, he would but half understand; goes home pleased with the consciousness

Wit and Wisdom of Samuel Johnson.

of a day well spent, lies down full of ideas, and rises in the morning empty as before.'

Idler, No. 48.

Calumny:

CALUMNY differs from most other injuries in this dreadful circumstance. He who commits it never can repair it. A false report may spread where a recantation never reaches; and an accusation must certainly fly faster than a defence while the greater part of mankind are base and wicked. The effects of a false report cannot be determined or circumscribed. It may check a hero in his attempts for the promotion of the happiness of his country, or a saint in his endeavours for the propagation of truth.

Works, ix. 449.

Cant:

BOSWELL. 'I wish much to be in Parliament, Sir.' JOHNSON. 'Why, Sir, unless you come resolved to support any administration, you would be the worse for being in Parliament, because you would be obliged to live more expensively.' BOSWELL. 'Perhaps, Sir, I should be the less happy for being in Parliament. I never would sell my vote, and I should be vexed if things went wrong.' JOHNSON. 'That's cant, Sir. It would not vex you more in the house than in the gallery: public affairs vex no man.' BOSWELL. 'Have not they vexed yourself a little, Sir? Have not you been vexed by all the turbulence of this reign, and by that absurd vote of the House of Commons, "That the influence of the Crown has increased, is increasing, and ought to be diminished?"' JOHNSON. 'Sir, I have never slept an hour less, nor eat an ounce less meat.

I would

I would have knocked the factious dogs on the head, to be sure; but I was not *vexed.*' BOSWELL. 'I declare, Sir, upon my honour, I did imagine I was vexed, and took a pride in it; but it *was*, perhaps, cant; for I own I neither ate less, nor slept less.' JOHNSON. 'My dear friend, clear your *mind* of cant. You may *talk* as other people do : you may say to a man, "Sir, I am your most humble servant." You are *not* his most humble servant. You may say, "These are bad times; it is a melancholy thing to be reserved to such times." You don't mind the times. You tell a man, "I am sorry you had such bad weather the last day of your journey, and were so much wet." You don't care sixpence whether he is wet or dry. You may *talk* in this manner; it is a mode of talking in Society : but don't *think* foolishly.'   Boswell's *Life of Johnson*, iv. 220.

Wit and
Wisdom
of
Samuel
Johnson.

.·.

WE are either born with such dissimilitude of temper and inclination, or receive so many of our ideas and opinions from the state of life in which we are engaged, that the griefs and cares of one part of mankind seem to the other hypocrisy, folly, and affectation. Every class of society has its cant of lamentation which is understood or regarded by none but themselves; and every part of life has its uneasinesses which those who do not feel them will not commiserate.   *Rambler*, No. 128.

Caricatures :

'IT was after the publication of the *Lives of the Poets* that Dr. Farr, being engaged to dine with Sir Joshua Reynolds, mentioned, on coming in, that in his way he had seen a
caricature,

caricature, which he thought clever, of the nine muses flogging Dr. Johnson round Parnassus. The admirers of Gray and others, who thought their favourites hardly treated in the *Lives*, were laughing at Dr. Farr's account of the print, when Dr. Johnson was himself announced. Dr. Farr being the only stranger, Sir Joshua introduced him, and, to Dr. Farr's infinite embarrassment, repeated what he had just been telling them. Johnson was not at all surly on the occasion, but said, turning to Dr. Farr, "Sir, I am very glad to hear this. I hope the day will never arrive when I shall neither be the object of calumny or ridicule, for then I shall be neglected and forgotten."'

Murray's *Johnsoniana*, p. 229.

Censure of a man's self:

ALL censure of a man's self is oblique praise. It is in order to show how much he can spare. It has all the invidiousness of self-praise, and all the reproach of false-hood.

Boswell's *Life of Johnson*, iii. 323.

Chance:

HE seldom lives frugally who lives by chance. Hope is always liberal; and they that trust her promises make little scruple of revelling to-day on the profits of the morrow.

Works, vii. 298.

Change:

SUCH is the state of life, that none are happy but by the anticipation of change: the change itself is nothing; when we have made it the next wish is to change again.

Rasselas, ch. 47.

Character:

Character:

AMONG the sentiments which almost every man changes as he advances into years, is the expectation of uniformity of character.   He that without acquaintance with the power of desire, the cogency of distress, the complications of affairs, or the force of partial influence, has filled his mind with the excellence of virtue, and, having never tried his resolution in any encounters with hope or fear, believes it able to stand firm whatever shall oppose it, will be always clamorous against the smallest failure, ready to exact the utmost punctualities of right, and to consider every man that fails in any part of his duty as without conscience and without merit; unworthy of trust or love, of pity or regard; as an enemy whom all should join to drive out of society, as a pest which all should avoid, or as a weed which all should trample.   It is not but by experience that we are taught the possibility of retaining some virtues and rejecting others, or of being good or bad to a particular degree.

Rambler, No. 70.

．∶．

DERRICK may do very well as long as he can outrun his character; but the moment his character gets up with him, it is all over.   Boswell's *Life of Johnson*, i. 394.

Charity:

BY charity is to be understood every assistance of weakness or supply of wants produced by a desire of benefiting others and of pleasing God.   Not every act of liberality, every increase of the wealth of another, not every flow of negligent profusion or thoughtless start of sudden munificence is to be dignified with this venerable name.   There are

many

many motives to the appearance of bounty very different from those of true charity and which, with whatever success they may be imposed upon mankind, will be distinguished at the last day by Him to whom all hearts are open. It is not impossible that men whose chief desire is esteem and applause, who court the favour of the multitude and think fame the great end of action, may squander their wealth in such a manner that some part of it may benefit the virtuous or the miserable; but as the guilt, so the virtue of every action arises from design; and those blessings which are bestowed by chance will be of very little advantage to him that scattered them with no other prospect than that of hearing his own praises; praises of which he will not be often disappointed, but of which our Lord has determined that they shall be his reward. If any man in the distribution of his favours finds the desire of engaging gratitude or gaining affection to predominate in his mind; if he finds his benevolence weakened by observing that his favours are forgotten, and that those whom he has most studiously benefited are often least zealous for his service, he ought to remember that he is not acting upon the proper motives of charity. For true charity arises from faith in the promises of God, and expects rewards only in a future state. To hope for our recompense in this life is not beneficence but usury.

Works, ix. 322.

.·.

WHAT stronger incitement can any man require to a due consideration of the poor and needy than that the Lord will deliver him in the day of trouble; in that day when the shadow of death shall compass him about, and all the vanities of the world shall fade away, when all the comforts

of

of this life shall forsake him, when pleasure shall no longer delight nor power protect him? In that dreadful hour shall the man whose care has been extended to the general happiness of mankind, whose charity has rescued sickness from the grave and poverty from the dungeon; who has heard the groans of the aged struggling with misfortunes, and the cries of infants languishing with hunger, find favour in the sight of the great Author of society, and his recompense shall flow upon him from the fountain of mercy; he shall stand without fear on the brink of life and pass into eternity with an humble confidence of finding that mercy which he has never denied. His righteousness shall go before him and the glory of the Lord shall be his rereward.

Works, ix. 324.

．•．

To enumerate the various modes of charity which true godliness may suggest, as it is difficult, would be useless. They are as extensive as want and as various as misery.

Ib. ix. 412.

．•．

SOME readily find out that where there is distress there is vice, and easily discover the crime of feeding the lazy or encouraging the dissolute. To promote vice is certainly unlawful; but we do not always encourage vice when we relieve the vicious. *Ib.* ix. 393.

Charms for distant admiration:

THERE are charms made only for distant admiration. No spectacle is nobler than a blaze. *Ib.* vii. 182.

Chesterfield,

Chesterfield, Earl of:

TO THE RIGHT HONOURABLE THE EARL OF CHESTERFIELD.

February 5, 1755.

MY LORD,

I have been lately informed, by the proprietor of the World, that two papers, in which my Dictionary is recommended to the public, were written by your Lordship. To be so distinguished is an honour which, being very little accustomed to favours from the great, I know not well how to receive, or in what terms to acknowledge.

When, upon some slight encouragement, I first visited your Lordship, I was overpowered, like the rest of mankind, by the enchantment of your address; and could not forbear to wish that I might boast myself *Le vainqueur du vainqueur de la terre*;—that I might obtain that regard for which I saw the world contending; but I found my attendance so little encouraged, that neither pride nor modesty would suffer me to continue it. When I had once addressed your Lordship in public, I had exhausted all the art of pleasing which a retired and uncourtly scholar can possess. I had done all that I could; and no man is well pleased to have his all neglected, be it ever so little.

Seven years, my Lord, have now passed since I waited in your outward rooms or was repulsed from your door; during which time I have been pushing on my work through difficulties of which it is useless to complain, and have brought it, at last, to the verge of publication, without one act of assistance, one word of encouragement, or one smile of favour. Such treatment I did not expect, for I never had a Patron before.

The

The shepherd in Virgil[1] grew at last acquainted with Love, and found him a native of the rocks.

Is not a Patron, my Lord, one who looks with unconcern on a man struggling for life in the water, and, when he has reached ground, encumbers him with help? The notice which you have been pleased to take of my labours, had it been early, had been kind; but it has been delayed till I am indifferent, and cannot enjoy it; till I am solitary, and cannot impart it; till I am known, and do not want it. I hope it is no very cynical asperity not to confess obligations where no benefit has been received, or to be unwilling that the Public should consider me as owing that to a Patron which Providence has enabled me to do for myself.

Having carried on my work thus far with so little obligation to any favourer of learning, I shall not be disappointed though I should conclude it, if less be possible, with less; for I have been long wakened from that dream of hope in which I once boasted myself with so much exultation,

My Lord,

Your Lordship's most humble

Most obedient servant,

SAM. JOHNSON.

Boswell's Life of Johnson, i. 261.

.˙.

JOHNSON having now explicitly avowed his opinion of Lord Chesterfield did not refrain from expressing himself concerning that nobleman with pointed freedom: 'This man

---

[1] Nunc scio quid sit Amor.—*Eclogues*, viii. 43.

said

(said he) I thought had been a Lord among wits; but I find he is only a wit among Lords!'

Boswell's Life of Johnson, i. 266.

.·.

JOHNSON, speaking of his refusal to dedicate his *Dictionary* to Lord . Chesterfield, said :—'Sir, I found I must have gilded a rotten post.'

Ib. i. 266 n. 1.

Childless people :

NOTHING seems to have been more universally dreaded by the ancients than orbity, or want of children; and indeed, to a man who has survived all the companions of his youth, all who have participated his pleasures and his cares, have been engaged in the same events and filled their minds with the same conceptions, this full-peopled world is a dismal solitude. He stands forlorn and silent, neglected or insulted, in the midst of multitudes, animated with hopes which he cannot share, and employed in business which he is no longer able to forward or retard; nor can he find any to whom his life or his death is of importance, unless he has secured some domestic gratifications, some tender employments, and endeared himself to some whose interest and gratitude may unite them to him.   *Rambler*, No. 69.

Children :

'DR. JOHNSON used to condemn me for putting Newbery's books into children's hands. "Babies do not want," said he, "to hear about babies; they like to be told of giants and castles, and of somewhat which can stretch and stimulate their little minds." When I would urge the numerous

editions

editions of *Tommy Prudent* or *Goody Two Shoes*; " Remember always," said he, " that the parents buy the books, and that the children never read them." '

Piozzi's *Anecdotes*, p. 16.

Wit and
Wisdom
of
Samuel
Johnson.

. *.

HE begins to reproach himself with neglect of * * * * * 's education, and censures that idleness or that deviation, by the indulgence of which he has left uncultivated such a fertile mind. I advised him to let the child alone; and told him that the matter was not great, whether he could read at the end of four years or of five, and that I thought it not proper to harass a tender mind with the violence of painful attention. I may perhaps procure both father and son a year of quiet : and surely I may rate myself among their benefactors.

Piozzi Letters, i. 322.

. *.

YOU teach your daughters the diameters of the planets, and wonder when you have done that they do not delight in your company. No science can be communicated by mortal creatures without attention from the scholar; no attention can be obtained from children without the infliction of pain, and pain is never remembered without resentment.

Piozzi's *Anecdotes*, p. 22.

. *.

YOUR treatment of little * * * * was undoubtedly right; when there is so strong a reason against any thing as unconquerable terror, there ought surely to be some weighty reason for it before it is done. But for putting into the water a child already well, it is not very easy to find any reason strong or weak. That the nurses fretted, will supply

me

me during life with an additional motive to keep every child, as far as is possible, out of a nurse's power.   A nurse made of common mould will have a pride in overpowering a child's reluctance.   There are few minds to which tyranny is not delightful; power is nothing but as it is felt, and the delight of superiority is proportionate to the resistance overcome. *Piozzi Letters*, ii. 67.

...

ALLOW children to be happy their own way, for what better way will they ever find ? *Ib.* ii. 165.

Choice of evil:

IF choice of evil be freedom, the felon in the galleys has his option of labour or of stripes. *Works*, vi. 229.

Christ's teaching:

OF the Divine Author of our religion it is impossible to peruse the evangelical histories without observing how little he favoured the vanity of inquisitiveness ; how much more rarely he condescended to satisfy curiosity than to relieve distress ; and how much he desired that his followers should rather excel in goodness than in knowledge.   His precepts tend immediately to the rectification of the moral principles, and the direction of daily conduct, without ostentation, without art, at once irrefragable and plain, such as well-meaning simplicity may readily conceive, and of which we cannot mistake the meaning but when we are afraid to find it. *Rambler*, No. 81.

Chronology:

IT should be diligently inculcated to the scholar, that unless he fixes in his mind some idea of the time in which

each

Wit and
Wisdom
of
Samuel
Johnson.

each man of eminence lived, and each action was performed, with some part of the contemporary history of the
rest of the world, he will consume his life in useless reading
and darken his mind with a crowd of unconnected events;
his memory will be perplexed with distant transactions
resembling one another, and his reflections be like a dream
in a fever, busy and turbulent, but confused and indistinct.

Works, v. 239.

Church:

To be of no church is dangerous. Religion, of which
the rewards are distant and which is animated only by faith
and hope, will glide by degrees out of the mind, unless it
be invigorated and reimpressed by external ordinances, by
stated calls to worship, and the salutary influence of
example. Milton, who appears to have had full conviction
of the truth of christianity, and to have regarded the Holy
Scriptures with the profoundest veneration, to have been
untainted by any heretical peculiarity of opinion, and to
have lived in a confirmed belief of the immediate and
occasional agency of providence, yet grew old without any
visible worship. In the distribution of his hours, there was
no hour of prayer, either solitary or with his household;
omitting public prayers, he omitted all.

Of this omission the reason has been sought upon a
supposition which ought never to be made, that men live
with their own approbation, and justify their conduct to
themselves. Prayer certainly was not thought superfluous
by him who represents our first parents as praying accept-
ably in the state of innocence, and efficaciously after their
fall. That he lived without prayer can hardly be affirmed;
his studies and meditations were an habitual prayer. The

neglect

neglect of it in his family was probably a fault for which he condemned himself, and which he intended to correct, but that death, as too often happens, intercepted his reformation.

Works, vii. 115.

Civilisation: its true test:

A DECENT provision for the poor is the true test of civilization [1].

Boswell's *Life of Johnson*, ii. 130.

Classes of mankind:

WE are by our occupations, education, and habits of life divided almost into different species which regard one another, for the most part, with scorn and malignity. Each of these classes of the human race has desires, fears, and conversation, vexations and merriment peculiar to itself; cares which another cannot feel; pleasures which he cannot partake; and modes of expressing every sensation which he cannot understand. That frolic which shakes one man with laughter will convulse another with indignation; the strain of jocularity which in one place obtains treats and patronage would in another be heard with indifference, and in a third with abhorrence.

Rambler, No. 160.

College tutors:

'"Τερψάμενος νεῖται, καὶ πλείονα εἰδώς [2] " (the offer of the Syren to Ulysses), any man who can promise that to another will preserve his respect.—Applied by Dr. Johnson to a college tutor.'

Croker's *Boswell*, 8vo. ed. p. 838.

---

[1] The word, no doubt, that Johnson used was *civility*; for he refused to admit *civilisation* into his *Dictionary*. See *post*, p. 66, *note*.

[2] *Odyssey*, xii. 188.

' Happier hence and wiser he departs.'

COWPER, *Odyssey*, xii. 222.

Colonies:

Colonies :

SOME colonies indeed have been established more peace-ably than others. The utmost extremity of wrong has not always been practised ; but those that have settled in the new world on the fairest terms have no other merit than that of a scrivener who ruins in silence, over a plunderer that seizes by force ; all have taken what had other owners, and all have had recourse to arms rather than quit the prey on which they had fastened. *Works,* vi. 115.

Comets and princes :

IMPROVISO translation of the following Distich on the Duke of Modena's running away from the comet in 1742 or 1743.

> *Se al venir vostro i principi sen' vanno*
> *Deh venga ogni dì——durate un' anno.*

If at your coming princes disappear,
Comets ! come ev'ry day—and stay a year.

Ib. i. 144.

Commentators :

IT is not easy to discover from what cause the acrimony of a scholiast can naturally proceed. The subjects to be discussed by him are of very small importance ; they involve neither property nor liberty ; nor favour the interest of sect or party. The various readings of copies, and different interpretations of a passage, seem to be questions that might exercise the wit, without engaging the passions. But whether it be that *small things make mean men proud* and vanity catches small occasions ; or that all contrariety of opinion, even in those that can defend it no longer,

E   makes

makes proud men angry; there is often found in commentators a spontaneous strain of invective and contempt, more eager and venomous than is vented by the most furious controvertist in politics against those whom he is hired to defame. *Works,* v. 143.

Common fame:

THE general regard which every wise man has for his character is a proof that in the estimation of all mankind the testimony of common fame is of too great importance to be disregarded. *Debates. Works,* x. 182.

.·.

COMMON fame is to every man only what he himself commonly hears. *Ib.* x. 212.

Common life:

THESE diminutive observations[1] seem to take away something from the dignity of writing, and therefore are never communicated but with hesitation, and a little fear of abasement and contempt. But it must be remembered that life consists not of a series of illustrious actions, or elegant enjoyments; the greater part of our time passes in compliance with necessities, in the performance of daily duties, in the removal of small inconveniences, in the procurement of petty pleasures; and we are well or ill at ease as the main stream of life glides on smoothly, or is ruffled by small obstacles and frequent interruption. The true state of every nation is the state of common life. The manners of a people are not to be found in the schools of

---

[1] Johnson had been describing 'the incommodiousness of the Scotch windows.'

earning

learning or the palaces of greatness, where the national character is obscured or obliterated by travel or instruction, by philosophy or vanity; nor is public happiness to be estimated by the assemblies of the gay, or the banquets of the rich. The great mass of nations is neither rich nor gay: they whose aggregate constitutes the people are found in the streets and the villages, in the shops and farms; and from them, collectively considered, must the measure of general prosperity be taken. As they approach to delicacy, a nation is refined; as their conveniences are multiplied, a nation, at least a commercial nation, must be denominated wealthy.

Works, ix. 18.

Companions:

You have more than once wondered at my complaint of solitude when you hear that I am crowded with visits. *Inopem me copia fecit.* Visitors are no proper companions in the chamber of sickness. They come when I could sleep or read, they stay till I am weary, they force me to attend when my mind calls for relaxation, and to speak when my powers will hardly actuate my tongue. The amusements and consolations of languor and depression are conferred by familiar and domestic companions, which can be visited or called at will and can occasionally be quitted or dismissed, who do not obstruct accommodation by ceremony, or destroy indolence by awakening effort.

Piozzi Letters, ii. 341.

．•．

There are many whose vanity always inclines them to associate with those from whom they have no reason to

Wit and
Wisdom
of
Samuel
Johnson.

fear mortification; and there are times in which the wise and the knowing are willing to receive praise without the labour of deserving it, in which the most elevated mind is willing to descend, and the most active to be at rest. All therefore are at some hour or another fond of companions whom they can entertain upon easy terms, and who will relieve them from solitude without condemning them to vigilance and caution. We are most inclined to love when we have nothing to fear, and he that encourages us to please ourselves, will not be long without preference in our affection to those whose learning holds us at the distance of pupils, or whose wit calls all attention from us, and leaves us without importance and without regard.　　*Rambler*, No. 72.

Complaints:

To hear complaints with patience, even when complaints are vain, is one of the duties of friendship; and though it must be allowed that he suffers most like a hero that hides his grief in silence,

Spem vultu simulat, premit altum corde dolorem [1]

His outward smiles conceal'd his inward smart—DRYDEN,

yet it cannot be denied that he who complains acts like a man, like a social being who looks for help from his fellow-creatures. Pity is to many of the unhappy a source of comfort in hopeless distresses, as it contributes to recommend them to themselves by proving that they have not lost the regard of others; and heaven seems to indicate the duty even of barren compassion by inclining us to weep for evils which we cannot remedy.　　*Ib.* No. 59.

---

[1] Virgil, *Æneid*, i. 209.

To

To the arguments which have been used against complaints under the miseries of life the philosophers have, I think, forgot to add the incredulity of those to whom we recount our sufferings. But if the purpose of lamentation be to excite pity it is surely superfluous for age and weakness to tell their plaintive stories; for pity presupposes sympathy, and a little attention will show them that those who do not feel pain seldom think that it is felt; and a short recollection will inform almost every man that he is only repaid the insult which he has given, since he may remember how often he has mocked infirmity, laughed at its cautions, and censured its impatience. *Rambler*, No. 48.

.·.

It is not sufficiently considered how much he assumes who dares to claim the privilege of complaining; for as every man has, in his own opinion, a full share of the miseries of life, he is inclined to consider all clamorous uneasiness as a proof of impatience rather than of affliction, and to ask What merit has this man to show by which he has acquired a right to repine at the distributions of nature? Or, why does he imagine that exemptions should be granted him from the general condition of man? *Ib.* No. 50.

Compliments:

Unusual compliments, to which there is no stated and prescriptive answer, embarrass the feeble who know not what to say, and disgust the wise who, knowing them to be false, suspect them to be hypocritical.

Boswell's *Life of Johnson*, v. 440 *n.* 2.

Composition:

Composition:

My advice is that you attempt, from time to time, an original sermon; and in the labour of composition do not burthen your mind with too much at once; do not exact from yourself at one effort of excogitation propriety of thought and elegance of expression. Invent first, and then embellish. The production of something, where nothing was before, is an act of greater energy than the expansion or decoration of the thing produced. Set down diligently your thoughts as they rise in the first words that occur; and, when you have matter, you will easily give it form: nor, perhaps, will this method be always necessary; for by habit your thoughts and diction will flow together.

Boswell's *Life of Johnson*, iii. 437.

Composition is for the most part an effort of slow diligence and steady perseverance, to which the mind is dragged by necessity or resolution, and from which the attention is every moment starting to more delightful amusements.

Adventurer, No. 138.

A man may write at any time if he will set himself doggedly to it.   Boswell's *Life of Johnson*, v. 40.

Computation:

Never think that you have arithmetic enough; when you have exhausted your master, buy books. Nothing amuses more harmlessly than computation, and nothing is oftener applicable to real business or speculative enquiries. A thousand stories which the ignorant tell and believe die away at once, when the computist takes them in his gripe.

Piozzi Letters, ii. 296.

Condescension:

Condescension:

THERE is nothing more likely to betray a man into absurdity than *condescension* when he seems to suppose his understanding too powerful for his company.

Boswell's *Life of Johnson*, iv. 3.

Confutation of Stupidity:

I HAVE thought it hypocrisy to treat stupidity with reverence, or to honour nonsense with the ceremony of a confutation. As knavery, so folly that is not reclaimable, is to be speedily dispatched; business is to be freed from obstruction and society from a nuisance. Nor when I am censured by those whom I may offend by the use of terms correspondent with my ideas will I by a tame and silent submission give reason to suspect that I am conscious of a fault, but will treat the accusation with open contempt, and show no greater regard to the abettors than to the authors of absurdity.

Debates. Works, x. 310.

Conscience:

CONSCIENCE is nothing more than a conviction felt by ourselves of something to be done or something to be avoided; and in questions of simple unperplexed morality, conscience is very often a guide that may be trusted. But before conscience can determine, the state of the question is supposed to be completely known. In questions of law, or of fact, conscience is very often confounded with opinion. No man's conscience can tell him the rights of another man; they must be known by rational investigation or historical enquiry.

Boswell's *Life of Johnson*, ii. 243.

' Speaking

'Speaking of the *inward light* to which some methodists pretended, Johnson said it was a principle utterly incompatible with social or civil security. "If a man (said he,) pretends to a principle of action of which I can know nothing, nay, not so much as that he has it, but only that he pretends to it; how can I tell what that person may be prompted to do? When a person professes to be governed by a written ascertained law I can then know where to find him." '

Boswell's Life of Johnson, ii. 126.

Contemporaries:

No man loves to be indebted to his contemporaries.

Works, viii. 254.

Contempt:

No man can fall into contempt but those who deserve it.

Debates. Works, x. 359.

.·.

CONTEMPT is a kind of gangrene which, if it seizes one part of a character, corrupts all the rest by degrees.

Works, viii. 47.

Controversy:

' JOHNSON said, " When a man voluntarily engages in an important controversy he is to do all he can to lessen his antagonist, because authority from personal respect has much weight with most people, and often more than reasoning. If my antagonist writes bad language, though that may not be essential to the question, I will attack him for his bad language." ADAMS[1]. "You would not jostle a chimney-sweeper." JOHNSON. "Yes, Sir, if it were necessary to jostle him *down*." '

Boswell's Life of Johnson, ii. 443.

---

[1] Dr. Adams, Master of Pembroke College.

Conversation:

Conversation:

THERE is nothing by which a man exasperates most people more than by displaying a superior ability or brilliancy in conversation. They seem pleased at the time, but their envy makes them curse him at their hearts.

Boswell's Life of Johnson, iv. 195.

Conversions:

THAT conversion will always be suspected that apparently concurs with interest. He that never finds his error till it hinders his progress towards wealth or honour will not be thought to love truth only for herself. Yet it may easily happen that information may come at a commodious time; and, as truth and interest are not by any fatal necessity at variance, that one may by accident introduce the other. When opinions are struggling into popularity, the arguments by which they are opposed or defended become more known; and he that changes his profession would perhaps have changed it before with the like opportunities of instruction.

Works, vii. 278.

Copyright:

'WHEN Dr. Johnson and I were left by ourselves I read to him my notes of the Opinions of our Judges upon the questions of Literary Property. He did not like them; and said, "they make me think of your Judges not with that respect which I should wish to do." To the argument of one of them, that there can be no property in blasphemy or nonsense, he answered, "then your rotten sheep are mine! By that rule, when a man's house falls into decay he must lose it."'

Boswell's Life of Johnson, v. 50.

Corruption:

Corruption:

A MAN cannot spend all this life in frolic: age, or disease, or solitude, will bring some hours of serious consideration, and it will then afford no comfort to think that he has extended the dominion of vice, that he has loaded himself with the crimes of others, and can never know the extent of his own wickedness, or make reparation for the mischief that he has caused. There is not, perhaps, in all the stores of ideal anguish, a thought more painful than the consciousness of having propagated corruption by vitiating principles, of having not only drawn others from the paths of virtue, but blocked up the way by which they should return, of having blinded them to every beauty but the paint of pleasure, and deafened them to every call but the alluring voice of the syrens of destruction.

Rambler, No. 31.

Counting and guessing:

To count is a modern practice, the ancient method was to guess; and when numbers are guessed they are always magnified.   *Works*, ix. 95.

Counting-houses:

THE counting-house of an accomplished merchant is a school of method where the great science may be learned of ranging particulars under generals, of bringing the different parts of a transaction together, and of showing at one view a long series of dealing and exchange.

Ib. v. 251.

Country:

No wise man will go to live in the country unless he has something to do which can be better done in the country.

For

For instance: if he is to shut himself up for a year to study a science, it is better to look out to the fields than to an opposite wall. Then, if a man walks out in the country, there is nobody to keep him from walking in again: but if a man walks out in London he is not sure when he shall walk in again. A great city is, to be sure, the school for studying life; and 'The proper study of mankind is man[1],' as Pope observes. *Boswell's Life of Johnson*, iii. 253.

Courting great men:

'I TALKED of the mode adopted by some to rise in the world by courting great men, and asked him whether he had ever submitted to it. JOHNSON. "Why, Sir, I never was near enough to great men to court them. You may be prudently attached to great men and yet independent. You are not to do what you think wrong; and, Sir, you are to calculate and not pay too dear for what you get. You must not give a shilling's worth of court for six-pence worth of good. But if you can get a shilling's worth of good for six-pence worth of court, you are a fool if you do not pay court."' *Ib.* ii. 10.

Cowardice:

'AT this time[2] fears of an invasion were circulated; to obviate which Mr. Spottiswoode observed that Mr. Fraser the engineer, who had lately come from Dunkirk, said that the French had the same fears of us. JOHNSON. "It is thus that mutual cowardice keeps us in peace. Were one half of mankind brave and one half cowards, the brave would be always beating the cowards. Were all brave,

---

[1] *Essay on Man*, ii. 2.   [2] Spring of 1778.

they

they would lead a very uneasy life; all would be continually fighting: but being all cowards, we go on very well."'

Boswell's Life of Johnson, iii. 326.

Criticism:

THE great contention of criticism is to find the faults of the moderns and the beauties of the ancients. While an author is yet living we estimate his powers by his worst performance; and when he is dead we rate them by his best.

Works, v. 103.

.·.

'I MENTIONED Mallet's tragedy of *Elvira* which had been acted the preceding winter at Drury-lane, and that the Honourable Andrew Erskine, Mr. Dempster, and myself, had joined in writing a pamphlet entitled *Critical Strictures* against it. That the mildness of Dempster's disposition had, however, relented; and he had candidly said, "We have hardly a right to abuse this tragedy: for bad as it is, how vain should either of us be to write one not near so good." JOHNSON. "Why no, Sir; this is not just reasoning. You *may* abuse a tragedy though you cannot write one. You may scold a carpenter who has made you a bad table, though you cannot make a table. It is not your trade to make tables."'

Boswell's Life of Johnson, i. 408.

.·.

ALL truth is valuable, and satirical criticism may be considered as useful when it rectifies error and improves judgment; he that refines the public taste is a public benefactor.

Works, viii. 338.

Critics:

Critics :

THERE is a certain race of men that either imagine it their duty, or make it their amusement, to hinder the reception of every work of learning or genius, who stand as sentinels in the avenues of fame, and value themselves upon giving Ignorance and Envy the first notice of a prey.

Rambler, No. 3.

. · .

' "THERE are," said Dr. Johnson, "three distinct kinds of judges upon all new authors or productions; the first are those who know no rules, but pronounce entirely from their natural taste and feelings; the second are those who know and judge by rules; and the third are those who know, but are above the rules. These last are those you should wish to satisfy. Next to them rate the natural judges; but ever despise those opinions that are formed by the rules. . . . The natural feelings of untaught hearers ought never to be slighted." '
Mme. D'Arblay's *Diary*, i. 180; ii. 128.

. · .

' "DR. Farmer," said Johnson, "you have done that which never was done before; that is, you have completely finished a controversy beyond all further doubt." "There are some critics," answered Farmer, "who will adhere to their old opinions." "Ah!" said Johnson, "that may be true; for the limbs will quiver and move when the soul is gone." '
Boswell's *Life of Johnson*, iii. 38 *n. 6.*

Cunning :

EVERY man wishes to be wise, and they who cannot be wise are almost always cunning. The less is the real discernment of those whom business or conversation brings

together,

together, the more illusions are practised, nor is caution ever so necessary as with associates or opponents of feeble minds.

Idler, No. 92.

.·.

CUNNING has effect from the credulity of others rather than from the abilities of those who are cunning. It requires no extraordinary talents to lie and deceive.

Boswell's *Life of Johnson*, v. 217.

Curiosity:

CURIOSITY is one of the permanent and certain characteristics of a vigorous intellect. Every advance into knowledge opens new prospects and produces new incitements to further progress. All the attainments possible in our present state are evidently inadequate to our capacities of enjoyment; conquest serves no purpose but that of kindling ambition, discovery has no effect but of raising expectation; the gratification of one desire encourages another; and after all our labours, studies, and inquiries, we are continually at the same distance from the completion of our schemes, have still some wish importunate to be satisfied, and some faculty restless and turbulent for want of its enjoyment.

Rambler, No. 103.

.·.

CURIOSITY is, in great and generous minds, the first passion and the last; and perhaps always predominates in proportion to the strength of the contemplative faculties.

Ib. No. 150.

Day dreams:

IN solitude we have our dreams to ourselves, and in company we agree to dream in concert. The end sought in both is forgetfulness of ourselves.

Idler, No. 32.

Dead

Dead languages:

WHEN the matter is low or scanty, a dead language, in which nothing is mean because nothing is familiar, affords great conveniences; and by the sonorous magnificence of Roman syllables the writer conceals penury of thought, and want of novelty, often from the reader and often from himself.

Works, vii. 421.

Death:

WRITE to me no more about *dying with a grace*; when you feel what I have felt in approaching eternity—in fear of soon hearing the sentence of which there is no revocation, you will know the folly; my wish is that you may know it sooner. The distance between the grave and the remotest point of human longevity is but a very little; and of that little no path is certain. You knew all this, and I thought that I knew it too; but I know it now with a new conviction. May that new conviction not be vain.

Piozzi Letters, ii. 354.

.·.

CUSTOM so far regulates the sentiments, at least of common minds, that I believe men may be generally observed to grow less tender as they advance in age. He who, when life was new, melted at the loss of every companion can look in time without concern upon the grave into which his last friend was thrown, and into which himself is ready to fall; not that he is more willing to die than formerly, but that he is more familiar to the death of others, and therefore is not alarmed so far as to consider how much nearer he approaches to his end. But this is to submit tamely to the tyranny of accident, and to suffer our reason

to

to lie useless.　Every funeral may justly be considered as a summons to prepare for that state into which it shows us that we must some time enter; and the summons is more loud and piercing as the event of which it warns us is at less distance.　To neglect at any time preparation for death is to sleep on our post at a siege; but to omit it in old age is to sleep at an attack.　　　*Rambler*, No. 78.

THE time will come to every human being when it must be known how well he can bear to die.　　　*Works*, vi. 499.

THE whole of life is but keeping away the thoughts of death.　　　Boswell's *Life of Johnson*, ii. 93.

THEY who most endeavour the happiness of others, who devote their thoughts to tenderness and pity, and studiously maintain the reciprocation of kindness, by degrees mingle their souls in such a manner as to feel from their separation a total destitution of happiness, a sudden abruption of all their prospects, a cessation of all their hopes, schemes, and desires.　The whole mind becomes a gloomy vacuity without any image or form of pleasure, a chaos of confused wishes directed to no particular end, or to that which, while we wish, we cannot hope to obtain; for the dead will not revive; those whom God has called away from the present state of existence can be seen no more in it; we must go to them but they cannot return to us.　　　*Works*, ix. 521.

WHEN a friend is carried to his grave we at once find excuses for every weakness, and palliations of every fault; we recollect a thousand endearments, which before glided

off

off our minds without impression, a thousand favours un-
repaid, a thousand duties unperformed, and wish, vainly
wish for his return, not so much that we may receive as
that we may bestow happiness, and recompense that kindness which before we never understood. There is not,
perhaps, to a mind well instructed, a more painful occur-
rence, than the death of one whom we have injured without
reparation. Our crime seems now irretrievable, it is in-
delibly recorded and the stamp of fate is fixed upon it.
We consider with the most afflictive anguish the pain
which we have given and now cannot alleviate, and the
losses which we have caused and now cannot repair.

Rambler No. 54.

.·.

MILTON has judiciously represented the father of mankind as seized with horror and astonishment at the sight of
death exhibited to him on the mount of vision[1]. For
surely nothing can so much disturb the passions, or perplex
the intellects of man, as the disruption of his union with
visible nature; a separation from all that has hitherto delighted or engaged him; a change not only of the place
but the manner of his being; an entrance into a state not
simply which he knows not, but which perhaps he has not
faculties to know; an immediate and perceptible com-
munication with the Supreme Being, and, what is above all
distressful and alarming, the final sentence and unalterable
allotment. Yet we to whom the shortness of life has given
frequent occasions of contemplating mortality can, without
emotion, see generations of men pass away, and are at
leisure to establish modes of sorrow and adjust the cere-

---

[1] *Paradise Lost*, xi. 448.

F

monial

monial of death. We can look upon funeral pomp as a common spectacle in which we have no concern, and turn away from it to trifles and amusements without dejection of look or inquietude of heart. *Rambler*, No. 78.

.·.

IF one was to think constantly of death the business of life would stand still. Boswell's *Life of Johnson*, v. 316.

.·.

MULTITUDES there must always be, and greater multitudes as arts and civility[1] prevail, who cannot wholly withdraw their thoughts from death. All cannot be distracted with business, or stunned with the clamours of assemblies or the shouts of armies. All cannot live in the perpetual dissipation of successive diversions, nor will all enslave their understandings to their senses, and seek felicity in the gross gratifications of appetite. . . . When the faculties were once put in motion, when the mind had broken loose from the shackles of sense and made excursions to remote consequences, the first consideration that would stop her course must be the incessant waste of life, the approach of age, and the certainty of death; the approach of that time in which strength must fail and pleasure fly away, and the certainty of that dissolution which shall put an end to all the prospects of this world. It is impossible to think and not sometimes to think on death. Hope indeed has many powers of delusion; whatever is possible, however unlikely, it will teach us to promise ourselves; but death no man has

---

[1] ' He (Johnson) would not admit *civilisation* [in his Dictionary] but only *civility*. With great deference to him I thought *civilisation* from *to civilise* better, in the sense opposed to *barbarity*, than *civility*.'— Boswell's *Life of Johnson*, ii. 155.

escaped,

escaped, and therefore no man can hope to escape it.
From this dreadful expectation no shelter or refuge can be
found. Whatever we see forces it upon us; whatever is,
new or old, flourishing or declining, either directly or by
very short deduction leads man to the consideration of his
end; and accordingly we find that the fear of death has
always been considered as the great enemy of human quiet,
the polluter of the feast of happiness and embitterer of the
cup of joy. The young man who rejoiceth in his youth
amidst his music and his gaiety has always been disturbed
with the thought that his youth will be quickly at an end.
The monarch to whom it is said that he is a god has always
been reminded by his own heart that he shall die like man.

Works, ix. 517.

．·．

THE uncertainty of death is in effect the great support
of the whole system of life.   *Ib.* ix. 382.

．·．

A VIOLENT death is never very painful; the only danger
is, lest it should be unprovided. But if a man can be supposed to make no provision for death in war, what can be
the state that would have awakened him to the care of
futurity? When would that man have prepared himself to
die who went to seek death without preparation? What
then can be the reason why we lament more him that dies
of a wound than him that dies of a fever? A man that
languishes with disease ends his life with more pain, but
with less virtue: he leaves no example to his friends, nor
bequeaths any honour to his descendants. The only reason
why we lament a soldier's death is that we think he might
have lived longer; yet this cause of grief is common to

many other kinds of death which are not so passionately bewailed. The truth is, that every death is violent which is the effect of accident; every death which is not gradually brought on by the miseries of age, or when life is extinguished for any other reason than that it is burnt out. He that dies before sixty of a cold or consumption, dies, in reality, by a violent death; yet his death is borne with patience only because the cause of his untimely end is silent and invisible. Let us endeavour to see things as they are, and then inquire whether we ought to complain. Whether to see life as it is will give us much consolation, I know not; but the consolation which is drawn from truth, if any there be, is solid and durable: that which may be derived from error must be, like its original, fallacious and fugitive.

Boswell's Life of Johnson, i. 338.

.•.

I READ the letters in which you relate your mother's death to Mrs. Strahan, and think I do myself honour when I tell you that I read them with tears; but tears are neither to *you* nor to *me* of any further use when once the tribute of nature has been paid. The business of life summons us away from useless grief and calls us to the exercise of those virtues of which we are lamenting our deprivation. The greatest benefit which one friend can confer upon another is to guard, and excite, and elevate his virtues. This your mother will still perform if you diligently preserve the memory of her life and of her death: a life, so far as I can learn, useful, wise, and innocent; and a death resigned, peaceful, and holy. I cannot forbear to mention that neither reason nor revelation denies you to hope that you may increase her happiness by obeying her precepts; and

that

that she may, in her present state, look with pleasure upon every act of virtue to which her instructions or example have contributed. Whether this be more than a pleasing dream, or a just opinion of separate spirits is, indeed, of no great importance to us, when we consider ourselves as acting under the eye of GOD: yet, surely, there is something pleasing in the belief that our separation from those whom we love is merely corporeal; and it may be a great incitement to virtuous friendship if it can be made probable that that union that has received the divine approbation shall continue to eternity.   Boswell's *Life of Johnson*, i. 212.

Wit and Wisdom of Samuel Johnson.

•••

NOTHING is more evident than that the decays of age must terminate in death; yet there is no man, says *Tully*, who does not believe that he may yet live another year; and there is none who does not, upon the same principle, hope another year for his parent or his friend: but the fallacy will be in time detected; the last year, the last day, must come. It has come and is past. The life which made my own life pleasant is at an end, and the gates of death are shut upon my prospects[1].   *Idler*, No. 41.

•••

HAVING myself suffered what you are now suffering, I well know the weight of your distress, how much need you have of comfort, and how little comfort can be given. A loss such as yours lacerates the mind, and breaks the whole system of purposes and hopes. It leaves a dismal vacuity in life which affords nothing on which the affections can fix, or to which endeavour may be directed. All this

---

[1] Johnson's mother died a few days before this number of *The Idler* was published.

I have

I have known, and it is now, in the vicissitude of things, your turn to know it.

But in the condition of mortal beings one must lose another. What would be the wretchedness of life if there was not something always in view, some Being immutable and unfailing, to whose mercy man may have recourse.

Croker's Boswell, 8vo. ed. p. 66[1].

.•.

HE that outlives a wife whom he has long loved sees himself disjoined from the only mind that has the same hopes, and fears, and interest; from the only companion with whom he has shared much good or evil; and with whom he could set his mind at liberty to retrace the past or anticipate the future. The continuity of being is lacerated; the settled course of sentiment and action is stopped; and life stands suspended and motionless till it is driven by external causes into a new channel. But the time of suspense is dreadful.

Our first recourse in this distressed solitude is, perhaps for want of habitual piety, to a gloomy acquiescence in necessity. Of two mortal beings, one must lose the other. But surely there is a higher and better comfort to be drawn from the consideration of that Providence which watches over all, and a belief that the living and the dead are equally in the hands of God who will reunite those whom he has separated, or who sees that it is best not to reunite.

Boswell's Life of Johnson, iii. 419[2].

---

[1] Written to Mr. James Elphinston.
[2] Written to Dr. Lawrence.

YOU

You know poor Mr. Dodsley has lost his wife; I believe he is much affected. I hope he will not suffer so much as I yet suffer for the loss of mine.

Οἴμοι· τί δ' οἴμοι; θνῆτα γὰρ πεπόνθαμεν [1].

I have ever since seemed to myself broken off from mankind; a kind of solitary wanderer in the wild of life, without any direction or fixed point of view; a gloomy gazer on a world to which I have little relation.

Boswell's Life of Johnson, i. 277.

Debauching the mind:

I HAVE heard of barbarians who, when tempests drive ships upon their coast, decoy them to the rocks that they may plunder their lading, and have always thought that wretches thus merciless in their depredations ought to be destroyed by a general insurrection of all social beings; yet how light is this guilt to the crime of him who, in the agitations of remorse, cuts away the anchor of piety and, when he has drawn aside credulity from the paths of virtue, hides the light of heaven which would direct her to return.

Rambler, No. 171.

Debt:

Do not accustom yourself to consider debt only as an inconvenience; you will find it a calamity. Poverty takes away so many means of doing good and produces so much inability to resist evil, both natural and moral, that it is by all virtuous means to be avoided. Consider a man whose fortune is very narrow; whatever be his rank by birth, or

---

[1] Alas! but wherefore alas? Man is born to sorrow.

whatever

Wit and
Wisdom
of
Samuel
Johnson.

whatever his reputation by intellectual excellence, what good can he do? or what evil can he prevent? That he cannot help the needy is evident; he has nothing to spare. But perhaps his advice or admonition may be useful. His poverty will destroy his influence: many more can find that he is poor than that he is wise; and few will reverence the understanding that is of so little advantage to its owner. I say nothing of the personal wretchedness of a debtor, which, however, has passed into a proverb[1]. Of riches it is not necessary to write the praise. Let it, however, be remembered that he who has money to spare has it always in his power to benefit others; and of such power a good man must always be desirous.   Boswell's *Life of Johnson*, iv. 152.

Debtors and creditors:

THOSE who made the laws have apparently supposed that every deficiency of payment is the crime of the debtor. But the truth is that the creditor always shares the act, and often more than shares the guilt, of improper trust. It seldom happens that any man imprisons another but for debts which he suffered to be contracted in hope of advantage to himself, and for bargains in which he proportioned his profit to his own opinion of the hazard; and there is no reason why one should punish the other for a contract in which both concurred. . . . The motive to credit is the hope of advantage. Commerce can never be at a stop while one man wants what another can supply; and credit will never be denied while it is likely to be repaid

---

[1] 'I never retired to rest without feeling the justness of the Spanish proverb, "Let him who sleeps too much borrow the pillow of a debtor." ' Johnson's *Works*. iv. 14.

with

with profit. He that trusts one whom he designs to sue is criminal by the act of trust; the cessation of such insidious traffic is to be desired, and no reason can be given why a change of the law should impair any other.

We see nation trade with nation where no payment can be compelled. Mutual convenience produces mutual confidence; and the merchants continue to satisfy the demands of each other though they have nothing to dread but the loss of trade.

It is vain to continue an institution which experience shows to be ineffectual. We have now imprisoned one generation of debtors after another, but we do not find that their numbers lessen. We have now learned that rashness and imprudence will not be deterred from taking credit; let us try whether fraud and avarice may be more easily restrained from giving it.

Idler, No. 22.

Deceptions:

I HAVE always considered it as treason against the great republic of human nature to make any man's virtues the means of deceiving him, whether on great or little occasions. All imposture weakens confidence and chills benevolence.

Rasselas, ch. 46.

Declamation and calculation:

WHEN you are declaiming, declaim; and when you are calculating, calculate.

Boswell's *Life of Johnson* ii . 49.

Dedications:

NOTHING has so much degraded literature from its natural rank as the practice of indecent and promiscuous dedication; for what credit can he expect who professes

himself

himself the hireling of vanity, however profligate, and without shame or scruple celebrates the worthless, dignifies the mean, and gives to the corrupt, licentious, and oppressive, the ornaments which ought only to add grace to truth and loveliness to innocence? Every other kind of adulteration, however shameful, however mischievous, is less detestable than the crime of counterfeiting characters, and fixing the stamp of literary sanction upon the dross and refuse of the world.

Rambler, No. 136.

'Derange':

'Johnson would not allow the word *derange* to be an English word. "Sir," said a gentleman who had some pretensions to literature, "I have seen it in a book." "Not in a *bound* book," said Johnson; "*disarrange* is the word we ought to use instead of it."' Boswell's *Life of Johnson*, iii. 319 *n*. 1.

Dialogue and action:

It is indeed much more easy to form dialogues than to contrive adventures. Every position makes way for an argument, and every objection dictates an answer. When two disputants are engaged upon a complicated and extensive question, the difficulty is not to continue, but to end the controversy. But whether it be that we comprehend but few of the possibilities of life, or that life itself affords little variety, every man who has tried knows how much labour it will cost to form such a combination of circumstances as shall have at once the grace of novelty and credibility, and delight fancy without violence to reason.

Works, vii. 150.

Difficulties:

Difficulties:

I am no friend to making religion appear too hard. Many good people have done harm by giving severe notions of it. In the same way as to learning: I never frighten young people with difficulties; on the contrary, I tell them that they may very easily get as much as will do very well. I do not indeed tell them that they will be *Bentleys*.

Boswell's *Life of Johnson*, v. 316.

Diffusion of mental powers:

A man may be so much of every thing that he is nothing of any thing.

Ib. iv. 176.

Dignity:

If we look without prejudice on the world, we shall find that men whose consciousness of their merit sets them above the compliances of servility are apt enough in their association with superiors to watch their own dignity with troublesome and punctilious jealousy, and in the fervour of independence to exact that attention which they refuse to pay.

Works, viii. 476.

Digressions:

I am well convinced how near indecency and faction are to one another, and how inevitably confusion produces obscurity; but I hope it will always be remembered that he who first infringes decency or deviates from method is to answer for all the consequences that may arise from the neglect of senatorial customs; for it is not to be expected that any man will bear reproaches without reply, or that he

who

who wanders from the question will not be followed in his digressions and hunted through his labyrinths.

Debates. Works, x. 358.

Diminishing the people:

NOTHING is less difficult than to procure one convenience by the forfeiture of another. A soldier may expedite his march by throwing away his arms. To banish the tacks-man [1] is easy; to make a country plentiful by diminishing the people is an expeditious mode of husbandry; but that abundance which there is nobody to enjoy contributes little to human happiness.

Works, ix. 84.

Disappointments:

BE alone as little as you can; when you are alone do not suffer your thoughts to dwell on what you might have done to prevent this disappointment. You perhaps could not have done what you imagine, or might have done it without effect. But even to think in the most reasonable manner is for the present not so useful as not to think. Remit yourself solemnly into the hands of God and then turn your mind upon the business and amusements which lie before you. 'All is best,' says Cheyne, 'as it has been excepting the errors of our own free will.' Burton concludes his long book upon melancholy with this important precept, 'Be not solitary; be not idle.' Remember Cheyne's position and observe Burton's precept.

Piozzi Letters, i. 202.

---

[1] The tacksmen in the Hebrides are the large leaseholders who let part of the land they rent to under-tenants.

Disappointing

Disappointing ourselves :

WE do not indeed so often disappoint others as ourselves. We not only think more highly than others of our own abilities, but allow ourselves to form hopes which we never communicate, and please our thoughts with employments which none ever will allot us, and with elevations to which we are never expected to rise; and when our days and years have passed away in common business or common amusements, and we find at last that we have suffered our purposes to sleep till the time of action is past, we are reproached only by our own reflections; neither our friends nor our enemies wonder that we live and die like the rest of mankind; that we live without notice and die without memorial; they know not what task we had proposed, and therefore cannot discern whether it is finished.   *Idler*, No. 88.

Discoveries of new lands :

IN 1463, in the third year of the reign of John II died prince Henry, the first encourager of remote navigation, by whose incitement, patronage and example, distant nations have been made acquainted with each other, unknown countries have been brought into general view, and the power of Europe has been extended to the remotest parts of the world. What mankind has lost and gained by the genius and designs of this prince it would be long to compare and very difficult to estimate. Much knowledge has been acquired, and much cruelty been committed; the belief of religion has been very little propagated, and its laws have been outrageously and enormously violated. The Europeans have scarcely visited any coast but to gratify avarice and extend corruption; to arrogate dominion

without

without right, and practise cruelty without incentive. Happy had it then been for the oppressed if the designs of Henry had slept in his bosom, and surely more happy for the oppressors. But there is reason to hope that out of so much evil good may sometimes be produced; and that the light of the gospel will at last illuminate the sands of Africa and the deserts of America, though its progress cannot but be slow when it is so much obstructed by the lives of christians.

Works, v. 219.

．˙．

To find a new country and invade it has always been the same.

Ib. v. 215.

Disputing with good humour:

'MR. Murray praised the ancient philosophers for the candour and good humour with which those of different sects disputed with each other. JOHNSON. "Sir, they disputed with good humour because they were not in earnest as to religion. Had the ancients been serious in their belief we should not have had their Gods exhibited in the manner we find them represented in the Poets. The people would not have suffered it. They disputed with good humour upon their fanciful theories because they were not interested in the truth of them: when a man has nothing to lose, he may be in good humour with his opponent. Accordingly you see in Lucian, the Epicurean, who argues only negatively, keeps his temper; the Stoic, who has something positive to preserve, grows angry. Being angry with one who controverts an opinion which you value is a necessary consequence of the uneasiness which you feel. Every man who attacks my belief

diminishes

diminishes in some degree my confidence in it, and there-fore makes me uneasy; and I am angry with him who makes me uneasy. Those only who believed in revelation have been angry at having their faith called in question; because they only had something upon which they could rest as matter of fact." MURRAY. "It seems to me that we are not angry at a man for controverting an opinion which we believe and value; we rather pity him." JOHNSON. "Why, Sir; to be sure when you wish a man to have that belief which you think is of infinite advantage, you wish well to him; but your primary consideration is your own quiet. If a madman were to come into this room with a stick in his hand, no doubt we should pity the state of his mind; but our primary consideration would be to take care of ourselves. We should knock him down first and pity him afterwards. No, Sir; every man will dispute with great good humour upon a subject in which he is not interested. I will dispute very calmly upon the probability of another man's son being hanged; but if a man zealously enforces the probability that my own son will be hanged, I shall certainly not be in a very good humour with him."...
MURRAY. "But, Sir, truth will always bear an examina-tion." JOHNSON. "Yes, Sir, but it is painful to be forced to defend it. Consider, Sir, how should you like, though conscious of your innocence, to be tried before a jury for a capital crime once a week?"'   Boswell's *Life of Johnson*, iii. 10.

Distance:

DISTANCE either of time or place is sufficient to reconcile weak minds to wonderful relations.

Works, v. 57.

IN

'In the evening[1] we went to the Town-hall which was converted into a temporary theatre, and saw *Theodosius*, with *The Stratford Jubilee*. I was happy to see Dr. Johnson sitting in a conspicuous part of the pit and receiving affectionate homage from all his acquaintance. We were quite gay and merry. I afterwards mentioned to him that I condemned myself for being so, when poor Mr. and Mrs. Thrale were in such distress. Johnson. "You are wrong, Sir; twenty years hence Mr. and Mrs. Thrale will not suffer much pain from the death of their son. Now, Sir, you are to consider that distance of place, as well as distance of time, operates upon the human feelings. I would not have you be gay in the presence of the distressed because it would shock them; but you may be gay at a distance. Pain for the loss of a friend, or of a relation whom we love, is occasioned by the want which we feel. In time the vacuity is filled with something else; or sometimes the vacuity closes up of itself." '   Boswell's *Life of Johnson*, ii. 471.

Distinctions :

Every man, however hopeless his pretensions may appear to all but himself, has some project by which he hopes to rise to reputation; some art by which he imagines that the notice of the world will be attracted; some quality good or bad which discriminates him from the common herd of mortals, and by which others may be persuaded to love or compelled to fear him.   *Rambler*, No. 164.

---

[1] Of the day on which the news reached Johnson in Lichfield of the death of Mr. Thrale's son.

THERE lurks, perhaps, in every human heart a desire of distinction which inclines every man first to hope, and then to believe, that Nature has given him something peculiar to himself.

Boswell's *Life of Johnson*, i. 474.

. .

SUCH seems to be the disposition of man that whatever makes a distinction produces rivalry.

Works, ix. 40.

Diurnal writers :

THE ostentatious and haughty display of themselves has been the usual refuge of diurnal writers, in vindication of whose practice it may be said that what it wants in prudence is supplied by sincerity, and who at least may plead that if their boasts deceive any into the perusal of their performances they defraud them of but little time.

> *Quid enim? Concurritur—horæ*
> *Momento cita mors venit, aut victoria læta.*
>
> HORACE [1].

The battle join, and in a moment's flight,
Death, or a joyful conquest, ends the fight.—FRANCIS.

The question concerning the merit of the day is soon decided, and we are not condemned to toil through half a folio to be convinced that the writer has broke his promise.

Rambler, No. 1.

Divine intimation of acceptance :

POSSIBLY it may please God to afford *us* some consolation, some secret intimations of acceptance and forgiveness. But these radiations of favour are not always felt by the

---

[1] 1 *Sat.* i. 7.

G

sincerest

sincerest penitents. To the greater part of those whom angels stand ready to receive nothing is granted in this world beyond rational hope ; and with hope, founded on promise, we may well be satisfied.   Boswell's *Life of Johnson*, iii. 295 *n.* 1.

Domestic greatness unattainable :

In the ancient celebration of victory a slave was placed on the triumphal car by the side of the general, who reminded him by a short sentence that he was a man. Whatever danger there might be lest a leader, in his passage to the capitol, should forget the frailties of his nature, there was surely no need of such an admonition ; the intoxication could not have continued long ; he would have been at home but a few hours before some of his dependants would have forgot his greatness and shown him that, notwithstanding his laurels, he was yet a man. There are some who try to escape this domestic degradation by labouring to appear always wise or always great ; but he that strives against nature will for ever strive in vain. To be grave of mien and slow of utterance ; to look with solicitude and speak with hesitation is attainable at will ; but the show of wisdom is ridiculous when there is nothing to cause doubt, as that of valour where there is nothing to be feared.

Idler, No. 51.

Domestic tyranny :

Offences against society in its greater extent are cognisable by human laws. No man can invade the property, or disturb the quiet of his neighbour, without subjecting himself to penalties and suffering in proportion to the injuries he has offered. But cruelty and pride, oppression and

partiality

partiality may tyrannise in private families without control; meekness may be trampled on and piety insulted without any appeal but to conscience and to heaven. A thousand methods of torture may be invented, a thousand acts of unkindness or disregard may be committed, a thousand innocent gratifications may be denied, and a thousand hardships imposed without any violation of national laws. Life may be imbittered with hourly vexation, and weeks, months and years be lingered out in misery without any legal cause of separation or possibility of judicial redress. Perhaps no sharper anguish is felt than that which cannot be complained of, nor any greater cruelties inflicted than some which no human authority can relieve. *Works* ix. 291.

Domestic virtue:

POPE's epitaph on Mrs. Corbet, who died of a cancer in her breast [1].

> Here rests a woman, good without pretence,
> Blest with plain reason, and with sober sense:
> No conquest she but o'er herself, desir'd;
> No arts essay'd, but not to be admir'd;
> Passion and pride were to her soul unknown,
> Convinc'd that Virtue only is our own.
> So unaffected, so compos'd a mind,
> So firm, yet soft, so strong, yet so refin'd,
> Heaven, as its purest gold, by tortures try'd;
> The saint sustain'd it, but the woman dy'd.

I have always considered this as the most valuable of all Pope's epitaphs; the subject of it is a character not discriminated by any shining or eminent peculiarities; yet that

---

[1] In the North aisle of the parish church of St. Margaret, Westminster.

which

which really makes though not the splendour, the felicity of life, and that which every wise man will choose for his final and lasting companion in the languor of age, in the quiet of privacy, when he departs weary and disgusted from the ostentatious, the volatile, and the vain. Of such a character, which the dull overlook and the gay despise, it was fit that the value should be made known and the dignity established. Domestic virtue, as it is exerted without great occasions or conspicuous consequences, in an even unnoted tenour, required the genius of Pope to display it in such a manner as might attract regard and enforce reverence. Who can forbear to lament that this amiable woman has no name in the verses?

Works, viii. 354.

Donne versus Pope:

'MR. CRAUFORD being engaged to dinner where Dr. Johnson was to be, resolved to pay his court to him; and having heard that he preferred Donne's Satires to Pope's version of them said, "Do you know, Dr. Johnson, that I like Dr. Donne's original Satires better than Pope's?" Johnson said, "Well, Sir, I can't help that."'

Murray's Johnsoniana, p. 427.

Dulness:

THIS fellow's dulness is elastic, and all we do is but like kicking at a woolsack.

Piozzi's Anecdotes, p. 217.

Duties:

MUCH of the prosperity of a trading nation depends upon duties properly apportioned; so that what is necessary may continue cheap, and what is of use only to luxury may in

some

some measure atone to the public for the mischief done to individuals. Duties may often be so regulated as to become useful even to those that pay them ; and they may be likewise so unequally imposed as to discourage honesty and depress industry, and give temptation to fraud and unlawful practices.   *Works*, v. 253.

Duty:

WHEN we act according to our duty we commit the event to Him by whose laws our actions are governed, and who will suffer none to be finally punished for obedience. When, in prospect of some good whether natural or moral, we break the rules prescribed us, we withdraw from the direction of superior wisdom and take all consequences upon ourselves.   Man cannot so far know the connexion of causes and events as that he may venture to do wrong in order to do right.   When we pursue our end by lawful means, we may always console our miscarriage by the hope of future recompense.   When we consult only our own policy, and attempt to find a nearer way to good by overleaping the settled boundaries of right and wrong, we cannot be happy even by success because we cannot escape the consciousness of our fault : but, if we miscarry, the disappointment is irremediably imbittered.   How comfortless is the sorrow of him who feels at once the pangs of guilt and the vexation of calamity which guilt has brought upon him !

Rasselas, ch. 34.

Eating:

'AT supper this night he talked of good eating with uncommon satisfaction. "Some people (said he) have a foolish way of not minding, or pretending not to mind,

what

Wit and
Wisdom
of
Samuel
Johnson.

what they eat.   For my part, I mind my belly very studiously and very carefully; for I look upon it that he who does not mind his belly will hardly mind anything else."'

Boswell's Life of Johnson, i. 7.

· ·. ·

'JOHNSON often said, "that wherever the dinner is ill got there is poverty, or there is avarice, or there is stupidity; in short, the family is somehow grossly wrong; for," continued he, "a man seldom thinks with more earnestness of anything than he does of his dinner; and if he cannot get that well dressed he should be suspected of inaccuracy in other things."'

Piozzi's Anecdotes, p. 149.

Education :

I HATE by-roads in education.   Education is as well known, and has long been as well known, as ever it can be. Endeavouring to make children prematurely wise is useless labour.   Suppose they have more knowledge at five or six years old than other children, what use can be made of it? It will be lost before it is wanted, and the waste of so much time and labour of the teacher can never be repaid.   Too much is expected from precocity, and too little performed.

Boswell's Life of Johnson, ii. 407.

·. ·

HE that supports an infant enables him to live here, but he that educates him assists him in his passage to a happier state and prevents that wickedness which is, if not the necessary, yet the frequent consequence of unenlightened infancy and vagrant poverty.   Nor does this charity terminate in the persons upon whom it is conferred, but extends its influence through the whole state, which has very frequently

quently

quently experienced how much is to be dreaded from men bred up without principles and without employment. He who begs in the street in his infancy learns only how to rob there in his manhood; and it is certainly very apparent with how much less difficulty evils are prevented than remedied.

Works, ix. 468.

.˙.

' MR. LANGTON told us he was about to establish a school upon his estate, but it had been suggested to him that it might have a tendency to make the people less industrious. JOHNSON. " No, Sir. While learning to read and write is a distinction, the few who have that distinction may be the less inclined to work; but when everybody learns to read and write, it is no longer a distinction. A man who has a laced waistcoat is too fine a man to work; but if everybody had laced waistcoats, we should have people working in laced waistcoats. There are no people whatever more industrious, none who work more than our manufacturers; yet they have all learnt to read and write. Sir, you must not neglect doing a thing immediately good from fear of remote evil,—from fear of its being abused. A man who has candles may sit up too late, which he would not do if he had not candles; but nobody will deny that the art of making candles, by which light is continued to us beyond the time that the sun gives us light, is a valuable art and ought to be preserved." '

Boswell's *Life of Johnson*, ii. 188.

.˙.

' JOHNSON advised me to-night not to *refine* in the education of my children. " Life (said he) will not bear refinement : you must do as other people do." '

Ib. iii. 169.

THE

THE purpose of Milton, as it seems, was to teach something more solid than the common literature of schools by reading those authors that treat of physical subjects, such as the georgic and astronomical treatises of the ancients. This was a scheme of improvement which seems to have busied many literary projectors of that age. Cowley, who had more means than Milton of knowing what was wanting to the embellishments of life, formed the same plan of education in his imaginary college.

But the truth is, that the knowledge of external nature, and the sciences which that knowledge requires or includes, are not the great or the frequent business of the human mind. Whether we provide for action or conversation, whether we wish to be useful or pleasing, the first requisite is the religious and moral knowledge of right and wrong; the next is an acquaintance with the history of mankind, and with those examples which may be said to embody truth, and prove by events the reasonableness of opinions. Prudence and justice are virtues and excellencies of all times and of all places; we are perpetually moralists, but we are geometricians only by chance. Our intercourse with intellectual nature is necessary; our speculations upon matter are voluntary, and at leisure. Physiological learning is of such rare emergence, that one may know another half his life, without being able to estimate his skill in hydrostatics or astronomy; but his moral and prudential character immediately appears.

Those authors, therefore, are to be read at schools that supply most axioms of prudence, most principles of moral truth, and most materials for conversation; and these purposes are best served by poets, orators, and historians.

Let

Let me not be censured for this digression as pedantic or paradoxical; for, if I have Milton against me, I have Socrates on my side. It was his labour to turn philosophy from the study of nature to speculations upon life; but the innovators whom I oppose are turning off attention from life to nature. They seem to think that we are placed here to watch the growth of plants, or the motions of the stars. Socrates was rather of opinion that what we had to learn was how to do good and avoid evil.

Ὅττι τοι ἐν μεγάροισι κακόντ' ἀγαθόντε τέτυκται[1].

Works, vii. 76.

.·.

' WE talked of the education of children, and I asked him what he thought was best to teach them first. JOHNSON. "Sir, it is no matter what you teach them first, any more than what leg you shall put into your breeches first. Sir, you may stand disputing which is best to put in first, but in the mean time your breech is bare. Sir, while you are considering which of two things you should teach your child first, another boy has learnt them both." '

Boswell's *Life of Johnson*, i. 452.

Eighteenth century:

THE present age, though not likely to shine hereafter among the most splendid periods of history, has yet given examples of charity which may be very properly recommended to imitation. The equal distribution of wealth which long commerce has produced does not enable any

---

[1] *Odyssey*, iv. 392.
' What good, what ill hath in thine house befallen.'

Cowper's *Translation*, iv. 478.

single

single hand to raise edifices of piety like fortified cities, to appropriate manors to religious uses, or deal out such large and lasting beneficence as was scattered over the land in ancient times by those who possessed counties or provinces. But no sooner is a new species of misery brought to view, and a design of relieving it professed, than every hand is open to contribute something, every tongue is busied in solicitation, and every art of pleasure is employed for a time in the interest of virtue. *Idler*, No. 4.

Emendations:

I HAVE always suspected that the reading is right which requires many words to prove it wrong, and the emendation wrong that cannot without so much labour appear to be right. The justness of a happy restoration strikes at once, and the moral precept may be well applied to criticism, *quod dubitas ne feceris.* *Works*, v. 150.

Emigration:

To hinder insurrection by driving away the people, and to govern peaceably by having no subjects, is an expedient that argues no great profundity of politics. To soften the obdurate, to convince the mistaken, to mollify the resentful, are worthy of a statesman; but it affords a legislator little self-applause to consider that where there was formerly an insurrection, there is now a wilderness. *Ib.* ix. 94.

THE great business of insular policy is now to keep the people in their own country. As the world has been let in upon them they have heard of happier climates and less arbitrary government; and if they are disgusted have

emissaries

emissaries among them ready to offer them land and houses as a reward for deserting their chief and clan. Many have departed both from the main of Scotland and from the islands; and all that go may be considered as subjects lost to the British crown; for a nation scattered in the boundless regions of America resembles rays diverging from a focus. All the rays remain, but the heat is gone. Their power consisted in their concentration: when they are dispersed they have no effect. It may be thought that they are happier by the change; but they are not happy as a nation, for they are a nation no longer. As they contribute not to the prosperity of any community they must want that security, that dignity, that happiness, whatever it be, which a prosperous community throws back upon individuals.

Works, ix. 128.

Employment:

EMPLOYMENT is the great instrument of intellectual dominion. The mind cannot retire from its enemy into total vacancy, or turn aside from one object but by passing to another. The gloomy and the resentful are always found among those who have nothing to do or who do nothing. We must be busy about good or evil, and he to whom the present offers nothing will often be looking backward on the past.

Idler, No. 72.

.·.

'SIR, (said Johnson,) you cannot give me an instance of any man who is permitted to lay out his own time contriving not to have tedious hours.'

Boswell's *Life of Johnson*, ii. 194.

England's

England's command of the Sea:

UPON the ocean we are allowed to be irresistible; to be able to shut up the ports of the continent, imprison the nations of Europe within the limits of their own territories, deprive them of all foreign assistance, and put a stop to the commerce of the world. It is allowed that we are placed the sentinels at the barriers of nature, and the arbiters of the intercourse of mankind.

Debates. Works, x. 466.

Enjoyment:

PROVIDENCE has fixed the limits of human enjoyment by immoveable boundaries, and has set different gratifications at such a distance from each other that no art or power can bring them together. This great law it is the business of every rational being to understand, that life may not pass away in an attempt to make contradictions consistent, to combine opposite qualities, and to unite things which the nature of their being must always keep asunder.

Rambler, No. 178.

Enthusiast:

SIR, he is an enthusiast by rule.

Boswell's *Life of Johnson,* iv. 33.

Epitaphs:

THE difficulty in writing epitaphs is to give a particular and appropriate praise. This, however, is not always to be performed, whatever be the diligence or ability of the writer; for the greater part of mankind *have no character at all,* have little that distinguishes them from others equally good or bad, and therefore nothing can be said of them

which

which may not be applied with equal propriety to a thousand more. It is indeed no great panegyric that there is inclosed in this tomb one who was born in one year and died in another: yet many useful and amiable lives have been spent which yet leave little materials for any other memorial.

Works, viii. 355.

. .

THOUGH a sepulchral inscription is professedly a panegyric and, therefore, not confined to historical impartiality, yet it ought always to be written with regard to truth. No man ought to be commended for virtues which he never possessed, but whoever is curious to know his faults must inquire after them in other places; the monuments of the dead are not intended to perpetuate the memory of crimes, but to exhibit patterns of virtue. On the tomb of Mæcenas his luxury is not to be mentioned with his munificence, nor is the proscription to find a place on the monument of Augustus. The best subject for epitaphs is private virtue; virtue exerted in the same circumstances in which the bulk of mankind are placed, and which, therefore, may admit of many imitators. He that has delivered his country from oppression, or freed the world from ignorance and error, can excite the emulation of a very small number; but he that has repelled the temptations of poverty and disdained to free himself from distress at the expence of his virtue, may animate multitudes by his example to the same firmness of heart and steadiness of resolution.

Ib. v. 265.

. .

THE writer of an epitaph should not be considered as saying nothing but what is strictly true. Allowance must

be

be made for some degree of exaggerated praise. In lapidary inscriptions a man is not upon oath.

Boswell's Life of Johnson, ii. 407.

Estimate of oneself:

THERE is no being so poor and so contemptible, who does not think there is somebody still poorer and still more contemptible.

Ib. ii. 13.

Eternal perdition:

IF he whose crimes have deprived him of the favour of God can reflect upon his conduct without disturbance, or can at will banish the reflection; if he who considers himself as suspended over the abyss of eternal perdition only by the thread of life which must soon part by its own weakness, and which the wing of every minute may divide, can cast his eyes round him without shuddering with horror or panting for security; what can he judge of himself but that he is not yet awakened to sufficient conviction, since every loss is more lamented than the loss of the divine favour, and every danger more dreadful than the danger of final condemnation?

Rambler, No. 110.

Ethics:

ETHICS, or *morality*, is one of the studies which ought to begin with the first glimpse of reason and only end with life itself.

Works, v. 243.

Exaggeration:

IN discussing exceptions from the course of nature, the first question is, whether the fact be justly stated. That which is strange is delightful, and a pleasing error is not

willingly

willingly detected.   Accuracy of narration is not very common, and there are few so rigidly philosophical as not to represent as perpetual what is only frequent, or as constant what is really casual.   *Works*, ix. 26.

.·.

EXAGGERATION and the absurdities ever faithfully attached to it are inseparable attributes of the ignorant, the empty, and the affected.   Hence those eloquent tropes so familiar in every conversation, *monstrously pretty, vastly little;* ... hence your *eminent shoe-maker, farriers, and undertakers.* ... It is to the same muddy source we owe the many falsehoods and absurdities we have been pestered with concerning Lisbon[1].   Thence your extravagantly sublime figures: *Lisbon is no more; can be seen no more*, etc., ... with all the other prodigal effusions of bombast beyond the stretch of time or temper to enumerate.

Boswell's *Life of Johnson*, i. 309 *n.* 3.

.·.

'I TOLD Dr. Johnson that I had travelled all the preceding night and gone to bed at Leek, in Staffordshire; and that when I rose to go to church in the afternoon, I was informed there had been an earthquake of which, it seems, the shock had been felt in some degree at Ashbourne.   JOHNSON. "Sir, it will be much exaggerated in popular talk: for, in the first place, the common people do not accurately adapt their thoughts to the objects; nor, secondly, do they accurately adapt their words to their thoughts: they do not mean to lie; but, taking no pains to be exact, they give you very false accounts.   A great part of their language is proverbial.   If anything rocks at

---

[1] The great earthquake of 1755 had lately happened.

all,

all, they say *it rocks like a cradle*; and in this way they go on."'

Boswell's *Life of Johnson*, iii. 136.

SELDOM any splendid story is wholly true.   *Works*, vii. 224.

Excise:

A HATEFUL tax levied upon commodities, and adjudged not by the common judges of property, but wretches hired by those to whom Excise is paid.

Dictionary.

Exclamations:

EXCLAMATION seldom succeeds in our language; and I think it may be observed that the particle O! used at the beginning of a sentence always offends.   *Works*, viii. 357.

Exercise:

SUCH is the constitution of man, that labour may be styled its own reward; nor will any external incitements be requisite if it be considered how much happiness is gained, and how much misery escaped, by frequent and violent agitation of the body. . . . Exercise cannot secure us from that dissolution to which we are decreed; but while the soul and body continue united it can make the association pleasing and give probable hopes that they shall be disjoined by an easy separation. It was a principle among the ancients that acute diseases are from heaven, and chronical from ourselves: the dart of death indeed falls from heaven, but we poison it by our own misconduct: to die is the fate of man, but to die with lingering anguish is generally his folly.

Rambler, No. 85.

I TAKE the true definition of exercise to be labour without weariness.

Boswell's *Life of Johnson*, iv. 151 *n*. 1.

Expectation:

Expectation:

PERHAPS I may not be more censured for doing wrong than for doing little; for raising in the public expectations which at last I have not answered. The expectation of ignorance is indefinite, and that of knowledge is often tyrannical. It is hard to satisfy those who know not what to demand, or those who demand by design what they think impossible to be done. I have indeed disappointed no opinion more than my own; yet I have endeavoured to perform my task with no slight solicitude.   *Works*, v. 151.

EXPECTATION, when her wings are once expanded, easily reaches heights which performance never will attain; and when she has mounted the summit of perfection derides her follower, who dies in the pursuit.   *Ib.* v. 2.

'PERCIVAL STOCKDALE records, that after he had entered on his charge as domestic tutor to Lord Craven's son he called on Johnson, who asked him how he liked his place. On his hesitating to answer he said:—"You must expect insolence." He added that in his youth he had entertained great expectations from a powerful family. "At length," he said, "I found that their promises, and consequently my expectations, vanished into air. . . . But, Sir, they would have treated me much worse if they had known that the motives from which I paid my court to them were purely selfish, and what opinion I had formed of them." He added that since he knew mankind he had not, on any occasion been the sport of such delusion; and that he had never been disappointed by anybody but himself.'   Boswell's *Life of Johnson*, i. 337 *n.* 1.

H   Faithfulness:

Faithfulness :

To know the condition to which a compliance with this motion[1] would reduce the British nation we need only turn our eyes downwards upon the hourly scenes of common life; we need only attend to the occurrences which crowd perpetually upon our view, and consider the calamitous state of that man of whom it is generally known that he cannot be trusted, and that secrets communicated to him are in reality scattered among mankind. *Debates. Works,* xi. 53.

Falsehoods :

To doubt whether a man of eminence[2] has told the truth about his own birth is, in appearance, to be very deficient in candour; yet nobody can live long without knowing that falsehoods of convenience or vanity, falsehoods from which no evil immediately visible ensues, except the general degradation of human testimony, are very lightly uttered, and once uttered are sullenly supported. Boileau, who desired to be thought a rigorous and steady moralist, having told a petty lie to Lewis XIV continued it afterwards by false dates; thinking himself obliged *in honour*, says his admirer, to maintain what, when he said it, was so well received. *Works,* viii. 23.

.'.

LARGE offers and sturdy rejections are among the most common topics of falsehood. *Ib.* vii. 98.

---

[1] On March 9, 1742, Lord Limerick made a motion for enquiring into the conduct of affairs at home and abroad during the last twenty years.

[2] Congreve was charged with having 'meanly disowned his native country' Ireland.

Falsifiers :

Falsifiers:

YOUR assent to a man whom you have never known to falsify is a debt; but after you have known a man to falsify, your assent to him then is a favour.

Boswell's *Life of Johnson*, iv. 320.

Falstaff:

BUT Falstaff, unimitated, unimitable Falstaff, how shall I describe thee? Thou compound of sense and vice; of sense which may be admired but not esteemed; of vice which may be despised but hardly detested. Falstaff is a character loaded with faults, and with those faults which naturally produce contempt. He is a thief and a glutton, a coward and a boaster, always ready to cheat the weak and prey upon the poor; to terrify the timorous and insult the defenceless. At once obsequious and malignant, he satirizes in their absence those whom he lives by flattering. He is familiar with the prince only as an agent of vice; but of this familiarity he is so proud as not only to be supercilious and haughty with common men, but to think his interest of importance to the duke of Lancaster. Yet the man thus corrupt, thus despicable, makes himself necessary to the prince that despises him by the most pleasing of all qualities, perpetual gaiety, by an unfailing power of exciting laughter, which is the more freely indulged as his wit is not of the splendid or ambitious kind, but consists in easy scapes and sallies of levity, which make sport but raise no envy. It must be observed that he is stained with no enormous or sanguinary crimes, so that his licentiousness is not so offensive but that it may be borne for his mirth. The moral to be drawn from this representation is, that no

Wit and Wisdom of Samuel Johnson.

H 2

man

man is more dangerous than he that, with a will to corrupt, hath the power to please ; and that neither wit nor honesty ought to think themselves safe with such a companion, when they see Henry seduced by Falstaff.   *Works*, v. 164.

Fame :

TIME quickly puts an end to artificial and accidental fame, and Addison is to pass through futurity protected only by his genius.   Every name which kindness or interest once raised too high is in danger lest the next age should by the vengeance of criticism sink it in the same proportion. A great writer has lately styled him 'an indifferent poet and a worse critic.'   *Ib.* vii. 451.

.˙.

IT is one of the innumerable absurdities of pride that we are never more impatient of direction than in that part of life when we need it most ; we are in haste to meet enemies whom we have not strength to overcome, and to undertake tasks which we cannot perform : and as he that once mis-carries does not easily persuade mankind to favour another attempt, an ineffectual struggle for fame is often followed by perpetual obscurity.   *Rambler*, No. 111.

.˙.

THIS ill economy of fame is sometimes the effect of stupidity.   Men whose perceptions are languid and sluggish, who lament nothing but loss of money and feel nothing but a blow, are often at a difficulty to guess why they are encompassed with enemies, though they neglect all those arts by which men are endeared to one another.   They comfort themselves that they have lived irreproachably ; that none can charge them with having endangered his life, or diminished his possessions ; and therefore conclude that

they

they suffer by some invincible fatality, or impute the malice of their neighbours to ignorance or envy. They wrap themselves up in their innocence, and enjoy the congratulations of their own hearts, without knowing or suspecting that they are every day deservedly incurring resentments by withholding from those with whom they converse that regard, or appearance of regard, to which every one is entitled by the customs of the world. *Rambler*, No. 56.

THOSE who are oppressed by their own reputation will, perhaps, not be comforted by hearing that their cares are unnecessary. But the truth is that no man is much regarded by the rest of the world. He that considers how little he dwells upon the condition of others will learn how little the attention of others is attracted by himself While we see multitudes passing before us, of whom, perhaps, not one appears to deserve our notice or excite our sympathy, we should remember that we likewise are lost in the same throng; that the eye which happens to glance upon us is turned in a moment on him that follows us, and that the utmost which we can reasonably hope or fear is, to fill a vacant hour with prattle and be forgotten. *Ib.* No. 159.

HE that pursues fame with just claims trusts his happiness to the winds; but he that endeavours after it by false merit has to fear, not only the violence of the storm, but the leaks of his vessel. *Ib.* No. 20.

IT seems not to be sufficiently considered how little renown can be admitted in the world. Mankind are kept perpetually busy by their fears or desires, and have not more leisure from their own affairs than to acquaint themselves

themselves with the accidents of the current day. Engaged in contriving some refuge from calamity, or in shortening the way to some new possession, they seldom suffer their thoughts to wander to the past or future; none but a few solitary students have leisure to inquire into the claims of ancient heroes or sages; and names which hoped to range over kingdoms and continents shrink at last into cloisters or colleges.

Rambler, No. 146.

. • .

' "You know what Johnson said to Boswell of preserving fame?" "No." "There were but two ways," he told him, "of preserving, one was by sugar, the other by salt. Now," says he, "as the sweet way, Bozzy, you are but little likely to attain, I would have you plunge into vinegar and get fairly pickled at once." '

Mme. D'Arblay's Diary, iv. 140.

Fancy and reason:

To what degree Fancy is to be admitted into religious offices it would require much deliberation to determine. I am far from intending totally to exclude it. Fancy is a faculty bestowed by our Creator, and it is reasonable that all His gifts should be used to His glory, that all our faculties should co-operate in His worship; but they are to co-operate according to the will of Him that gave them, according to the order which His wisdom has established. As ceremonies prudential or convenient are less obligatory than positive ordinances, as bodily worship is only the token to others or ourselves of mental adoration, so Fancy is always to act in subordination to Reason. We may take Fancy for a companion, but must follow Reason as our guide. We may allow Fancy to suggest certain ideas in certain places; but Reason must always be heard when she tells us that

those

those ideas and those places have no natural or necessary relation. When we enter a church we habitually recall to mind the duty of adoration, but we must not omit adoration for want of a temple ; because we know, and ought to remember, that the Universal Lord is everywhere present; and that, therefore, to come to Iona or to Jerusalem, though it may be useful, cannot be necessary.

Boswell's Life of Johnson, ii. 276.

Favourite :

ONE chosen as a companion by a superior; a mean wretch whose whole business is by any means to please.

Dictionary.

Favours :

HE only confers favours generously who appears, when they are once conferred, to remember them no more.

Works, ix. 467.

Fear:

ALL fear is in itself painful, and when it conduces not to safety is painful without use. Every consideration therefore by which groundless terrors may be removed adds something to human happiness. Rambler, No. 29.

Fiction and passion :

WHERE there is fiction there is no passion : he that describes himself as a shepherd and his Neæra or Delia as a shepherdess, and talks of goats and lambs, feels no passion. He that courts his mistress with Roman imagery deserves to lose her; for she may with good reason suspect his sincerity. Works, viii. 91.

Fictions :

Fictions of the last age:

I REMEMBER a remark made by Scaliger upon Pontanus that all his writings are filled with the same images; and that if you take from him his lilies and his roses, his satyrs and his dryads, he will have nothing left that can be called poetry.   In like manner almost all the fictions of the last age will vanish if you deprive them of a hermit and a wood, a battle and a shipwreck.

Rambler, No. 4.

Fiddle-de-dee:

‘ IT was near the close of Johnson's life that two young ladies, who were warm admirers of his works but had never seen himself, went to Bolt Court and, asking if he was at home, were shown upstairs where he was writing.   He laid down his pen on their entrance; and, as they stood before him, one of the females repeated a speech of some length previously prepared for the occasion.   It was an enthusiastic effusion which, when the speaker had finished, she panted for her idol's reply.   What was her mortification when all he said was, “ Fiddle-de-dee, my dear.” ’

Murray's *Johnsoniana*, p. 230.

Fiddling:

THERE is nothing, I think, in which the power of art is shown so much as in playing on the fiddle.   In all other things we can do something at first.   Any man will forge a bar of iron if you give him a hammer; not so well as a smith, but tolerably.   A man will saw a piece of wood and make a box, though a clumsy one; but give him a fiddle and a fiddle-stick, and he can do nothing.

Boswell's *Life of Johnson*, ii. 226.

Finery:

Finery:

‘WHEN talking of dress, he said, “Sir, were I to have anything fine, it should be very fine. Were I to wear a ring, it should not be a bauble, but a stone of great value. Were I to wear a laced or embroidered waistcoat, it should be very rich. I had once a very rich laced waistcoat which I wore the first night of my tragedy.” ’

Boswell's *Life of Johnson*, v. 364.

Flattery:

HE that is much flattered soon learns to flatter himself; we are commonly taught our duty by fear or shame, and how can they act upon the man who hears nothing but his own praises?

Works, viii. 217.

．·．

IN order that all men may be taught to speak truth it is necessary that all likewise should learn to hear it; for no species of falsehood is more frequent than flattery, to which the coward is betrayed by fear, the dependant by interest, and the friend by tenderness. Those who are neither servile nor timorous are yet desirous to bestow pleasure; and while unjust demands of praise continue to be made, there will always be some whom hope, fear, or kindness, will dispose to pay them.

Rambler, No. 96.

．·．

‘AT Sir Joshua Reynolds’s one evening Hannah More met Dr. Johnson. She very soon began to pay her court to him in the most fulsome strain. “Spare me, I beseech you, dear Madam,” was his reply. She still *laid it on*. “Pray, Madam, let us have no more of this;” he rejoined. Not paying any attention to these warnings, she continued

still

still her eulogy.　At length, provoked by this indelicate and *vain* obtrusion of compliment, he exclaimed, "Dearest lady, consider with yourself what your flattery is worth before you bestow it so freely." '　　　　　Boswell's *Life of Johnson*, iv. 341.

FLATTERY pleases very generally.　In the first place, the flatterer may think what he says to be true : but, in the second place, whether he thinks so or not, he certainly thinks those whom he flatters of consequence enough to be flattered.　　　　　　　　　　*Ib.* ii. 364.

Flogging :

THERE is now less flogging in our great public schools than formerly, but then less is learned there ; so that what the boys get at one end they lose at the other.　　*Ib.* ii. 407.

Floundering well :

'GOLDSMITH ridiculously asserted, that Warburton was a weak writer.　This misapplied characteristic Dr. Johnson refuted.　I shall never forget one of the happy metaphors with which he strengthened and illustrated his refutation. "Warburton," said he, "may be absurd, but he will never be weak : he *flounders* well." '　　　　*Johnsoniana*, p. 354.

Forgetfulness :

IT may be doubted whether we should be more bene-fitted by the art of memory or the art of forgetfulness . . . All useless misery is certainly folly, and he that feels evils before they come may be deservedly censured ; yet surely to dread the future is more reasonable than to lament the past.　The business of life is to go forwards : he who sees evil in prospect meets it in his way ; but he who catches it by retrospection turns back to find it.　That which is

feared

feared may sometimes be avoided, but that which is re-gretted to-day may be regretted again to-morrow. Regret is indeed useful and virtuous, and not only allowable but necessary, when it tends to the amendment of life or to admonition of error which we may be again in danger of committing. But a very small part of the moments spent in meditation on the past produce any reasonable caution or salutary sorrow. Most of the mortifications that we have suffered arose from the concurrence of local and temporary circumstances, which can never meet again; and most of our disappointments have succeeded those expectations which life allows not to be formed a second time. It would add much to human happiness, if an art could be taught of forgetting all of which the remembrance is at once useless and afflictive, if that pain which never can end in pleasure could be driven totally away, that the mind might perform its functions without incumbrance, and the past might no longer encroach upon the present. *Idler*, No. 72.

Forgiveness:

OF him that hopes to be forgiven it is indispensably re-quired that he forgive. It is therefore superfluous to urge any other motive. On this great duty eternity is suspended, and to him that refuses to practise it the throne of mercy is inaccessible, and the Saviour of the world has been born in vain. *Rambler*, No. 185.

Forms:

' IN answer to the arguments urged by Puritans, Quakers, etc., against showy decorations of the human figure, I once heard him exclaim :—" Oh, let us not be found, when our
Master

Master calls us, ripping the lace off our waistcoats, but the spirit of contention from our souls and tongues ! . . . Alas ! Sir, a man who cannot get to heaven in a green coat will not find his way thither the sooner in a grey one." '

Piozzi's Anecdotes, p. 109.

Fortitude :

THE arguments by which Lady Macbeth persuades her husband to commit the murder afford a proof of Shakespeare's knowledge of human nature. She urges the excellence and dignity of courage, a glittering idea which has dazzled mankind from age to age, and animated sometimes the housebreaker, and sometimes the conqueror : but this sophism Macbeth has for ever destroyed by distinguishing true from false fortitude, in a line and a half; of which it may almost be said, that they ought to bestow immortality on the author, though all his other productions had been lost.

> I dare do all that may become a man.
> Who dares do more is none [1].

Works, v. 69.

Fortune :

IT may be remarked that they whose condition has not afforded them the light of moral or religious instruction, and who collect all their ideas by their own eyes and digest them by their own understandings, seem to consider those who are placed in ranks of remote superiority as almost another and higher species of beings. As themselves have known little other misery than the consequences of want, they are with difficulty persuaded that where there is wealth

---

[1] Act 1, sc. 7.

there

there can be sorrow, or that those who glitter in dignity, and glide along in affluence, can be acquainted with pains and cares like those which lie heavy upon the rest of mankind.

Rambler, No. 58.

Wit and Wisdom of Samuel Johnson.

• •

So powerful is genius when it is invested with the glitter of affluence! Men willingly pay to fortune that regard which they owe to merit, and are pleased when they have an opportunity at once of gratifying their vanity and practising their duty.

Works, viii. 125.

Fraud:

THE nature of fraud as distinct from other violations of right or property seems to consist in this, that the man injured is induced to concur in the act by which the injury is done. Thus to take away anything valuable without the owner's knowledge is a theft; to take it away against his consent by threats or force is a robbery; to borrow it without intention of returning it is a fraud, because the owner consents to the act by which it passed out of his own hands.

Ib. ix. 454.

• •

THIS is a stratagem [1] by which an author, panting for fame and yet afraid of seeming to challenge it, may at once gratify his vanity and preserve the appearance of modesty;

---

[1] Browne's *Religio Medici* had been published, it was said, without the author's knowledge. Johnson says: 'There is surely some reason to doubt the truth of the complaint so frequently made of surreptitious editions. . . It is easy to convey an imperfect book by a distant hand to the press, and plead the circulation of a false copy as an excuse for publishing the true.'

may

may enter the lists and secure a retreat : and this candour might suffer to pass undetected as an innocent fraud, but that indeed no fraud is innocent ; for the confidence which makes the happiness of society is in some degree diminished by every man whose practice is at variance with his words.

                                         Works, vi. 478.

Friendship :

IN youth we are apt to be too rigorous in our expectations, and to suppose that the duties of life are to be performed with unfailing exactness and regularity; but in our progress through life we are forced to abate much of our demands, and to take friends such as we can find them, not as we would make them. These concessions every wise man is more ready to make to others, as he knows that he shall often want them for himself; and when he remembers how often he fails in the observance of a cultivation of his best friends, is willing to suppose that his friends may in their turn neglect him without any intention to offend him.

                                 Croker's *Boswell*, p. 146.

.˙.

'"CLING to those who cling to you," said the immortal Johnson to your mother [1], when she uttered something that seemed fastidious relative to a person whose partiality she did not prize.'

                           Mme. D'Arblay's *Diary*, vii. 255.

.˙.

FRIENDSHIP, like love, is destroyed by long absence, though it may be increased by short intermissions. What we have missed long enough to want it, we value more

---

[1] Written to Mme. D'Arblay's son.

                                         when

when it is regained ; but that which has been lost till it is forgotten will be found at last with little gladness, and with still less if a substitute has supplied the place.   *Idler*, No. 23.

Wit and
Wisdom
of
Samuel
Johnson.

．•．

THE necessities of our condition require a thousand offices of tenderness, which mere regard for the species will never dictate.   Every man has frequent grievances which only the solicitude of friendship will discover and remedy, and which would remain for ever unheeded in the mighty heap of human calamity, were it only surveyed by the eye of general benevolence equally attentive to every misery.

Rambler, No. 99.

．•．

IF a man does not make new acquaintance as he advances through life, he will soon find himself left alone.   A man, Sir, should keep his friendship *in constant repair.*

Boswell's *Life of Johnson*, i. 300.

．•．

MEN engaged, by moral or religious motives, in contrary parties, will generally look with different eyes upon every man, and decide almost every question upon different principles.   When such occasions of dispute happen, to comply is to betray our cause and to maintain friendship by ceasing to deserve it ; to be silent is to lose the happiness and dignity of independence, to live in perpetual constraint, and to desert, if not to betray: and who shall determine which of two friends shall yield, where neither believes himself mistaken and both confess the importance of the question? What then remains but contradiction and debate? and from those what can be expected but acrimony and vehemence, the insolence of triumph, the vexation of defeat,

and,

and, in time, a weariness of contest and an extinction of benevolence ? *Rambler*, No. 64.

THOSE that have loved longest love best. A sudden blaze of kindness may by a single blast of coldness be extinguished, but that fondness which length of time has connected with many circumstances and occasions ; though it may for a while be suppressed by disgust or resentment, with or without a cause, is hourly revived by accidental recollection. To those that have lived long together, every thing heard and every thing seen recalls some pleasure communicated, or some benefit conferred, some petty quarrel, or some slight endearment. Esteem of great powers, or amiable qualities newly discovered, may embroider a day or a week, but a friendship of twenty years is interwoven with the texture of life. A friend may be often found and lost, but an *old friend* never can be found, and nature has provided that he cannot easily be lost. *Piozzi Letters*, ii. 325.

THE most generous and disinterested friendship must be resolved at last into the love of ourselves ; he therefore whose reputation or dignity inclines us to consider his esteem as a testimonial of desert will always find our hearts open to his endearments. *Rambler*, No. 166.

Future :

IT may be observed, in general, that the future is purchased by the present. It is not possible to secure distant or permanent happiness but by the forbearance of some immediate gratification. *Ib.* No. 178.

Future life :

Future life :

YOU know I never thought confidence with respect to futurity any part of the character of a brave, a wise, or a good man. Bravery has no place where it can avail nothing ; wisdom impresses strongly the consciousness of those faults of which it is itself perhaps an aggravation ; and goodness, always wishing to be better and imputing every deficience to criminal negligence and every fault to voluntary corruption, never dares to suppose the condition of forgiveness fulfilled, nor what is wanting in the crime supplied by penitence. This is the state of the best : but what must be the condition of him whose heart will not suffer him to rank himself among the best, or among the good ? Such must be his dread of the approaching trial as will leave him little attention to the opinion of those whom he is leaving for ever ; and the serenity that is not felt it can be no virtue to feign.   *Piozzi Letters*, ii. 350.

. ˙ .

THE miseries of life may, perhaps, afford some proof of a future state, compared as well with the mercy as the justice of God. It is scarcely to be imagined that Infinite Benevolence would create a being capable of enjoying so much more than is here to be enjoyed, and qualified by nature to prolong pain by remembrance, and anticipate it by terror, if he was not designed for something nobler and better than a state in which many of his faculties can serve only for his torment ; in which he is to be importuned by desires that never can be satisfied, to feel many evils which he had no power to avoid, and to fear many which he shall never feel : there will surely come a time when every capacity of

happiness

I

happiness shall be filled, and none shall be wretched but by his own fault.

Adventurer, No. 120.

Garrick:

' "David, Madam," said the Doctor, "looks much older than he is; for his face has had double the business of any other man's; it is never at rest; when he speaks one minute he has quite a different countenance to what he assumes the next; I don't believe he ever kept the same look for half-an-hour together in the whole course of his life; and such an eternal, restless, fatiguing play of the muscles must certainly wear out a man's face before its real time." '

Mme. D'Arblay's *Diary*, i. 64.

.·.

' "They say," cried Mrs. Thrale, "that Garrick was extremely hurt by the coldness of the King's applause[1]." "He has been so long accustomed," said Mr. Seward, "to the thundering acclamation of a theatre, that mere calm approbation must necessarily be insipid, nay, dispiriting to him." "Sir," said Dr. Johnson, "he has no right, in a royal apartment, to expect the hallooing and clamour of the one-shilling gallery. The King, I doubt not, gave him as much applause as was rationally his due. And, indeed, great and uncommon as is the merit of Mr. Garrick, no man will be bold enough to assert that he has not had his just proportion both of fame and profit. He has long reigned the unequalled favourite of the public; and therefore nobody, we may venture to say, will mourn his hard lot, if the King and the Royal Family were not transported into rapture upon hearing him read *Lethe*! But yet, Mr. Garrick will complain

---

[1] Garrick had read *Lethe* in character before the Court.

to

to his friends ; and his friends will lament the King's want
of feeling and taste.   But then—Mr. Garrick will kindly
excuse the King.   He will say that his Majesty—might,
perhaps, be thinking of something else !   That the affairs
of America might possibly occur to him—or some other
subject of state more important—perhaps—than *Lethe.*
But though he will candidly say this himself—he will not
easily forgive his friends if they do not contradict him." '

Memoirs of Dr. Burney, ii. 97.

.·.

'Both Johnson and Garrick used to talk pleasantly of
this their first journey to London.   Garrick, evidently
meaning to embellish a little, said one day in my hearing,
"we rode and tied."   And the Bishop of Killaloe informed
me that at another time, when Johnson and Garrick were
dining together in a pretty large company, Johnson humor-
ously ascertaining the chronology of something, expressed
himself thus: "that was the year when I came to London
with two-pence half-penny in my pocket."   Garrick over-
hearing him exclaimed, " eh ? what do you say? with two-
pence half-penny in your pocket ?"—Johnson, " Why yes ;
when I came with two-pence half-penny in *my* pocket, and
thou, Davy, with three half-pence in thine." '

Boswell's *Life of Johnson,* i. 101 *n.* 1.

Gelidus :

Gelidus is a man of great penetration and deep researches.   Having a mind naturally formed for the abstruser
sciences, he can comprehend intricate combinations without
confusion, and being of a temper naturally cool and equal,
he is seldom interrupted by his passions in the pursuit of

I 2   the

the longest chain of unexpected consequences. He has, therefore, a long time indulged hopes that the solution of some problems, by which the professors of science have been hitherto baffled, is reserved for his genius and industry. He spends his time in the highest room of his house into which none of his family are suffered to enter; and when he comes down to his dinner, or his rest, he walks about like a stranger that is there only for a day, without any tokens of regard or tenderness. He has totally divested himself of all human sensations; he has neither eye for beauty nor ear for complaint; he neither rejoices at the good fortune of his nearest friend nor mourns for any public or private calamity. Having once received a letter and given it his servant to read, he was informed that it was written by his brother who, being shipwrecked, had swum naked to land, and was destitute of necessaries in a foreign country. Naked and destitute! says Gelidus, reach down the last volume of meteorological observations, extract an exact account of the wind, and note it carefully in the diary of the weather.

The family of Gelidus once broke into his study to show him that a town at a small distance was on fire; and in a few moments a servant came to tell him that the flame had caught so many houses on both sides that the inhabitants were confounded, and began to think of rather escaping with their lives than saving their dwellings. What you tell me, says Gelidus, is very probable, for fire naturally acts in a circle.

Thus lives this great philosopher, insensible to every spectacle of distress, and unmoved by the loudest call of social nature for want of considering that men are designed

for

for the succour and comfort of each other; that though there are hours which may be laudably spent upon knowledge not immediately useful, yet the first attention is due to practical virtue; and that he may be justly driven out from the commerce of mankind, who has so far abstracted himself from the species, as to partake neither of the joys nor griefs of others, but neglects the endearments of his wife and the caresses of his children to count the drops of rain, note the changes of the wind, and calculate the eclipses of the moons of Jupiter.   *Rambler*, No. 24.

Genius:

OF all the bugbears by which the *Infantes barbati*, boys both young and old, have been hitherto frighted from digressing into new tracts of learning, none has been more mischievously efficacious than an opinion that every kind of knowledge requires a peculiar genius, or mental constitution, framed for the reception of some ideas and the exclusion of others; and that to him whose genius is not adapted to the study which he prosecutes, all labour shall be vain and fruitless, vain as an endeavour to mingle oil and water, or, in the language of chemistry, to amalgamate bodies of heterogeneous principles.   *Ib.* No. 25.

IN the window of his[1] mother's apartment lay Spenser's Fairy Queen, in which he very early took delight to read, till by feeling the charms of verse he became, as he relates, irrecoverably a poet. Such are the accidents which, sometimes remembered and perhaps sometimes forgotten, produce that particular designation of mind, and propensity for some certain science or employment, which is commonly

---

[1] Cowley's.

called

called genius. The true genius is a mind of large general powers, accidentally determined to some particular direction. Sir Joshua Reynolds, the great painter of the present age, had the first fondness for his art excited by the perusal of Richardson's treatise.   *Works*, vii. 1.

.·.

'No, Sir,' said Johnson, 'people are not born with a particular genius for particular employments or studies, for it would be like saying that a man could see a great way east, but could not west. It is good sense applied with diligence to what was at first a mere accident, and which by great application grew to be called by the generality of mankind, a particular genius.'   Boswell's *Life of Johnson*, ii. 437 *n*. 2.

.·.

OF his[1] intellectual character, the constituent and fundamental principle was good sense, a prompt and intuitive perception of consonance and propriety. He saw immediately of his own conceptions what was to be chosen and what to be rejected, and in the works of others what was to be shunned and what was to be copied. But good sense alone is a sedate and quiescent quality, which manages its possessions well but does not increase them; it collects few materials for its own operations, and preserves safety but never gains supremacy. Pope had likewise genius; a mind active, ambitious, and adventurous, always investigating, always aspiring; in its widest searches still longing to go forward, in its highest flights still wishing to be higher; always imagining something greater than it knows, always endeavouring more than it can do.   *Works*, viii. 320.

---

[1] Pope's.

Do not let such evils overwhelm you as thousands have suffered, and thousands have surmounted; but turn your thoughts with vigour to some other plan of life, and keep always in your mind that, with due submission to Providence, a man of genius has been seldom ruined but by himself.   Boswell's *Life of Johnson*, i. 381.

Gentlemen:

'OFFICERS (Dr. Johnson said) were falsely supposed to have the carriage of gentlemen; whereas no profession left a stronger brand behind it than that of a soldier; and it was the essence of a gentleman's character to bear the visible mark of no profession whatever.'   Piozzi's *Anecdotes*, p. 156.

Ghosts:

'THAT the dead are seen no more,' said Imlac, 'I will not undertake to maintain against the concurrent and unvaried testimony of all ages and of all nations.   There is no people rude or learned among whom apparitions of the dead are not related and believed.   This opinion, which perhaps prevails as far as human nature is diffused, could become universal only by its truth: those that never heard of one another would not have agreed in a tale which nothing but experience can make credible.   That it is doubted by single cavillers can very little weaken the general evidence, and some who deny it with their tongues confess it by their fears.'   *Rasselas*, ch. 31.

.·.

'TALKING of ghosts, Dr. Johnson said, "It is wonderful that five thousand years have now elapsed since the creation of the world, and still it is undecided whether or not there

has

has ever been an instance of the spirit of any person appearing after death.　All argument is against it ; but all
belief is for it." '　　　　　　　Boswell's *Life of Johnson*, iii. 230.

. · .

'OF apparitions, Dr. Johnson observed, " A total dis-
belief of them is adverse to the opinion of the existence of
the soul between death and the last day; the question
simply is, whether departed spirits ever have the power of
making themselves perceptible to us ; a man who thinks he
has seen an apparition can only be convinced himself; his
authority will not convince another, and his conviction, if
rational, must be founded on being told something which
cannot be known but by supernatural means." '　　*Ib.* iv. 94.

Gluttony :

GLUTTONY is, I think, less common among women than
among men.　Women commonly eat more sparingly, and
are less curious in the choice of meat; but if once you find
a woman gluttonous, expect from her very little virtue.　Her
mind is enslaved to the lowest and grossest temptation.
A friend of mine who courted a lady of whom he did not
know much was advised to see her eat, and, if she was
voluptuous at table, to forsake her.　He married her, however, and in a few weeks came to his adviser with this
exclamation, ' It is the disturbance of my life to see this
woman eat.'　She was, as might be expected, selfish and
brutal ; and after some years of discord they parted and,
I believe, came together no more.　　　*Piozzi Letters*, ii. 298.

God's mercy :

THAT God will forgive may, indeed, be established as
the first and fundamental truth of religion ; for though the
knowledge

knowledge of His existence is the origin of philosophy, yet
without the belief of His mercy it would have little influence
upon our moral conduct.   There could be no prospect of
enjoying the protection or regard of him whom the least
deviation from rectitude made inexorable for ever, and
every man would naturally withdraw his thoughts from the
contemplation of a Creator whom he must consider as a
governor too pure to be pleased and too severe to be
pacified; as an enemy infinitely wise and infinitely powerful, whom he could neither deceive, escape, nor resist.

Rambler, No. 110.

Good humour:

A MAN grows better humoured as he grows older.   He
improves by experience.   When young, he thinks himself of great consequence and everything of importance.
As he advances in life, he learns to think himself of no
consequence and little things of little importance; and so
he becomes more patient and better pleased.   All good-
humour and complaisance are acquired.   Naturally a child
seizes directly what it sees, and thinks of pleasing itself
only.   By degrees it is taught to please others and to
prefer others, and that this will ultimately produce the
greatest happiness.   If a man is not convinced of that, he
will never practise it.   Boswell's *Life of Johnson*, v. 211.

Good and ill breeding:

THE difference between a well-bred and an ill-bred man
is this: One immediately attracts your liking, the other
your aversion.   You love the one till you find reason to
hate him; you hate the other till you find reason to love
him.   *Ib.* iv. 319.

Government:

Government:

OUR desires are not the measure of equity. It were to be desired that power should be only in the hands of the merciful, and riches in the possession of the generous; but the law must leave both riches and power where it finds them, and must often leave riches with the covetous, and power with the cruel. Convenience may be a rule in little things, where no other rule has been established. But as the great end of government is to give every man his own, no inconvenience is greater than that of making right uncertain. Nor is any man more an enemy to public peace than he who fills weak heads with imaginary claims, and breaks the series of civil subordination by inciting the lower classes of mankind to encroach upon the higher.

Boswell's Life of Johnson, ii. 244.

Governors:

GOVERNORS, being accustomed to hear of more crimes than they can punish and more wrongs than they can redress, set themselves at ease by indiscriminate negligence, and presently forget the request when they lose sight of the petitioner. Rasselas, ch. 34.

Grammarians:

No man forgets his original trade: the rights of nations and of kings sink into questions of grammar if grammarians discuss them. Works, vii. 85.

Gratitude:

THERE are minds so impatient of inferiority that their gratitude is a species of revenge, and they return benefits,

not

not because recompense is a pleasure, but because obligation is a pain.

Rambler, No. 87.

Wit and
Wisdom
of
Samuel
Johnson.

.˙.

GRATITUDE is a species of justice. *Works*, ix. 509.

Great enterprises:

THERE are some men of narrow views and grovelling conceptions who, without the instigation of personal malice, treat every new attempt as wild and chimerical, and look upon every endeavour to depart from the beaten track as the rash effort of a warm imagination, or the glittering speculation of an exalted mind that may please and dazzle for a time, but can produce no real or lasting advantage. These men value themselves upon a perpetual scepticism, upon believing nothing but their own senses, upon calling for demonstration where it cannot possibly be obtained, and sometimes upon holding out against it when it is laid before them; upon inventing arguments against the success of any new undertaking, and, where arguments cannot be found, upon treating it with contempt and ridicule. Such have been the most formidable enemies of the great benefactors to mankind, . . . for their notions and discourse are so agreeable to the lazy, the envious, and the timorous, that they seldom fail of becoming popular and directing the opinions of mankind. *Works*, vi. 338.

Great people:

MUCH has been said of the equality and independence which Swift preserved in his conversation with the ministers, of the frankness of his remonstrances and the familiarity of his friendship. In accounts of this kind a few single incidents are set against the general tenour of behaviour.

No

No man, however, can pay a more servile tribute to the Great than by suffering his liberty in their presence to aggrandize him in his own esteem. Between different ranks of the community there is necessarily some distance; he who is called by his superior to pass the interval may properly accept the invitation; but petulance and obtrusion are rarely produced by magnanimity; nor have often any nobler cause than the pride of importance and the malice of inferiority. He who knows himself necessary may set, while that necessity lasts, a high value upon himself; as in a lower condition a servant eminently skilful may be saucy, but he is saucy only because he is servile. Swift appears to have preserved the kindness of the great when they wanted him no longer; and therefore it must be allowed that the childish freedom to which he seems enough inclined was overpowered by his better qualities. . . . It may be justly supposed that there was in his conversation what appears so frequently in his letters, an affectation of familiarity with the Great, an ambition of momentary equality sought and enjoyed by the neglect of those ceremonies which custom has established as the barriers between one order of society and another. This transgression of regularity was by himself and his admirers termed greatness of soul. But a great mind disdains to hold anything by courtesy, and therefore never usurps what a lawful claimant may take away. He that encroaches on another's dignity puts himself in his power; he is either repelled with helpless indignity, or endured by clemency and condescension.

Works, viii. 204, 225.

. .

THE civilities of the great are never thrown away.

Ib. vi. 446.
EVERY

EVERY great man, of whatever kind be his greatness, has among his friends those who officiously or insidiously quicken his attention to offences, heighten his disgust, and stimulate his resentment. *Works*, viii. 266.

.˙.

POPE's scorn of the Great is too often repeated to be real; no man thinks much of that which he despises.

Ib. viii. 316.

Great things:

A MAN would never undertake great things, could he be amused with small. Boswell's *Life of Johnson*, iii. 242.

Greatness:

THE first step to greatness is to be honest. *Works*, vi. 311.

Grief:

GRIEF is a species of idleness. *Piozzi Letters*, i. 76.

.˙.

WHERE there is leisure for fiction there is little grief.

Works, vii. 119.

Grub-street:

GRUB-STREET, the name of a street in London much inhabited by writers of small histories, *dictionaries*, and temporary poems; whence any mean production is called *Grub-street*.

> Χαῖρ' Ἰθάκη μετ' ἄεθλα, μετ' ἄλγεα πικρὰ
> Ἀσπασίως τεὸν οὖδας ἱκάνομαι.

Dictionary.

.˙.

'DR. JOHNSON offered to take me with him to Grub-street to see the ruins of the house demolished there in the

late

late riots[1] by a mob that, as he observed, could be no friend to the Muses! He inquired if I had ever yet visited Grub-street? but was obliged to restrain his anger when I answered "No," because he acknowledged he had never paid his respects to it himself.

"However," says he, "you and I, Burney, will go together; we have a very good right to go, so we'll visit the mansions of our progenitors, and take up our own freedom together."'

Mme. D'Arblay's Diary, i. 415.

Habits:

I BELIEVE most men may review all the lives that have passed within their observation, without remembering one efficacious resolution, or being able to tell a single instance of a course of practice suddenly changed in consequence of a change of opinion or an establishment of determination. Many indeed alter their conduct, and are not at fifty what they were at thirty; but they commonly varied imperceptibly from themselves, followed the train of external causes, and rather suffered reformation than made it.   *Idler*, No. 27.

Happiness:

EVERY period of life is obliged to borrow its happiness from the time to come. In youth we have nothing past to entertain us, and in age we derive little from retrospect but hopeless sorrow. Yet the future likewise has its limits, which the imagination dreads to approach but which we see to be not far distant. The loss of our friends and companions impresses hourly upon us the necessity of our own departure; we know that the schemes of man are quickly at an end, that we must soon lie down in the grave with the

---

[1] The Gordon riots of June, 1780.

forgotten

forgotten multitudes of former ages, and yield our place to others who, like us, shall be driven a while by hope or fear about the surface of the earth, and then like us be lost in the shades of death. *Rambler*, No. 203.

* *

'EVERY man,' said Imlac, 'may, by examining his own mind, guess what passes in the minds of others : when you feel that your own gaiety is counterfeit, it may justly lead you to suspect that of your companions not to be sincere. Envy is commonly reciprocal. We are long before we are convinced that happiness is never to be found, and each believes it possessed by others to keep alive the hope of obtaining it for himself. In the assembly, where you passed the last night, there appeared such sprightliness of air, and volatility of fancy, as might have suited beings of a higher order, formed to inhabit serener regions inaccessible to care or sorrow : yet believe me, prince, there was not one who did not dread the moment when solitude should deliver him to the tyranny of reflection.' *Rasselas*, ch. 16.

* *

'ON necessary and inevitable evils which overwhelm kingdoms at once all disputation is vain : when they happen they must be endured. But it is evident that these bursts of universal distress are more dreaded than felt ; thousands and ten thousands flourish in youth and wither in age without the knowledge of any other than domestic evils, and share the same pleasures and vexations whether their kings are mild or cruel, whether the armies of their country pursue their enemies or retreat before them. While courts are disturbed with intestine competitions, and am-bassadors are negociating in foreign countries, the smith

still

still plies his anvil and the husbandman drives his plough forward; the necessaries of life are required and obtained; and the successive business of the seasons continues to make its wonted revolutions.

Rasselas, ch. 28.

I WILL not trouble you with speculations about peace and war. The good or ill success of battles and embassies extends itself to a very small part of domestic life: we all have good and evil, which we feel more sensibly than our petty part of public miscarriage or prosperity.

Boswell's *Life of Johnson*, i. 381.

'WHETHER perfect happiness would be procured by perfect goodness,' said Nekayah, 'this world will never afford an opportunity of deciding. But this at least may be maintained, that we do not always find visible happiness in proportion to visible virtue. All natural, and almost all political evils, are incident alike to the bad and good; they are confounded in the misery of a famine and not much distinguished in the fury of a faction; they sink together in a tempest and are driven together from their country by invaders. All that virtue can afford is quietness of conscience and a steady prospect of a happier state; this may enable us to endure calamity with patience; but remember that patience must suppose pain.'

Rasselas, ch. 27.

IT has been the boast of some swelling moralists that every man's fortune was in his own power, that prudence supplied the place of all other divinities, and that happiness is the unfailing consequence of virtue. But surely the

quiver

quiver of Omnipotence is stored with arrows against which the shield of human virtue, however adamantine it has been boasted, is held up in vain; we do not always suffer by our crimes; we are not always protected by our innocence.

Adventurer, No. 120.

Wit and Wisdom of Samuel Johnson.

.·.

DR. JOHNSON this day enlarged upon Pope's melancholy remark,

> 'Man never *is*, but always *to be* blest[1].'

He asserted that *the present* was never a happy state to any human being; but that, as every part of life of which we are conscious was at some point of time a period yet to come in which felicity was expected, there was some happiness produced by hope. Being pressed upon this subject and asked if he really was of opinion that though, in general, happiness was very rare in human life, a man was not sometimes happy in the moment that was present, he answered, 'Never, but when he is drunk.' Boswell's *Life of Johnson*, ii. 350.

.·.

THAT man is never happy for the present is so true that all his relief from unhappiness is only forgetting himself for a little while. Life is a progress from want to want, not from enjoyment to enjoyment.

Ib. iii. 53.

Hasty expressions:

HE[2] may perhaps, in the ardour of his imagination, have hazarded an expression which a mind intent upon faults may interpret into heresy, if considered apart from the rest of his discourse; but a phrase is not to be opposed to volumes.

Works, vi. 502.

---

[1] *Essay on Man*, i. 95. [2] Sir Thomas Browne.

K

Hatred:

Hatred and contempt :

THERE are men whom public hatred affects less sensibly than public contempt, and who would rather be convicted of a crime than charged with an absurdity.

Debates. Gent. Mag. xiii. 349.

Health :

HEALTH is indeed so necessary to all the duties, as well as pleasures of life, that the crime of squandering it is equal to the folly; and he that for a short gratification brings weakness and diseases upon himself, and for the pleasure of a few years passed in the tumults of diversion and clamours of merriment condemns the maturer and more experienced part of his life to the chamber and the couch, may be justly reproached not only as a spendthrift of his own happiness, but as a robber of the public; as a wretch that has voluntarily disqualified himself for the business of his station and refused that part which Providence assigns him in the general task of human nature.   *Rambler*, No. 48.

Hebrideans :

THE general conversation of the islanders has nothing particular. I did not meet with the inquisitiveness of which I have read, and suspect the judgment to have been rashly made. A stranger of curiosity comes into a place where a stranger is seldom seen ; he importunes the people with questions of which they cannot guess the motive, and gazes with surprise on things which they, having had them always before their eyes, do not suspect of anything wonderful. He appears to them like some being of another world, and then thinks it peculiar that they take their turn to inquire whence he comes, and whither he is going.

Works, ix. 100.

Heirs :

Heirs:

Every day sends out in quest of pleasure and distinction some heir fondled in ignorance and flattered into pride.

Rambler, No. 175.

Heroes and conquerors:

I am far from intending to vindicate the sanguinary projects of heroes and conquerors, and would wish rather to diminish the reputation of their success than the infamy of their miscarriages: for I cannot conceive why he that has burnt cities, wasted nations, and filled the world with horror and desolation, should be more kindly regarded by mankind than he that died in the rudiments of wickedness; why he that accomplished mischief should be glorious, and he that only endeavoured it should be criminal. I would wish Cæsar and Catiline, Xerxes and Alexander, Charles and Peter, huddled together in obscurity or detestation.

Adventurer, No. 99.

History:

The general and rapid narratives of history, which involve a thousand fortunes in the business of a day and complicate innumerable incidents in one great transaction, afford few lessons applicable to private life, which derives its comforts and its wretchedness from the right or wrong management of things, which nothing but their frequence makes considerable, *Parva si non fiunt quotidie*, says Pliny, and which can have no place in those relations which never descend below the consultation of senates, the motions of armies, and the schemes of conspirators. *Rambler*, No. 60.

There

THERE are some works which the authors must consign unpublished to posterity, however uncertain be the event, however hopeless be the trust. He that writes the history of his own times, if he adheres steadily to truth, will write that which his own times will not easily endure. He must be content to reposit his book till all private passions shall cease, and love and hatred give way to curiosity.

Idler, No. 65.

Hoarding:

Do not discourage your children from hoarding if they have a taste to it: whoever lays up his penny rather than part with it for a cake at least is not the slave of gross appetite: and shows besides a preference always to be esteemed of the future to the present moment. Such a mind may be made a good one; but the natural spend-thrift, who grasps his pleasures greedily and coarsely, and cares for nothing but immediate indulgence, is very little to be valued above a negro.   Piozzi's *Anecdotes*, p. 153.

Holding your tongue when you are beaten:

'I MADE one day very minute inquiries about the tale of his knocking down Tom Osborne the bookseller. "And how was that affair? in earnest? do tell me, Mr. Johnson." "There is nothing to tell, dearest lady, but that he was insolent and I beat him, and that he was a blockhead and told of it, which I should never have done. I have beat many a fellow, but the rest had the wit to hold their tongues."'   Piozzi's *Anecdotes*, p. 232.

Honesty

Honesty and elegance:

HONESTY is not greater where elegance is less.

Works, ix. 38.

Hope:

OF a certain player[1] Dr. Johnson remarked, that his conversation usually threatened and announced more than it performed; that he fed you with a continual renovation of hope to end in a constant succession of disappointment.

Boswell's *Life of Johnson*, ii. 122.

∴

WHATEVER enlarges hope will exalt courage.

Works, ix. 161.

∴

IT is necessary to hope though hope should always be deluded; for hope itself is happiness, and its frustrations, however frequent, are yet less dreadful than its extinction.

Idler, No. 58.

∴

HOPE is itself a species of happiness, and, perhaps, the chief happiness which this world affords: but, like all other pleasures immoderately enjoyed, the excesses of hope must be expiated by pain; and expectations improperly indulged must end in disappointment. If it be asked what is the improper expectation which it is dangerous to indulge, experience will quickly answer, that it is such expectation as is dictated not by reason but by desire; expectation raised not by the common occurrences of life, but by the wants of the expectant; an expectation that requires the common course of things to be changed, and the general rules of action to be broken. Boswell's *Life of Johnson*, i. 368.

---

[1] Thomas Sheridan.

GAY

GAY is represented as a man easily incited to hope and deeply depressed when his hopes were disappointed. This is not the character of a hero; but it may naturally imply something more generally welcome, a soft and civil companion. Whoever is apt to hope good from others is diligent to please them; but he that believes his powers strong enough to force their own way commonly tries only to please himself.   *Works*, viii. 64.

⁂

THE natural flights of the human mind are not from pleasure to pleasure but from hope to hope.   *Rambler*, No. 2.

⁂

To this test[1] let every man bring his imaginations before they have been too long predominant in his mind. Whatever is true will bear to be related, whatever is rational will endure to be explained; but when we delight to brood in secret over future happiness and silently to employ our meditations upon schemes of which we are conscious that the bare mention would expose us to derision and contempt, we should then remember that we are cheating ourselves by voluntary delusions; and giving up to the unreal mockeries of fancy those hours in which solid advantages might be attained by sober thought and rational assiduity.

Adventurer, No. 69.

⁂

A GENTLEMAN who had been very unhappy in marriage married immediately after his wife died: Johnson said, it was the triumph of hope over experience.

Boswell's *Life of Johnson*, ii. 128.

---

[1] The test of an accurate statement in writing.

Human

Human beings:

THE two lowest of all human beings are a scribbler for a party and a commissioner of excise. *Idler*, No. 65.

.·.

EVERY man should endeavour to maintain in himself a favourable opinion of the powers of the human mind; which are perhaps in every man greater than they appear, and might by diligent cultivation be exalted to a degree beyond what their possessor presumes to believe. *Adventurer*, No. 81.

.·.

'THOUGH a stern *true-born Englishman*, and fully prejudiced against all other nations, Dr. Johnson had discernment enough to see, and candour enough to censure, the cold reserve too common among Englishmen towards strangers: "Sir, (said he,) two men of any other nation who are shown into a room together at a house where they are both visitors will immediately find some conversation.   But two Englishmen will probably go each to a different window, and remain in obstinate silence.   Sir, we as yet do not enough understand the common rights of humanity."'
Boswell's *Life of Johnson*, iv. 191.

Humility:

EVERY man acquainted with the common principles of human action will look with veneration on the writer[1], who is at one time combating Locke, and at another making a catechism for children in their fourth year.   A voluntary descent from the dignity of science is perhaps the hardest lesson that humility can teach. *Works*, viii. 384.

---

[1] Isaac Watts.

Hypocrisy:

Hypocrisy:

IT is not uncommon to charge the difference between promise and performance, between profession and reality, upon deep design and studied deceit; but the truth is that there is very little hypocrisy in the world; we do not so often endeavour or wish to impose on others as on ourselves; we resolve to do right, we hope to keep our resolutions, we declare them to confirm our own hope, and fix our own inconstancy by calling witnesses of our actions; but at last habit prevails and those whom we invited to our triumph laugh at our defeat.

Idler, No. 27.

Hypothetical possibility:

HE who will determine against that which he knows because there may be something which he knows not; he that can set hypothetical possibility against acknowledged certainty is not to be admitted among reasonable beings. All that we know of matter is that matter is inert, senseless, and lifeless; and if this conviction cannot be opposed but by referring us to something that we know not, we have all the evidence that human intellect can admit. If that which is known may be overruled by that which is unknown, no being not omniscient can arrive at certainty.

Rasselas, ch. 48.

Hypocrites of learning:

SEVERE and connected attention is preserved but for a short time; and when a man shuts himself up in his closet, and bends his thoughts to the discussion of any abstruse question, he will find his faculties continually stealing away to

more

more pleasing entertainments. He often perceives himself transported, he knows not how, to distant tracts of thought, and returns to his first object as from a dream, without knowing when he forsook it or how long he has been abstracted from it. It has been observed that the most studious are not always the most learned. . . . . Many impose upon the world, and many upon themselves by an appearance of severe and exemplary diligence, when they, in reality, give themselves up to the luxury of fancy, please their minds with regulating the past or planning the future; place themselves at will in varied situations of happiness, and slumber away their days in voluntary visions. . . . .

There is nothing more fatal to a man whose business is to think, than to have learned the art of regaling his mind with those airy gratifications. Other vices or follies are restrained by fear, reformed by admonition, or rejected by the conviction which the comparison of our conduct with that of others may in time produce. But this invisible riot of the mind, this secret prodigality of being, is secure from detection and fearless of reproach. The dreamer retires to his apartments, shuts out the cares and interruptions of mankind, and abandons himself to his own fancy; new worlds rise up before him, one image is followed by another, and a long succession of delights dances round him. He is at last called back to life by nature or by custom, and enters peevish into society, because he cannot model it to his own will. He returns from his idle excursions with the asperity, though not with the knowledge of a student, and hastens again to the same felicity with the eagerness of a man bent upon the advancement of some favourite science. The infatuation strengthens by degrees and, like the poison of opiates, weakens his powers without any external symptoms

of

of malignity. It happens, indeed, that these hypocrites of learning are in time detected, and convinced by disgrace and disappointment of the difference between the labour of thought and the sport of musing. But this discovery is often not made till it is too late to recover the time that has been fooled away.

Rambler, No. 89.

Idleness and poverty:

To be idle and to be poor have always been reproaches, and therefore every man endeavours with his utmost care to hide his poverty from others, and his idleness from himself.

Idler, No. 17.

'If the man who turnips cries':

If the man who turnips cries
Cry not when his father dies,
'Tis a proof that he had rather
Have a turnip than his father.

Piozzi's *Anecdotes*, p. 67.

Ignorance:

' A LADY once asked Johnson how he came to define *Pastern* the *knee* of a horse: instead of making an elaborate defence, as she expected, he at once answered, " Ignorance, Madam, pure ignorance." '

Boswell's *Life of Johnson*, i. 293.

.·.

' MR. BEAUCLERK told Dr. Johnson that Dr. James said to him he knew more Greek than Mr. Walmesley. " Sir," said he, " Dr. James did not know enough of Greek to be sensible of his ignorance of the language. Walmesley did." '

Ib. iv. 33 *n.* 3.

' A CERTAIN

'A CERTAIN young clergyman used to come about Dr. Johnson. The Doctor said it vexed him to be in his company, his ignorance was so hopeless. "Sir," said Mr. Langton, "his coming about you shows he wishes to help his ignorance." "Sir," said the Doctor, "his ignorance is so great I am afraid to show him the bottom of it."'

Boswell's *Life of Johnson*, iv. 33, n. 3.

IF obedience to the will of God be necessary to happiness, and knowledge of His will be necessary to obedience, I know not how he that withholds this knowledge, or delays it, can be said to love his neighbour as himself. He that voluntarily continues ignorance is guilty of all the crimes which ignorance produces; as to him that should extinguish the tapers of a lighthouse might justly be imputed the calamities of shipwrecks. Christianity is the highest perfection of humanity. . . . Let it, however, be remembered that the efficacy of ignorance has been long tried, and has not produced the consequence expected. Let knowledge, therefore, take its turn; and let the patrons of privation stand awhile aside, and admit the operation of positive principles.

Ib. ii. 27.

Ignorant people cunning:

To help the ignorant commonly requires much patience, for the ignorant are always trying to be cunning.

Ib. v. 217 *n.* 1.

Illiterate nations:

IN nations where there is hardly the use of letters what is once out of sight is lost for ever. They think but little, and of their few thoughts none are wasted on the past in which they are neither interested by fear nor hope. Their

only

only registers are stated observances and practical representations. For this reason an age of ignorance is an age of ceremony. Pageants and processions and commemorations gradually shrink away, as better methods come into use of recording events and preserving rights.   *Works*, ix. 61.

Imitation:

No man ever yet became great by imitation.

Rambler, No. 154.

.˙.

WHEN Lee was once told by a critic that it was very easy to write like a madman, he answered that it was difficult to write like a madman, but easy enough to write like a fool; and I hope to be excused by my kind contributors if, in imitation of this great author, I presume to remind them that it is much easier not to write like a man than to write like a woman.   *Rambler*, No. 20.

Impertinent fellow:

'CUMBERLAND, in his *Feast of Reason*, introduces Johnson annoyed by an impertinent fellow, and saying to him:— "Have I said anything, good Sir, that you do not comprehend?" "No, no," replied he, "I perfectly well comprehend every word you have been saying." "Do you so, Sir?" said the philosopher, "then I heartily ask pardon of the company for misemploying their time so egregiously."'

Boswell's *Life of Johnson*, iv. 64 *n.* 2.

Imposing words for ideas:

I DO not mean to reproach this author[1] for not knowing what is equally hidden from learning and from ignorance.

---

[1] Soame Jenyns.

The

The shame is to impose words for ideas upon ourselves or others; to imagine that we are going forward when we are only turning round; to think that there is any difference between him that gives nb reason and him that gives a reason, which by his own confession cannot be conceived.

Works, vi. 64.

Impossible:

MEN are generally idle and ready to satisfy themselves and intimidate the industry of others by calling that impossible which is only difficult. *Ib.* vi. 285.

Inaccuracy of narrators:

I CANNOT forbear to hint to this writer[1] and all others the danger and weakness of trusting too readily to information. Nothing but experience could evince the frequency of false information, or enable any man to conceive that so many groundless reports should be propagated as every man of eminence may hear of himself. Some men relate what they think as what they know; some men of confused memories and habitual inaccuracy ascribe to one man what belongs to another, and some talk on without thought or care. A few men are sufficient to broach falsehoods, which are afterwards innocently diffused by successive relaters.

Works, vi. 42.

Incivility:

A MAN has no more right to *say* an uncivil thing than to *act* one; no more right to say a rude thing to another than to knock him down. Boswell's *Life of Johnson,* iv. 28.

---

[1] Dr. Joseph Warton, author of an *Essay on the Writings and Genius of Pope.*

Inconsistencies:

Inconsistencies :

INCONSISTENCIES cannot both be right, but imputed to man they may both be true.   *Rasselas*, ch. 8.

Indolence :

INDOLENCE is one of the vices from which those whom it once infects are seldom reformed. Every other species of luxury operates upon some appetite that is quickly satiated, and requires some concurrence of art or accident which every place will not supply; but the desire of ease acts equally at all hours, and the longer it is indulged is the more increased. To do nothing is in every man's power; we can never want an opportunity of omitting duties.

Rambler, No. 155.

.˙.

YOU are not oppressed by sickness, you are not distracted by business : if you are sick, you are sick of leisure :—And allow yourself to be told that no disease is more to be dreaded or avoided. Rather to do nothing than to do good is the lowest state of a degraded mind. Boileau says to his pupil,

> ' *Que les vers ne soient pas votre éternel emploi,*
> *Cultivez vos amis* [1].'

That voluntary debility which modern language is content to term indolence will, if it is not counteracted by resolution, render in time the strongest faculties lifeless, and turn the flame to the smoke of virtue.

Boswell's *Life of Johnson*, iv. 352.

---

[1] Boileau, *Art Poétique*, chant iv.

Influence :

Influence :

IT is a maxim that no man ever was enslaved by influence while he was fit to be free.   *Boswell's Life of Johnson*, iii. 205 *n.* 4.

Innocence :

THESE reasoners frequently confound innocence with the mere incapacity of guilt. He that never saw, or heard, or thought of strong liquors, cannot be proposed as a pattern of sobriety.   *Works*, vi. 367.

Insults :

THERE are innumerable modes of insult and tokens of contempt for which it is not easy to find a name, which vanish to nothing in an attempt to describe them, and yet may, by continual repetition, make day pass after day in sorrow and in terror. Phrases of cursory compliment and established salutation may, by a different modulation of the voice or cast of the countenance, convey contrary meanings and be changed from indications of respect to expressions of scorn. The dependant who cultivates delicacy in himself very little consults his own tranquillity. *Rambler*, No. 149.

Integrity and Knowledge :

INTEGRITY without knowledge is weak and useless, and knowledge without integrity is dangerous and dreadful.

Rasselas, ch. 41.

Interest :

THERE is a kind of mercantile speculation which ascribes every action to interest, and considers interest as only another name for pecuniary advantage. But the boundless

variety

variety of human affections is not to be thus easily circumscribed.

Works, ix. 500.

Intimacy :

THE worst way of being intimate is by scribbling.

Boswell's *Life of Johnson*, v. 93.

Intoxication :

' I CALLED on Dr. Johnson one morning, when Mrs.
Williams, the blind lady, was conversing with him. She was
telling him where she had dined the day before. "There
were several gentlemen there," said she, " and when some
of them came to the tea-table, I found that there had been
a good deal of hard drinking." She closed this observation
with a trite moral reflection ; " I wonder what pleasure men
can take in making beasts of themselves !" " I wonder,
Madam," replied the Doctor, "that you have not penetration
enough to see the strong inducement to this excess ; for he
who makes a *beast* of himself gets rid of the pain of being a
man." '

Murray's *Johnsoniana*, p. 356.

Invasion :

WOULD not any stranger imagine that we were a nation
infected with a general phrensy, that cowardice had perverted
our imaginations, filled us with apprehensions of impossible
invasions, raised phantoms before our eyes and distracted
us with wild ideas of slavery and tyranny, oppression and
persecution ? I have dwelt thus long on this point because
I know the Pretender is the last refuge of those who defend
a standing army ; not that I propose to convince any man
of the folly of such apprehensions or to fortify him against
such terrors for the time to come ; for if any man in reality

now

now dreads the Pretender, fear must be his distemper; he is doomed to live in terrors, and it is of no importance whether he dreads an invasion or a goblin, whether he is afraid to disband the army or to put out his candle in the night; his imagination is tainted and he must be cured not by argument but by physic.

Debates. Works, x. 54.

Ireland :

'DR. JOHNSON had great compassion for the miseries and distresses of the Irish nation, particularly the Papists; and severely reprobated the barbarous debilitating policy of the British government, which, he said, was the most detestable mode of persecution. To a gentleman who hinted such policy might be necessary to support the authority of the English government, he replied by saying, " Let the authority of the English government perish rather than be maintained by iniquity. Better would it be to restrain the turbulence of the natives by the authority of the sword, and to make them amenable to law and justice by an effectual and vigorous police, than to grind them to powder by all manner of disabilities and incapacities. Better," said he, "to hang or drown people at once than, by an unrelenting persecution, to beggar and starve them."'

Boswell's *Life of Johnson*, ii. 121.

'Irene':

'I WAS told,' wrote Sir Walter Scott, 'that a gentleman called Pot, or some such name, was introduced to Johnson as a particular admirer of his. The Doctor growled and took no further notice. " He admires in especial your *Irene* as the finest tragedy of modern times;" to which the Doctor replied :—" If Pot says so, Pot lies !" and relapsed into his reverie.'

Ib. iv. 5, *n.* 1.

L   Jealousy :

Jealousy :

LITTLE people are apt to be jealous : but they should not be jealous ; for they ought to consider that superior attention will necessarily be paid to superior fortune or rank. Two persons may have equal merit, and on that account may have an equal claim to attention ; but one of them may have also fortune and rank, and so may have a double claim.

Boswell's Life of Johnson, iii. 55.

Jesting :

'MR. JOHNSON liked a frolic or a jest well enough ; though he had strange serious rules about it too : and very angry was he if anybody offered to be merry when he was disposed to be grave. " You have an ill-founded notion (said he) that it is clever to turn matters off with a joke (as the phrase is) ; whereas nothing produces enmity so certain as one person's showing a disposition to be merry when another is inclined to be either serious or displeased." '

Piozzi's Anecdotes, p. 116.

Judgment of other people :

' SEEING Mr. Johnson justly delighted with Dr. Solander's conversation, I observed once that he was a man of great parts who talked from a full mind. " It may be so (said Mr. Johnson), but you cannot know it yet, nor I neither : the pump works well, to be sure ! but how, I wonder, are we to decide in so very short an acquaintance whether it is supplied by a spring or a reservoir ? " '

Ib. p. 195.

.·.

PRIOR had apparently such rectitude of judgment as secured him from everything that approached to the ridiculous

or

or absurd; but as laws operate in civil agency not to the excitement of virtue, but the repression of wickedness, so judgment in the operations of intellect can hinder faults, but not produce excellence. *Works*, viii. 20.

Kings:

HE[1] may be said to owe to the difficulties of his youth an advantage less frequently obtained by princes than literature and mathematics. The necessity of passing his time without pomp, and of partaking of the pleasures and labours of a lower station, made him acquainted with the various forms of life, and with the genuine passions, interests, desires, and distresses of mankind. Kings, without this help from temporary infelicity, see the world in a mist, which magnifies everything near them and bounds their view to a narrow compass which few are able to extend by the mere force of curiosity. I have always thought that what Cromwell had more than our lawful kings he owed to the private condition in which he first entered the world, and in which he long continued: in that state he learned his art of secret transaction, and the knowledge by which he was able to oppose zeal to zeal, and make one enthusiast destroy another. *Ib.* vi. 440.

Knowledge:

ALL knowledge is of itself of some value. There is nothing so minute or inconsiderable, that I would not rather know it than not. In the same manner all power, of whatever sort, is of itself desirable. A man would not submit to learn to hem a ruffle of his wife, or his wife's maid; but if a

---

[1] Frederick the Great.

L 2

mere

mere wish could attain it, he would rather wish to be able to hem a ruffle.

Boswell's *Life of Johnson*, ii. 357.

.·.

OF whatever we see we always wish to know; always congratulate ourselves when we know that of which we perceive another to be ignorant.   Take therefore all opportunities of learning that offer themselves, however remote the matter may be from common life or common conversation.   Look in Herschel's telescope; go into a chemist's laboratory; if you see a manufacturer at work, remark his operations.   By this activity of attention you will find in every place diversion and improvement.

Piozzi Letters, ii. 357.

.·.

'ON Saturday, July 30 [1763], Dr. Johnson and I took a sculler at the Temple-stairs, and set out for Greenwich.   I asked him if he really thought a knowledge of the Greek and Latin languages an essential requisite to a good education.   JOHNSON. "Most certainly, Sir; for those who know them have a very great advantage over those who do not.   Nay, Sir, it is wonderful what a difference learning makes upon people even in the common intercourse of life, which does not appear to be much connected with it."   "And yet (said I) people go through the world very well, and carry on the business of life to good advantage, without learning."   JOHNSON. "Why, Sir, that may be true in cases where learning cannot possibly be of any use; for instance, this boy rows us as well without learning as if he could sing the song of Orpheus to the Argonauts, who were the first sailors."   He then called to the boy, "What would you give, my lad, to know about the Argonauts?"   "Sir (said the boy), I would give what I have."   Johnson was much

pleased

pleased with his answer, and we gave him a double fare. Dr. Johnson then turning to me, "Sir (said he), a desire of knowledge is the natural feeling of mankind; and every human being whose mind is not debauched will be willing to give all that he has to get knowledge." '

Boswell's Life of Johnson, i. 457.

Wit and
Wisdom
of
Samuel
Johnson.

KNOWLEDGE is certainly one of the means of pleasure, as is confessed by the natural desire which every mind feels of increasing its ideas.   Ignorance is mere privation by which nothing can be produced : it is a vacuity in which the soul sits motionless and torpid for want of attraction ; and, without knowing why, we always rejoice when we learn and grieve when we forget.   I am therefore inclined to conclude that if nothing counteracts the natural consequence of learning we grow more happy as our minds take a wider range.

Rasselas, ch. 11.

MAN is not weak ; knowledge is more than equivalent to force.   The master of mechanics laughs at strength.

Ib. ch. 13.

Laced coats :

'SIR JOSHUA REYNOLDS said one day, that *nobody* wore laced coats now; and that once everybody wore them. "See now (says Johnson), how absurd that is; as if the bulk of mankind consisted of fine gentlemen that came to him to sit for their pictures.   If every man who wears a laced coat (that he can pay for) was extirpated, who would miss them ?" '

Piozzi's Anecdotes, p. 155.

'IT was at Admiral Walsingham's table that Dr. Johnson

made

made that excellent reply to a pert coxcomb who baited him during dinner. "Pray now," said he to the Doctor, "what would you give, old gentleman, to be as young and sprightly as I am?" "Why, Sir, I think," replied Johnson, "I would almost be content to be as foolish."'

Boswell's Life of Johnson, iii. 21, n. 2.

Lade, Sir John:

LONG-EXPECTED one-and-twenty,
    Ling'ring year, at length is flown;
Pride and pleasure, pomp and plenty,
    Great * * * * * * *[1], are now your own.

Loosen'd from the Minor's tether,
    Free to mortgage or to sell,
Wild as wind, and light as feather,
    Bid the sons of thrift farewell.

Call the Betseys, Kates, and Jennies,
    All the names that banish care;
Lavish of your grandsire's guineas,
    Show the spirit of an heir.

All that prey on vice or folly
    Joy to see their quarry fly;
There the gamester, light and jolly,
    There the lender, grave and sly.

Wealth, my lad, was made to wander,
    Let it wander as it will;
Call the jockey, call the pander,
    Bid them come and take their fill.

When the bonny blade carouses,
    Pockets full, and spirits high—
What are acres? what are houses?
    Only dirt, or wet or dry.

---

[1] Sir John.

Should

> Should the guardian friend or mother
> Tell the woes of wilful waste ;
> Scorn their counsel, scorn their pother—
> You can hang or drown at last.

Boswell's Life of Johnson, iv. 413.

Language :

THERE is no tracing the connection of ancient nations but by language ; and therefore I am always sorry when any language is lost, because languages are the pedigree of nations.

Ib. v. 225.

Last :

THERE are few things not purely evil of which we can say without some emotion of uneasiness *this is the last.* Those who never could agree together shed tears when mutual discontent has determined them to final separation ; of a place which has been frequently visited, though without pleasure, the last look is taken with heaviness of heart ; and the *Idler*, with all his chillness of tranquillity, is not wholly unaffected by the thought that his last essay is now before him. This secret horror of the last is inseparable from a thinking being whose life is limited and to whom death is dreadful. We always make a secret comparison between a part and the whole ; the termination of any period of life reminds us that life itself has likewise its termination ; when we have done anything for the last time we involuntarily reflect that a part of the days allotted to us is past, and that as more is past there is less remaining.

Idler, No. 103.

Latin :

'DR. JOHNSON's opinion [was] that I could not name above five of my college acquaintances who read Latin with ease

sufficient

sufficient to make it pleasurable. The difficulty of the language overpowers the desire to read the author.'

Windham's Diary, p. 17.

Laws:

As manners make laws, manners likewise repeal them.

Boswell's Life of Johnson, ii. 419.

Learned ambition:

THE miscarriages of the great designs of princes are recorded in the histories of the world but are of little use to the bulk of mankind, who seem very little interested in admonitions against errors which they cannot commit. But the fate of learned ambition is a proper subject for every scholar to consider ; for who has not had occasion to regret the dissipation of great abilities in a boundless multiplicity of pursuits, to lament the sudden desertion of excellent designs upon the offer of some other subject made inviting by its novelty, and to observe the inaccuracy and deficiencies of works left unfinished by too great an extension of the plan ?

Rambler, No. 17.

IT will I believe be found invariably true that learning was never decried by any learned man.   Adventurer, No. 85.

WHOEVER considers the revolutions of learning and the various questions of greater or less importance upon which wit and reason have exercised their powers, must lament the unsuccessfulness of inquiry and the slow advances of truth, when he reflects that great part of the labour of every writer is only the destruction of those that went before him.

The

The first care of the builder of a new system is to demolish the fabrics which are standing. The chief desire of him that comments an author is to show how much other commentators have corrupted and obscured him. The opinions prevalent in one age as truths above the reach of controversy are confuted and rejected in another and rise again to reception in remoter times. Thus the human mind is kept in motion without progress. Thus sometimes truth and error, and sometimes contrarieties of error, take each other's place by reciprocal invasion. The tide of seeming knowledge, which is poured over one generation, retires and leaves another naked and barren; the sudden meteors of intelligence which for a while appear to shoot their beams into the regions of obscurity on a sudden withdraw their lustre and leave mortals again to grope their way.

Works, v. 140.

Letters :

It has been so long said as to be commonly believed that the true characters of men may be found in their letters, and that he who writes to his friend lays his heart open before him. But the truth is that such were the simple friendships of the 'Golden Age,' and now the friendships only of children. Very few can boast of hearts which they dare lay open to themselves, and of which, by whatever accident exposed, they do not shun a distinct and continued view; and certainly what we hide from ourselves we do not show to our friends. There is, indeed, no transaction which offers stronger temptations to fallacy and sophistication than epistolary intercourse. In the eagerness of conversation the first emotions of the mind often burst out before they are considered; in the tumult of

business

business interest and passion have their genuine effect;
but a friendly letter is a calm and deliberate performance
in the cool of leisure, in the stillness of solitude, and surely
no man sits down to depreciate by design his character.

Works, viii. 314.

Levellers :

'DR. JOHNSON again insisted on the duty of maintaining
subordination of rank. "Sir, I would no more deprive a
nobleman of his respect, than of his money. I consider
myself as acting a part in the great system of society, and I
do to others as I would have them to do to me. I would
behave to a nobleman as I should expect he would behave
to me were I a nobleman and he Sam. Johnson. Sir, there
is one Mrs. Macaulay in this town, a great republican. One
day when I was at her house, I put on a very grave countenance, and said to her, 'Madam, I am now become a convert
to your way of thinking. I am convinced that all mankind
are upon an equal footing; and to give you an unquestionable proof, Madam, that I am in earnest, here is a very
sensible, civil, well-behaved fellow-citizen, your footman; I
desire that he may be allowed to sit down and dine with
us.' I thus, Sir, showed her the absurdity of the levelling
doctrine. She has never liked me since. Sir, your levellers
wish to level *down* as far as themselves; but they cannot
bear levelling *up* to themselves. They would all have some
people under them; why not then have some people above
them?" I mentioned a certain author who disgusted me
by his forwardness, and by showing no deference to noble-
men into whose company he was admitted. JOHNSON.
"Suppose a shoemaker should claim an equality with him,
as he does with a Lord; how he would stare. 'Why, Sir,
do

do you stare? (says the shoemaker,) I do great service to society. 'Tis true I am paid for doing it; but so are you, Sir: and I am sorry to say it, paid better than I am for doing something not so necessary. For mankind could do better without your books than without my shoes.' Thus, Sir, there would be a perpetual struggle for precedence were there no fixed invariable rules for the distinction of rank, which creates no jealousy, as it is allowed to be accidental." '

Boswell's Life of Johnson, i. 447.

Levett, Robert:

CONDEMN'D to Hope's delusive mine,
    As on we toil from day to day,
By sudden blast or slow decline
    Our social comforts drop away.

Well try'd through many a varying year,
    See Levett to the grave descend;
Officious, innocent, sincere,
    Of every friendless name the friend.

Yet still he fills affection's eye,
    Obscurely wise, and coarsely kind;
Nor, letter'd arrogance, deny
    Thy praise to merit unrefin'd.

When fainting Nature call'd for aid,
    And hov'ring Death prepar'd the blow,
His vigorous remedy display'd
    The power of art without the show.

In Misery's darkest caverns known,
    His ready help was ever nigh,
Where hopeless Anguish pour'd his groan,
    And lonely want retir'd to die.

No summons mock'd by chill delay,
    No petty gains disdain'd by pride;
The modest wants of every day
    The toil of every day supply'd.

His

His virtues walk'd their narrow round,
  Nor made a pause, nor left a void ;
And sure the Eternal Master found
  His single talent well employ'd.

The busy day, the peaceful night,
  Unfelt, uncounted, glided by ;
His frame was firm, his powers were bright,
  Though now his eightieth year was nigh.

Then, with no throbs of fiery pain,
  No cold gradations of decay,
Death broke at once the vital chain,
  And freed his soul the nearest way.

Boswell's Life of Johnson, iv. 137.

Lexicographer :

LEXICOGRAPHER, a writer of dictionaries, a harmless
drudge.   *Dictionary.*

Lexicography :

SUCH is the fate of hapless lexicography that not only
darkness but light impedes and distresses it ; things may be
not only too little but too much known to be happily
illustrated. To explain requires the use of terms less
abstruse than that which is to be explained, and such terms
cannot always be found ; for as nothing can be proved but
by supposing something intuitively known and evident without proof, so nothing can be defined but by the use of
words too plain to admit a definition.   *Works,* v. 34.

Liars :

'TALKING of an acquaintance of ours whose narratives,
which abounded in curious and interesting topics, were
unhappily found to be very fabulous ; I mentioned Lord
Mansfield's having said to me, "Suppose we believe one

half

half of what he tells." JOHNSON. "Ay; but we don't know *which* half to believe. By his lying we lose not only our reverence for him, but all comfort in his conversation." BOSWELL. "May we not take it as amusing fiction?" JOHNSON. "Sir, the misfortune is, that you will insensibly believe as much of it as you incline to believe." '

Boswell's Life of Johnson, iv. 178.

Libelling the dead:

' I MENTIONED Mr. Maclaurin's uneasiness on account of a degree of ridicule carelessly thrown on his deceased father, in Goldsmith's *History of Animated Nature*, in which that celebrated mathematician is represented as being subject to fits of yawning so violent as to render him incapable of proceeding in his lecture; a story altogether unfounded, but for the publication of which the law would give no reparation. This led us to agitate the question, whether legal redress could be obtained, even when a man's deceased relation was calumniated in a publication. Mr. Murray maintained there should be reparation, unless the author could justify himself by proving the fact. JOHNSON. "Sir, it is of so much more consequence that truth should be told than that individuals should not be made uneasy, that it is much better that the law does not restrain writing freely concerning the characters of the dead. Damages will be given to a man who is calumniated in his life-time, because he may be hurt in his worldly interest, or at least hurt in his mind: but the law does not regard that uneasiness which a man feels on having his ancestor calumniated. That is too nice. Let him deny what is said, and let the matter have a fair chance by discussion. But, if a man could say nothing against a character but what he can

prove,

prove, history could not be written; for a great deal is known of men of which proof cannot be brought. A minister may be notoriously known to take bribes, and yet you may not be able to prove it." Mr. Murray suggested that the author should be obliged to show some sort of evidence, though he would not require a strict legal proof: but Johnson firmly and resolutely opposed any restraint whatever, as adverse to a free investigation of the characters of mankind.'

Boswell's Life of Johnson, iii. 15.

Liberty:

'LORD GRAHAM commended Dr. Drummond at Naples, as a man of extraordinary talents; and added, that he had a great love of liberty. JOHNSON. "He is *young*, my Lord; (looking to his Lordship with an arch smile) all *boys* love liberty, till experience convinces them they are not so fit to govern themselves as they imagined. We are all agreed as to our own liberty; we would have as much of it as we can get; but we are not agreed as to the liberty of others; for in proportion as we take, others must lose. I believe we hardly wish that the mob should have liberty to govern us. When that was the case some time ago, no man was at liberty not to have candles in his windows." '

Ib. iii. 383.

∴

THE *Letters*[1] have something of that indistinct and headstrong ardour for liberty which a man of genius always catches when he enters the world, and always suffers to cool as he passes forward.

Works, viii. 488.

---

[1] *The Persian Letters* by the first Lord Lyttelton.

LIBERTY is to the lowest rank of every nation little more than the choice of working or starving; and this choice is, I suppose, equally allowed in every country.   *Works*, vi. 151.

.˙.

THE notion of liberty amuses the people of England, and helps to keep off the *tædium vitæ*. When a butcher tells you that *his heart bleeds for his country* he has, in fact, no uneasy feeling.   Boswell's *Life of Johnson*, i. 394.

.˙.

HE[1] published about the same time his 'Areopagitica, a speech of Mr. John Milton for the liberty of unlicensed printing.' The danger of such unbounded liberty, and the danger of bounding it, have produced a problem in the science of government, which human understanding seems hitherto unable to solve. If nothing may be published but what civil authority shall have previously approved, power must always be the standard of truth: if every dreamer of innovations may propagate his projects, there can be no settlement; if every murmurer at government may diffuse discontent, there can be no peace; and if every sceptic in theology may teach his follies, there can be no religion. The remedy against these evils is to punish the authors; for it is yet allowed that every society may punish, though not prevent, the publication of opinions which that society shall think pernicious; but this punishment, though it may crush the author, promotes the book; and it seems not more reasonable to leave the right of printing unrestrained because writers may be afterwards censured, than it would

---

[1] Milton.

Wit and
Wisdom
of
Samuel
Johnson.

be to sleep with doors unbolted, because by our laws we can hang a thief. *Works*, vii. 82.

Lichfield Cathedral:

'In Lichfield Cathedral porch, a gentleman, who might, perhaps, be too ambitious to be thought an acquaintance of the great Literary Oracle, ventured to say, "Dr. Johnson, we have had a most excellent discourse to-day"; to which he replied, "That may be, Sir, but it is impossible for you to know it."' Boswell's *Life of Johnson*, ii. 466 *n.* 3.

Lies:

'Johnson told me, that he went up thither [to his library in the garret story] without mentioning it to his servant, when he wanted to study, secure from interruption; for he would not allow his servant to say he was not at home when he really was. "A servant's strict regard for truth (said he) must be weakened by such a practice. A philosopher may know that it is merely a form of denial; but few servants are such nice distinguishers. If I accustom a servant to tell a lie for *me*, have I not reason to apprehend that he will tell many lies for *himself*?"' *Ib.* i. 436.

.·.

'There are (said Johnson) inexcusable lies and consecrated lies. For instance, we are told that on the arrival of the news of the unfortunate battle of Fontenoy, every heart beat, and every eye was in tears. Now we know that no man eat his dinner the worse, but there *should* have been all this concern; and to say there *was* (smiling) may be reckoned a consecrated lie.' *Ib.* i. 355.

Life:

Life :

I HAVE often thought those happy that have been fixed, from the first dawn of thought, in a determination to some state of life by the choice of one whose authority may preclude caprice, and whose influence may prejudice them in favour of his opinion. The general precept of consulting the genius is of little use unless we are told how the genius can be known. If it is to be discovered only by experiment, life will be lost before the resolution can be fixed; if any other indications are to be found they may, perhaps, be very early discerned. At least, if to miscarry in an attempt be a proof of having mistaken the direction of the genius, men appear not less frequently deceived with regard to themselves than to others; and therefore no one has much reason to complain that his life was planned out by his friends, or to be confident that he should have had either more honour or happiness by being abandoned to the chance of his own fancy. . . . Of two states of life equally consistent with religion and virtue, he who chooses earliest chooses best.

Rambler, No. 19.

. .

'WHEN professions were talked of, "Scorn (said Mr. Johnson) to put your behaviour under the dominion of canters; never think it clever to call physic a mean study or law a dry one, or ask a baby of seven years old which way *his genius* leads him, when we all know that a boy of seven years old has no *genius* for anything except a peg-top and an apple-pie; but fix on some business where much money may be got and little virtue risked: follow that business steadily, and do not live as Roger Ascham says

M   the

the wits do, *men know not how ; and at last die obscurely, men mark not where."* '
    Piozzi's *Anecdotes*, p. 251.

．˙．

LIFE is not long, and too much of it must not pass in idle deliberation how it shall be spent; deliberation, which those who begin it by prudence and continue it with subtlety must, after long expense of thought, conclude by chance. To prefer one future mode of life to another, upon just reasons, requires faculties which it has not pleased our Creator to give us.

' If, therefore, the profession you have chosen has some unexpected inconveniences, console yourself by reflecting that no profession is without them; and that all the importunities and perplexities of business are softness and luxury, compared with the incessant cravings of vacancy, and the unsatisfactory expedients of idleness.
    Boswell's *Life of Johnson*, ii. 22.

．˙．

' "To him that lives well," answered the hermit, "every form of life is good; nor can I give any other rule for choice than to remove from all apparent evil." '
    Rasselas, ch. 21.

．˙．

THE main of life is, indeed, composed of small incidents and petty occurrences; of wishes for objects not remote, and grief for disappointments of no fatal consequence; of insect vexations which sting us and fly away, impertinences which buzz awhile about us, and are heard no more; of meteorous pleasures which dance before us and are dissipated; of compliments which glide off the soul like other music, and are forgotten by him that gave and him that received them. Such is the general heap out of which

every

every man is to cull his own condition; for, as the chemists tell us that all bodies are resolvable into the same elements, and that the boundless variety of things arises from the different proportions of very few ingredients; so a few pains and a few pleasures are all the materials of human life, and of these the proportions are partly allotted by Providence, and partly left to the arrangement of reason and of choice. As these are well or ill disposed, man is for the most part happy or miserable. For very few are involved in great events, or have their thread of life entwisted with the chain of causes on which armies or nations are suspended; and even those who seem wholly busied in public affairs, and elevated above low cares or trivial pleasures, pass the chief part of their time in familiar and domestic scenes; from these they came into public life, to these they are every hour recalled by passions not to be suppressed; in these they have the reward of their toils, and to these at last they retire. The great end of prudence is to give cheerfulness to those hours which splendour cannot gild and acclamation cannot exhilarate; those soft intervals of unbended amusement, in which a man shrinks to his natural dimensions and throws aside the ornaments or disguises which he feels in privacy to be useless incumbrances, and to lose all effect when they become familiar. To be happy at home is the ultimate result of all ambition, the end to which every enterprise and labour tends, and of which every desire prompts the prosecution. *Rambler*, No. 68.

.·.

THE reigning error of mankind is that we are not content with the conditions on which the goods of life are granted.

Ib. No. 178.

 EVERY

EVERY man is to take existence on the terms on which it is given to him. To some men it is given on condition of not taking liberties which other men may take without much harm. One may drink wine and be nothing the worse for it; on another, wine may have effects so inflammatory as to injure him both in body and mind, and perhaps, make him commit something for which he may deserve to be hanged.   Boswell's *Life of Johnson*, iii. 58.

.·.

To strive with difficulties, and to conquer them, is the highest human felicity; the next is to strive and deserve to conquer: but he whose life has passed without a contest, and who can boast neither success nor merit, can survey himself only as a useless filler of existence; and if he is content with his own character, must owe his satisfaction to insensibility.   *Adventurer*, No. 111.

.·.

WHEN such is the condition of beings, not brute and savage, but endowed with reason and united in society, who would not expect that they should join in a perpetual confederacy against the certain or fortuitous troubles to which they are exposed? that they should universally co-operate in the proportion [? promotion] of universal felicity? that every man should easily discover that his own happiness is connected with that of every other man? that thousands and millions should continue together as partakers of one common nature? and that every eye should be vigilant and every hand active for the confirmation of ease and the prevention of misfortune? This expectation might be formed by speculative wisdom, but experience will soon dissipate the pleasing illusion. A slight survey of life

will

will show that, instead of hoping to be happy in the general felicity, every man pursues a private and independent interest, proposes to himself some peculiar convenience, and prizes it more as it is less attainable by others.

Works, ix. 496.

.•.

WHEN you favoured me with your letter, you seemed to be in want of materials to fill it, having met with no great adventures either of peril or delight, nor done or suffered anything out of the common course of life.   When you have lived longer and considered more you will find the common course of life very fertile of observation and reflection.   Upon the common course of life must our thoughts and our conversation be generally employed.   Our general course of life must denominate us wise or foolish; happy or miserable: if it is well regulated we pass on prosperously and smoothly; as it is neglected we live in embarrassment, perplexity, and uneasiness. . . . A letter may be always made out of the books of the morning or talk of the evening.   *Piozzi Letters*, ii. 290.

.•.

To improve the golden moment of opportunity, and catch the good that is within our reach, is the great art of life.   *Works*, vi. 214.

.•.

[1] TAKE all opportunities of filling your mind with genuine scenes of nature ; description is always fallacious ; at least till you have seen realities you cannot know it to be true. This observation might be extended to life, but life cannot

---

[1] Written to a young lady.

be surveyed with the same safety as nature, and it is better to know vice and folly by report than by experience. A painter, says Sidney, mingled in the battle that he might know how to paint it; but his knowledge was useless, for some mischievous sword took away his head. They whose speculation upon characters leads them too far into the world may lose that nice sense of good and evil by which characters are to be tried. Acquaint yourself therefore both with the pleasing and the terrible parts of nature, but in life wish to know only the good. *Piozzi Letters*, ii. 308.

．·．

Such is the course of nature, that whoever lives long must outlive those whom he loves and honours. Such is the condition of our present existence, that life must one time lose its associations, and every inhabitant of the earth must walk downward to the grave alone and unregarded, without any partner of his joy or grief, without any interested witness of his misfortunes or success. Misfortune, indeed, he may yet feel; for where is the bottom of the misery of man? But what is success to him that has none to enjoy it? Happiness is not found in self-contemplation; it is perceived only when it is reflected from another.

Idler, No. 41.

．·．

The love of life is necessary to the vigorous prosecution of any undertaking. *Rambler*, No. 59.

．·．

Life is not the object of science: we see a little, very little; and what is beyond we only can conjecture. If we inquire of those who have gone before us, we receive small satisfaction; some have travelled life without observation,

and

and some willingly mislead us. The only thought, therefore, on which we can repose with comfort is that which presents to us the care of Providence, whose eye takes in the whole of things and under whose direction all involuntary errors will terminate in happiness. *Adventurer*, No. 107.

.˙.

IT is said, and said truly, that experience is the best teacher; and it is supposed that as life is lengthened experience is increased. But a closer inspection of human life will discover that time often passes without any incident which can much enlarge knowledge or ratify judgment. When we are young we learn much, because we are universally ignorant, we observe every thing because every thing is new. But after some years, the occurrences of daily life are exhausted; one day passes like another in the same scene of appearances, in the same course of transactions; we have to do what we have often done, and what we do not try, because we do not wish, to do much better; we are told what we already know, and therefore what repetition cannot make us know with greater certainty. *Piozzi Letters*, i. 298.

.˙.

SOME desire is necessary to keep life in motion, and he whose real wants are supplied must admit those of fancy. *Rasselas*, ch. 8.

.˙.

HUMAN life is everywhere a state in which much is to be endured and little to be enjoyed. *Ib.* ch. 11.

.˙.

How evil came into the world; for what reason it is that life is overspread with such boundless varieties of misery;

why

why the only thinking being of this globe is doomed to think merely to be wretched, and to pass his time from youth to age in fearing or in suffering calamities, is a question which philosophers have long asked, and which philosophy could never answer.   *Idler*, No. 89.

.˙.

HE that wanders about the world sees new forms of human misery; and if he chances to meet an old friend, meets a face darkened with troubles.   *Piozzi Letters*, i. 107.

.˙.

ALL here is gloomy; a faint struggle with the tediousness of time; a doleful confession of present misery, and the approach seen and felt of what is most dreaded and most shunned. But such is the lot of man.   *Ib.* ii. 209.

.˙.

THE freaks and humours and spleen and vanity of women, as they embroil families in discord, and fill houses with disquiet do more to obstruct the happiness of life in a year than the ambition of the clergy in many centuries. It has been well observed that the misery of man proceeds not from any single crush of overwhelming evil, but from small vexations continually repeated.   *Works*, viii. 333.

.˙.

MISERY is caused, for the most part, not by a heavy crush of disaster, but by the corrosion of less visible evils which canker enjoyment and undermine security. The visit of an invader is necessarily rare, but domestic animosities allow no cessation.   *Ib.* ix. 89.

THE

THE miseries of life would be increased beyond all human power of endurance if we were to enter the world with the same opinions as we carry from it. *Rambler*, No. 196.

Literary Catalogues:

NOR is the use of catalogues of less importance to those whom curiosity has engaged in the study of literary history, and who think the intellectual revolutions of the world more worthy of their attention than the ravages of tyrants, the desolation of kingdoms, the rout of armies, and the fall of empires. Those who are pleased with observing the first birth of new opinions, their struggles against opposition, their silent progress under persecution, their general reception, and their gradual decline or sudden extinction; those that amuse themselves with remarking the different periods of human knowledge, and observe how darkness and light succeed each other; by what accident the most gloomy nights of ignorance have given way to the dawn of science, and how learning has languished and decayed for want of patronage and regard, or been overborne by the prevalence of fashionable ignorance, or lost amidst the tumults of invasion and the storms of violence—all those who desire any knowledge of the literary transactions of past ages may find in catalogues, like this[1] at least, such an account as is given by annalists and chronologers of civil history.

Works, v. 183.

Literature:

' DR. WATSON observed that Glasgow University had fewer home-students since trade increased, as learning was rather

---

[1] The Harleian Catalogue.

incompatible

incompatible with it. JOHNSON. " Why, Sir, as trade is now carried on by subordinate hands, men in trade have as much leisure as others ; and now learning itself is a trade. A man goes to a bookseller and gets what he can. We have done with patronage. In the infancy of learning we find some great man praised for it. This diffused it among others. When it becomes general an author leaves the great and applies to the multitude." BOSWELL. " It is a shame that authors are not now better patronized." JOHNSON. " No, Sir. If learning cannot support a man, if he must sit with his hands across till somebody feeds him, it is as to him a bad thing, and it is better as it is. With patronage, what flattery ! what falsehood ! While a man is in equilibrio, he throws truth among the multitude and lets them take it as they please : in patronage he must say what pleases his patron, and it is an equal chance whether that be truth or falsehood." WATSON. " But is not the case now, that, instead of flattering one person, we flatter the age ? " JOHNSON. " No, Sir. The world always lets a man tell what he thinks his own way. I wonder, however, that so many people have written who might have let it alone. That people should endeavour to excel in conversation I do not wonder, because in conversation praise is instantly reverberated." '

Boswell's *Life of Johnson,* v. 58.

.˙.

' ON Mr. Barclay's becoming a partner in the brewery[1], Johnson advised him not to allow his commercial pursuits to divert his attention from his studies. " A mere literary

---

[1] The brewery which had belonged to Mr. Thrale, and which was on his death bought by Messrs. Barclay and Perkins.

man,"

man," said the Doctor, "is a *dull* man; a man who is solely a man of business is a *selfish* man; but when literature and commerce are united they make a *respectable* man." '

Croker's Boswell (8vo. ed.), p. 837.

Little things:

LITTLE things are not valued but when they are done by those who can do greater. Works, viii. 395.

Living for others:

EVERY man has in the present state of things wants which cannot wait for public plenty, and vexations which must be quieted before the days of universal peace. And no man can live only for others unless he could persuade others to live only for him. Ib. ix. 497.

Local emotion:

WE were now treading that illustrious island which was once the luminary of the Caledonian regions, whence savage clans and roving barbarians derived the benefits of knowledge and the blessings of religion. To abstract the mind from all local emotion would be impossible if it were endeavoured, and would be foolish if it were possible. Whatever withdraws us from the power of our senses, whatever makes the past, the distant, or the future predominate over the present, advances us in the dignity of thinking beings. Far from me and from my friends be such frigid philosophy as may conduct us indifferent and unmoved over any ground which has been dignified by wisdom, bravery, or virtue. That man is little to be envied whose patriotism

would

would not gain force upon the plain of Marathon, or whose piety would not grow warmer among the ruins of Iona.

Works, ix. 145.

Looking close to the ground:

'WHEN Mr. Bickerstaff's flight confirmed the report of his guilt, and my husband said in answer to Johnson's astonishment, that he had long been a suspected man: " By those who look close to the ground dirt will be seen, Sir, (was the lofty reply); I hope I see things from a greater distance." '

Piozzi's *Anecdotes*, p. 168.

Love:

UPON every other stage [but Shakespeare's] the universal agent is love, by whose power all good and evil is distributed, and every action quickened or retarded. To bring a lover, a lady, and a rival into the fable; to entangle them in contradictory obligations, perplex them with oppositions of interest, and harass them with violence of desires inconsistent with each other; to make them meet in rapture and part in agony; to fill their mouths with hyperbolical joy and outrageous sorrow; to distress them as nothing human ever was distressed; to deliver them as nothing human ever was delivered, is the business of a modern dramatist. For this probability is violated, life is misrepresented, and language is depraved. But love is only one of many passions; and as it has no great influence upon the sum of life it has little operation in the dramas of a poet, who caught his ideas from the living world and exhibited only what he saw before him. He knew that any other passion, as it was regular or exorbitant, was a cause of happiness or calamity.

Works, v. 107.

OF

OF your love I know not the propriety, nor can estimate the power; but in love, as in every other passion of which hope is the essence, we ought always to remember the uncertainty of events. There is, indeed, nothing that so much seduces reason from vigilance as the thought of passing life with an amiable woman; and if all would happen that a lover fancies, I know not what other terrestrial happiness would deserve pursuit. But love and marriage are different states. Those who are to suffer the evils together and to suffer often for the sake of one another, soon lose that tenderness of look and that benevolence of mind which arose from the participation of unmingled pleasure and successive amusement. A woman, we are sure, will not be always fair; we are not sure she will always be virtuous: and man cannot retain through life that respect and assiduity by which he pleases for a day or for a month. I do not, however, pretend to have discovered that life has anything more to be desired than a prudent and virtuous marriage; therefore know not what counsel to give you.

Boswell's *Life of Johnson*, i. 381.

Luxury:

IT is generally supposed that life is longer in places where there are few opportunities of luxury; but I found no instance here[1] of extraordinary longevity. A cottager grows old over his oaten cakes like a citizen at a turtle feast. He is indeed seldom incommoded by corpulence. Poverty preserves him from sinking under the burden of himself, but he escapes no other injury of time. Instances of long life are often related, which those who hear them

---

[1] In the Western Islands.

are more willing to credit than examine. To be told that any man has attained a hundred years gives hope and comfort to him who stands trembling on the brink of his own climacteric.

Works, ix. 81.

THERE is no snare more dangerous to busy and excursive minds than the cobwebs of petty inquisitiveness, which entangle them in trivial employments and minute studies, and detain them in a middle state between the tediousness of total inactivity, and the fatigue of laborious efforts, enchant them at once with ease and novelty, and vitiate them with the luxury of learning. The necessity of doing something and the fear of undertaking much sinks the historian to a genealogist, the philosopher to a journalist of the weather, and the mathematician to a constructor of dials.

Rambler, No. 103.

Macpherson, James:

' I DESCRIBED to him an impudent fellow [1] from Scotland who affected to be a savage, and railed at all established systems. JOHNSON. " There is nothing surprising in this, Sir. He wants to make himself conspicuous. He would tumble in a hogstye as long as you looked at him and called to him to come out. But let him alone, never mind him, and he'll soon give it over."

' I added that the same person maintained that there was no distinction between virtue and vice. JOHNSON. " Why, Sir, if the fellow does not think as he speaks, he is lying, and I see not what honour he can propose to himself from having the character of a liar. But if he does really think

---

[1] James Macpherson, the author of *Ossian*.

that

that there is no distinction between virtue and vice, why, Sir, when he leaves our houses let us count our spoons." '

Boswell's Life of Johnson, i. 432.

.·.

Mr. James Macpherson,

I received your foolish and impudent letter. Any violence offered me I shall do my best to repel; and what I cannot do for myself the law shall do for me. I hope I shall never be deterred from detecting what I think a cheat by the menaces of a ruffian.

What would you have me retract? I thought your book an imposture; I think it an imposture still. For this opinion I have given my reasons to the public, which I here dare you to refute. Your rage I defy. Your abilities since your Homer[1] are not so formidable, and what I hear of your morals inclines me to pay regard not to what you shall say, but to what you shall prove. You may print this if you will. Sam. Johnson.

Ib. ii. 298.

Madness:

'Of the uncertainties of our present state,' said Imlac, 'the most dreadful and alarming is the uncertain continuance of reason.' . . . Rasselas inquired of him whether he thought such maladies of the mind frequent, and how they were contracted? 'Disorders of intellect,' answered Imlac, 'happen much more often than superficial observers will easily believe. Perhaps, if we speak with rigorous exactness, no human mind is in its right state. There is no man whose imagination does not sometimes predominate

---

[1] A translation of the Iliad.

over his reason, who can regulate his attention wholly by his will, and whose ideas will come and go at his command. No man will be found in whose mind airy notions do not sometimes tyrannise, and force him to hope or fear beyond the limits of sober probability. All power of fancy over reason is a degree of insanity; but while this power is such as we can control and repress it is not visible to others, nor considered as any depravation of the mental faculties: it is not pronounced madness but when it becomes ungovernable, and apparently influences speech or action.

Rasselas, chs. 43 and 44.

THE moralists all talk of the uncertainty of fortune and the transitoriness of beauty, but it is yet more dreadful to consider that the powers of the mind are equally liable to change; that understanding may make its appearance and depart, that it may blaze and expire.

Croker's *Boswell* (8vo ed.), p. 102.

How little can we venture to exult in any intellectual powers or literary attainments when we consider the condition of poor Collins! I knew him a few years ago full of hopes and full of projects, versed in many languages, high in fancy, and strong in retention. This busy and forcible mind is now under the government of those who lately would not have been able to comprehend the least and most narrow of its designs.

Ib. p. 82.

MADMEN are all sensual in the lower stages of the distemper. They are eager for gratifications to soothe their minds and divert their attention from the misery which they suffer; but when they grow very ill pleasure is too

weak

weak for them, and they seek for pain. Employment and hardships prevent melancholy. I suppose in all our army in America there was not one man who went mad.

Boswell's Life of Johnson, iii. 176.

Magnificence:

MAGNIFICENCE cannot be cheap, for what is cheap cannot be magnificent.

Works, v. 458.

Man of the world:

ONE may be so much a man of the world as to be nothing in the world.

Boswell's Life of Johnson, iii. 375.

Man:

EVERYTHING that enlarges the sphere of human powers, that shows man he can do what he thought he could not do, is valuable. The first man who balanced a straw upon his nose; Johnson, who rode upon three horses at a time; in short, all such men deserved the applause of mankind, not on account of the use of what they did but of the dexterity which they exhibited.

Ib. iii. 231.

.·.

PERHAPS man is the only being that can properly be called idle, that does by others what he might do himself, or sacrifices duty or pleasure to the love of ease.

Idler, No. 1.

.·.

WHERE there is no education, as in savage countries, men will have the upper hand of women. Bodily strength, no doubt, contributes to this; but it would be so exclusive of that, for it is mind that always governs. When it comes to dry understanding man has the better.

Boswell's Life of Johnson, iii. 52.

MILTON

MILTON thought women made only for obedience, and man only for rebellion.

Works, vii. 116.

Mankind:

WE are to consider mankind not as we wish them but as we find them, frequently corrupt and always fallible.

Debates. Works, xi. 174.

SURELY we may be content to credit the general voice of mankind complaining incessantly of general infelicity; and when we see the restlessness of the young and peevishness of the old, when we find the daring and the active combating misery, and the calm and humble lamenting it; when the vigorous are exhausting themselves in struggles with their own condition, and the old and the wise retiring from the contest in weariness and despondency, we may be content at last to conclude that if happiness had been to be found some would have found it, and that it is vain to search longer for what all have missed.

Works, ix. 395.

DR. JOHNSON advised me when I was moving about to read diligently the great book of mankind.

Boswell's *Life of Johnson*, i. 464.

THE history of mankind is little else than a narrative of designs which have failed, and hopes that have been disappointed.

Works, ix. 398.

THIS[1] is only one of the innumerable artifices practised in the universal conspiracy of mankind against themselves;

---

[1] The refusal to see the approach of death.

every

every age and every condition indulges some darling fallacy; every man amuses himself with projects which he knows to be improbable, and which, therefore, he resolves to pursue without daring to examine them.   *Adventurer*, No. 69.

⁂

THE utmost excellence at which humanity can arrive is a constant and determinate pursuit of virtue without regard to present dangers or advantage; a continual reference of every action to the divine will; an habitual appeal to everlasting justice; and an unvaried elevation of the intellectual eye to the reward which perseverance only can obtain.

Rambler, No. 185.

⁂

As I know more of mankind I expect less of them, and am ready now to call a man *a good man* upon easier terms than I was formerly.   Boswell's *Life of Johnson*, iv. 239.

Managers of theatres:

OF all authors those are the most wretched who exhibit their productions on the theatre, and who are to propitiate first the manager and then the public. Many an humble visitant have I followed to the doors of these lords of the drama, seen him touch the knocker with a shaking hand, and after long deliberation adventure to solicit entrance by a single knock; but I never staid to see them come out from their audience because my heart is tender and, being subject to frights in bed, I would not willingly dream of an author.

Works, v. 360.

Marriage:

THEY [the unmarried] dream away their time without friendship, without fondness, and are driven to rid themselves of the day, for which they have no use, by childish amusements or vicious delights. They act as beings under the constant sense of some known inferiority that fills their minds with rancour and their tongues with censure. They are peevish at home and malevolent abroad ; and, as the outlaws of human nature, make it their business and their pleasure to disturb that society which debars them from its privileges. To live without feeling or exciting sympathy, to be fortunate without adding to the felicity of others, or afflicted without tasting the balm of pity is a state more gloomy than solitude : it is not retreat but exclusion from mankind. Marriage has many pains but celibacy has no pleasures.

Rasselas, ch. 26.

AN accurate view of the world will confirm [the opinion] that marriage is not commonly unhappy otherwise than as life is unhappy, and that most of those who complain of connubial miseries have as much satisfaction as their nature would have admitted, or their conduct procured in any other condition.

Rambler, No. 45.

IT may be urged in extenuation of this crime[1], which parents, not in any other respect to be numbered with robbers and assassins, frequently commit, that in their estimation riches and happiness are equivalent terms. They have passed their lives with no other wish than of adding acre to acre and filling one bag after another, and imagine the advantage of a daughter sufficiently considered when they have secured her a large jointure, and given her reasonable expectations of living in the midst of those pleasures with which she had seen her father and mother solacing their age.

Rambler, No. 39.

---

[1] The crime of forcing children to marry against their will.

UNLIMITED

UNLIMITED obedience is due only to the Universal Father of Heaven and Earth. My parents may be mad or foolish; may be wicked and malicious; may be erroneously religious or absurdly scrupulous. I am not bound to compliance with mandates either positive or negative, which either religion condemns, or reason rejects. There wanders about the world a wild notion which extends over marriage more than over any other transaction. If Miss * * * followed a trade, would it be said that she was bound in conscience to give or refuse credit at her father's choice? And is not marriage a thing in which she is more interested, and has therefore more right of choice? When I may suffer for my own crimes, when I may be sued for my own debts, I may judge by parity of reason for my own happiness. The parent's moral right can arise only from his kindness, and his civil right only from his money. Conscience cannot dictate obedience to the wicked or compliance with the foolish; and of interest mere prudence is the judge.

Piozzi Letters, i. 83.

. . .

IT is dangerous for a man and woman to suspend their fate upon each other at a time when opinions are fixed and habits are established; when friendships have been contracted on both sides; when life has been planned into method and the mind has long enjoyed the contemplation of its own prospects. . . . I believe it will be found that those who marry late are best pleased with their children, and those who marry early with their partners.

Rasselas, ch. 29.

. . .

SUCH is the common process of marriage. A youth or maiden meeting by chance, or brought together by artifice,

exchange

exchange glances, reciprocate civilities, go home and dream of one another. Having little to divert attention or diversify thought they find themselves uneasy when they are apart, and therefore conclude that they shall be happy together. They marry and discover what nothing but voluntary blindness before had concealed ; they wear out life in altercations and charge nature with cruelty. *Rasselas*, ch. 29.

BOSWELL. ' Pray, Sir, do you not suppose that there are fifty women in the world, with any one of whom a man may be as happy as with any one woman in particular ? ' JOHNSON. ' Ay, Sir, fifty thousand.' BOSWELL. ' Then, Sir, you are not of opinion with some who imagine that certain men and certain women are made for each other ; and that they cannot be happy if they miss their counterparts.' JOHNSON. ' To be sure not, Sir. I believe marriages would in general be as happy, and often more so, if they were all made by the Lord Chancellor, upon a due consideration of characters and circumstances, without the parties having any choice in the matter.' Boswell's *Life of Johnson*, ii. 461.

' ONE day at Streatham, when Dr. Johnson was musing over the fire, a young gentleman called to him suddenly, and I suppose he thought disrespectfully, in these words :— " Mr. Johnson, would you advise me to marry ? " " I would advise no man to marry, Sir," returns for answer in a very angry tone Dr. Johnson, " who is not likely to propagate understanding." ' Piozzi's *Anecdotes*, p. 97.

' DR. JOHNSON said, " It is commonly a weak man who
marries

marries for love." We then talked of marrying women of fortune; and I mentioned a common remark, that a man may be, upon the whole, richer by marrying a woman with a very small portion, because a woman of fortune will be proportionally expensive; whereas a woman who brings none will be very moderate in expenses. JOHNSON. "Depend upon it, Sir, this is not true. A woman of fortune being used to the handling of money spends it judiciously; but a woman who gets the command of money for the first time upon her marriage has such a gust in spending it, that she throws it away with great profusion."'

Boswell's Life of Johnson, iii. 3.

Masters:

IT is not uncommon for those who have grown wise by the labour of others to add a little of their own and overlook their masters. Works, vii. 470.

Mean minds:

IT is dangerous for mean minds to venture themselves within the sphere of greatness. Stupidity is soon blinded by the splendour of wealth, and cowardice is easily fettered in the shackles of dependence. To solicit patronage is, at least in the event, to set virtue to sale. None can be pleased without praise, and few can be praised without falsehood; few can be assiduous without servility, and none can be servile without corruption. Rambler, No. 104.

Meanness:

AN infallible characteristic of meanness is cruelty.

Works, vi. 176.

Medicine:

Medicine :

THAT it should be imagined that the greatest physician of the age[1] arrived at so high a degree of skill without any assistance from his predecessors, and that a man eminent for integrity practised medicine by chance and grew wise only by murder, is not to be considered without astonishment.

Works, vi. 409.

Meeting fools in heaven :

'MRS. KNOWLES, "I hope, Doctor, thou wilt not remain unforgiving ; and that you will renew your friendship, and joyfully meet at last in those bright regions where pride and prejudice can never enter." Dr. Johnson, "Meet *her*[2]! I never desire to meet fools anywhere."'

Boswell's *Life of Johnson*, iii. 299 *n*. 2.

Melancholy :

'TALKING of constitutional melancholy, Johnson observed, "A man so afflicted, Sir, must divert distressing thoughts, and not combat with them." BOSWELL. "May not he think them down, Sir?" JOHNSON. "No, Sir. To attempt to *think them down* is madness. He should have a lamp constantly burning in his bed-chamber during the night, and if wakefully disturbed take a book and read, and compose himself to rest. To have the management of the mind is a great art, and it may be attained in a considerable degree

---

[1] It had been reported that Dr. Sydenham 'engaged in the practice of physic without any acquaintance with the theory, or knowledge of the opinions or precepts of former writers.'

[2] Miss Jane Harry, who had offended Johnson by becoming a proselyte to Quakerism.

by

by experience and habitual exercise." BOSWELL. "Should not he provide amusements for himself? Would it not, for instance, be right for him to take a course of chemistry?" JOHNSON. "Let him take a course of chemistry, or a course of rope-dancing, or a course of anything to which he is inclined at the time. Let him contrive to have as many retreats for his mind as he can, as many things to which it can fly from itself."'

Boswell's *Life of Johnson*, ii. 440.

.·.

WHEN any fit of anxiety, or gloominess, or perversion of mind lays hold upon you, make it a rule not to publish it by complaints, but exert your whole care to hide it; by endeavouring to hide it you will drive it away. Be always busy.

Ib. iii. 368.

.·.

YOU are always complaining of melancholy, and I conclude from those complaints that you are fond of it. No man talks of that which he is desirous to conceal, and every man desires to conceal that of which he is ashamed. Do not pretend to deny it; *manifestum habemus furem.* Make it an invariable and obligatory law to yourself never to mention your own mental diseases. If you are never to speak of them, you will think on them but little; and if you think little of them they will molest you rarely. When you talk of them it is plain that you want either praise or pity: for praise there is no room, and pity will do you no good; therefore from this hour speak no more, think no more, about them.

Ib. iii. 421.

Memory:

THE true art of memory is the art of attention.

Idler, No. 74.

IT

It is, I believe, much more common for the solitary and thoughtful to amuse themselves with schemes of the future than reviews of the past. For the future is pliant and ductile, and will be easily moulded by a strong fancy into any form. But the images which memory presents are of a stubborn and untractable nature, the objects of remembrance have already existed, and left their signature behind them impressed upon the mind, so as to defy all attempts of rasure or of change. As the satisfactions, therefore, arising from memory are less arbitrary, they are more solid, and are, indeed, the only joys which we can call our own. Whatever we have once reposited, as Dryden expresses it, 'in the sacred treasure of the past,' is out of the reach of accident or violence, nor can be lost either by our own weakness or another's malice.

Rambler, No. 41.

Men who cannot bear their own company:

It may be laid down as a position which will seldom deceive, that when a man cannot bear his own company, there is something wrong.

Ib. No. 5.

Mental repose:

To play with important truths, to disturb the repose of established tenets, to subtilize objections, and elude proof, is too often the sport of youthful vanity, of which maturer experience commonly repents. There is a time when every man is weary of raising difficulties only to task himself with the solution, and desires to enjoy truth without the labour or hazard of contest.

Works, vi. 497.

Mental

Mental superiority:

SUCH is the delight of mental superiority, that none on whom nature or study has conferred it would purchase the gifts of fortune by its loss. *Rambler*, No. 150.

Merit set against fortune:

'ROUSSEAU'S treatise on the inequality of mankind was at this time a fashionable topic. It gave rise to an observation by Mr. Dempster that the advantages of fortune and rank were nothing to a wise man, who ought to value only merit. JOHNSON. " If a man were a savage, living in the woods by himself, this might be true; but in civilized society we all depend upon each other, and our happiness is very much owing to the good opinion of mankind. Now, Sir, in civilized society, external advantages make us more respected. A man with a good coat upon his back meets with a better reception than he who has a bad one. Sir, you may analyse this, and say what is there in it? But that will avail you nothing, for it is a part of a general system. Pound St. Paul's Church into atoms, and consider any single atom; it is, to be sure, good for nothing: but put all these atoms together, and you have St. Paul's Church. So it is with human felicity, which is made up of many ingredients, each of which may be shown to be very insignificant. In civilized society, personal merit will not serve you so much as money will. Sir, you may make the experiment. Go into the street, and give one man a lecture on morality and another a shilling, and see which will respect you most. If you wish only to support nature, Sir William Petty fixes your allowance at three pounds a year; but as times are much altered, let us call it six pounds.

pounds. This sum will fill your belly, shelter you from the weather, and even get you a strong lasting coat, supposing it to be made of good bull's hide. Now, Sir, all beyond this is artificial, and is desired in order to obtain a greater degree of respect from our fellow-creatures. And, Sir, if six hundred pounds a year procure a man more consequence, and, of course, more happiness than six pounds a year, the same proportion will hold as to six thousand, and so on as far as opulence can be carried. Perhaps he who has a large fortune may not be so happy as he who has a small one; but that must proceed from other causes than from his having the large fortune: for, *caeteris paribus*, he who is rich in a civilized society, must be happier than he who is poor; as riches, if properly used, (and it is a man's own fault if they are not,) must be productive of the highest advantages. Money, to be sure, of itself is of no use; for its only use is to part with it. Rousseau, and all those who deal in paradoxes, are led away by a childish desire of novelty. When I was a boy, I used always to choose the wrong side of a debate, because most ingenious things, that is to say most new things, could be said upon it. Sir, there is nothing for which you may not muster up more plausible arguments, than those which are urged against wealth and other external advantages. Why, now, there is stealing; why should it be thought a crime? When we consider by what unjust methods property has been often acquired, and that what was unjustly got it must be unjust to keep, where is the harm in one man's taking the property of another from him? Besides, Sir, when we consider the bad use that many people make of their property, and how much better use the thief may make of it, it may be defended as a very allowable practice. Yet, Sir, the

experience

experience of mankind has discovered stealing to be so very
bad a thing that they make no scruple to hang a man for it.
When I was running about this town a very poor fellow,
I was a great arguer for the advantages of poverty; but
I was, at the same time, very sorry to be poor. Sir, all the
arguments which are brought to represent poverty as no
evil show it to be evidently a great evil. You never find
people labouring to convince you that you may live very
happily upon a plentiful fortune.—So you hear people talking how miserable a king must be; and yet they all wish to
be in his place.' Boswell's *Life of Johnson*, i. 439.

Milton:

THAT this relation[1] is true cannot be questioned: but
surely the honour of letters, the dignity of sacred poetry, the
spirit of the English nation, and the glory of human nature,
require that it should be true no longer. In an age in which
statues are erected to the honour of this great writer, in
which his effigy has been diffused on medals, and his work
propagated by translations and illustrated by commentaries;
in an age which, amidst all its vices and all its follies, has
not become infamous for want of charity; it may be surely
allowed to hope that the living remains of Milton will be no
longer suffered to languish in distress. It is yet in the power
of a great people to reward the poet whose name they boast,
and from their alliance to whose genius they claim some
kind of superiority to every other nation of the earth; that
poet, whose works may possibly be read when every other
monument of British greatness shall be obliterated; to reward him, not with pictures or with medals which, if he

---

[1] Of the distress in which Milton's granddaughter was.

sees,

sees, he sees with contempt, but with tokens of gratitude which he, perhaps, may even now consider as not unworthy the regard of an immortal spirit. And surely to those who refuse their names to no other scheme of expense, it will not be unwelcome that a subscription is proposed for relieving, in the languor of age, the pains of disease, and the contempt of poverty, the grand-daughter of the author of Paradise Lost.

Works, v. 270.

Mind :

THE true strong and sound mind is the mind that can embrace equally great things and small.

Boswell's *Life of Johnson*, iii. 334.

.•.

SUCH was the criticism to which the genius of Dryden could be reduced between rage and terror; rage with little provocation, and terror with little danger. To see the highest mind thus levelled with the meanest may produce some solace to the consciousness of weakness, and some mortification to the pride of wisdom. But let it be remembered that minds are not levelled in their powers but when they are first levelled in their desires. Dryden and Settle had both placed their happiness in the claps of multitudes.

Works, vii. 257.

Mirth :

REAL mirth must be always natural, and nature is uniform. Men have been wise in very different modes; but they have always laughed the same way. *Ib.* vii. 34.

.•.

THE size of a man's understanding may always be justly measured by his mirth.

Piozzi's *Anecdotes*, p. 298.

Misfortunes :

Misfortunes:

DEPEND upon it that if a man *talks* of his misfortunes, there is something in them that is not disagreeable to him; for where there is nothing but pure misery, there never is any recourse to the mention of it.

Boswell's *Life of Johnson*, iv. 31.

Missionaries:

THE first propagators of christianity recommended their doctrines by their sufferings and virtues; they entered no defenceless territories with swords in their hands; they built no forts upon ground to which they had no right, nor polluted the purity of religion with the avarice of trade or insolence of power.

Works, v. 221.

Moderation:

MODERATION is commonly firm, and firmness is commonly successful.

Ib. vi. 194.

Monastic life:

I DO not wonder that, where the monastic life is permitted, every order finds votaries, and every monastery inhabitants. Men will submit to any rule by which they may be exempted from the tyranny of caprice and of chance. They are glad to supply by external authority their own want of constancy and resolution, and court the government of others when long experience has convinced them of their own inability to govern themselves. If I were to visit Italy, my curiosity would be more attracted by convents than by palaces; though I am afraid that I should find expectation in both places equally disappointed, and life in both places

supported

supported with impatience and quitted with reluctance. That it must be so soon quitted is a powerful remedy against impatience ; but what shall free us from reluctance? Those who have endeavoured to teach us to die well have taught few to die willingly: yet I cannot but hope that a good life might end at last in a contented death.

Boswell's *Life of Johnson*, i. 365.

.˙.

It is as unreasonable for a man to go into a Carthusian convent for fear of being immoral, as for a man to cut off his hands for fear he should steal. There is, indeed, great resolution in the immediate act of dismembering himself; but when that is once done, he has no longer any merit: for though it is out of his power to steal, yet he may all his life be a thief in his heart. So when a man has once become a Carthusian, he is obliged to continue so whether he chooses it or not. Their silence, too, is absurd. We read in the Gospel of the apostles being sent to preach, but not to hold their tongues. All severity that does not tend to increase good, or prevent evil, is idle. I said to the Lady Abbess of a convent, 'Madam, you are here not for the love of virtue but the fear of vice.' She said she should remember this as long as she lived.

Ib. ii. 435.

.˙.

Of these recluses it may without uncharitable censure be affirmed, that they have secured their innocence by the loss of their virtue ; that to avoid the commission of some faults they have made many duties impracticable ; and that, lest they should do what they ought *not* to do, they leave much *undone* which they ought to *do*.

Works, ix. 313.

Money:

Money:

THERE are few ways in which a man can be more in-nocently employed than in getting money.

Boswell's *Life of Johnson*, ii. 323.

.·.

GETTING money is not all a man's business: to cultivate kindness is a valuable part of the business of life.

Ib. iii. 182.

.·.

THERE is no condition which is not disquieted either with the care of gaining or of keeping money; and the race of man may be divided in a political estimate between those who are practising fraud, and those who are repelling it.

Rambler, No. 131.

.·.

'WHEN a gentleman told Dr. Johnson he had bought a suit of lace for his lady, he said "Well, Sir, you have done a good thing and a wise thing." "I have done a good thing," said the gentleman, "but I do not know that I have done a wise thing." JOHNSON. "Yes, Sir, no money is better spent than what is laid out for domestic satisfaction. A man is pleased that his wife is drest as well as other people; and a wife is pleased that she is drest."'

Boswell's *Life of Johnson*, ii. 352.

.·.

MANY there are who openly and almost professedly regulate all their conduct by their love of money; who have no other reason for action or forbearance, for compliance or refusal, than that they hope to gain more by one than by the other. These are indeed the meanest and cruellest of human beings, a race with whom, as with some pestiferous

O animals,

animals, the whole creation seems to be at war; but who, however detested or scorned, long continue to add heap to heap, and when they have reduced one to beggary, are still permitted to fasten on another.

Rambler, No. 175.

∴

MONEY and time are the heaviest burdens of life, and the unhappiest of all mortals are those who have more of either than they know how to use.

Idler, No. 30.

Morality of an action:

THE morality of an action depends on the motive from which we act. If I fling half-a-crown to a beggar with intention to break his head, and he picks it up and buys victuals with it, the physical effect is good; but, with respect to me, the action is very wrong. So religious exercises, if not performed with an intention to please God, avail us nothing. As our Saviour says of those who perform them from other motives, 'Verily they have their reward.'

Boswell's *Life of Johnson*, i. 397.

Moral good and physical evil:

ALMOST all the moral good which is left among us is the apparent effect of physical evil.

Idler, No. 89.

Music:

'UPON his hearing a celebrated performer go through a hard composition, and hearing it remarked that it was very difficult, Dr. Johnson said, "I would it had been impossible."'

Boswell's *Life of Johnson*, ii. 409 *n*. 1.

National

National debt:

NOTHING is more easy than to clear debts by borrowing, or to borrow when a nation is mortgaged for the payment.

Debates. Works, x. 179.

. · .

WE ought to be honest at all events; we are at liberty likewise to be generous at our own expense, but I think we have hardly a right to boast of our liberality when we contract debts for the advantage of the House of Austria, and leave them to be paid by the industry or frugality of succeeding ages.

Ib. xi. 219.

. · .

SPEAKING of the national debt Dr. Johnson said, it was an idle dream to suppose that the country could sink under it. Let the public creditors be ever so clamorous the interest of millions must ever prevail over that of thousands.

Boswell's *Life of Johnson*, ii. 127.

Native place:

EVERY man has a lurking wish to appear considerable in his native place.

Ib. ii. 141.

Nature:

NATURE never gives everything at once.

Works, ix. 29.

Neatness in excess:

' I asked Mr. Johnson if he ever disputed with his wife. " Perpetually," said he ; " my wife had a particular reverence for cleanliness, and desired the praise of neatness in her dress and furniture, as many ladies do, till they become trouble-some to their best friends, slaves to their own besoms, and

only

only sigh for the hour of sweeping their husbands out of the house as dirt and useless lumber. A clean floor is so comfortable, she would say sometimes by way of twitting; till at last I told her that I thought we had had talk enough about the floor, we would now have a touch at the ceiling." I asked him if he ever huffed his wife about his dinner. "So often," replied he, "that at last she called to me and said, Nay, hold Mr. Johnson, and do not make a farce of thanking God for a dinner which in a few minutes you will protest not eatable."'

Piozzi's Anecdotes, pp. 146, 150.

'Needs'—a young lady's 'needs':

'DURING a visit of Miss Brown's to Streatham, Dr. Johnson was enquiring of her several things that she could not answer; and, as he held her so cheap in regard to books, he began to question her concerning domestic affairs,—puddings, pies, plain work, and so forth. Miss Brown, not at all more able to give a good account of herself in these articles than in the others, began all her answers with "Why, Sir, one need not be obliged to do so,—or so," whatever was the thing in question. When he had finished his interrogatories, and she had finished her " need nots," he ended the discourse with saying, "As to your needs, my dear, they are so very many, that you would be frightened yourself if you knew half of them."'

Mme. D'Arblay's Diary, i. 104.

New things and familiar things:

IN this work[1] are exhibited, in a very high degree, the

---

[1] *The Rape of the Lock.*

two

two most engaging powers of an author. New things are made familiar, and familiar things are made new.

Works, viii. 332.

Newspapers:

JOURNALS are daily multiplied without increase of knowledge. The tale of the morning paper is told again in the evening, and the narratives of the evening are bought again in the morning. These repetitions, indeed, waste time but they do not shorten it. The most eager peruser of news is tired before he has completed his labour; and many a man who enters the coffee-house in his night-gown[1] and slippers is called away to his shop, or his dinner, before he has well considered the state of *Europe*. It is discovered by *Reaumur* that spiders might make silk if they could be persuaded to live in peace together. The writers of news, if they could be confederated, might give more pleasure to the public. The morning and evening authors might divide an event between them; a single action, and that not of much importance, might be gradually discovered so as to vary a whole week with joy, anxiety, and conjecture.

Idler, No. 7.

Newswriters:

To write news in its perfection requires such a combination of qualities that a man completely fitted for the task is not always to be found. In Sir *Henry Wotton's* jocular definition, *An ambassador* is said to be *a man of virtue sent abroad to tell lies for the advantage of his country;* a newswriter is *a man without virtue, who writes lies at home for his own profit.*

Ib. No. 30.

---

[1] Dressing-gown.

No

No turn to Economy:

'MRS. THRALE asked whether Mr. Langton took any better care of his affairs than formerly? " No, Madam," cried the doctor, " and never will ; he complains of the ill effects of habit, and rests contentedly upon a confessed indolence.　He told his father himself that he had ' no turn to economy'; but a thief might as well plead that he had no turn to honesty."'

Mme. D'Arblay's Diary, i. 75.

Notes :

NOTES are often necessary, but they are necessary evils. Let him that is yet unacquainted with the powers of Shakespeare, and who desires to feel the highest pleasure that the drama can give, read every play, from the first scene to the last, with utter negligence of all his commentators.　When his fancy is once on the wing let it not stoop at correction or explanation.　When his attention is strongly engaged let it disdain alike to turn aside to the name of Theobald and of Pope.　Let him read on through brightness and obscurity, through integrity and corruption; let him preserve his comprehension of the dialogue and his interest in the fable.　And when the pleasures of novelty have ceased let him attempt exactness and read the commentators.

Works, v. 152.

IF my readings are of little value they have not been ostentatiously displayed or importunately obtruded.　I could have written longer notes, for the art of writing notes is not of difficult attainment.　The work is performed first by railing at the stupidity, negligence, ignorance, and asinine tastelessness of the former editors, and showing, from all

that

that goes before and all that follows, the inelegance and absurdity of the old reading; then by proposing something which to superficial readers would seem specious, but which the editor rejects with indignation; then by producing the true reading with a long paraphrase, and concluding with loud acclamations on the discovery, and a sober wish for the advancement and prosperity of genuine criticism.

Works, v. 149.

Novels:

IT is not a sufficient vindication of a character, that it is drawn as it appears; for many characters ought never to be drawn: nor of a narrative, that the train of events is agreeable to observation and experience; for that observation which is called knowledge of the world will be found much more frequently to make men cunning than good. . . . Many writers, for the sake of following nature, so mingle good and bad qualities in their principal personages that they are both equally conspicuous; and as we accompany them through their adventures with delight, and are led by degrees to interest ourselves in their favour, we lose the abhorrence of their faults because they do not hinder our pleasure, or, perhaps, regard them with some kindness for being united with so much merit. . . . . Vice, for vice is necessary to be shown, should always disgust; nor should the graces of gaiety or the dignity of courage be so united with it, as to reconcile it to the mind. Wherever it appears, it should raise hatred by the malignity of its practices and contempt by the meanness of its stratagems: for while it is supported by either parts or spirit, it will be seldom heartily abhorred. The Roman tyrant was content to be hated if he was but

feared;

feared; and there are thousands of the readers of romances willing to be thought wicked if they may be allowed to be wits. It is therefore to be steadily inculcated, that virtue is the highest proof of understanding and the only solid basis of greatness, and that vice is the natural consequence of narrow thoughts; that it begins in mistake and ends in ignominy. *Rambler*, No. 4.

Oats:

A GRAIN which in England is generally given to horses, but in Scotland supports the people. *Dictionary.*

Objections:

OBJECTIONS crowd upon us without being sought, and instead of exercising our sagacity weary our attention.

Debates. Works, x. 344.

. · .

'JOHNSON observed that so many objections might be made to everything, that nothing could overcome them but the necessity of doing something. No man would be of any profession, as simply opposed to not being of it: but every one must do something.' Boswell's *Life of Johnson*, ii. 128.

Obligations:

To be obliged is to be in some respect inferior to another; and few willingly indulge the memory of an action which raises one whom they have always been accustomed to think below them, but satisfy themselves with faint praise and penurious payment, and then drive it from their own minds and endeavour to conceal it from the knowledge of others. *Rambler*, No. 166.

Ocean:

Ocean:

'A GENTLEMAN once told Dr. Johnson that a friend of his, looking into the Dictionary which the Doctor had lately published, could not find the word *ocean*. "Not find ocean," exclaimed our Lexicographer; "Sir, I doubt the veracity of your information!" He instantly stalked into his library and, opening the work in question with the utmost impatience, at last triumphantly put his finger upon the subject of research, adding, "There, Sir; there is *ocean*!" The gentleman was preparing to apologise for the mistake; but Dr. Johnson good-naturedly dismissed the subject with "Never mind it, Sir; perhaps your friend spells *ocean* with an *s*."'

Murray's Johnsoniana, p. 423.

Old age:

AT length weariness succeeds to labour, and the mind lies at ease in the contemplation of her own attainments without any desire of new conquests or excursions. This is the age of recollection and narrative; the opinions are settled and the avenues of apprehension shut against any new intelligence; the days that are to follow must pass in the inculcation of precepts already collected, and assertion of tenets already received; nothing is henceforward so odious as opposition, so insolent as doubt, or so dangerous as novelty.

Rambler, No. 151.

. • .

IN the decline of life shame and grief are of short duration; whether it be that we bear easily what we have borne long, or that, finding ourselves in age less regarded, we less regard others; or, that we look with slight regard

upon

upon afflictions to which we know that the hand of death is about to put an end.

Rasselas, ch. 4.

Old men:

THERE is nothing against which an old man should be so much upon his guard as putting himself to nurse.

Boswell's *Life of Johnson*, ii. 474.

THERE is a wicked inclination in most people to suppose an old man decayed in his intellects. If a young or middle-aged man, when leaving a company, does not recollect where he laid his hat, it is nothing; but if the same inattention is discovered in an old man, people will shrug up their shoulders, and say 'His memory is going.'

Ib. iv. 181.

Omens:

THEY returned to their work day after day, and in a short time found a fissure in the rock which enabled them to pass far with very little obstruction. This Rasselas considered as a good omen. 'Do not disturb your mind,' said Imlac, 'with other hopes or fears than reason may suggest; if you are pleased with prognostics of good you will be terrified likewise with tokens of evil, and your whole life will be a prey to superstition. Whatever facilitates our work is more than an omen, it is a cause of success.

Rasselas, ch. 13.

Opinions:

THE greatest part of mankind have no other reason for their opinions than that they are in fashion.　　*Works*, v. 58.

THE

THE opinions of every man must be learned from himself: concerning his practice it is safest to trust the evidence of others. Where these testimonies concur no higher degree of historical certainty can be obtained. *Works*, vi. 503.

Overlooking the boundaries:

EVEN those that have most reverence for the laws of right are pleased with showing that not fear, but choice, regulates their behaviour; and would be thought to comply rather than obey. We love to overlook the boundaries which we do not wish to pass; and as the Roman satirist remarks, he that has no design to take the life of another is yet glad to have it in his hands. *Rambler*, No. 114.

Over-work:

WHOEVER takes up life beforehand by depriving himself of rest and refreshment must not only pay back the hours, but pay them back with usury. *Ib.* No. 48.

Pain:

INFELICITY is involved in corporeal nature and interwoven with our being; all attempts therefore to decline it wholly are useless and vain: the armies of pain send their arrows against us on every side, the choice is only between those which are more or less sharp or tinged with poison of greater or less malignity; and the strongest armour which reason can supply will only blunt their points but cannot repel them. *Ib.* No. 32.

.·.

OUR sense is so much stronger of what we suffer than of what we enjoy, that the ideas of pain predominate in almost every mind. What is recollection but a revival of vexations, or history but a record of wars, treasons and calamities? Death, which is considered as the greatest evil, happens to all. The greatest good, be it what it will, is the lot but of a part.

Works, ix. 105.

Paradise Lost:

The plan of *Paradise Lost* has this inconvenience, that it comprises neither human actions nor human manners. The man and woman who act and suffer are in a state which no other man or woman can ever know. The reader finds no transaction in which he can be engaged; beholds no condition in which he can by any effort of imagination place himself; he has therefore little natural curiosity or sympathy. We all, indeed, feel the effects of Adam's disobedience; we all sin like Adam and like him must all bewail our offences; we have restless and insidious enemies in the fallen angels; and in the blessed spirits we have guardians and friends; in the redemption of mankind we hope to be included; and in the description of heaven and hell we are surely interested, as we are all to reside hereafter either in the regions of horror or of bliss. But these truths are too important to be new; they have been taught to our infancy; they have mingled with our solitary thoughts and familiar conversations and are habitually interwoven with the whole texture of life. Being therefore not new they raise no unaccustomed emotion in the mind; what we knew before we cannot learn; what is not unexpected cannot surprise.

Ib. vii. 134.

Paraphrases:

'Returning through the house, Johnson stepped into a small study or book room. The first book he laid his hands

upon

upon was Harwood's *Liberal Translation of the New Testament*. The passage which first caught his eye was from that sublime apostrophe in St. John upon the raising of Lazarus, "Jesus wept;" which Harwood had conceitedly rendered "and Jesus, the Saviour of the world, burst into a flood of tears." He contemptuously threw the book aside, exclaiming, "Puppy!" I then showed him Sterne's Sermons. "Sir," said he, "do you ever read any others?" "Yes, Doctor: I read Sherlock, Tillotson, Beveridge, and others." "Ay, Sir, *there* you drink the cup of salvation to the bottom; here you have merely the froth from the surface."'

Croker's Boswell, 8vo ed. p. 836.

Parents :

In general those parents have most reverence who most deserve it; for he that lives well cannot be despised.

Rasselas, ch. 26.

. . .

The unjustifiable severity of a parent is loaded with this aggravation, that those whom he injures are always in his sight. The injustice of a prince is often exercised upon those of whom he never had any personal or particular knowledge; and the sentence which he pronounces, whether of banishment, imprisonment, or death, removes from his view the man whom he condemns. But the domestic oppressor dooms himself to gaze upon those faces which he clouds with terror and with sorrow; and beholds every moment the effects of his own barbarities. He that can bear to give continual pain to those who surround him and can walk with satisfaction in the gloom of his own presence; he that can see submissive misery without relenting, and meet without emotion the eye that implores mercy or

demands

demands justice, will scarcely be amended by remonstrance or admonition; he has found means of stopping the avenues of tenderness and arming his heart against the force of reason.

Rambler, No. 148.

Parliament:

IF such petitions as these[1] are admitted, if the legislature shall submit to receive laws, and subjects resume at pleasure the power with which the government is vested, what is this assembly but a convention of empty phantoms whose determinations are nothing more than a mockery of state? Every insult upon this house is a violation of our constitution; and the constitution, like every other fabric, by being often battered must fall at last. It is indeed already destroyed if there be in the nation any body of men who shall with impunity refuse to comply with the laws, plead the great charter of liberty against those powers that made it, and fix the limits of their own obedience.

Debates. Works, x. 362.

Parodies:

'JOHNSON was present when a tragedy was read in which there occurred this line :—

"Who rules o'er freemen should himself be free."

The company having admired it much, "I cannot agree with you (said Johnson :) it might as well be said,—

Who drives fat oxen should himself be fat."'

Boswell's Life of Johnson, iv. 312.

---

[1] In a petition from certain inhabitants of Gloucestershire against the Seamen's Bill of 1741, it was stated that 'such a law could never be obeyed, or much blood would be shed in consequence of it.'—Works, x. 362.

I PUT

I PUT my hat upon my head
  And walked into the Strand,
And there I met another man
  With his hat in his hand.

Boswell's Life of Johnson, ii. 136 n. 4.

.˙.

I THEREFORE pray thee, Renny dear,
  That thou wilt give to me,
With cream and sugar soften'd well,
  Another dish of tea.

Nor fear that I, my gentle maid,
  Shall long detain the cup,
When once unto the bottom I
  Have drunk the liquor up.

Yet hear, alas! this mournful truth,
  Nor hear it with a frown;—
Thou canst not make the tea so fast
  As I can gulp it down.

Murray's Johnsoniana, p. 175.

.˙.

'HERMIT hoar, in solemn cell,
  Wearing out life's evening gray;
Smite thy bosom, sage, and tell
  What is bliss? and which the way?'

Thus I spoke; and speaking sigh'd;
  —Scarce repress'd the starting tear;—
When the smiling sage reply'd—
  '—Come, my lad, and drink some beer.'

Boswell's Life of Johnson, iii. 159.

.˙.

THE tender infant, meek and mild,
  Fell down upon the stone;
The nurse took up the squealing child,
  But still the child squealed on.

Piozzi's Anecdotes, p. 66.

LINES

LINES written in ridicule of certain Poems published in
1777[1].

> Wheresoe'er I turn my view,
> All is strange, yet nothing new;
> Endless labour all along,
> Endless labour to be wrong;
> Phrase that time hath flung away,
> Uncouth words in disarray,
> Trick'd in antique ruff and bonnet,
> Ode, and elegy, and sonnet.

Piozzi's Anecdotes, p. 64.

Party:

HE that changes his party by his humour is not more
virtuous than he that changes it by his interest: he loves
himself rather than truth.   Works, vii. 81.

. . .

'DR. JOHNSON said a certain eminent political friend of
ours[2] was wrong in his maxim of sticking to a certain set
of *men* on all occasions. "I can see that a man may do
right to stick to a *party* (said he;) that is to say, he is a
Whig, or he is a *Tory*, and he thinks one of those parties
upon the whole the best, and that to make it prevail, it
must be generally supported, though in particulars it may
be wrong. He takes its faggot of principles, in which there
are fewer rotten sticks than in the other, though some rotten
sticks to be sure; and they cannot well be separated. But,
to bind one's self to one man, or one set of men, (who may
be right to-day and wrong to-morrow,) without any general
preference of system, I must disapprove."'

Boswell's Life of Johnson, v. 36.

---

[1] By Thomas Warton.   [2] Edmund Burke.

Pastorals:

Pastorals:

THERE is something in the poetical *Arcadia* so remote from known reality and speculative possibility that we can never support its representation through a long work. A Pastoral of a hundred lines may be endured; but who will hear of sheep and goats, and myrtle bowers and purling rivulets through five acts? Such scenes please barbarians in the dawn of literature and children in the dawn of life; but will be for the most part thrown away as men grow wise and nations grow learned. *Works*, viii. 71.

Patience:

LEST we should think ourselves too soon entitled to the mournful privileges of irresistible misery, it is proper to reflect that the utmost anguish which human wit can contrive, or human malice can inflict, has been borne with constancy; and that if the pains of disease be, as I believe they are, sometimes greater than those of artificial torture, they are therefore in their own nature shorter: the vital frame is quickly broken or the union between soul and body is for a time suspended by insensibility, and we soon cease to feel our maladies when they once become too violent to be borne. I think there is some reason for questioning whether the body and mind are not so pro-portioned that the one can bear all that can be inflicted on the other, whether virtue cannot stand its ground as long as life, and whether a soul well principled will not be separated sooner than subdued. *Rambler*, No. 32.

Patriotism:

PATRIOTISM is the last refuge of a scoundrel.

Boswell's Life of Johnson, ii. 348.

PATRIOTISM is not necessarily included in rebellion. A
man may hate his king yet not love his country.

Works, vi. 216.

Pedantry:

THE general reproach with which ignorance revenges the
superciliousness of learning is that of pedantry; a censure
which every man incurs who has at any time the misfortune
to talk to those who cannot understand him, and by which
the modest and timorous are sometimes frighted from the
display of their acquisitions and the exertion of their powers.

Rambler, No. 173.

Peevishness:

KNOWLEDGE and genius are often enemies to quiet by
suggesting ideas of excellence which men and the performances of men cannot attain. But let no man rashly determine that his unwillingness to be pleased is a proof of
understanding unless his superiority appears from less
doubtful evidence; for though peevishness may sometimes
justly boast its descent from learning or from wit, it is much
oftener of a base extraction, the child of vanity and nursling
of ignorance.   *Rambler*, No. 74.

Pen:

TOM [BIRCH] is a lively rogue; he remembers a great
deal, and can tell many pleasant stories; but a pen is to
Tom a torpedo, the touch of it benumbs his hand and his
brain.   Boswell's *Life of Johnson*, i. 159 *n.* 4.

Penal laws:

MAN is for the most part equally unhappy when subjected
without redress to the passions of another, or left without

control

control to the dominion of his own. This every man, however unwilling he may be to own it of himself, will very readily acknowledge of his neighbour. No man knows any one except himself whom he judges fit to be set free from the coercion of laws, and to be abandoned entirely to his own choice. By this consideration have all civilized nations been induced to the enactions of penal laws, laws by which every man's danger becomes every man's safety and by which though all are restrained yet all are benefited. *Works,* ix. 507.

Penitence :

'UPON the question whether a man who had been guilty of vicious actions would do well to force himself into solitude and sadness; JOHNSON. "No, Sir, unless it prevent him from being vicious again. With some people, gloomy penitence is only madness turned upside down. A man may be gloomy till, in order to be relieved from gloom, he has recourse again to criminal indulgencies." '

Boswell's *Life of Johnson,* iii. 27.

Pension :

AN allowance made to any one without an equivalent. In England it is generally understood to mean pay given to a state hireling for treason to his country. *Dictionary.*

Penuriousness :

'TALKING of a penurious gentleman of our acquaintance, Johnson said, "Sir, he is narrow, not so much from avarice as from impotence to spend his money. He cannot find in his heart to pour out a bottle of wine; but he would not much care if it should sour." '

Boswell's *Life of Johnson,* iii. 40.

Penury :

Penury:

RICHES cannot be within the reach of great numbers, because to be rich is to possess more than is commonly placed in a single hand; and, if many could obtain the sum which now makes a man wealthy, the name of wealth must then be transferred to still greater accumulation. But I am not certain that it is equally impossible to exempt the lower classes of mankind from poverty; because, though whatever be the wealth of the community, some will always have least, and he that has less than any other is comparatively poor; yet I do not see any coactive necessity that many should be without the indispensable conveniencies of life; but am sometimes inclined to imagine that, casual calamities excepted, there might by universal prudence be procured an universal exemption from want; and that he who should happen to have least, might notwithstanding have enough. . . . The prospect of penury in age is so gloomy and terrifying that every man who looks before him must resolve to avoid it; and it must be avoided generally by the science of sparing. For, though in every age there are some, who by bold adventures or by favourable accidents, rise suddenly to riches, yet it is dangerous to indulge hopes of such rare events: and the bulk of mankind must owe their affluence to small and gradual profits, below which their expense must be resolutely reduced.

Rambler, No. 57.

People:

THE princess found their [1] thoughts narrow, their wishes low, and their merriment often artificial. Their pleasures, poor as they were, could not be preserved pure, but were

---

[1] People of middle fortune.

embittered

embittered by petty competitions and worthless emulation. They were always jealous of the beauty of each other; of a quality to which solicitude can add nothing, and from which detraction can take nothing away. Many were in love with triflers like themselves, and many fancied that they were in love when in truth they were only idle. Their affection was not fixed on sense or virtue, and therefore seldom ended but in vexation. Their grief, however, like their joy, was transient; everything floated in their mind unconnected with the past or future, so that one desire easily gave way to another, as a second stone cast into the water effaces and confounds the circles of the first.

Rasselas, ch. 25.

I BELIEVE it will always be found that it is dangerous to gratify the people at their own expense, and to sacrifice their interest to their caprices. *Debates. Works*, xi. 177.

THE people are starving by thousands and murmuring by millions. *Ib.* x. 209.

I HAVE found reason to pay great regard to the voice of the people in cases where knowledge has been forced upon them by experience, without long deductions or deep researches. *Rambler*, No. 25.

Performance and possibility:

THE distance is commonly very great between actual performances and speculative possibility. It is natural to suppose that as much as has been done to-day may be

done

done to-morrow: but on the morrow some difficulty emerges, or some external impediment obstructs. Indolence, interruption, business, and pleasure, all take their turns of retardation; and every long work is lengthened by a thousand causes that can, and ten thousand that cannot, be recounted. Perhaps no extensive and multifarious pèrformance was ever effected within the term originally fixed in the undertaker's mind. He that runs against Time has an antagonist not subject to casualties.

Works, viii. 255.

Perseverance:

ALL the performances of human art at which we look with praise or wonder are instances of the resistless force of perseverance; it is by this that the quarry becomes a pyramid, and that distant countries ar united with canals. If a man was to compare the effect of a single stroke of the pickaxe, or of one impression of the spade, with the general design and last result, he would be overwhelmed by the sense of their disproportion; yet these petty operations, incessantly continued, in time surmount the greatest difficulties, and mountains are levelled and oceans bounded by the slender force of human beings.   *Rambler,* No. 43.

Petitioning:

THIS petitioning is a new mode of distressing government, and a mighty easy one. I will undertake to get petitions either against quarter-guineas or half-guineas, with the help of a little hot wine. There must be no yielding to encourage this. The object is not important enough. We are not to blow up half a dozen palaces because one cottage is burning.   Boswell's *Life of Johnson,* ii. 90.

THE

THE progress of a petition is well known. An ejected placeman goes down to his county or his borough, tells his friends of his inability to serve them ; and his constituents, of the corruption of the government. His friends readily understand that he who can get nothing will have nothing to give. They agree to proclaim a meeting; meat and drink are plentifully provided ; a crowd is easily brought together, and those who think that they know the reason of their meeting undertake to tell those who know it not. Ale and clamour unite their powers ; the crowd, condensed and heated, begins to ferment with the leaven of sedition. All see a thousand evils though they cannot show them, and grow impatient for a remedy though they know not what. A speech is then made by the Cicero of the day ; he says much and suppresses more ; and credit is equally given to what he tells and what he conceals. The petition is read and universally approved. Those who are sober enough to write add their names, and the rest would sign it if they could. Every man goes home and tells his neighbour of the glories of the day ; how he was consulted and what he advised ; how he was invited into the great room, where his lordship called him by his name ; how he was caressed by Sir Francis, Sir Joseph, or Sir George ; how he ate turtle and venison, and drank unanimity to the three brothers.

The poor loiterer, whose shop had confined him or whose wife had locked him up, hears the tale of luxury with envy, and at last inquires what was their petition. Of the petition nothing is remembered by the narrator, but that it spoke much of fears and apprehensions and something very alarming, and that he is sure it is against the government; the other is convinced that it must be right,

and

and wishes he had been there, for he loves wine and venison, and is resolved as long as he lives to be against the government.   The petition is then handed from town to town, and from house to house; and wherever it comes, the inhabitants flock together that they may see that which must be sent to the king.   Names are easily collected. One man signs because he hates the papists, another because he has vowed destruction to the turnpikes; one because it will vex the parson, another because he owes his landlord nothing; one because he is rich, another because he is poor; one to show that he is not afraid, and another to show that he can write.   *Works*, vi. 172.

Piety:

A WICKED fellow is the most pious when he takes to it. He'll beat you all at piety.   Boswell's *Life of Johnson*, iv. 289.

Pilgrimages:

'PILGRIMAGE,' said Imlac, 'like many other acts of piety, may be reasonable or superstitious, according to the principles upon which it is performed.   Long journeys in search of truth are not commanded.   Truth, such as is necessary to the regulation of life, is always found where it is honestly sought.   Change of place is no natural cause of the increase of piety, for it inevitably produces dissipation of mind.   Yet, since men go every day to view the fields where great actions have been performed, and return with stronger impressions of the event, curiosity of the same kind may naturally dispose us to view that country whence our religion had its beginning; and I believe no man surveys those awful scenes without some

confirmation

confirmation of holy resolutions. That the Supreme Being may be more easily propitiated in one place than in another is the dream of idle superstition; but that some places may operate upon our own minds in an uncommon manner is an opinion which hourly experience will justify. He who supposes that his vices may be more successfully combated in Palestine, will, perhaps, find himself mistaken, yet he may go thither without folly: he who thinks they will be more freely pardoned, dishonours at once his reason and religion.'

Rasselas, ch. 11.

Wit and Wisdom of Samuel Johnson.

Place and power:

To be out of place is not necessarily to be out of power.

Debates. Works, xi. 111.

Plantation:

PLANTATION is naturally the employment of a mind un-burdened with care and vacant to futurity, saturated with present good, and at leisure to derive gratification from the prospect of posterity. He that pines with hunger is in little care how others shall be fed. The poor man is seldom studious to make his grandson rich.

Works, ix. 137.

Pleasing:

MEN may be convinced, but they cannot be pleased, against their will.

Ib. viii. 26.

.·.

WE all live upon the hope of pleasing somebody.

Boswell's *Life of Johnson,* ii. 22.

Pleased

Pleased with oneself:

HE that is pleased with himself easily imagines that he shall please others.

Works, viii. 237.

Pleasure :

THERE are goods so opposed that we cannot seize both, but, by too much prudence, may pass between them at too great a distance to reach either. This is often the fate of long consideration ; he does nothing who endeavours to do more than is allowed to humanity. Flatter not yourself with contrarieties of pleasure. Of the blessings set before you make your choice and be content. No man can taste the fruits of autumn while he is delighting his scent with the flowers of the spring : no man can, at the same time, fill his cup from the source and from the mouth of the Nile.

Rasselas, ch. 29.

.·.

'TALKING of a man's resolving to deny himself the use of wine from moral and religious considerations, Dr. Johnson said, "He must not doubt about it. When one doubts as to pleasure we know what will be the conclusion. I now no more think of drinking wine than a horse does. The wine upon the table is no more for me than for the dog that is under the table [1]."'

Boswell's *Life of Johnson*, iii. 250.

.·.

IT is well known that the most certain way to give any man pleasure is to persuade him that you receive pleasure from him, to encourage him to freedom and confidence, and

---

[1] Johnson for many years abstained from all intoxicating liquors.

to

to avoid any such appearance of superiority as may overbear and depress him. We see many that by this art only spend their days in the midst of caresses, invitations, and civilities; and without any extraordinary qualities or attainments are the universal favourites of both sexes, and certainly find a friend in every place. *Rambler*, No. 72.

No man is a hypocrite in his pleasures.

Boswell's *Life of Johnson*, iv. 316.

THE public pleasures of far the greater part of mankind are counterfeit. *Idler*, No. 18.

THE general employment of mankind is to increase pleasure or remove the pressure of pain. These are the vital principles of action that fill ports with ships, shops with manufactures, and fields with husbandmen, that keep the statesman diligent in attendance and the trader active in his business. *Works*, ix. 452.

Poets:

NEW arts are long in the world before poets describe them; for they borrow everything from their predecessors, and commonly derive very little from nature or from life.

Works, vii. 316.

To a poet nothing can be useless. *Rasselas*, ch. 10.

IT may have been observed by every reader that there are certain topics which never are exhausted. Of some

images

images and sentiments the mind of man may be said to be enamoured; it meets them, however often they occur, with the same ardour which a lover feels at the sight of his mistress, and parts from them with the same regret when they can no longer be enjoyed. . . . When night overshadows a romantic scene, all is stillness, silence, and quiet; the poets of the grove cease their melody, the moon towers over the world in gentle majesty, men forget their labours and their cares, and every passion and pursuit is for a while suspended. All this we know already, yet we hear it repeated without weariness; because such is generally the life of man, that he is pleased to think on the time when he shall pause from a sense of his condition. *Adventurer*, No. 108.

Poetry:

PLEASURE and terror are indeed the genuine sources of poetry; but poetical pleasure must be such as human imagination can at least conceive; and poetical terror such as human strength and fortitude may combat. The good and evil of eternity are too ponderous for the wings of wit; the mind sinks under them in passive helplessness, content with calm belief and humble adoration. *Works*, vii. 135.

. · .

No poem should be long of which the purpose is only to strike the fancy, without enlightening the understanding by precept, ratiocination, or narrative. A blaze first pleases, and then tires the sight. *Ib*. viii. 59.

. · .

WORDS too familiar or too remote defeat the purpose of a poet. From those sounds which we hear on small or on coarse occasions, we do not easily receive strong impres-

sions

sions or delightful images; and words to which we are nearly strangers whenever they occur, draw that attention on themselves which they should transmit to things.

Works, vii. 308.

Pointed axioms and acute replies:

POINTED axioms and acute replies fly loose about the world, and are assigned successively to those whom it may be the fashion to celebrate.

Ib. vii. 200.

Policy and morality:

GOVERNMENT will not perhaps soon arrive at such purity and excellence but that some connivance at least will be indulged to the triumphant robber and successful cheat. He that brings wealth home is seldom interrogated by what means it was obtained. This, however, is one of those modes of corruption with which mankind ought always to struggle, and which they may in time hope to overcome. There is reason to expect that as the world is more enlightened, policy and morality will at last be reconciled, and that nations will learn not to do what they would not suffer.

Works, vi. 183.

Politeness:

THE universal axiom in which all complaisance is included, and from which flow all the formalities which custom has established in civilized nations, is, *That no man shall give any preference to himself.* A rule so comprehensive and certain that, perhaps, it is not easy for the mind to image an incivility without supposing it to be broken.

Rambler, No. 98.

POLITENESS

POLITENESS is fictitious benevolence. It supplies the place of it amongst those who see each other only in public or but little. Depend upon it, the want of it never fails to produce something disagreeable to one or other. I have always applied to good breeding what Addison, in his *Cato*[1], says of honour :—

> ' Honour 's a sacred tie; the law of Kings;
> The noble mind's distinguishing perfection,
> That aids and strengthens Virtue where it meets her;
> And imitates her actions where she is not.'

Boswell's Life of Johnson, v. 82.

Political second sight:

IT is said of those who have the wonderful power called second sight, that they seldom see anything but evil: political second sight has the same effect; we hear of nothing but of an alarming crisis, of violated rights and expiring liberties. The morning rises upon new wrongs, and the dreamer passes the night in imaginary shackles. The sphere of anxiety is now enlarged; he that hitherto cared only for himself now cares for the public; for he has learned that the happiness of individuals is comprised in the prosperity of the whole, and that his country never suffers but he suffers with it, however it happens that he feels no pain. Fired with this fever of epidemic patriotism, the tailor slips his thimble, the draper drops his yard, and the blacksmith lays down his hammer; they meet at an honest alehouse, consider the state of the nation, read or hear the last petition, lament the miseries of the time, are alarmed at the dreadful crisis, and subscribe to the support of the bill of rights.

Works, vi. 170.

---

[1] Act ii. sc. 5.

Posterity:

Posterity:

POSTERITY is always the author's favourite.

Piozzi Letters, ii. 14.

.·.

LAWS are formed by the manners and exigencies of particular times, and it is but accidental that they last longer than their causes : the limitation of feudal succession to the male arose from the obligation of the tenant to attend his chief in war. As times and opinions are always changing, I know not whether it be not usurpation to prescribe rules to posterity, by presuming to judge of what we cannot know; and I know not whether I fully approve either your[1] design or your father's, to limit that succession which descended to you unlimited. If we are to leave *sartum tectum*[2] to posterity, what we have without any merit of our own received from our ancestors, should not choice and free-will be kept unviolated? Is land to be treated with more reverence than liberty?

Boswell's Life of Johnson, ii. 416.

Poverty:

IT will be found upon a nearer view that they who extol the happiness of poverty, do not mean the same state with those who deplore its miseries. Poets have their imaginations filled with ideas of magnificence; and being accustomed to contemplate the downfall of empires, or to contrive forms of lamentations for monarchs in distress, rank all the classes of mankind in a state of poverty who make no approaches to the dignity of crowns. To be poor,

---

[1] Boswell's.

[2] The technical term in Roman law for a building in good repair.

in

in the epic language, is only not to command the wealth of nations, nor to have fleets and armies in pay.

Rambler, No. 202.

.˙.

POVERTY has, in large cities, very different appearances: it is often concealed in splendour, and often in extravagance. It is the care of a very great part of mankind to conceal their indigence from the rest : they support themselves by temporary expedients, and every day is lost in contriving for the morrow.   *Rasselas*, ch. 25.

.˙.

THE inevitable consequence of poverty is dependence.

Works, vii. 299.

.˙.

POVERTY is very gently paraphrased by want of riches. In that sense almost every man may in his own opinion be poor. But there is another poverty which is want of competence of all that can soften the miseries of life, of all that can diversify attention or delight imagination. There is yet another poverty which is want of necessaries, a species of poverty which no care of the public, no charity of particulars, can preserve many from feeling openly and many secretly. That hope and fear are inseparably or very frequently connected with poverty and riches my surveys of life have not informed me. The milder degrees of poverty are sometimes supported by hope, but the more severe often sink down in motionless despondence. Life must be seen before it can be known. This author[1] and Pope[2] perhaps never saw the

---

[1] Soame Jenyns, author of *A Free Enquiry into the Nature and Origin of Evil.*

[2] Pope in the *Essay on Man*, Epistle III, shows that ‘ the whole

miseries

miseries which they imagine thus easy to be borne. The poor indeed are insensible of many little vexations which sometimes imbitter the possessions and pollute the enjoyments of the rich. They are not pained by casual incivility or mortified by the mutilation of a compliment; but this happiness is like that of a malefactor who ceases to feel the cords that bind him when the pincers are tearing his flesh.

Works, vi. 54.

THERE is a degree of want by which the freedom of agency is almost destroyed. *Ib.* viii. 402.

A MAN guilty of poverty easily believes himself suspected.

Rambler, No. 26.

RESOLVE not to be poor: whatever you have, spend less. Poverty is a great enemy to human happiness; it certainly destroys liberty, and it makes some virtues impracticable and others extremely difficult. Boswell's *Life of Johnson,* iv. 157.

POVERTY, like many other miseries of life, is often little more than an imaginary calamity. Men often call themselves poor, not because they want necessaries, but because they have not more than they want. *Works,* ix. 336.

THOUGH it should be granted that those who *are born to poverty and drudgery* should not be *deprived* by an *improper education* of the *opiate of ignorance,* even this concession will not be of much use to direct our practice unless it be

---

universe is one system of society,' that 'nothing is made wholly for itself, nor yet wholly for another,' and that 'the happiness of animals is mutual.' Jenyns quotes lines 27-40 of this Epistle.

Q   determined

determined who are those that are *born to poverty*. To entail irreversible poverty upon generation after generation only because the ancestor happened to be poor is in itself cruel, if not unjust, and is wholly contrary to the maxims of a commercial nation, which always suppose and promote a rotation of property, and offer every individual a chance of mending his condition by his diligence. Those who communicate literature to the son of a poor man consider him as one not born to poverty, but to the necessity of deriving a better fortune from himself. In this attempt, as in others, many fail and many succeed. Those that fail will feel their misery more acutely; but since poverty is now confessed to be such a calamity as cannot be borne without the opiate of insensibility, I hope the happiness of those whom education enables to escape from it may turn the balance against that exacerbation which the others suffer.

I am always afraid of determining on the side of envy or cruelty. The privileges of education may sometimes be improperly bestowed, but I shall always fear to withhold them lest I should be yielding to the suggestions of pride, while I persuade myself that I am following the maxims of policy; and under the appearance of salutary restraints should be indulging the lust of dominion and that malevolence which delights in seeing others depressed !

Works, vi. 56.

Power:

WHEN the power of birth and station ceases no hope remains but from the prevalence of money. Power and wealth supply the place of each other. Power confers the ability of gratifying our desire without the consent of others. Wealth enables us to obtain the consent of others to our gratification.

tion. Power, simply considered, whatever it confers on one must take from another. Wealth enables its owner to give to others by taking only from himself. Power pleases the violent and proud : wealth delights the placid and the timorous. Youth therefore flies at power, and age grovels after riches.

Works, ix. 91.

Praise :

JUST praise is only a debt, but flattery is a present.

Rambler, No. 155.

. : .

To charge all unmerited praise with the guilt of flattery, and to suppose that the encomiast always knows and feels the falsehoods of his assertions is surely to discover great ignorance of human nature and human life. In determinations depending not on rules but on experience and comparison, judgment is always in some degree subject to affection. Very near to admiration is the wish to admire.

Works, vii. 396.

. : .

No man can observe without indignation on what names, both of ancient and modern times, the utmost exuberance of praise has been lavished, and by what hands it has been bestowed. It has never yet been found that the tyrant, the plunderer, the oppressor, the most hateful of the hateful, the most profligate of the profligate, have been denied any celebrations which they were willing to purchase, or that wickedness and folly have not found correspondent flatterers through all their subordinations, except when they have been associated with avarice or poverty, and have wanted either inclination or ability to hire a panegyrist. As there

Wit and
Wisdom
of
Samuel
Johnson.

is no character so deformed as to fright away from it the prostitutes of praise, there is no degree of encomiastic veneration which pride has refused. The emperors of Rome suffered themselves to be worshipped in their lives with altars and sacrifices; and in an age more enlightened the terms peculiar to the praise and worship of the Supreme Being have been applied to wretches whom it was the reproach of humanity to number among men; and whom nothing but riches or power hindered those that read or wrote their deification from hunting into the toils of justice as disturbers of the peace of nature.   *Rambler*, No. 104.

PRAISE and money [are] the two powerful corrupters of mankind.   Boswell's *Life of Johnson*, iv. 242.

HE who praises everybody praises nobody.   *Ib.* iii. 225, *n.* 3.

MEN are seldom satisfied with praise introduced or followed by any mention of defect.   *Works*, viii. 297.

Prayer:

THE principle upon which extemporary prayer was originally introduced is no longer admitted. The minister formerly in the effusion of his prayer expected immediate and perhaps perceptible inspiration, and therefore thought it his duty not to think before what he should say. It is now universally confessed that men pray as they speak on other occasions, according to the general measure of their abilities and attainments. Whatever each may think of a form prescribed by another he cannot but believe that he can himself

compose

compose by study and meditation a better prayer than will rise in his mind at a sudden call; and if he has any hope of supernatural help why may he not as well receive it when he writes as when he speaks?   *Works,* ix. 102.

.•.

LET no man imagine that he may indulge his malice, his avarice, or his ambition at the expense of others; that he may raise himself to wealth and honour by the breach of every law of heaven and earth, then retire laden with the plunder of the miserable, spend his life in fantastic penances or false devotion, and by his compliance with the external duties of religion atone for withholding what he has torn away from the lawful possessor by rapine and extortion : let him not flatter himself with false persuasions that prayer and mortification can alter the great and invariable rules of reason and justice: let him not think that he can acquire a right to keep what he had no right to take away, or that frequent prostrations before God will justify his perseverance in oppressing men : let him be assured that his presence profanes the temple, and that his prayer will be turned into sin.   *Ib.* ix. 305.

Preaching:

'I TALKED of preaching and of the great success which those called Methodists have. JOHNSON. "Sir, it is owing to their expressing themselves in a plain and familiar manner, which is the only way to do good to the common people, and which clergymen of genius and learning ought to do from a principle of duty when it is suited to their congregations ; a practice for which they will be praised by men of sense. To insist against drunkenness as a crime because it

debases

debases reason, the noblest faculty of man, would be of no service to the common people: but to tell them that they may die in a fit of drunkenness, and show them how dreadful that would be, cannot fail to make a deep impression. Sir, when your Scotch clergy give up their homely manner religion will soon decay in that country."'

Boswell's Life of Johnson, i. 458.

Precedency:

'JOHNSON, for sport perhaps, or from the spirit of contradiction, eagerly maintained that Derrick had merit as a writer. Mr. Morgann argued with him directly in vain. At length he had recourse to this device, "Pray, Sir, (said he,) whether do you reckon Derrick or Smart[1] the best poet?" Johnson at once felt himself roused, and answered, "Sir, there is no settling the point of precedency between a louse and a flea."'

Ib. iv. 192.

Prejudices:

To be prejudiced is always to be weak; yet there are prejudices so near to laudable that they have been often praised and are always pardoned.

Works, vi. 225.

Prices[2]:

To fix the price of any commodity of which the quantity and the use may vary their proportions is the most excessive degree of ignorance. No man can determine the price of

---

[1] A writer in the *European Magazine* says that it was Boyce, and not Smart, who was compared with Derrick.

[2] In the bill of 1741 'for the encouragement of sailors,' one of the clauses fixed the maximum rate of wages for sailors in the merchant service.

corn

corn unless he can regulate the harvest and keep the number of the people for ever at a stand. . . . The other clauses of this bill complicated at once with cruelty and folly have been treated with becoming indignation ; but this may be considered with less ardour of resentment and fewer emotions of zeal because, though perhaps equally iniquitous, it will do no harm, for a law that can never be executed can never be felt. That it will consume the manufacture of paper and swell the books of statutes is all the good or hurt that can be hoped or feared from a law like this; a law which fixes what is in its own nature mutable, which prescribes rules to the seasons and limits to the winds.

Debates. Works, x. 341, 344.

Pride :

PRIDE is seldom delicate, it will please itself with very mean advantages ; and envy feels not its own happiness but when it may be compared with the misery of others.

Rasselas, ch. 9.

. * .

PRIDE is a vice which pride itself inclines every man to find in others and to overlook in himself.   *Works*, vi. 498.

. * .

HE that overvalues himself will undervalue others, and he that undervalues others will oppress them.   *Ib.* ix. 344.

Princes :

PRINCES have this remaining of humanity that they think themselves obliged not to make war without a reason.

Ib. vi. 463.

THE

THE studies of princes seldom produce great effects, for princes draw with meaner mortals the lot of understanding.

Works, vi. 439.

Prodigies :

PRODIGIES are always seen in proportion as they are expected. .

Ib. v. 58.

Profession :

'DR. JOHNSON has often been heard by me to observe that it was the greatest misfortune which could befall a man to have been bred to no profession, and pathetically to regret that this misfortune was his own.'

More's Practical Piety, p. 313.

Projects :

WHATEVER is attempted without previous certainty of success may be considered as a project, and amongst narrow minds may therefore expose its author to censure and contempt ; and if the liberty of laughing be once indulged every man will laugh at what he does not understand, every project will be considered as madness, and every great or new design will be censured as a project.   *Adventurer*, No. 99.

.˙.

PROJECTS of future piety are perhaps not less common than of future pleasure, and are, as there is reason to fear, not less commonly interrupted.   *Works*, ix. 383.

The Public :

THE majority of a society is the true definition of *the public.*   *Debates. Works*, xi. 116.

Punishment :

Punishment :

THE power of punishment is to silence, not to confute.

Works, ix. 499.

. · .

THEY who would rejoice at the correction of a thief are yet shocked at the thought of destroying him. His crime shrinks to nothing compared with his misery; and severity defeats itself by exciting pity. *Rambler*, No. 114.

Pupillage :

STUDY is laborious, and not always satisfactory; and conversation has its pains as well as pleasures; we are willing to learn but not willing to be taught; we are pained by ignorance but pained yet more by another's knowledge. From the vexation of pupillage men commonly set themselves free about the middle of life, by shutting up the avenues of intelligence, and resolving to rest in their present state; and they whose ardour of inquiry continues longer find themselves insensibly forsaken by their instructors. As every man advances in life, the proportion between those that are younger and that are older than himself is continually changing; and he that has lived half a century finds few that do not require from him that information which he once expected from those that went before him.

Idler, No. 44.

Purposes :

LIFE, to be worthy of a rational being, must be always in progression; we must always purpose to do more or better than in time past. The mind is enlarged and elevated by mere purposes, though they end as they began by airy contemplation. We compare and judge though we do not practise. *Piozzi Letters*, ii. 334.

Pyramids :

Pyramids :

IT seems [1] to have been erected only in compliance with that hunger of imagination which preys incessantly upon life, and must be always appeased by some employment. Those who have already all that they can enjoy must enlarge their desires. He that has built for use till use is supplied must begin to build for vanity, and extend his plan to the utmost power of human performance, that he may not be soon reduced to form another wish. I consider this mighty structure as a monument of the insufficiency of human enjoyments. A king whose power is unlimited and whose treasures surmount all real and imaginary wants is compelled to solace, by the erection of a pyramid, the satiety of dominion and tastelessness of pleasures, and to amuse the tediousness of declining life by seeing thousands labouring without end, and one stone for no purpose laid upon another. Whoever thou art that, not content with a moderate condition, imaginest happiness in royal magnificence, and dreamest that command or riches can feed the appetite of novelty with perpetual gratifications, survey the pyramids and confess thy folly !

Rasselas, ch. 32.

Questioning :

QUESTIONING is not the mode of conversation among gentlemen. It is assuming a superiority, and it is particularly wrong to question a man concerning himself. There may be parts of his former life which he may not wish to be made known to other persons, or even brought to his own recollection.

Boswell's *Life of Johnson*, ii. 472.

---

[1] The Great Pyramid.

Race

Race of life:

THERE is an honest contention for preference and superiority by which the powers of greater minds are pushed into action and the ancient boundaries of science are overpast.

Works, ix. 498.

Rascal:

'MR. WINDHAM, before he set out for Ireland as Secretary to Lord Northington when Lord Lieutenant, expressed to the Sage some modest and virtuous doubts, whether he could bring himself to practise those arts which it is supposed a person in that situation has occasion to employ. " Don't be afraid, Sir, (said Johnson with a pleasant smile,) you will soon make a very pretty rascal[1]." '

Boswell's *Life of Johnson*, iv. 200.

Reading:

'HE said that, for general improvement, a man should read whatever his immediate inclination prompts him to; though to be sure, if a man has a science to learn, he must regularly and resolutely advance. He added, " what we read with inclination makes a much stronger impression.

---

[1] I find in Mr. Windham's private diary the following memoranda of Dr. Johnson's advice: 'I have no great timidity in my own disposition, and am no encourager of it in others. Never be afraid to think yourself fit for any thing for which your friends think you fit. *You will become an able negotiator—a very pretty rascal.* No one in Ireland wears even the mask of incorruption; no one professes to do for sixpence what he can get a shilling for doing. Set sail, and see where the winds and the waves will carry you. Every day will improve another. *Dies diem docet*, by observing at night where you failed in the day, and by resolving to fail so no more.'—Croker's *Boswell*, p. 724.

If we read without inclination half the mind is employed in fixing the attention; so there is but one half to be employed on what we read." He told us he read Fielding's *Amelia* through without stopping. He said, "If a man begins to read in the middle of a book and feels an inclination to go on, let him not quit it to go to the beginning. He may perhaps not feel again the inclination."'

Boswell's *Life of Johnson*, iii. 43.

' DR. JOHNSON advised me to-day to have as many books about me as I could; that I might read upon any subject upon which I had a desire for instruction at the time. " What you read *then* (said he) you will remember; but if you have not a book immediately ready, and the subject moulds in your mind, it is a chance if you again have a desire to study it." He added, "If a man never has an eager desire for instruction, he should prescribe a task for himself. But it is better when a man reads from immediate inclination."'

Ib. iii. 193.

I AM always for getting a boy forward in his learning; for that is a sure good. I would let him at first read *any* English book which happens to engage his attention; because you have done a great deal when you have brought him to have entertainment from a book. He'll get better books afterwards.

Ib. iii. 385.

SNATCHES of reading will not make a Bentley or a Clarke. They are, however, in a certain degree advantageous. I would put a child into a library (where no unfit books are) and let him read at his choice. A child should not be

discouraged

discouraged from reading anything that he takes a liking to from a notion that it is above his reach. If that be the case, the child will soon find it out and desist ; if not, he of course gains the instruction, which is so much the more likely to come from the inclination with which he takes up the study.   Boswell's *Life of Johnson*, iv. 21.

.˙.

'JOHNSON took occasion to enlarge on the advantages of reading, and combated the idle superficial notion that knowledge enough may be acquired in conversation. " The foundation (said he) must be laid by reading. General principles must be had from books, which however must be brought to the test of real life. In conversation you never get a system. What is said upon a subject is to be gathered from a hundred people. The parts of a truth which a man gets thus are at such a distance from each other that he never attains to a full view." '   *Ib.* ii. 361.

.˙.

IT is strange that there should be so little reading in the world, and so much writing. People in general do not willingly read if they can have anything else to amuse them. There must be an external impulse ; emulation, or vanity, or avarice. The progress which the understanding makes through a book has more pain than pleasure in it. Language is scanty, and inadequate to express the nice gradations and mixtures of our feelings. No man reads a book of science from pure inclination. The books that we do read with pleasure are light compositions, which contain a quick succession of events.   *Ib.* iv. 218.

.˙.

'WHEN some one asked Johnson whether they should

introduce

introduce Hugh Kelly to him, "No, Sir," says he, "I never desire to converse with a man who has written more than he has read."'

Boswell's *Life of Johnson*, ii. 48, *n.* 2.

Recluses:

HE that can only converse upon questions about which only a small part of mankind has knowledge sufficient to make them curious must lose his days in unsocial silence and live in the crowd of life without a companion.

Rambler, No. 137.

Relief of enemies:

THAT charity is best of which the consequences are most extensive: the relief of enemies[1] has a tendency to unite mankind in fraternal affection; to soften the acrimony of adverse nations, and dispose them to peace and amity; in the mean time, it alleviates captivity and takes away something from the miseries of war. The rage of war, however mitigated, will always fill the world with calamity and horror: let it not then be unnecessarily extended; let animosity and hostility cease together; and no man be longer deemed an enemy than while his sword is drawn against us.

Works, vi. 148.

Religion:

'A PHYSICIAN being mentioned who had lost his practice, because his whimsically changing his religion had made people distrustful of him, I maintained that this was unreasonable, as religion is unconnected with medical skill. JOHNSON. "Sir, it is not unreasonable; for when people see

---

[1] In 1759 a Committee had been formed to raise subscriptions for the French prisoners of war in England. See Boswell's *Life of Johnson*, i. 353.

a man

a man absurd in what they understand, they may conclude the same of him in what they do not understand. If a physician were to take to eating of horse-flesh, nobody would employ him: though one may eat horse-flesh and be a very skilful physician. If a man were educated in an absurd religion, his continuing to profess it would not hurt him, though his changing to it would."'

Boswell's Life of Johnson, ii. 466.

. .

SURELY there is no man who thus afflicted[1] does not seek succour in the *Gospel*, which has brought *life and immortality to light*. The precepts of Epicurus, who teaches us to endure what the laws of the universe make necessary, may silence, but not content us. The dictates of Zeno, who commands us to look with indifference on external things, may dispose us to conceal our sorrow, but cannot assuage it. Real alleviation of the loss of friends and rational tranquillity in the prospect of our own dissolution can be received only from the promises of Him in whose hands are life and death, and from the assurance of another and better state in which all tears will be wiped from the eyes and the whole soul shall be filled with joy. Philosophy may infuse stubbornness, but Religion only can give patience.

Idler, No. 41.

. .

IN childhood, while our minds are yet unoccupied, religion is impressed upon them, and the first years of almost all who have been well educated are passed in a regular discharge of the duties of piety. But as we advance forward into the crowds of life, innumerable delights solicit

---

[1] Afflicted by the death of a friend.

our

our inclinations, and innumerable cares distract our attention; the time of youth is passed in noisy frolics; manhood
is led on from hope to hope and from project to project;
the dissoluteness of pleasure, the inebriation of success, the
ardour of expectation, and the vehemence of competition,
chain down the mind alike to the present scene; nor is it
remembered how soon this mist of trifles must be scattered,
and the bubbles that float upon the rivulet of life be lost for
ever in the gulf of eternity. To this consideration scarcely
any man is awakened but by some pressing and resistless
evil. The death of those from whom he derived his
pleasures or to whom he destined his possessions, some
disease which shows him the vanity of all external acquisitions, or the gloom of age which intercepts his prospects of
long enjoyment, forces him to fix his hopes upon another
state, and when he has contended with the tempests of
life till his strength fails him, he flies at last to the shelter
of religion. *Idler*, No 89.

RELIGION is not only neglected by the projector and
adventurer, by men who suspend their happiness on the
slender thread of artifice, or stand tottering upon the point
of chance. For if we visit the most cool and regular parts
of the community, if we turn our eye to the farm or to the
shop, where one year glides uniformly after another and
nothing new or important is either expected or dreaded, yet
still the same indifference about eternity will be found.
There is no interest so small, nor engagement so slight, but
that, if it be followed and expanded, it may be sufficient to
keep religion out of the thoughts. Many men may be
observed, not agitated by very violent passions, nor over-

borne

borne by any powerful habits, nor depraved by any great degrees of wickedness; men who are honest dealers, faithful friends, and inoffensive neighbours, who yet have no vital principle of religion, who live wholly without self-examination, and indulge any desire that happens to arise with very little resistance or compunction, who hardly know what it is to combat a temptation or to repent of a fault; but go on neither self-approved nor self-condemned, not endeavouring after any excellence nor reforming any vicious practice or irregular desire.

Works, ix. 381.

.˙.

FOR a man to revile and insult that God whose power he allows, to ridicule that revelation of which he believes the authority divine, to dare the vengeance of Omnipotence and cry 'Am not I in sport?' is an infatuation incredible, a degree of madness without a name. Yet there are men who by walking after their own lusts and indulging their passions have reached this stupendous height of wickedness. They have dared to teach falsehoods which they do not themselves believe; and to extinguish in others that conviction which they cannot suppress in themselves.

The motive of their proceeding is sometimes a desire of promoting their own pleasures by procuring accomplices in vice. Man is so far formed for society that even solitary wickedness quickly disgusts; and debauchery requires its combinations and confederacies which, as intemperance diminishes their numbers, must be filled up with new proselytes.

Let those who practise this dreadful method of depraving the morals and ensnaring the soul consider what they are engaged in. Let them consider what they are promoting and what means they are employing. Let them pause and reflect a little before they do an injury that can never be repaired, before they take away what cannot be restored; before they corrupt the heart of their companion by perverting his opinions, before they lead him into sin, and by destroying his reverence for religion take away every motive to repentance and all the means of reformation. This is a degree of guilt before which robbery, perjury, and murder vanish into nothing. No mischief of which the consequences terminate in our present state bears any proportion to the crime of decoying our brother into the broad way of eternal misery and stopping his ears against that holy voice that recalls him to salvation. *Works,* ix. 478.

IT has happened to ————, as to many active and prosperous men, that his mind has been wholly absorbed in business, or at intervals dissolved in amusement; and habituated so long to certain modes of employment or diversion, that in the decline of life it can no more receive a new train of images than the hand can acquire dexterity in a new mechanical operation. For this reason a religious education is so necessary. Spiritual ideas may be recollected in old age but can hardly be acquired. *Piozzi Letters,* ii. 82.

THAT we are fallen upon an age in which corruption is barely not universal is universally confessed. Venality sculks no longer in the dark but snatches the bribe in public, and prostitution issues forth without shame, glittering with the ornaments of successful wickedness. Rapine preys on the public without opposition, and perjury betrays it without inquiry. Irreligion is not only avowed but boasted, and the

pestilence

pestilence that used to walk in darkness is now destroying at noon-day. Shall this be the state of the English nation, and shall her law-givers behold it without regard? Must the torrent continue to roll on till it shall sweep us into the gulf of perdition? Surely there will come a time when the careless shall be frighted and the sluggish shall be roused; when every passion shall be put upon the guard by the dread of general depravity; when he who laughs at wickedness in his companion shall start from it in his child; when the man who fears not for his soul shall tremble for his possessions; when it shall be discovered that religion only can secure the rich from robbery and the poor from oppression, can defend the state from treason and the throne from assassination.

Works, v. 436.

Reputation:

'AGAINST personal abuse Johnson was ever armed by a reflection that I have heard him utter:—"Alas! reputation would be of little worth were it in the power of every concealed enemy to deprive us of it."'

Hawkins's Life of Johnson, p. 348.

Resentment:

RESENTMENT gratifies him who intended an injury, and pains him unjustly who did not intend it.

Boswell's Life of Johnson, iv. 367.

Resisting power:

HE that has once concluded it lawful to resist power when it wants merit will soon find a want of merit to justify his resistance of power.

Works, ix. 503.

R 2   Restitution:

Restitution:

THERE is, indeed, a partial restitution with which many have attempted to quiet their consciences, and have betrayed their own souls. When they are sufficiently enriched by wicked practices and leave off to rob from satiety of wealth, or are awakened to reflection upon their own lives by danger, adversity or sickness, they then become desirous to be at peace with God, and hope to obtain by refunding part of their acquisitions a permission to enjoy the rest. In pursuance of this view churches are built, schools endowed, the poor clothed, and the ignorant educated; works indeed highly pleasing to God when performed in concurrence with the other duties of religion, but which will never atone for the violation of justice. To plunder one man for the sake of relieving another is not charity; to build temples with the gains of wickedness is to endeavour to bribe the Divinity. This ought ye to have done and not left the other undone. Ye ought doubtless to be charitable, but ye ought first to be just. There are others who consider God as a judge still more easily reconciled to crimes, and therefore perform their acts of atonement after death, and destine their estates to charity when they can serve the end of luxury or vanity no longer. But whoever he be that has loaded his soul with the spoils of the unhappy, and riots in affluence by cruelty and injustice, let him not be deceived. God is not mocked. Restitution must be made to those who have been wronged, and whatever he withholds from them he withholds at the hazard of eternal happiness.

Works, ix. 306.

Rhetorical

Rhetorical action:

THE use of *English* oratory is only at the bar, in the parliament and in the church. Neither the judges of our laws nor the representatives of our people would be much affected by laboured gesticulation, or believe any man the more because he rolled his eyes, or puffed his cheeks, or spread abroad his arms, or stamped the ground, or thumped his breast, or turned his eyes sometimes to the ceiling and sometimes to the floor. Upon men intent only upon truth the arm of an orator has little power; a credible testimony or a cogent argument will overcome all the art of modulation, and all the violence of contortion. *Idler*, No. 90.

Rhetoricians:

CHILDREN fly from their own shadow, and rhetoricians are frighted by their own voices. *Works*, vi. 262.

Rich:

IT is better to *live* rich than to *die* rich.

Boswell's *Life of Johnson*, iii. 304.

.˙.

No scheme of policy has in any country yet brought the rich and poor on equal terms into courts of judicature. Perhaps experience improving on experience may in time effect it. *Works*, ix. 90.

.˙.

BENEFITS which are received as gifts from wealth are exacted as debts from indigence; and he that in a high station is celebrated for superfluous goodness would in a

meaner

meaner condition have barely been confessed to have done
his duty.   *Rambler*, No. 166.

Richardson and his flatterers:

' DR. JOHNSON said, that if Mr. Richardson had lived till
I[1] came out, my praises would have added two or three
years to his life. "For," says Dr. Johnson, "that fellow
died merely from want of change among his flatterers: he
perished for want of *more*, like a man obliged to breathe
the same air till it is exhausted." '

Boswell's *Life of Johnson*, v. 396, *n.* 1.

Riches:

ACQUISITIONS long enjoyed are with great difficulty
quitted; with so great difficulty that we seldom, very
seldom, meet with true repentance in those whom the
desire of riches has betrayed to wickedness. Men who
could willingly resign the luxuries and sensual pleasures of
a large fortune cannot consent to live without the grandeur
and the homage.   *Works*, ix. 309.

.·.

RICHES, perhaps, do not so often produce crimes as
incite accusers.   *Rambler*, No. 172.

Ridicule:

AKENSIDE adopted Shaftesbury's foolish assertion of the
efficacy of ridicule for the discovery of truth. For this he
was attacked by Warburton and defended by Dyson: Warburton afterwards reprinted his remarks at the end of his

---

[1] Mrs. Thrale.

dedication

dedication to his Freethinkers. The result of all the arguments which have been produced in a long and eager discussion of this idle question may easily be collected. If ridicule be applied to any position as the test of truth it will then become a question whether such ridicule be just; and this can only be decided by the application of truth as the test of ridicule. Two men fearing, one a real and the other a fancied danger, will be for a while equally exposed to the inevitable consequences of cowardice, contemptuous censure, and ludicrous representation; and the true state of both cases must be known before it can be decided whose terror is rational and whose is ridiculous; who is to be pitied and who to be despised. Both are for a while equally exposed to laughter, but both are not therefore equally contemptible.   *Works,* viii. 470.

Rising in the world:

'A LARGE number of friends, such as Johnson, Mr. Burke, and Mr. Murphy, dined at Garrick's at Christmas, 1760. Foote was then in Dublin. It was said at table that he had been horse-whipped by an apothecary for taking him off upon the stage. "But I wonder," said Garrick, "that any man would show so much resentment to Foote; nobody ever thought it worth his while to quarrel with him in London." "And I am glad," said Johnson, "to find that the man is rising in the world."'   Boswell's *Life of Johnson,* ii. 155, *n.* 2.

Romances:

IN the romances formerly written every transaction and sentiment was so remote from all that passes among men that the reader was in very little danger of making any applications to himself; the virtues and crimes were equally

beyond

beyond his sphere of activity, and he amused himself with heroes and with traitors, deliverers and persecutors, as with beings of another species, whose actions were regulated upon motives of their own, and who had neither faults nor excellences in common with himself. But when an adventurer is levelled with the rest of the world and acts in such scenes of the universal drama as may be the lot of any other man, young spectators fix their eyes upon him with closer attention and hope, by observing his behaviour and success, to regulate their own practices when they shall be engaged in the like part. *Rambler*, No. 4.

Romantic virtue:

NARRATIONS of romantic and impracticable virtue will be read with wonder, but that which is unattainable is recommended in vain. That good may be endeavoured it must be shown to be possible. *Works*, viii. 292.

.˙.

'DR. JOHNSON used to advise his friends to be upon their guard against romantic virtue as being founded upon no settled principle. "A plank," said he, "that is tilted up at one end must, of course, fall down on the other."'

Boswell's *Life of Johnson*, vi. xlviii.

Round numbers:

ROUND numbers are always false. *Ib*. iii. 226, *n*. 4.

Ruling passion:

IN this poem[1] Pope has endeavoured to establish and

---

[1] *Characters of Men.*

exemplify

exemplify his favourite theory of the *ruling Passion*, by which he means an original direction of desire to some particular object; an innate affection, which gives all action a determinate and invariable tendency and operates upon the whole system of life, either openly or more secretly, by the intervention of some accidental or subordinate propension. Of any passion thus innate and irresistible the existence may reasonably be doubted. Human characters are by no means constant; men change by change of place, of fortune, of acquaintance; he who is at one time a lover of pleasure is at another a lover of money. Those indeed who attain any excellence commonly spend life in one pursuit, for excellence is not often gained upon easier terms. But to the particular species of excellence men are directed not by an ascendant planet or predominating humour, but by the first book which they read, some early conversation which they heard, or some accident which excited ardour and emulation.

It must at least be allowed that this *ruling Passion*, antecedent to reason and observation, must have an object independent on human contrivance, for there can be no natural desire of artificial good. No man therefore can be born, in the strict acceptation, a lover of money, for he may be born where money does not exist: nor can he be born, in a moral sense, a lover of his country, for society politically regulated is a state contradistinguished from a state of nature; and any attention to that coalition of interests which makes the happiness of a country is possible only to those whom enquiry and reflection have enabled to comprehend it. This doctrine is in itself pernicious as well as false; its tendency is to produce the belief of a kind of moral predestination, or overruling principle which cannot

be

be resisted; he that admits it is prepared to comply with every desire that caprice or opportunity shall excite, and to flatter himself that he submits only to the lawful dominion of nature, in obeying the resistless authority of his *ruling Passion.*

Works, viii. 292.

Sailors:

' DR. JOHNSON took occasion to enlarge, as he often did, upon the wretchedness of a sea-life. " A ship is worse than a gaol. There is in a gaol better air, better company, better conveniency of every kind; and a ship has the additional disadvantage of being in danger. When men come to like a sea-life they are not fit to live on land."—" Then (said I) it would be cruel in a father to breed his son to the sea." JOHNSON. " It would be cruel in a father who thinks as I do. Men go to sea before they know the unhappiness of that way of life; and when they have come to know it they cannot escape from it because it is then too late to choose another profession; as indeed is generally the case with men when they have once engaged in any particular way of life." '

Boswell's *Life of Johnson,* ii. 438.

. · .

No man will be a sailor who has contrivance enough to get himself into a gaol; for being in a ship is being in a gaol, with the chance of being drowned.

Ib. v. 137.

Sanctuary for fugitives:

THE State has not a right to erect a general sanctuary for fugitives, or give protection to such as have forfeited their lives by crimes against the laws of common morality equally acknowledged by all nations, because no people can with-

out

out infraction of the universal league of social beings incite, by prospects of impunity and safety, those practices in another dominion which they would themselves punish in their own.

Rambler, No. 81.

Satiety:

NOTHING was seen on every side but multitudes wandering about they knew not whither, in quest they knew not of what; no voice was heard but of complaints that mentioned no pain, and murmurs that could tell of no misfortune.

Ib. No. 33.

Savage life:

THE traveller wanders through a naked desert, gratified sometimes, but rarely, with the sight of cows, and now and then finds a heap of loose stones and turf in a cavity between rocks, where a being born with all those powers which education expands and all those sensations which culture refines, is condemned to shelter itself from the wind and rain. Philosophers there are who try to make themselves believe that this life is happy, but they believe it only while they are saying it, and never yet produced conviction in a single mind; he whom want of words or images sunk into silence still thought, as he thought before, that privation of pleasure can never please, and that content is not to be much envied when it has no other principle than ignorance of good.

Piozzi Letters, i. 150.

Scarcity of food:

SCARCITY is an evil that extends at once to the whole community; that neither leaves quiet to the poor nor

safety

safety to the rich; that in its approaches distresses all the subordinate ranks of mankind, and in its extremity must subvert government, drive the populace upon their rulers, and end in bloodshed and massacre. Those who want the supports of life will seize them wherever they can be found. If in any place there are more than can be fed some must be expelled or some must be destroyed.

Works, v. 321.

Scenery:

I SAT down on a bank[1], such as a writer of romance might have delighted to feign. I had, indeed, no trees to whisper over my head, but a clear rivulet streamed at my feet. The day was calm, the air was soft, and all was rudeness, silence, and solitude. Before me, and on either side, were high hills which, by hindering the eye from ranging, forced the mind to find entertainment for itself. Whether I spent the hour well I know not, for here I first conceived the thought of this narration[2].   *Ib.* ix. 36.

.˙.

THE night came on while we had yet a great part of the way to go, though not so dark but that we could discern the cataracts which poured down the hills on one side, and fell into one general channel that ran with great violence on the other. The wind was loud, the rain was heavy, and the whistling of the blast, the fall of the shower, the rush of the cataracts, and the roar of the torrent, made a nobler chorus of the rough music of nature than it had ever been my chance to hear before.   *Ib.* ix. 155.

---

[1] In a valley in the Highlands.
[2] *A Journey to the Western Islands.*

THE

THE day soon failed us, and the moon presented a very solemn and pleasing scene. The sky was clear, so that the eye commanded a wide circle: the sea was neither still nor turbulent; the wind neither silent nor loud. We were never far from one coast or another, on which, if the weather had become violent, we could have found shelter, and therefore contemplated at ease the region through which we glided in the tranquillity of the night, and saw now a rock and now an island grow gradually conspicuous and gradually obscure.

Works, ix. 145.

Schemes of merriment:

NOTHING is more hopeless than a scheme of merriment.

Idler, No. 58.

Schemes of political improvement:

MOST schemes of political improvement are very laughable things.

Boswell's *Life of Johnson*, ii. 102.

Scholars:

' SIR,' said Imlac, ' my history will not be long: the life that is devoted to knowledge passes silently away, and is very little diversified by events. To talk in public, to think in solitude, to read and to hear, to inquire and answer inquiries, is the business of a scholar. He wanders about the world without pomp or terror, and is neither known nor valued but by men like himself.'

Rasselas, ch. 8.

Schoolboys' happiness:

' DR. JOHNSON maintained that a boy at school was the happiest of human beings. I supported a different opinion,

from

from which I have never yet varied, that a man is happier ; and I enlarged upon the anxiety and sufferings which are endured at school. JOHNSON. "Ah! Sir, a boy's being flogged is not so severe as a man's having the hiss of the world against him. Men have a solicitude about fame ; and the greater share they have of it the more afraid they are of losing it." '

Ib. i. 451.

Schoolmasters :

' JOHNSON used to say that schoolmasters were worse than the Egyptian task-masters of old. " No boy," says he, " is sure any day he goes to school to escape a whipping. How can the schoolmaster tell what the boy has really forgotten and what he has neglected to learn ? " '

Ib. ii. 146, *n.* 4.

Schools :

' IT having been mentioned to Dr. Johnson that a gentleman who had a son whom he imagined to have an extreme degree of timidity resolved to send him to a public school that he might acquire confidence ;—" Sir, (said Johnson,) this is a preposterous expedient for removing his infirmity ; such a disposition should be cultivated in the shade. Placing him at a public school is forcing an owl upon day." '

Boswell's *Life of Johnson,* iv. 312.

. ˙.

AT a great school there is all the splendour and illumination of many minds ; the radiance of all is concentrated in

each,

each, or at least reflected upon each. But we must own that neither a dull boy nor an idle boy will do so well at a great school as at a private one. For at a great school there are always boys enough to do well easily, who are sufficient to keep up the credit of the school; and after whipping being tried to no purpose, the dull or idle boys are left at the end of a class, having the appearance of going through the course, but learning nothing at all. Such boys may do good at a private school, where constant attention is paid to them and they are watched. So that the question of public or private education is not properly a general one; but whether one or the other is best for *my son*. *Ib.* v. 85.

.·.

NOT to name the school or the masters of men illustrious for literature is a kind of historical fraud by which honest fame is injuriously diminished. *Works*, vii. 418.

Scoffers:

THE talents which qualify a man for a disputant and a buffoon seem very different; and an unprejudiced person would be inclined to form contrary ideas of an argument and a jest. . . . These men [the scoffers] have discovered, it seems, a more compendious way to knowledge. They decide the most momentous questions amidst the jollity of feasts and the excesses of riots. They have found that an adversary is more easily silenced than confuted. They insult instead of vanquishing their antagonists, and decline the battle to hasten to the triumph. *Works*, ix. 474.

Scotch

Wit and
Wisdom
of
Samuel
Johnson.

Scotch learning :

THEIR learning is like bread in a besieged town ; every man gets a little, but no man gets a full meal.

Boswell's *Life of Johnson*, ii. 363.

.⋅.

'WHEN a Scotchman was talking against Warburton, Johnson said he had more literature than had been imported from Scotland since the days of Buchanan. Upon the other's mentioning other eminent writers of the Scotch ; "These will not do," said Johnson, "Let us have some more of your northern lights; these are mere farthing candles."'

Ib. v. 57 *n.* 3.

Scotchmen :

A SCOTCHMAN must be a very sturdy moralist who does not love Scotland better than truth ; he will always love it better than inquiry : and if falsehood flatters his vanity, will not be very diligent to detect it.   *Works,* ix. 116.

.⋅.

'MR. OGILVIE was unlucky enough to choose for the topic of his conversation the praises of his native country. He began with saying that there was very rich land round Edinburgh. Goldsmith, who had studied physic there, contradicted this, very untruly, with a sneering laugh. Disconcerted a little by this, Mr. Ogilvie then took new ground where, I suppose, he thought himself perfectly safe ; for he observed that Scotland had a great many noble wild prospects. JOHNSON. "I believe, Sir, you have a great many. Norway, too, has noble wild prospects ; and Lapland is remarkable for prodigious noble wild prospects. But Sir, let me tell you, the noblest prospect which

a Scotchman

a Scotchman ever sees, is the high road that leads him to England!"'

Boswell's Life of Johnson, i. 425.

Scruples:

'DR. JOHNSON ridiculed a friend who, looking out on Streatham Common from our windows, lamented the enormous wickedness of the times because some bird-catchers were busy there one fine Sunday morning. "While half the Christian world is permitted," said Johnson, "to dance and sing and celebrate Sunday as a day of festivity, how comes your puritanical spirit so offended with frivolous and empty deviations from exactness? Whoever loads life with unnecessary scruples, Sir," continued he, "provokes the attention of others on his conduct, and incurs the censure of singularity, without reaping the reward of superior virtue."'

Piozzi's Anecdotes, p. 227.

Seasons and weather:

THIS dependance of the soul upon the seasons, those temporary and periodical ebbs and flows of intellect, may, I suppose, justly be derided as the fumes of vain imagination. *Sapiens dominabitur astris.* The author that thinks himself weather-bound will find, with a little help from hellebore, that he is only idle or exhausted. But while this notion has possession of the head, it produces the inability which it supposes. Our powers owe much of their energy to our hopes: *possunt quia posse videntur.* When success seems attainable diligence is enforced; but when it is admitted that the faculties are suppressed by a cross wind or a cloudy sky, the day is given up with-

S

out

out resistance; for who can contend with the course of Nature?

Works, vii. 102.

Secrecy:

THE rules that I shall propose concerning secrecy, and from which I think it not safe to deviate without long and exact deliberation are—Never to solicit the knowledge of a secret. Not willingly, nor without many limitations, to accept such confidence when it is offered. When a secret is once admitted, to consider the trust as of a very high nature, important as society and sacred as truth, and therefore not to be violated for any incidental convenience, or slight appearance of contrary fitness.

Rambler, No. 13.

Self-accusations:

No man is obliged to accuse himself of crimes which are known to God alone; even the fear of hurting others ought often to restrain him from it, since to confess crimes may be in some measure to teach them, and those may imitate him in wickedness who will not follow him in his repentance.

Works, ix. 303.

Self-confidence:

SELF-CONFIDENCE is the first requisite to great undertakings. He, indeed, who forms his opinion of himself in solitude without knowing the powers of other men, is very liable to error: but it was the felicity of Pope to rate himself at his real value.

Ib. viii. 237.

Self-deception:

IT is generally not so much the desire of men sunk into

into

into depravity to deceive the world as themselves, for
when no particular circumstances make them dependent on
others, infamy disturbs them little, but as it revives their
remorse and is echoed to them from their own hearts.

Rambler, No. 76.

⁂

THOSE whom their virtue restrains from deceiving others
are often disposed by their vanity to deceive themselves.

Works, viii. 39.

⁂

THERE are men who always confound the praise of
goodness with the practice, and who believe themselves
mild and moderate, charitable and faithful, because they
have exerted their eloquence in commendation of mildness,
fidelity, and other virtues. This is an error almost universal among those that converse much with dependents,
with such whose fear or interest disposes them to a seeming reverence for any declamation, however enthusiastic,
and submission to any boast, however arrogant. Having
none to recall their attention to their lives, they rate themselves by the goodness of their opinions, and forget how
much more easily men may show their virtue in their talk
than in their actions.

Rambler, No. 28.

Self-love:

SELF-LOVE, co-operating with an imagination vigorous
and fertile as that of Browne, will find or make objects of
astonishment in every man's life[1]; and perhaps there is no
human being, however hid in the crowd from the observa-

---

[1] Sir Thomas Browne had stated in the *Religio Medici* that 'his
life had been a miracle of thirty years.'

tion

tion of his fellow mortals, who, if he has leisure and disposition to recollect his own thoughts and actions, will not conclude his life in some sort a miracle, and imagine himself distinguished from all the rest of his species by many discriminations of nature or of fortune. *Works*, vi. 480.

.˙.

PERSONAL resentment[1], though no laudable motive to satire, can add great force to general principle.　Self-love is a busy prompter. *Ib.* vii. 323.

Self-satisfaction:

To have attempted much is always laudable, even when the enterprise is above the strength that undertakes it. To rest below his own aim is incident to every one whose fancy is active, and whose views are comprehensive; nor is any man satisfied with himself because he has done much, but because he can conceive little. *Ib.* v. 42.

Servants:

THE highest panegyric that private virtue can receive is the praise of servants.　For, however vanity or insolence may look down with contempt on the suffrage of men undignified by wealth and unenlightened by education, it very seldom happens that they commend or blame without justice.　Vice and virtue are easily distinguished.　Oppression, according to Harrington's aphorism, will be felt by those that cannot see it; and, perhaps, it falls out very often that, in moral questions, the philosophers in the gown

---

[1] Dryden had gratified his resentment towards Settle and Shadwell by inserting in Tate's second part of *Absalom and Achitophel* an attack on them ‘which for poignancy of satire exceeds any part of the former.’

and

and in the livery differ not so much in their sentiments as in their language, and have equal power of discerning right though they cannot point it out to others with equal address. *Rambler*, No. 68.

Shakespeare :

A QUIBBLE is to Shakespeare what luminous vapours are to the traveller : he follows it at all adventures ; it is sure to lead him out of his way and sure to engulf him in the mire. It has some malignant power over his mind, and its fascinations are irresistible. Whatever be the dignity or profundity of his disquisitions, whether he be enlarging knowledge or exalting affection, whether he be amusing attention with incidents, or enchaining it in suspense, let but a quibble spring up before him, and he leaves his work unfinished. A quibble is the golden apple for which he will always turn aside from his career, or stoop from his elevation. A quibble, poor and barren as it is, gave him such delight, that he was content to purchase it by the sacrifice of reason, propriety, and truth. A quibble was to him the fatal Cleopatra for which he lost the world and was content to lose it. *Works*, v. 118.

.·.

YET it must be at last confessed that, as we owe every thing to him, he owes something to us ; that, if much of his praise is paid by perception and judgment, much is likewise given by custom and veneration. We fix our eyes upon his graces and turn them from his deformities, and endure in him what we should in another loathe or despise. *Ib.* v. 133.

Shallows

Shallows are clear:

'Dr. Johnson one evening roundly asserted in his rough way that "Swift was a shallow fellow; a very shallow fellow." Mr. Sheridan replied warmly but modestly, "Pardon me, Sir, for differing from you, but I always thought the Dean a very clear writer." Johnson vociferated "All shallows are clear."'

Boswell's Life of Johnson, v. 44, n. 3.

Sheridan, Thomas:

'He laughed heartily when I mentioned to him a saying of his concerning Mr. Thomas Sheridan which Foote took a wicked pleasure to circulate. "Why, Sir, Sherry is dull, naturally dull; but it must have taken him a great deal of pains to become what we now see him. Such an excess of stupidity, Sir, is not in Nature." "So (said he), I allowed him all his own merit." He now added, "Sheridan cannot bear me. I bring his declamation to a point. I ask him a plain question, What do you mean to teach? Besides, Sir, what influence can Mr. Sheridan have upon the language of this great country by his narrow exertions? Sir, it is burning a farthing candle at Dover to show light at Calais."'

Ib. i. 453.

Shops:

To a man that ranges the streets of London, where he is tempted to contrive wants for the pleasure of supplying them, a shop affords no image worthy of attention; but in an island it turns the balance of existence between good and evil. To live in perpetual want of little things is a state not indeed of torture, but of constant vexation. I have

in

in Sky had some difficulty to find ink for a letter; and if a woman breaks her needle, the work is at a stop.

Works, ix. 127.

Sick chamber:

IT may be said that disease generally begins that equality which death completes; the distinctions which set one man so much above another are very little perceived in the gloom of a sick chamber, where it will be vain to expect entertainment from the gay or instruction from the wise; where all human glory is obliterated, the wit is clouded, the reasoner perplexed, and the hero subdued; where the highest and brightest of mortal beings finds nothing left him but the consciousness of innocence. *Rambler*, No. 48.

． ・ ．

THE only conviction that rushes upon the soul and takes away from our appetites and passions the power of resistance is to be found where I have received it, at the bed of a dying friend. To enter this school of wisdom is not the peculiar privilege of geometricians; the most sublime and important precepts require no uncommon opportunities nor laborious preparations; they are enforced without the aid of eloquence, and understood without skill in analytic science. Every tongue can utter them, and every understanding can conceive them. He that wishes in earnest to obtain just sentiments concerning his condition, and would be intimately acquainted with the world, may find instructions on every side. He that desires to enter behind the scene which every art has been employed to decorate and every passion labours to illuminate, and wishes to see life stripped of those ornaments which make it glitter on the stage, and exposed

in

in its natural meanness, impotence, and nakedness, may find all the delusion laid open in the chamber of disease: he will there find vanity divested of her robes, power deprived of her sceptre, and hypocrisy without her mask.

Rambler, No. 54.

Silence:

IT is always observable that silence propagates itself, and that the longer talk has been suspended, the more difficult it is to find anything to say.   *Adventurer*, No. 84.

Singularity:

WHATEVER he[1] did, he seemed willing to do in a manner peculiar to himself, without sufficiently considering that singularity, as it implies a contempt of the general practice, is a kind of defiance which justly provokes the hostility of ridicule ; he therefore who indulges peculiar habits is worse than others, if he be not better.   *Works,* viii. 223.

. . .

THERE is in human nature a general inclination to make people stare ; and every wise man has himself to cure of it, and does cure himself. If you wish to make people stare by doing better than others, why, make them stare till they stare their eyes out. But consider how easy it is to make people stare by being absurd. I may do it by going into a drawing-room without my shoes. You remember the gentleman in *The Spectator*[2], who had a commission of lunacy taken out against him for his extreme singularity, such as never wearing a wig, but a night-cap. Now, Sir, abstractedly,

---

[1] Swift.   [2] No. 576.

the

the night-cap was best, but relatively, the advantage was overbalanced by his making the boys run after him.

Boswell's Life of Johnson, ii. 74.

Sleeplessness :

KEEP yourself cheerful. Lie in bed with a lamp, and when you cannot sleep and are beginning to think, light your candle and read. At least light your candle; a man is perhaps never so much harassed by his own mind in the light as in the dark.

Ib. iv. 409, n. 1.

Soldiers :

I WAS the second son of a gentleman whose estate was barely sufficient to support himself and his heir in the dignity of killing game. He therefore made use of the interest which the alliances of his family afforded him to procure me a post in the army. I passed some years in the most contemptible of all human stations, that of a soldier in time of peace. I wandered with the regiment as the quarters were changed, without opportunity for business, taste for knowledge, or money for pleasure. Wherever I came, I was for some time a stranger without curiosity, and afterwards an acquaintance without friendship. Having nothing to hope in these places of fortuitous residence, I resigned my conduct to chance; I had no intention to offend, I had no ambition to delight. I suppose every man is shocked when he hears how frequently soldiers are wishing for war. The wish is not always sincere; the greater part are content with sleep and lace, and counterfeit an ardour which they do not feel; but those who desire it most are neither prompted by malevolence nor patriotism; they neither pant for laurels nor delight in blood; but long to be

Wit and
Wisdom
of
Samuel
Johnson.

be delivered from the tyranny of idleness and restored to
the dignity of active beings.   *Idler*, No. 21.

. .

OUR nation may boast beyond any other people in the
world of a kind of epidemic bravery, diffused equally through
all its ranks. We can show a peasantry of heroes, and fill
our armies with clowns whose courage may vie with that of
their general. . . . The equality of English privileges, the
impartiality of our laws, the freedom of our tenures, and
the prosperity of our trade, dispose us very little to reverence
superiors. It is not to any great esteem of the officers that
the English soldier is indebted for his spirit in the hour
of battle; for perhaps it does not often happen that he
thinks much better of his leader than of himself. The
French count, who has lately published the Art of War,
remarks how much soldiers are animated when they see all
their dangers shared by those who were born to be their
masters, and whom they consider as beings of a different
rank. The Englishman despises such motives of courage:
he was born without a master; and looks not on any man,
however dignified by lace or titles, as deriving from nature
any claims to his respect, or inheriting any qualities superior
to his own. . . . Whence then is the courage of the English
vulgar? It proceeds, in my opinion, from that dissolution
of dependence which obliges every man to regard his own
character. While every man is fed by his own hands he
has no need of any servile arts; he may always have wages
for his labour, and is no less necessary to his employer
than his employer is to him. While he looks for no protection from others, he is naturally roused to be his own
protector; and having nothing to abate his esteem of himself,

he

he consequently aspires to the esteem of others. Thus every man that crowds our streets is a man of honour, disdainful of obligation, impatient of reproach, and desirous of extending his reputation among those of his own rank; and as courage is in most frequent use, the fame of courage is most eagerly pursued. From this neglect of subordination I do not deny that some inconveniences may from time to time proceed: the power of the law does not always sufficiently supply the want of reverence, or maintain the proper distinction between different ranks; but good and evil will grow up in this world together; and they who complain in peace of the insolence of the populace must remember that their insolence in peace is bravery in war.

Works, vi. 149-152.

Soldiers and sailors:

'WE talked of war. JOHNSON. "Every man thinks meanly of himself for not having been a soldier, or not having been at sea." BOSWELL. "Lord Mansfield does not." JOHNSON. "Sir, if Lord Mansfield were in a company of General Officers and Admirals who have been in service, he would shrink; he'd wish to creep under the table." BOSWELL. "No; he'd think he could *try* them all." JOHNSON. "Yes, if he could catch them: but they'd try him much sooner. No, Sir; were Socrates and Charles the Twelfth of Sweden both present in any company, and Socrates to say, 'Follow me, and hear a lecture on philosophy;' and Charles, laying his hand on his sword, to say, 'Follow me, and dethrone the Czar;' a man would be ashamed to follow Socrates. Sir, the impression is universal: yet it is strange. As to the sailor, when you look down from the quarter deck to the

space

space below, you see the utmost extremity of human misery ; such crowding, such filth, such stench !" BOSWELL. " Yet sailors are happy." JOHNSON. " They are happy as brutes are happy, with a piece of fresh meat,—with the grossest sensuality. But, Sir, the profession of soldiers and sailors has the dignity of danger. Mankind reverence those who have got over fear, which is so general a weakness." SCOTT[1]. " But is not courage mechanical, and to be acquired ? " JOHNSON. " Why yes, Sir, in a collective sense. Soldiers consider themselves only as parts of a great machine." SCOTT. " We find people fond of being sailors." JOHNSON. " I cannot account for that any more than I can account for other strange perversions of imagination." '

Boswell's Life of Johnson, iii. 265.

Solitude :

I[2] HAVE been for some time unsettled and distracted: my mind is disturbed with a thousand perplexities of doubt and vanities of imagination which hourly prevail upon me, because I have no opportunities of relaxation or diversion. I am sometimes ashamed to think that I could not secure myself from vice but by retiring from the exercise of virtue, and begin to suspect that I was rather impelled by resentment than led by devotion into solitude. My fancy riots in scenes of folly, and I lament that I have lost so much and have gained so little. In solitude, if I escape the example of bad men, I want likewise the counsel and conversation of the good. I have been long comparing the evils with the advantages of society, and resolve to return into the world

---

[1] Afterwards Lord Stowell.   [2] The hermit in *Rasselas*.

to-morrow.

to-morrow. The life of a solitary man will be certainly miserable, but not certainly devout. *Rasselas*, ch. 21.

Something done :

No man can perform so little as not to have reason to congratulate himself on his merits when he beholds the multitudes that live in total idleness and have never yet endeavoured to be useful. *Rambler*, No. 83.

Sonorous sentences :

SOMETIMES the reader is suddenly ravished with a sonorous sentence, of which, when the noise is past, the meaning does not long remain. *Works*, vi. 15.

Sorrow :

SORROW is not that regret for negligence or error which may animate us to future care or activity, or that repentance of crimes for which, however irrevocable, our Creator has promised to accept it as an atonement ; the pain which arises from these causes has very salutary effects, and is every hour extenuating itself by the reparation of those miscarriages that produce it. Sorrow is properly that state of mind in which our desires are fixed upon the past, without looking forward to the future, an incessant wish that something were otherwise than it has been, a tormenting and harassing want of some enjoyment or possession which we have lost, and which no endeavours can possibly regain. . . . The safe and general antidote against sorrow is employment. It is commonly observed that, among soldiers and seamen, though there is much kindness, there is little grief ; they see their friend fall without any of that lamentation which is

indulged

indulged in security and idleness because they have no leisure to spare from the care of themselves ; and whoever shall keep his thoughts equally busy will find himself equally unaffected with irretrievable losses.　*Rambler*, No. 47.

'WE talked of Lady Tavistock, who grieved herself to death for the loss of her husband [1].—"She was rich and wanted employment (says Johnson), so she cried till she lost all power of restraining her tears : other women are forced to outlive their husbands, who were just as much beloved, depend on it ; but they have no time for grief ; and I doubt not, if we had put my Lady Tavistock into a small chandler's shop, and given her a nurse-child to tend, her life would have been saved.　The poor and the busy have no leisure for sentimental sorrow."'　Piozzi's *Anecdotes*, p. 153.

'"SORROW," as Dr. Johnson said, "is the mere rust of the soul.　Activity will cleanse and brighten it."'

Mme. D'Arblay's *Diary*, vii. 357.

To grieve for evils is often wrong ; but it is much more wrong to grieve without them.　All sorrow that lasts longer than its cause is morbid, and should be shaken off as an attack of melancholy, as the forerunner of a greater evil than poverty or pain.　*Piozzi Letters*, ii. 23.

'THE state of a mind oppressed with a sudden calamity,' said Imlac, 'is like that of the fabulous inhabitants of the

---

[1] The Marquis of Tavistock, the fourth Duke of Bedford's only son, was killed by a fall from his horse in 1767.

new

new created earth who, when the first night came upon them, supposed that day would never return [1]. When the clouds of sorrow gather over us we see nothing beyond them, nor can imagine how they will be dispelled: yet a new day succeeded to the night, and sorrow is never long without a dawn of ease. But they who restrain themselves from receiving comfort do as the savages would have done had they put out their eyes when it was dark. Our minds, like our bodies, are in continual flux; something is hourly lost, and something acquired. To lose much at once is inconvenient to either, but while the vital powers remain uninjured, nature will find the means of reparation. Distance has the same effect on the mind as on the eye, and while we glide along the stream of time, whatever we leave behind us is always lessening, and that which we approach increasing in magnitude. Do not suffer life to stagnate; it will grow muddy for want of motion: commit yourself again to the current of the world.'

Rasselas, ch. 35.

THERE is no wisdom in useless and hopeless sorrow; but there is something in it so like virtue, that he who is wholly without it cannot be loved, nor will by me at least be thought worthy of esteem.

Piozzi Letters, ii. 198.

LIFE occupies us all too much to leave us room for any

---

[1] This passage might have suggested Blanco White's beautiful sonnet which begins:—

'Mysterious night! when our first parent knew
Thee from report divine, and heard thy name,
Did he not tremble for this lovely frame,
This glorious canopy of light and blue?'

care

care of others beyond what duty enjoins, and no duty enjoins sorrow or anxiety that is at once troublesome and useless.   I would readily help the poor lady[1], but if I cannot do her good by assisting her, I shall not disturb myself by lamenting her.

Piozzi Letters, i. 365.

.˙.

TEARS are often to be found where there is little sorrow, and the deepest sorrow without any tears.

Works, ix. 304.

Southwark Election:

'A BOROUGH election once showed me Mr. Johnson's toleration of boisterous mirth.   A rough fellow, a hatter by trade, seeing his beaver in a state of decay, seized it suddenly with one hand, and clapping him on the back with the other, "Ah, Master Johnson," says he, " this is no time to be thinking about *hats*." "No, no, Sir," replies our Doctor in a cheerful tone, "hats are of no use now, as you say, except to throw up in the air and huzza with," accompanying his words with the true election halloo.'

Piozzi's *Anecdotes*, p. 214.

Sovereignty:

IN sovereignty there are no gradations.   There may be limited royalty, there may be limited consulship; but there can be no limited government.   There must in every society be some power or other from which there is no appeal, which admits no restrictions, which pervades the whole mass of the community, regulates and adjusts all subordination, enacts laws or repeals them, erects or annuls judicatures,

---

[1] A lady whose son was very dangerously ill.

extends

extends or contracts privileges, exempt itself from question or control, and bounded only by physical necessity.

Works, vi. 234.

Speaking of a man in his own presence:

NEVER speak of a man in his own presence. It is always indelicate, and may be offensive.

Boswell's *Life of Johnson,* ii. 472.

Speculation:

IF there were no other end of life than to find some adequate solace for every day, I know not whether any condition could be preferred to that of the man who involves himself in his own thoughts, and never suffers experience to show him the vanity of speculation; for no sooner are notions reduced to practice, than tranquillity and confidence forsake the breast; every day brings its task, and often without bringing abilities to perform it : difficulties embarrass, uncertainty perplexes, opposition retards, censure exasperates, or neglect depresses. We proceed because we have begun; we complete our design that the labour already spent may not be vain : but as expectation gradually dies away, the gay smile of alacrity disappears, we are compelled to implore severer powers and trust the event to patience and constancy. When once our labour has begun, the comfort that enables us to endure it is the prospect of its end; for though in every long work there are some joyous intervals of self-applause, when the attention is recreated by unexpected facility and the imagination soothed by incidental excellencies; yet the toil with which performance struggles after idea is so irksome and disgusting, and so frequent is the necessity of resting below that perfection

Wit and
Wisdom
of
Samuel
Johnson.

T   which

which we imagined within our reach, that seldom any man
obtains more from his endeavours than a painful conviction
of his defects, and a continual resuscitation of desires which
he feels himself unable to gratify.   *Rambler*, No. 207.

Speculations and practice :

NOT only our speculations influence our practice, but
our practice reciprocally influences our speculations. We
not only do what we approve, but there is danger lest in
time we come to approve what we do, though for no other
reason but that we do it. A man is always desirous of being
at peace with himself, and when he cannot reconcile his
passions to his conscience he will attempt to reconcile his
conscience to his passions ; he will find reason for doing
what he resolved to do, and rather than not ' walk after his
own lusts' will scoff at religion.   *Works*, ix. 4:2.

The stage :

IT will be asked how the drama moves if it is not
credited. It is credited with all the credit due to a drama.
It is credited, whenever it moves, as a just picture of a real
original ; as representing to the auditor what he would himself feel if he were to do or suffer what is there feigned to
be suffered or to be done. The reflection that strikes the
heart is not that the evils before us are real evils, but that
they are evils to which we ourselves may be exposed. If
there be any fallacy, it is not that we fancy the players, but
that we fancy ourselves unhappy for a moment ; but we
rather lament the possibility than suppose the presence of
misery, as a mother weeps over her babe when she remembers that death may take it from her. The delight of tragedy

proceeds

proceeds from our consciousness of fiction; if we thought murders and treasons real they would please no more.

Works, v. 121.

. · .

SUCH is the triumphant language with which a critic exults over the misery of an irregular poet, and exults commonly without resistance or reply. It is time, therefore, to tell him by the authority of Shakespeare that he assumes, as an unquestionable principle, a position which, while his breath is forming it into words, his understanding pronounces to be false. It is false that any representation is mistaken for reality; that any dramatic fable in its materiality was ever credible, or, for a single moment was ever credited. The objection arising from the impossibility of passing the first hour at Alexandria and the next at Rome supposes that, when the play opens, the spectator really imagines himself at Alexandria, and believes that his walk to the theatre has been a voyage to Egypt, and that he lives in the days of Antony and Cleopatra. Surely he that imagines this may imagine more. He that can take the stage at one time for the palace of the Ptolemies may take it in half an hour for the promontory of Actium. Delusion, if delusion be admitted, has no certain limitation; if the spectator can be once persuaded that his old acquaintance are Alexander and Caesar, that a room illuminated with candles is the plain of Pharsalia, or the bank of Granicus, he is in a state of elevation above the reach of reason or of truth, and from the heights of empyrean poetry may despise the circumscriptions of terrestrial nature. There is no reason why a mind thus wandering in ecstacy should count the clock, or why an hour should not be a century in that calenture of the brain that can make the stage a field. The

truth

Wit and
Wisdom
of
Samuel
Johnson.

truth is that the spectators are always in their senses, and know, from the first act to the last, that the stage is only a stage, and that the players are only players. *Works,* v. 120.

.˙.

FAMILIAR comedy is often more powerful on the theatre than in the page; imperial tragedy is always less. *Ib.* v. 122.

'Strutting dignity:

HE[1] has a kind of strutting dignity, and is tall by walking on tiptoe. *Ib.* viii. 487.

Style:

COLLINS affected the obsolete when it was not worthy of revival; and he puts his words out of the common order, seeming to think, with some later candidates for fame, that not to write prose is certainly to write poetry.

Works, viii. 404.

.˙.

LEVITY of thought naturally produced familiarity of language, and the familiar part of language continues long the same; the dialogue of comedy, when it is transcribed from popular manners and real life, is read from age to age with equal pleasure. The artifices of inversion, by which the established order of words is changed, or of innovation, by which new words or meanings of words are introduced, is practised, not by those who talk to be understood, but by those who write to be admired. *Ib.* vii. 34.

.˙.

A MOTHER tells her infant that *two and two make four*;

---

[1] Thomas Gray, in his Odes.

the

the child remembers the proposition, and is able to count four to all the purposes of life, till the course of his education brings him among philosophers, who fright him from his former knowledge by telling him that four is a certain aggregate of units ; that all numbers being only the repetition of an unit, which, though not a number itself, is the parent, root, or original of all number, *four* is the denomination assigned to a certain number of such repetitions. The only danger is lest, when he first hears these dreadful sounds, the pupil should run away; if he has but the courage to stay till the conclusion he will find that, when speculation has done its worst, two and two still make four.

Idler, No. 36.

THE great pest of speech is frequency of translation. No book was ever turned from one language into another without imparting something of its native idiom ; this is the most mischievous and comprehensive innovation ; single words may enter by thousands and the fabric of the tongue continue the same, but new phraseology changes much at once ; it alters not the single stones of the building, but the order of the columns. If an academy should be established for the cultivation of our style, which I, who can never wish to see dependence multiplied, hope the spirit of English liberty will hinder or destroy, let them, instead of compiling grammars and dictionaries, endeavour with all their influence to stop the licence of translators, whose idleness and ignorance, if it be suffered to proceed, will reduce us to babble a dialect of France.   *Works*, v. 48.

FEW faults of style, whether real or imaginary, excite the malignity of a more numerous class of readers than the use

Wit and
Wisdom
of
Samuel
Johnson.

of hard words. . . . Among the hard words which are no longer to be used it has been long the custom to number terms of art. 'Every man' (says Swift) 'is more able to explain the subject of an art than its professors; a farmer will tell you in two words that he has broken his leg, but a surgeon, after a long discourse, shall leave you as ignorant as you were before.' This could only have been said by such an exact observer of life in gratification of malignity, or in ostentation of acuteness. Every hour produces instances of the necessity of terms of art. Mankind could never conspire in uniform affectation; it is not but by necessity that every science and every trade has its peculiar language.

Idler, No. 70.

THE imitators of Spenser are indeed not very rigid censors of themselves, for they seem to conclude that when they have disfigured their lines with a few obsolete syllables they have accomplished their design, without considering that they ought not only to admit old words but to avoid new. The laws of imitation are broken by every word introduced since the time of Spenser, as the character of Hector is violated by quoting Aristotle in the play. It would, indeed, be difficult to exclude from a long poem all modern phrases, though it is easy to sprinkle it with gleanings of antiquity. Perhaps, however, the style of Spenser might by long labour be justly copied; but life is surely given us for higher purposes than to gather what our ancestors have wisely thrown away, and to learn what is of no value but because it has been forgotten.   *Rambler*, No. 121.

IF there be, what I believe there is, in every nation a style which

which never becomes obsolete, a certain mode of phraseology so consonant and congenial to the analogy and principles of its respective language as to remain settled and unaltered; this style is probably to be sought in the common intercourse of life, among those who speak only to be understood, without ambition of elegance. The polite are always catching modish innovations, and the learned depart from established forms of speech in hope of finding or making better; those who wish for distinction forsake the vulgar when the vulgar is right; but there is a conversation above grossness and below refinement where propriety resides, and where this poet[1] seems to have gathered his comic dialogue. He is therefore more agreeable to the ears of the present age than any other author equally remote, and among his other excellencies deserves to be studied as one of the original masters of our language. *Works*, v. 114.

Wit and
Wisdom
of
Samuel
Johnson.

.˙.

COWLEY'S diction was in his own time censured as negligent. He seems not to have known, or not to have considered, that words being arbitrary must owe their power to association, and have the influence, and that only, which custom has given them. Language is the dress of thought: and as the noblest mien or most graceful action would be degraded and obscured by a garb appropriated to the gross employments of rustics or mechanics, so the most heroic sentiments will lose their efficacy, and the most splendid ideas drop their magnificence, if they are conveyed by words used commonly upon low and trivial occasions, debased by vulgar mouths, and contaminated by inelegant applications. Truth indeed is always truth, and reason is always reason;

---

[1] Shakespeare.

they

they have an intrinsic and unalterable value, and constitute that intellectual gold which defies destruction: but gold may be so concealed in baser matter that only a chemist can recover it; sense may be so hidden in unrefined and plebeian words that none but philosophers can distinguish it; and both may be so buried in impurities as not to pay the cost of their extraction. The diction, being the vehicle of the thoughts, first presents itself to the intellectual eye; and if the first appearance offends, a further knowledge is not often sought. Whatever professes to benefit by pleasing must please at once. The pleasures of the mind imply something sudden and unexpected: that which elevates must always surprise. What is perceived by slow degrees may gratify us with the consciousness of improvement, but will never strike with the sense of pleasure.

Works, vii. 51.

• • •

The words[1] are multiplied till the sense is hardly perceived; attention deserts the mind and settles in the ear. The reader wanders through the gay diffusion, sometimes amazed and sometimes delighted, but, after many turnings in the flowery labyrinth, comes out as he went in. He remarked little, and laid hold on nothing.   *Ib.* viii. 473.

• • •

The rules of style, like those of law, arise from precedents often repeated.   *Works*, v. 16.

• • •

It is indeed not easy to distinguish affectation from habit; he that has once studiously formed a style rarely writes afterwards with complete ease.   *Ib.* viii. 284.

---

[1] In Akenside's *Pleasures of Imagination.*

THAT

THAT the vulgar express their thoughts clearly is far from true; and what perspicuity can be found among them proceeds not from the easiness of their language, but the shallowness of their thoughts.

Idler, No. 70.

.˙.

' DR. JOHNSON'S opinion that there were three ways in which writings may be unnatural: by being *bombastic* and above nature—*affected* and beside it, fringing every event with ornaments which nature did not afford—or *weak* and below nature. That neither of the first would please long. That the third might indeed please a good while, or at least many; because imbecility, and consequently a love of imbecility, might be found in many.'

Windham's *Diary*, p. 18.

Subordination :

As the great end of government is to give every man his own no inconvenience is greater than that of making right uncertain. Nor is any man more an enemy to public peace than he who fills weak heads with imaginary claims, and breaks the series of civil subordination by inciting the lower classes of mankind to encroach upon the higher.

Works, v. 478.

Suicide :

' WE talked of a man's drowning himself. JOHNSON. " I should never think it time to make away with myself." I put the case of Eustace Budgell, who was accused of forging a will, and sunk himself in the Thames before the trial of its authenticity came on. " Suppose, Sir, (said I,) that a man is absolutely sure that if he lives a few days longer he shall be detected in a fraud, the consequence of which will be utter

disgrace

disgrace and expulsion from society." JOHNSON. "Then, Sir, let him go abroad to a distant country; let him go to some place where he is *not* known.   Don't let him go to the devil where he *is* known!"'

Boswell's *Life of Johnson*, v. 54.

SUICIDE is always to be had [1] without expense of thought.

Works, viii. 486.

Superiority of understanding :

As many more can discover that a man is richer than that he is wiser than themselves, superiority of understanding is not so readily acknowledged as that of fortune; nor is that haughtiness which the consciousness of great abilities incites borne with the same submission as the tyranny of affluence.

Ib. viii. 162.

Superstition and melancholy :

No disease of the imagination is so difficult of cure as that which is complicated with the dread of guilt; fancy and conscience then act interchangeably upon us, and so often shift their places that the illusions of one are not distinguished from the dictates of the other.   If fancy presents images not moral or religious the mind drives them away when they give it pain, but when melancholic notions take the form of duty they lay hold on the faculties without opposition because we are afraid to exclude or banish them. For this reason the superstitious are often melancholy, and the melancholy almost always superstitious.　*Rasselas*, ch. 46.

Suspicion :

WHEN a young man not distinguished by vigour of intellect comes into the world full of scruples and diffidence;

---

[1] By authors in their plots.

makes

makes a bargain with many provisional limitations; hesitates in his answer to a common question lest more should be intended than he can immediately discover; has a long reach in detecting the projects of his acquaintance; considers every caress as an act of hypocrisy, and feels neither gratitude nor affection from the tenderness of his friends because he believes no one to have any real tenderness but for himself; whatever expectations this early sagacity may raise of his future eminence or riches I can seldom forbear to consider him as a wretch incapable of generosity or benevolence; as a villain early completed beyond the need of common opportunities and gradual temptations. . . . It is better to suffer wrong than to do it, and happier to be sometimes cheated than not to trust.   *Rambler*, No. 79.

.•.

IT is seldom that the great or the wise suspect that they are despised or cheated.   *Works*, viii. 264.

.•.

Do not fancy that an intermission of writing is a decay of kindness. No man is always in a disposition to write; nor has any man at all times something to say. That distrust which intrudes so often on your mind is a mode of melancholy which, if it be the business of a wise man to be happy, it is foolish to indulge; and if it be a duty to preserve our faculties entire for their proper use it is criminal. Suspicion is very often an useless pain.   Boswell's *Life of Johnson*, iii. 135.

Sympathy:

'TALKING of our feeling for the distresses of others;—
JOHNSON. "Why, Sir, there is much noise made about it,
but

but it is greatly exaggerated. No, Sir, we have a certain degree of feeling to prompt us to do good : more than that Providence does not intend. It would be misery to no purpose." BOSWELL. "But suppose now, Sir, that one of your intimate friends were apprehended for an offence for which he might be hanged." JOHNSON. "I should do what I could to bail him and give him any other assistance ; but if he were once fairly hanged I should not suffer." BOSWELL. "Would you eat your dinner that day, Sir?" JOHNSON. "Yes, Sir; and eat it as if he were eating it with me. Why there's Baretti, who is to be tried for his life to-morrow, friends have risen up for him on every side ; yet if he should be hanged none of them will eat a slice of plum-pudding the less. Sir, that sympathetic feeling goes a very little way in depressing the mind." I told him that I had dined lately at Foote's, who showed me a letter which he had received from Tom Davies, telling him that he had not been able to sleep from the concern which he felt on account of " *This sad affair of Baretti*," begging of him to try if he could suggest anything that might be of service ; and, at the same time, recommending to him an industrious young man who kept a pickle-shop. JOHNSON. "Ay, Sir, here you have a specimen of human sympathy; a friend hanged and a cucumber pickled. We know not whether Baretti or the pickle-man has kept Davies from sleep ; nor does he know himself. And as to his not sleeping, Sir : Tom Davies is a very great man ; Tom has been upon the stage and knows how to do those things. I have not been upon the stage and cannot do those things." BOSWELL. "I have often blamed myself, Sir, for not feeling for others as sensibly as many say they do." JOHNSON. "Sir, don't be duped by them any more. You will find these very feeling people

are

are not very ready to do you good.   They *pay* you by *feeling*." '

Boswell's *Life of Johnson*, ii. 94.

. • .

' I SAID it was lucky he was not present when this misfortune[1] happened.   JOHNSON. "It is lucky for *me*. People in distress never think that you feel enough."   BOSWELL. " And, Sir, they will have the hope of seeing you which will be a relief in the meantime ; and when you get to them the pain will be so far abated that they will be capable of being consoled by you, which in the first violence of it I believe would not be the case."   JOHNSON. "No, Sir ; violent pain of mind like violent pain of body *must* be severely felt."   BOSWELL. " I own, Sir, I have not so much feeling for the distress of others as some people have, or pretend to have : but I know this that I would do all in my power to relieve them."   JOHNSON. "Sir, it is affectation to pretend to feel the distress of others as much as they do themselves.   It is equally so as if one should pretend to feel as much pain while a friend's leg is cutting off as he does.   No, Sir ; you have expressed the rational and just nature of sympathy. I would have gone to the extremity of the earth to have preserved this boy."

Ib. ii. 469.

. • .

To feel sincere and honest joy at the success of another, though it is necessary to true friendship, is perhaps neither very common nor very easy.   There is in every mind implanted by nature a desire of superiority which counteracts the pleasure which the sight of success and happiness ought always to impart.

Works, ix. 389.

---

[1] The death of Mr. Thrale's son.

System

System of life :

LET fanciful men do as they will, depend upon it it is difficult to disturb the system of life.

Boswell's Life of Johnson, ii. 102.

Talk :

SUCH tattle as filled your last sweet letter prevents one great inconvenience of absence, that of returning home a stranger and an inquirer. The variations of life consist of little things. Important innovations are soon heard and easily understood. Men that meet to talk of physics or metaphysics, or law or history, may be immediately acquainted. We look at each other in silence only for want of petty talk upon slight occurrences.　　Piozzi Letters, i. 354.

．・．

HE[1] shuffles between cowardice and veracity, and talks big when he says nothing.　　　　　Works, viii. 213.

．・．

A MAN who always talks for fame never can be pleasing. The man who talks to unburthen his mind is the man to delight you.　　　　　Boswell's Life of Johnson, iii. 247.

．・．

' MR. JOHNSON, when enumerating our Club, observed of some of us that they talked from books,—Langton in particular. "Garrick," he said, " would talk from books if he talked seriously." " *I*," said he, " do not talk from books ; *you* do not talk from books." '

Ib. v. 378, n. 4.

---

[1] Swift, who had been charged with writing a letter to Queen Caroline, 'not so much entreating as requiring her patronage of Mrs. Barber.'

Tame

Tame animals :

I BELIEVE no generous or benevolent man can see the vilest animal courting his regard and shrinking at his anger, playing his gambols of delight before him, calling on him in distress, and flying to him in danger without more kindness than he can persuade himself to feel for the wild and un-social inhabitants of the air and water.   We naturally endear to ourselves those to whom we impart any kind of pleasure because we imagine their affection and esteem secured to us by the benefits which they receive.   *Rambler*, No. 148.

Tavern life :

'WE dined at an excellent inn at Chapel-house, where Dr. Johnson expatiated on the felicity of England in its taverns and inns, and triumphed over the French for not having in any perfection the tavern life. " There is no private house (said he) in which people can enjoy themselves so well as at a capital tavern.   Let there be ever so great plenty of good things, ever so much grandeur, ever so much elegance, ever so much desire that every body should be easy; in the nature of things it cannot be : there must always be some degree of care and anxiety. The master of the house is anxious to entertain his guests ; the guests are anxious to be agreeable to him : and no man but a very impudent dog indeed can as freely command what is in another man's house as if it were his own. Whereas at a tavern there is a general freedom from anxiety. You are sure you are welcome : and the more noise you make, the more trouble you give, the more good things you call for, the welcomer you are. No servants will attend you with the alacrity which waiters do who are incited by the prospect of an immediate

reward

reward in proportion as they please. No, Sir; there is nothing which has yet been contrived by man by which so much happiness is produced as by a good tavern or inn." He then repeated with great emotion Shenstone's lines :—

> " Whoe'er has travell'd life's dull round,
>   Where'er his stages may have been,
>   May sigh to think he still has found
>   The warmest welcome at an inn." '

Boswell's Life of Johnson, ii. 451.

.˙.

'IN contradiction to those who, having a wife and children, prefer domestic enjoyments to those which a tavern affords, I have heard Johnson assert *that a tavern chair was the throne of human felicity*.—"As soon," said he, "as I enter the door of a tavern I experience an oblivion of care and a freedom from solicitude : when I am seated I find the master courteous and the servants obsequious to my call, anxious to know and ready to supply my wants : wine there exhilarates my spirits, and prompts me to free conversation and an interchange of discourse with those whom I most love : I dogmatise and am contradicted, and in this conflict of opinions and sentiments I find delight." '

Hawkins's Life of Johnson, p. 87.

Tea :

'I REMEMBER when Sir Joshua Reynolds at my house reminded Dr. Johnson that he had drunk eleven cups, he replied :—"Sir, I did not count your glasses of wine, why should you number up my cups of tea?" And then laughing in perfect good humour he added :—"Sir, I should have released the lady from any further trouble if it had not been for your remark; but you have reminded me that I want

one

one of the dozen, and I must request Mrs. Cumberland to round up my number."'

Cumberland's Memoirs, i. 357.

.˙.

'IT is related that at Dunvegan Lady Macleod, having poured out for Dr. Johnson sixteen cups of tea, asked him if a small basin would not save him trouble and be more agreeable. "I wonder, Madam," answered he roughly, "why all the ladies ask me such questions. It is to save yourselves trouble, Madam, and not me." The lady was silent and resumed her task.'

Northcote's Life of Reynolds, i. 81.

Teachers of morality:

BE not too hasty to trust or to admire the teachers of morality: they discourse like angels but they live like men.

Rasselas, ch. 18.

Teaching:

THERE is no employment in which men are more easily betrayed to indecency and impatience than in that of teaching; in which they necessarily converse with those who are their inferiors in the relation by which they are connected, and whom it may be sometimes proper to treat with that dignity which too often swells into arrogance; and to restrain with such authority as not every man has learnt to separate from tyranny. In this state of temporary honour a proud man is too willing to exert his prerogative and too ready to forget that he is dictating to those who may one day dictate to him. He is inclined to wonder that what he comprehends himself is not equally clear to others; and often reproaches the intellects of his auditors when he ought to blame the confusion of his own ideas and the improprieties

U   of

of his own language. He reiterates therefore his positions without elucidation, and enforces his assertions by his frown when he finds arguments less easy to be supplied. Thus forgetting that he had to do with men whose passions are perhaps equally turbulent with his own he transfers by degrees to his instruction the prejudices which are first raised by his behaviour; and having forced upon his pupils an hatred of their teacher he sees it quickly terminate in a contempt of the precept. *Works*, ix. 366.

Tedious, but not long:

AN hour may be tedious but cannot be long.

Idler, No. 71.

Telling tales against oneself:

A MAN should be careful never to tell tales of himself to his own disadvantage. People may be amused and laugh at the time, but they will be remembered and brought out against him upon some subsequent occasion.

Boswell's *Life of Johnson*, ii. 472.

Testimony:

To persuade common and uninstructed minds to the belief of any fact we may every day perceive that the testimony of one man whom they think worthy of credit has more force than the arguments of a thousand reasoners, even when the arguments are such as they may be imagined completely qualified to comprehend. *Works*, ix. 519.

Tenderness:

WANT of tenderness is want of parts, and is no less a proof of stupidity than depravity. Boswell's *Life of Johnson*, ii. 122.

The

The latter, the former:

THE Rev. T. Twining, one of Dr. Burney's friends, wrote in 1779:—'You use a form of reference that I abominate, i. e. the latter, the former. "As long as you have the use of your tongue and your pen," said Dr. Johnson to Dr. Burney, "never, Sir, be reduced to that shift."'

Boswell's Life of Johnson, iv. 190, n. 2.

Thinking indistinctly:

MOST men think indistinctly and therefore cannot speak with exactness.   Works, v. 43.

Thinking justly but faintly:

HE[1] thinks justly; but he thinks faintly.   Ib. vii. 452.

Thought:

THOUGHT is always troublesome to him who lives without his own approbation.   Ib. ix. 317.

Threatening the world:

POPE, in one of his Letters complaining of the treatment which his poem had found, 'owns that such critics can intimidate him, nay almost persuade him to write no more, which is a compliment this age deserves.' The man who threatens the world is always ridiculous; for the world can easily go on without him, and in a short time will cease to miss him. I have heard of an idiot who used to revenge his vexations by lying all night upon the bridge. 'There is nothing,' says Juvenal, 'that a man will not believe in his

---

[1] Addison, as a poet.

U 2

own

Wit and Wisdom of Samuel Johnson.

own favour [1].' Pope had been flattered till he thought him-self one of the moving powers in the system of life.   When he talked of laying down his pen, those who sat round him entreated and implored; and self-love did not suffer him to suspect that they went away and laughed.   *Works*, viii. 280.

Time:

So little do we accustom ourselves to consider the effects of time, that things necessary and certain often surprise us like unexpected contingencies.   We leave the beauty in her bloom, and after an absence of twenty years wonder at our return to find her faded.   We meet those whom we left children and can scarcely persuade ourselves to treat them as men.   The traveller visits in age those countries through which he rambled in his youth and hopes for merriment at the old place.   The man of business wearied with unsatis-factory prosperity retires to the town of his nativity, and expects to play away the last years with the companions of his childhood, and recover youth in the fields where he once was young.   *Idler*, No. 43.

IT is well known that time once past never returns; and that the moment which is lost is lost for ever.   Time there-fore ought, above all other kinds of property, to be free from invasion; and yet there is no man who does not claim the power of wasting that time which is the right of others. This usurpation is so general that a very small part of the year is spent by choice; scarcely anything is done when it is intended, or obtained when it is desired.   Life is con-tinually ravaged by invaders; one steals away an hour and

---

[1] *Satires*, iv. 70.

another

Wit and Wisdom of Samuel Johnson.

another a day; one conceals the robbery by hurrying us into business, another by lulling us with amusement; the depredation is continued through a thousand vicissitudes of tumult and tranquillity till, having lost all, we can lose no more.

Idler, No. 14.

.·.

WHATEVER we see on every side reminds us of the lapse of time and the flux of life. The day and night succeed each other, the rotation of seasons diversifies the year; the sun rises, attains the meridian, declines and sets; and the moon every night changes its form. The day has been considered as an image of the year, and the year as the representation of life. The morning answers to the spring, and the spring to childhood and youth; the noon corresponds to the summer, and the summer to the strength of manhood. The evening is an emblem of autumn, and autumn of declining life. The night with its silence and darkness shows the winter in which all the powers of vegetation are benumbed; and the winter points out the time when life shall cease with its hopes and pleasures.

Ib. No. 43.

Timidity:

IT is the advantage of vehemence and activity that they are always hastening to their own reformation; because they incite us to try whether our expectations are well grounded, and therefore detect the deceits which they are apt to occasion. But timidity is a disease of the mind more obstinate and fatal; for a man once persuaded that any impediment is insuperable, has given it, with respect to himself, that strength and weight which it had not before. He can scarcely strive with vigour and perseverance when

he

he has no hope of gaining the victory; and since he never will try his strength can never discover the unreasonableness of his fears.

Rambler, No. 25.

Toleration:

'TALKING on the subject of toleration one day when some friends were with him in his study, Dr. Johnson made his usual remark, that the State has a right to regulate the religion of the people, who are the children of the State. A clergyman having readily acquiesced in this, Johnson, who loved discussion, observed, "But, Sir, you must go round to other States than our own. You do not know what a Bramin has to say for himself. In short, Sir, I have got no further than this: Every man has a right to utter what he thinks truth, and every other man has a right to knock him down for it. Martyrdom is the test." '

Boswell's *Life of Johnson*, iv. 12.

To-morrow:

TO-MORROW is an old deceiver, and his cheat never grows stale.

Piozzi Letters, i. 94.

COMPLAINTS are vain; we will try to do better another time. To-morrow and to-morrow. A few designs and a few failures, and the time of designing is past.

Ib. i. 53.

Traders:

'At breakfast, I asked, "What is the reason that we are angry at a trader's having opulence?" JOHNSON. "Why, Sir, the reason is, (though I don't undertake to prove that there is a reason,) we see no qualities in trade that should

entitle

entitle a man to superiority. We are not angry at a soldier's getting riches, because we see that he possesses qualities which we have not. If a man returns from a battle, having lost one hand and with the other full of gold, we feel that he deserves the gold; but we cannot think that a fellow by sitting all day at a desk is entitled to get above us." BOSWELL. "But, Sir, may we not suppose a merchant to be a man of an enlarged mind, such as Addison in the *Spectator* describes Sir Andrew Freeport to have been?" JOHNSON. "Why, Sir, we may suppose any fictitious character. We may suppose a philosophical day-labourer, who is happy in reflecting that, by his labour, he contributes to the fertility of the earth and to the support of his fellow-creatures; but we find no such philosophical day-labourer. A merchant may, perhaps, be a man of an enlarged mind; but there is nothing in trade connected with an enlarged mind."'

Boswell's Life of Johnson, v. 327.

Tragedy-writers:

'MRS. BROOKE asked Johnson to look over her *Siege of Sinope*; he always found means to evade it. At last she pressed him so closely that he refused to do it, and told her that she herself, by carefully looking it over, would be able to see if there was anything amiss as well as he could. "But, Sir," said she, "I have no time. I have already so many irons in the fire." "Why then, Madam," said he quite out of patience, "the best thing I can advise you to do is to put your tragedy along with your irons."'

Hannah More's Memoirs, i. 200.

.˙.

'THE conversation turning on the merits of a certain dramatic

dramatic writer, Johnson said: "I never did the man an injury; but he would persist in reading his tragedy to me." '

Boswell's *Life of Johnson*, iv. 244, *n.* 2.

Travels:

HE that would travel for the entertainment of others should remember that the great object of remark is human life.

Idler, No. 97.

...

HE who has not made the experiment or who is not accustomed to require rigorous accuracy from himself, will scarcely believe how much a few hours take from certainty of knowledge and distinctness of imagery; how the succession of objects will be broken, how separate parts will be confused, and how many particular features and discriminations will be compressed and conglobated into one gross and general idea. To this dilatory notation must be imputed the false relations of travellers where there is no imaginable motive to deceive. They trusted to memory what cannot be trusted safely but to the eye, and told by guess what a few hours before they had known with certainty. Thus it was that Wheeler and Spon[1] described with irreconcilable contrariety things which they surveyed together, and which both undoubtedly designed to show as they saw them.

Works, ix. 144.

...

BOOKS of travels will be good in proportion to what a man has previously in his mind; his knowing what to observe; his power of contrasting one mode of life with another. As the Spanish proverb says, 'He who would bring home the wealth of the Indies must carry the wealth

---

[1] Travellers in the East in the seventeenth century.

of

of the Indies with him.' So it is in travelling ; a man must carry knowledge with him, if he would bring home knowledge.

Boswell's *Life of Johnson*, iii. 301.

Trifling :

THERE must be a time in which every man trifles ; and the only choice that nature offers us is to trifle in company or alone. To join profit with pleasure has been an old precept among men who have had very different conceptions of profit. All have agreed that our amusements should not terminate wholly in the present moment, but contribute more or less to future advantage. He that amuses himself among well-chosen companions can scarcely fail to receive from the most careless and obstreperous merriment which virtue can allow some useful hints ; nor can converse on the most familiar topics without some casual information. The loose sparkles of thoughtless wit may give new light to the mind, and the gay contention for paradoxical positions rectify the opinions. This is the time in which those friendships that give happiness or consolation, relief or security, are generally formed. A wise and good man is never so amiable as in his unbended and familiar intervals. Heroic generosity or philosophical discoveries may compel veneration and respect, but love always implies some kind of natural or voluntary equality, and is only to be excited by that levity and cheerfulness which disencumber all minds from awe and solicitude, invite the modest to freedom and exalt the timorous to confidence.

Rambler, No. 89.

Trustfulness :

Trustfulness:

WE are inclined to believe those whom we do not know
because they have never deceived us.   *Idler*, No. 80.

Truth:

THE value of every story depends on its being true.   A
story is a picture either of an individual or of human nature
in general: if it be false, it is a picture of nothing.   For
instance: suppose a man should tell that Johnson, before
setting out for Italy, as he had to cross the Alps, sat down
to make himself wings.   This many people would believe;
but it would be a picture of nothing.

Boswell's Life of Johnson, ii. 433.

∴

'"A STORY," says Johnson, "is a specimen of human
manners, and derives its sole value from its truth.   When
Foote has told me something, I dismiss it from my mind
like a passing shadow; when Reynolds tells me something,
I consider myself as possessed of an idea the more."'

Piozzi's Anecdotes, p. 116.

∴

HE[1] appears indeed to have been willing to pay labour
for truth.   *Works*, vi. 483.

∴

AGAINST the inconveniencies and vexations of long life
may be set the pleasure of discovering truth, perhaps the
only pleasure that age affords.   *Debates. Works*, xi. 5.

---

[1] Sir Thomas Browne.

NOBODY

NOBODY has a right to put another under such a difficulty that he must either hurt the person by telling the
truth, or hurt himself by telling what is not true.

Boswell's Life of Johnson, iii. 320.

.·.

DECENCY is a proper circumstance, but liberty is the
essence of senatorial disquisitions. Liberty is the parent
of truth, but truth and decency are sometimes at variance;
all men and all propositions are to be treated here[1] as they
deserve, and there are many who have no claim either to
respect or decency.   Debates. Works, x. 310.

.·.

'NEXT morning, while we were at breakfast, Johnson
gave a very earnest recommendation of what he himself
practised with the utmost conscientiousness: I mean a
strict attention to truth even in the most minute particulars. "Accustom your children (said he) constantly to
this; if a thing happened at one window and they, when
relating it, say that it happened at another, do not let it
pass, but instantly check them; you do not know where
deviation from truth will end." BOSWELL. "It may come
to the door: and when once an account is at all varied in
one circumstance, it may by degrees be varied so as to be
totally different from what really happened." Our lively
hostess[2], whose fancy was impatient of the rein, fidgeted at
this, and ventured to say, "Nay, this is too much. If
Mr. Johnson should forbid me to drink tea, I would
comply, as I should feel the restraint only twice a day;
but little variations in narrative must happen a thousand

---

[1] In the House of Commons.   [2] Mrs. Thrale.

times

times a day if one is not perpetually watching." JOHN-SON. "Well, Madam, and you *ought* to be perpetually watching. It is more from carelessness about truth than from intentional lying that there is so much falsehood in the world."'

Boswell's Life of Johnson, iii. 228.

Twalmley the Great:

'ONCE, when checking my boasting too frequently of myself in company, he said to me, "Boswell, you often vaunt so much as to provoke ridicule. You put me in mind of a man who was standing in the kitchen of an inn with his back to the fire, and thus accosted the person next him, "Do you know, Sir, who I am?" "No, Sir, (said the other,) I have not that advantage." "Sir, (said he,) I am the *great* TWALMLEY, who invented the New Floodgate Iron."'

Ib. iv. 193.

Tyranny:

THERE is a remedy in human nature against tyranny that will keep us safe under every form of government.

Ib. ii. 170.

Unclubable:

'DR. JOHNSON said that Sir John Hawkins and he once belonged to the same club, but that as he [Hawkins] eat no supper after the first night of his admission, he desired to be excused paying his share. "And was he excused?" "O yes; for no man is angry at another for being inferior to himself! we all scorned him, and admitted his plea. For my part I was such a fool as to pay my share for wine, though I never tasted any. But Sir John was a most *un-clubable* man."'

Mme. D'Arblay's Diary, i. 65.

Universities:

Universities:

IT is too common for those who have been bred to scholastic professions, and passed much of their time in academies where nothing but learning confers honours, to disregard every other qualification, and to imagine that they shall find mankind ready to pay homage to their knowledge and to crowd about them for instruction. They therefore step out from their cells into the open world with all the confidence of authority and dignity of importance ; they look round about them at once with ignorance and scorn on a race of beings to whom they are equally un- known and equally contemptible, but whose manners they must imitate, and with whose opinions they must comply if they desire to pass their time happily among them.

Rambler, No. 137.

. ∴ .

THE most frequent reproach of the scholastic race is the want of fortitude, not martial but philosophic. Men bred in shades and silence, taught to immure themselves at sunset, and accustomed to no other weapon than syllo- gism, may be allowed to feel terror at personal danger, and to be disconcerted by tumult and alarm. But why should he whose life is spent in contemplation, and whose business is only to discover truth, be unable to rectify the fallacies of imagination, or contend successfully against prejudice and passion? To what end has he read and meditated if he gives up his understanding to false appearances, and suffers himself to be enslaved by fear of evils to which only folly or vanity can expose him, or elated by advantages to which, as they are equally conferred upon the good and bad, no real dignity is annexed. Such, however, is the

state

state of the world, that the most obsequious of the slaves of pride, the most rapturous of the gazers upon wealth, the most officious of the whisperers of greatness, are collected from seminaries appropriated to the study of wisdom and of virtue, where it was intended that appetite should learn to be content with little, and that hope should aspire only to honours which no human power can give or take away.

Rambler, No. 180.

.·.

THE great advantage of a university is that a person lives in a place where his reputation depends on his learning.

Windham's *Diary*, p. 19.

Unhappy people hated:

THE world will never be long without some good reason to hate the unhappy: their real faults are immediately detected; and if those are not sufficient to sink them into infamy, an additional weight of calumny will be superadded; he that fails in his endeavours after wealth or power will not long retain either honesty or courage.

Adventurer, No. 99.

Unpleasing ideas obtruded:

UNNECESSARILY to obtrude unpleasing ideas is a species of oppression. It is little more criminal to deprive another of some real advantage, than to interrupt that forgetfulness of its absence which is the next happiness to actual possession.

Rambler, No. 98.

Use and wont:

'I PITIED a friend before Dr. Johnson who had a whining wife that found everything painful to her and nothing

pleasing.

pleasing. "He does not know that she whimpers (says Johnson); when a door has creaked for a fortnight together, you may observe the master will scarcely give sixpence to get it oiled." '

Piozzi's Anecdotes, p. 169.

Vanity:

THE greatest human virtue bears no proportion to human vanity. We always think ourselves better than we are, and are generally desirous that others should think us still better than we think ourselves. To praise us for actions or dispositions which deserve praise is not to confer a benefit, but to pay a tribute. We have always pretensions to fame which, in our own hearts, we know to be disputable, and which we are desirous to strengthen by a new suffrage; we have always hopes which we suspect to be fallacious, and of which we eagerly snatch at every confirmation.

Rambler, No. 104.

.·.

WHEN any one complains of the want of what he is known to possess in an uncommon degree, he certainly waits with impatience to be contradicted. When the trader pretends anxiety about the payment of his bills, or the beauty remarks how frightfully she looks, then is the lucky moment to talk of riches or of charms, of the death of lovers or the honour of a merchant.

Ib. No. 193.

.·.

EVERY man is of importance to himself, and therefore, in his own opinion, to others; and, supposing the world already acquainted with all his pleasures and his pains, is perhaps the first to publish injuries or misfortunes which had never been known unless related by himself, and at

which

which those that hear them will only laugh; for no man sympathizes with the sorrows of vanity. *Works*, viii. 276.

Variety:

THE great source of pleasure is variety. Uniformity must tire at last, though it be uniformity of excellence. We love to expect; and when expectation is disappointed or gratified, we want to be again expecting. For this impatience of the present, whoever would please must make provision. The skilful writer *irritat, mulcet*[1], makes a due distribution of the still and animated parts. It is for want of this artful intertexture, and those necessary changes, that the whole of a book may be tedious though all the parts are praised. *Ib.* vii. 151.

Virtue:

THE philosophers of the heathen world seemed to hope that man might be flattered into virtue, and therefore told him much of his rank and of the meanness of degeneracy; they asserted indeed with truth that all greatness was in the practice of virtue, but of virtue their notions were narrow; and pride, which their doctrine made its chief support, was not of power sufficient to struggle with sense or passion. *Ib.* ix. 311.

Virtues and vices:

NEITHER our virtues nor vices are all our own.

Rambler, No. 180.

Virtuosoes:

THE virtuoso cannot be said to be wholly useless; but perhaps he may be sometimes culpable for confining him-

---

[1] Horace, 2 *Epis.* i. 212.

self

self to business below his genius, and losing in petty speculations those hours by which, if he had spent them in nobler studies, he might have given new light to the intellectual world. It is never without grief that I find a man capable of ratiocination or invention enlisting himself in this secondary class of learning; for when he has once discovered a method of gratifying his desire of eminence by expence rather than by labour, and known the sweets of a life blest at once with the ease of idleness and the reputation of knowledge, he will not easily be brought to undergo again the toil of thinking, or leave his toys and trinkets for arguments and principles, arguments which require circumspection and vigilance, and principles which cannot be obtained but by the drudgery of meditation. *Rambler*, No. 83.

Vivite laeti:

WHAT can be done you must do for yourself; do not let any uneasy thought settle in your mind. Cheerfulness and exercise are your great remedies. Nothing is for the present worth your anxiety. *Vivite laeti*[1] is one of the great rules of health. I believe it will be good to ride often, but never to weariness, for weariness is itself a temporary resolution of the nerves, and is therefore to be avoided. Labour is exercise continued to fatigue—exercise is labour used only while it produces pleasure.

Piozzi Letters, ii. 54.

Vows:

ALL unnecessary vows are folly, because they suppose a prescience of the future which has not been given us.

---

[1] 'Mr. Burke once admirably counselled a grave and anxious gentleman "live pleasant."'—Boswell's *Life of Johnson*, i. 344.

X

They

They are, I think, a crime, because they resign that life to chance which God has given us to be regulated by reason; and superinduce a kind of fatality, from which it is the great privilege of our nature to be free.　　*Piozzi Letters*, i. 83.

Wag:

'DR. JOHNSON said, "Every man has some time in his life an ambition to be a wag."'　　Mme. D'Arblay's *Diary*, v. 307.

War:

IT is wonderful with what coolness and indifference the greater part of mankind see war commenced. Those that hear of it at a distance, or read of it in books, but have never presented its evils to their minds, consider it as little more than a splendid game, a proclamation, an army, a battle, and a triumph. Some indeed must perish in the most successful field; but they die upon the bed of honour, 'resign their lives amidst the joys of conquest and, filled with England's glory, smile in death.' The life of a modern soldier is ill represented by heroic fiction. War has means of destruction more formidable than the cannon and the sword. Of the thousands and ten thousands that perished in our late contests with France and Spain, a very small part ever felt the stroke of an enemy; the rest languished in tents and ships, amidst damps and putrefaction; pale, torpid, spiritless and helpless; gasping and groaning, unpitied among men made obdurate by long continuance of hopeless misery; and were at last whelmed in pits or heaved into the ocean, without notice and without remembrance. By incommodious encampments and unwholesome stations, where courage is useless and

enterprise

enterprise impracticable, fleets are silently dispeopled and armies sluggishly melted away. *Works,* vi. 199.

· ·

IT affords a generous and manly pleasure to conceive a little nation gathering its fruits and tending its herds with fearless confidence, though it lies open on every side to invasion. Where in contempt of walls and trenches, every man sleeps securely with his sword beside him; where all on the first approach of hostility came together at the call to battle, as at a summons to a festal show; and committing their cattle to the care of those whom age or nature has disabled, engaged the enemy with that competition for hazard and for glory which operate in men that fight under the eye of those whose dislike or kindness they have always considered as the greatest evil or the greatest good. This was, in the beginning of the present century, the state of the Highlands. Every man was a soldier who partook of national confidence and interested himself in national honour. To lose this spirit is to lose what no small advantage will compensate. It may likewise deserve to be inquired whether a great nation ought to be totally commercial? whether, amidst the uncertainty of human affairs, too much attention to one mode of happiness may not endanger others? whether the pride of riches must not sometimes have recourse to the protection of courage? and whether, if it be necessary to preserve in some part of the empire the military spirit, it can subsist more commodiously in any place, than in remote and unprofitable provinces, where it can commonly do little harm, and whence it may be called forth at any sudden exigence? It must however

be

be confessed that a man who places honour only in successful violence is a very troublesome and pernicious animal in
time of peace; and that the martial character cannot prevail
in a whole people, but by the diminution of all other virtues.
He that is accustomed to resolve all right into conquest
will have very little tenderness or equity. All the friendship
in such a life can be only a confederacy of invasion, or alliance of defence. The strong must flourish by force, and
the weak subsist by stratagem. *Works*, ix. 88.

.˙.

'JOHNSON laughed much at Lord Kames's opinion that
war was a good thing occasionally, as so much valour and
virtue were exhibited in it. "A fire," says Johnson, "might
as well be thought a good thing; there is the bravery and
address of the firemen employed in extinguishing it; there
is much humanity exerted in saving the lives and properties
of the poor sufferers; yet after all this, who can say a fire
is a good thing?"' Boswell's *Life of Johnson*, i. 393, *n.* 2.

Warburton and Thomas Edwards:

'SOON after Edwards's *Canons of Criticism* came out,
Johnson was dining at Tonson's the bookseller, with
Hayman the painter and some more company. Hayman
related to Sir Joshua Reynolds that, the conversation having
turned upon Edwards's book, the gentlemen praised it
much and Johnson allowed its merit. But when they went
farther, and appeared to put that author upon a level with
Warburton, "Nay, (said Johnson,) he has given him some
smart hits to be sure; but there is no proportion between the
two men; they must not be named together. A fly, Sir, may

sting

sting a stately horse and make him wince; but one is but an insect, and the other is a horse still." '

Boswell's Life of Johnson, i. 263, n. 3.

Wealth:

THEIR [1] arguments have been indeed so unsuccessful that I know not whether it can be shown that by all the wit and reason which this favourite cause has called forth, a single convert was ever made; that even one man has refused to be rich, when to be rich was in his power, from the conviction of the greater happiness of a narrow fortune; or disburthened himself of wealth when he had tried its inquietudes, merely to enjoy the peace and leisure and security of a mean and unenvied state.   Rambler, No. 58.

WEALTH cannot confer greatness, for nothing can make that great which the decree of nature has ordained to be little. The bramble may be placed in a hot-bed, but can never become an oak. Even royalty itself is not able to give that dignity which it happens not to find, but oppresses feeble minds, though it may elevate the strong. The world has been governed in the name of kings whose existence has scarcely been perceived by any real effects beyond their own palaces.   Ib.

EVERY man is rich or poor according to the proportion between his desires and enjoyments; any enlargement of wishes is therefore equally destructive to happiness with the diminution of possession; and he that teaches another to long for what he never shall obtain is no less an enemy

---

[1] The moralists who inveigh against riches.

to his quiet than if he had robbed him of part of his
patrimony.

Rambler, No. 163.

Weather:

AN *Englishman's* notice of the weather is the natural
consequence of changeable skies and uncertain seasons.
In many parts of the world wet weather and dry are
regularly expected at certain periods; but in our island
every man goes to sleep, unable to guess whether he shall
behold in the morning a bright or cloudy atmosphere,
whether his rest shall be lulled by a shower or broken by
a tempest. We therefore rejoice mutually at good weather
as at an escape from something that we feared; and mutually
complain of bad, as of the loss of something that we hoped.
Such is the reason of our practice; and who shall treat it
with contempt? Surely not the attendant on a court whose
business is to watch the looks of a being weak and foolish as
himself, and whose vanity is to recount the names of men
who might drop into nothing and leave no vacuity; nor
the proprietor of funds who stops his acquaintance in the
street to tell him of the loss of half-a-crown; nor the
inquirer after news who fills his head with foreign events
and talks of skirmishes and sieges, of which no consequence
will ever reach his hearers or himself. The weather is a
nobler and more interesting subject; it is the present state
of the skies and of the earth, on which plenty and famine
are suspended, on which millions depend for the necessaries
of life.

Idler, No. 11.

Wife:

‘ BUT surely,’ interposed the prince [1], ‘you suppose the

---

[1] Rasselas.

chief

chief motive of choice forgotten or neglected. Whenever I shall seek a wife, it shall be my first question, whether she be willing to be led by reason?' 'Thus it is,' said Nekayah, 'that philosophers are deceived. There are a thousand familiar disputes which reason never can decide; questions that elude investigation, and make logic ridiculous; cases where something must be done, and where little can be said. Consider the state of mankind, and inquire how few can be supposed to act upon any occasions, whether small or great, with all the reasons of action present to their minds. Wretched would be the pair above all names of wretchedness who should be doomed to adjust by reason every morning all the minute detail of a domestic day.'

Rasselas, ch. 29.

.˙.

' "SOME cunning men choose fools for their wives, thinking to manage them, but they always fail. There is a spaniel fool and a mule fool. The spaniel fool may be made to do by beating. The mule fool will neither do by words or blows; and the spaniel fool often turns mule at last: and suppose a fool to be made do pretty well, you must have the continual trouble of making her do. Depend upon it, no woman is the worse for sense and knowledge." Whether afterwards he meant merely to say a polite thing, or to give his opinion, I could not be sure; but he added, "Men know that women are an over-match for them, and therefore they choose the weakest or most ignorant. If they did not think so, they could never be afraid of women knowing as much as themselves." '   Boswell's Life of Johnson, v. 226.

Wit and
Wisdom
of
Samuel
Johnson.

Wilkes's

Wilkes's mob :

' JOHNSON had a sovereign contempt for Wilkes and his party, whom he looked upon as a mere rabble. " Sir," said he, " had Wilkes's mob prevailed against government, this nation had died of *phthiriasis*." The expression *morbus pediculosus*, as being better known would strike more.'

Boswell's Life of Johnson, iii. 183, n. 2.

Wine :

' DESIROUS of calling Johnson forth to talk and exercise his wit, though I should myself be the object of it, I resolutely ventured to undertake the defence of convivial indulgence in wine, though he was not to-night in the most genial humour. After urging the common plausible topics, I at last had recourse to the maxim *in vino veritas*, a man who is well warmed with wine will speak truth. JOHNSON. " Why, Sir, that may be an argument for drinking if you suppose men in general to be liars. But, Sir, I would not keep company with a fellow who lies as long as he is sober, and whom you must make drunk before you can get a word of truth out of him." '

Ib. ii. 187.

WINE gives great pleasure, and every pleasure is of itself a good. It is a good unless counterbalanced by evil. A man may have a strong reason not to drink wine, and that may be greater than the pleasure. Wine makes a man better pleased with himself. I do not say that it makes him more pleasing to others. Sometimes it does. But the danger is, that while a man grows better pleased with himself he may be growing less pleasing to others. Wine gives a man nothing. It neither gives him knowledge nor wit ; it only animates a man, and enables him to bring out what

a dread

a dread of the company has repressed. It only puts in motion what has been locked up in frost. But this may be good, or it may be bad. Boswell's *Life of Johnson*, iii. 327.

Wit and
Wisdom
of
Samuel
Johnson.

Wisdom:

DAILY business adds no more to wisdom than daily lesson to the learning of the teacher. . . . Far the greater part of human minds never endeavour their own improvement. Opinions once received from instruction, or settled by whatever accident, are seldom recalled to examination; having been once supposed to be right they are never discovered to be erroneous, for no application is made of any thing that time may present, either to shake or to confirm them. From this acquiescence in preconceptions none are wholly free; between fear of uncertainty and dislike of labour every one rests while he might yet go forward, and they that were wise at thirty-three are very little wiser at forty-five. *Piozzi Letters*, i. 300.

To what purpose is observation if we must shut our eyes against it and appeal for ever to the wisdom of our ancestors? If we must fall into error merely because they were mistaken, and rush upon rocks out of veneration to those who were wrecked against them? *Debates. Works*, x. 307.

Wishing young ladies well:

' A LITTLE while after Dr. Johnson drank Miss Thrale's health and mine, and then added: " 'Tis a terrible thing that we cannot wish young ladies well without wishing them to become old women!" ' Mme. D'Arblay's *Diary*, i. 63.

Wit:

Wit :

NOTHING was ever said with uncommon felicity but by the co-operation of chance; and therefore wit as well as valour must be content to share its honours with fortune.

Idler, No. 58.

Wits :

THE task of every other slave has an end. The rower in time reaches the port; the lexicographer at last finds the conclusion of his alphabet; only the hapless wit has his labour always to begin, the call for novelty is never satisfied, and one jest only raises expectation of another.

Rambler, No. 141.

Women :

WOMEN have a perpetual envy of our vices; they are less vicious than we, not from choice, but because we restrict them; they are the slaves of order and fashion; their virtue is of more consequence to us than our own, so far as concerns this world.   Boswell's *Life of Johnson*, iv. 291.

. · .

WOMEN, by whatever fate, always judge absurdly of the intellects of boys. The vivacity and confidence which attract female admiration are seldom produced in the early part of life, but by ignorance at least, if not by stupidity; for they proceed not from confidence of right, but fearlessness of wrong.   *Rambler*, No. 194.

. · .

' JOHNSON, upon hearing a lady commended for her learning, said :—" A man is in general better pleased when he has a good dinner upon his table than when his wife

talks

talks Greek. My old friend, Mrs. Carter, could make a pudding as well as translate Epictetus."'

Boswell's Life of Johnson, i. 122, n. 4.

.˙.

A WOMAN's preaching is like a dog's walking on his hinder legs. It is not done well; but you are surprised to find it done at all. *Ib. i. 463.*

.˙.

As the faculty of writing has been chiefly a masculine endowment, the reproach of making the world miserable has been always thrown upon the women. *Rambler, No. 18.*

.˙.

NATURE has given women so much power that the law has very wisely given them little.

Boswell's Life of Johnson, v. 226, n. 2.

Wonder:

THAT wonder is the effect of ignorance has been often observed. The awful stillness of attention with which the mind is overspread at the first view of an unexpected effect ceases when we have leisure to disentangle complications and investigate causes. Wonder is a pause of reason, a sudden cessation of the mental progress which lasts only while the understanding is fixed upon some single idea, and is at an end when it recovers force enough to divide the object into its parts, or mark the intermediate gradations from the first agent to the last consequence.

Rambler, No. 137.

Wonders:

THERE is not, perhaps, among the multitudes of all conditions that swarm upon the earth a single man who does

not

not believe that he has something extraordinary to relate of himself, and who does not at one time or other summon the attention of his friends to the casualties of his adventures, and the vicissitudes of his fortune: casualties and vicissitudes that happen alike in lives uniform and diversified; to the commander of armies and the writer at a desk; to the sailor who resigns himself to the wind and water, and the farmer whose longest journey is to the market. In the present state of the world man may pass through *Shakespeare's* seven stages of life, and meet nothing singular or wonderful. But such is every man's attention to himself, that what is common and unheeded when it is only seen becomes remarkable and peculiar when we happen to feel it.

Idler, No. 50.

∴

It is the great failing of a strong imagination to catch greedily at wonders.

Works, vi. 455.

∴

Wonders are willingly told and willingly heard.

Ib. viii. 292.

Words:

Don't accustom yourself to use big words for little matters.

Boswell's *Life of Johnson*, i. 471.

∴

When we see men grow old and die at a certain time one after another, from century to century, we laugh at the elixir that promises to prolong life to a thousand years; and with equal justice may the lexicographer be derided who, being able to produce no example of a nation that has preserved their words and phrases from mutability, shall

imagine

imagine that his dictionary can embalm his language and secure it from corruption and decay; that it is in his power to change sublunary nature, and clear the world at once from folly, vanity, and affectation. With this hope, however, academies have been instituted to guard the avenues of their languages, to retain fugitives and repulse intruders, but their vigilance and activity have hitherto been vain; sounds are too volatile and subtile for legal restraints; to enchain syllables and to lash the wind are equally the undertakings of pride unwilling to measure its desires by its strength. *Works*, v. 46.

Workmen and their tools:

NOTHING is to be expected from the workman whose tools are for ever to be sought. I was once told by a great master that no man ever excelled in painting who was eminently curious about pencils and colours. *Idler*, No. 31.

World:

ALL the complaints which are made of the world are unjust. I never knew a man of merit neglected: it was generally by his own fault that he failed of success. A man may hide his head in a hole: he may go into the country and publish a book now and then which nobody reads, and then complain he is neglected. There is no reason why any person should exert himself for a man who has written a good book: he has not written it for any individual. I may as well make a present to the postman who brings me a letter. When patronage was limited an author expected to find a Mæcenas, and complained if he did not

find

find one. Why should he complain? This Mæcenas has others as good as he, or others who have got the start of him.

Boswell's Life of Johnson, iv. 172.

.·.

THE world in its best state is nothing more than a larger assembly of beings combining to counterfeit happiness which they do not feel, employing every art and contrivance to embellish life, and to hide their real condition from the eyes of one another. *Adventurer*, No. 120.

.·.

IT is impossible for those that have only known affluence and prosperity to judge rightly of themselves or others. The rich and the powerful live in a perpetual masquerade in which all about them wear borrowed characters; and we only discover in what estimation we are held when we can no longer give hopes or fears. *Rambler*, No. 75.

.·.

BY the common sense of readers uncorrupted with literary prejudices, after all the refinements of subtilty and the dogmatism of learning, must be finally decided all claim to poetical honours. *Works*, viii. 487.

.·.

ABOUT things on which the public thinks long it commonly attains to think right. *Ib.* vii. 456.

.·.

THE world is not so unjust or unkind as it is peevishly represented. Those who deserve well seldom fail to receive from others such services as they can perform; but few

have

have much in their power, or are so stationed as to have great leisure from their own affairs, and kindness must be commonly the exuberance of content. The wretched have no compassion ; they can do good only from strong principles of duty. *Piozzi Letters*, ii. 199.

* * *

OF things that terminate in human life the world is the proper judge ; to despise its sentence if it were possible is not just ; and if it were just is not possible. *Works*, viii. 316.

* * *

THE world has always a right to be regarded.

Boswell's *Life of Johnson*, ii. 74, *n.* 3.

* * *

IN my younger days it is true I was much inclined to treat mankind with asperity and contempt ; but I found it answered no good end. I thought it wiser and better to take the world as it goes. Besides, as I have advanced in life I have had more reason to be satisfied with it. Mankind have treated me with more kindness, and of course I have more kindness for them. Croker's *Boswell* 8vo. ed., p. 832.

Writing without thinking :

NEXT to the crime of writing contrary to what a man thinks is that of writing without thinking. *Works*, viii. 128.

Wrong by halves :

MEN are wrong for want of sense, but they are wrong by halves for want of spirit. *Ib.* vi. 242.

Young

Young men :

YOUNG men in haste to be renowned too frequently talk of books which they have scarcely seen.

Works, vi. 43.

Young and old :

FEW parents act in such a manner as much to enforce their maxims by the credit of their lives. The old man trusts wholly to slow contrivance and gradual progression : the youth expects to force his way by genius, vigour, and precipitance. The old man pays regard to riches, and the youth reverences virtue. The old man deifies prudence : the youth commits himself to magnanimity and chance. The young man who intends no ill believes that none is intended, and therefore acts with openness and candour : but his father having suffered the injuries of fraud is impelled to suspect, and too often allured to practise it. Age looks with anger on the temerity of youth, and youth with contempt on the scrupulosity of age. Thus parents and children for the greatest part live on to love less and less : and if those whom nature has thus closely united are the torments of each other, where shall we look for tenderness and consolation ?

Rasselas, ch. 26.

Youth :

THE first years of man must make provision for the last. He that never thinks never can be wise. Perpetual levity must end in ignorance ; and intemperance, though it may fire the spirits for an hour, will make life short or miserable. Let us consider that youth is of no long duration, and that in maturer age, when the enchantments of fancy shall cease, and phantoms of delight dance no more about us, we shall

have

have no comforts but the esteem of wise men and the means of doing good. Let us therefore stop, while to stop is in our power : let us live as men who are some time to grow old, and to whom it will be the most dreadful of all evils to count their past years by follies, and to be reminded of their former luxuriance of health only by the maladies which riot has produced. *Rasselas*, ch. 17.

.˙.

SIR, the atrocious crime of being a young man which the honourable gentleman has with such spirit and decency charged upon me I shall neither attempt to palliate nor deny, but content myself with wishing that I may be one of those whose follies may cease with their youth, and not of that number who are ignorant in spite of experience. Whether youth can be imputed to any man as a reproach I will not, Sir, assume the province of determining; but surely age may become justly contemptible if the opportunities which it brings have passed away without improvement, and vice appears to prevail when the passions have subsided. The wretch that after having seen the consequences of a thousand errors continues still to blunder, and whose age has only added obstinacy to stupidity is surely the object of either abhorrence or contempt, and deserves not that his grey head should secure him from insults. Much more is he to be abhorred who as he has advanced in age has receded from virtue, and becomes more wicked with less temptation ; who prostitutes himself for money which he cannot enjoy, and spends the remains of his life in the ruin of his country. *Debates. Works*, x. 355.

.˙.

EVERY man who has been engaged in teaching knows

with

with how much difficulty youthful minds are confined to close application, and how readily they deviate to anything rather than attend to that which is imposed as a task. That this disposition when it becomes inconsistent with the forms of education is to be checked will readily be granted; but since, though it may be in some degree obviated it cannot wholly be suppressed, it is surely rational to turn it to advantage by taking care that the mind shall never want objects on which its faculties may be usefully employed. It is not impossible that this restless desire of novelty which gives so much trouble to the teacher may be often the struggle of the understanding starting from that to which it is not by nature adapted, and travelling in search of something on which it may fix with greater satisfaction. For without supposing each man particularly marked out by his genius for particular performances, it may be easily conceived that when a numerous class of boys is confined indiscriminately to the same forms of composition, the repetition of the same words or the explication of the same sentiments, the employment must either by nature or accident be less suitable to some than others; that the ideas to be contemplated may be too difficult for the apprehension of one, and too obvious for that of another: they may be such as some understandings cannot reach, though others look down upon them as below their regard. Every mind in its progress through the different stages of scholastic learning must be often in one of these conditions, must either flag with the labour or grow wanton with the facility of the work assigned; and in either state it naturally turns aside from the track before it. Weariness looks out for relief and leisure for employment, and surely it is rational to indulge the wander-

ings

ings of both.   For the faculties which are too lightly bur-
dened with the business of the day may with great propriety
add to it some other inquiry; and he that finds himself
over-wearied by a task which perhaps with all his efforts
he is not able to perform is undoubtedly to be justified in
addicting himself rather to easier studies, and endeavouring
to quit that which is above his attainment for that which
nature has not made him incapable of pursuing with advantage. *Works*, v. 232.

Zeal in Religion:

To be strictly religious is difficult; but we may be zealously religious at little expense.   By expressing on all occasions our detestation of heresy and popery and all other
horrors we erect ourselves into champions for truth without
much hazard or trouble.   The hopes of zeal are not wholly
groundless.   Indifference in questions of importance is no
amiable quality.   He that is warm for truth and fearless in
its defence performs one of the duties of a good man; he
strengthens his own conviction and guards others from delusion; but steadiness of belief and boldness of profession
are yet only part of the form of godliness which may be
attained by those who deny the power. *Ib.* ix. 409.

THE END.